CABFLARE

A blazing flash lit the cab's interior, glancing inward from the glass dome of the cab. Kendall watched, amazed, as ionized light crawled along the metal of the walls, touching every frame and dial-rim with a shimmering glow. A moment later, a cacophony of alarms blared from the control-panel as high-energy particles pierced the magnetic shielding, flooding the enclosed space of the cab with secondary radiation. Another alarm shrieked as the flare's gamma flux flattened the cab's magnetic shield nearly to roof-level.

Kendall shuddered as the deadly light built still higher, one minute, two minutes, three minutes of an ever-brightening brilliance, forcing him at last to hide his eyes.

Oh, Lord, he prayed in his terror, save us from the fire . . .

By Paula E. Downing
Published by Ballantine Books:

RINN'S STAR
FLARE STAR

FLARE STAR

Paula E. Downing

A Del Rey Book
BALLANTINE BOOKS • NEW YORK

A Del Rey Book
Published by Ballantine Books

Copyright © 1992 by Paula E. Downing

All rights reserved under International and Pan-American Copyright Conventions. Published in the United States of America by Ballantine Books, a division of Random House, Inc., New York, and simultaneously in Canada by Random House of Canada Limited, Toronto.

Library of Congress Catalog Card Number: 91-93146

ISBN 0-345-37165-8

Manufactured in the United States of America

First Edition: April 1992

Cover Art by Michael Herring

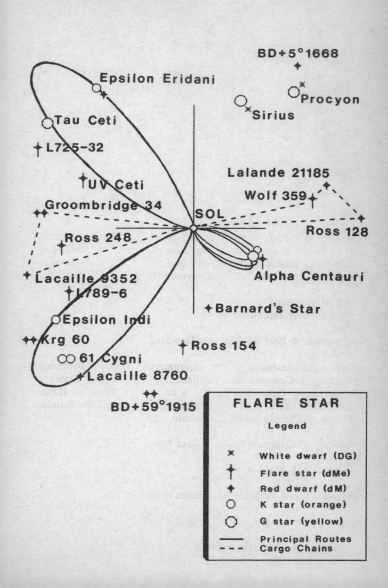

BD+5°1668

Epsilon Eridani

Procyon

Sirius

Tau Ceti

L725-32

Lalande 21185

UV Ceti

Wolf 359

Groombridge 34

SOL

Ross 248

Ross 128

Lacaille 9352

L789-6

Alpha Centauri

Epsilon Indi

Barnard's Star

Krg 60

61 Cygni

Ross 154

Lacaille 8760

BD+59°1915

FLARE STAR

Legend

✷	White dwarf (DG)
†	Flare star (dMe)
✦	Red dwarf (dM)
○	K star (orange)
⬡	G star (yellow)
——	Principal Routes
- - -	Cargo Chains

Prologue

Wolf 359, dwarf star dM8e, position 1056n0710 in Leo, 7.7 light-years from Earth.

Nearly eight light-years from Earth, the red dwarf star named Wolf 359 stirred restlessly. At long intervals in her far longer life, the Wolf star slipped into a deep sleep uncommon to a flare star, temporarily quiescent through a span of centuries, unusually mild in her temperament, almost benign in her solar dangers. In time, however, inevitably, the drowsing star awoke to renewed violence, rivaling the most dangerous of her flare star brethren, UV Ceti. In that awakening, Wolf accelerated her own substance into a delicate wind of atomic particles whipped by her contorted magnetic forces to nearly light-speed. As the flare ruptured the star's magnetic field, Wolf reached out with her gossamer fingers to caress the three planets of her tiny system, bathing their airless and crater-pocked plains, altering rock, changing atomic structures into odd and short-lived primal molecules, warming her children against the cold of space.

Only a tenth of Sol's mass, barely edging the barrier between star and planet, the flare stars lived a life of intense violence, seemingly poised on the verge of self-destruction with each massive flare yet finding stability in that constant release of stresses. In sleep, Wolf touched her children rarely, her caress as light as Sol's touch on Earth. But awake, her flares would inundate near space with a violent wind of heavy particles, intense gamma rays, and the odd unseen tachyons that defied the limits of space and time. Yet throughout human observation the sleeping Wolf's flares had leapt but a single magnitude, unlike the several-hundredfold flash of UV Ceti and other flare stars in Sol's vicinity. And so, when humanity expanded outward to nearby stars early in the twenty-third century and Earth's infant ship technology needed an interim stop on the way to two other small stars beyond Wolf, EuroCom took the risk and founded a colony station on Wolf's second planet.

In the twelfth year of the Wolf colony, a ten-thousand-year cycle completed itself deep in the star's ruby heart. The star stirred uneasily as convection cells lifted high-energy plasma to the formerly impenetrable barrier between interior and surface and pressed for release. As Wolf rotated on her axis, the differential rotation at equator and poles wrapped her magnetic lines into a bewildering confusion, winding Wolf like a top. Starspots, the visible mark of a star's magnetic stress, darkened her ruddy face and spread inexorably from the equator toward the poles. The decompressing flare, inhibited by the rising plasma, became dangerously delayed.

After ten thousand years, a cycle had ended. Deep within Wolf, her forces began building, shuddering upward through the gas layers, rousing the sleeper . . .

Chapter 1

Cargo-chain freighter Ceti Flag, *EuroCom registry, 90 hours to Wolf II colony station, A.D. 2246.*

Jason Roarke, first pilot of the *Ceti Flag*, lay comfortably on his bunk, smoking a vile cigar. The fumes swirled upward, adding a disapproving ratchety-ratch to the ceiling fan's customary hum. Jason blew a smoke ring at the fan and watched it tear the ring into fragments.

"Why do you smoke those awful things?" Helena asked.

She watched him from the upholstered armchair across the room, her nude body a study in intersecting curves, slender legs tucked neatly beneath her. Jason turned his head lazily to admire the view.

"Basic causation, love," he replied. "Egg to chicken, pig to ham, sex to a cigar."

Helena scowled, but he saw the smile tugging at her lips. She shook it away with a toss of her blond hair. "Men have one-track minds," she said, "also a basic causation. Too much testosterone. Have you considered having some of yours removed?"

"Ah, but it matches so nicely with female hormones, such as yours. Why don't you come back over here and we'll compare chemistry."

"We have duty in half an hour," she reproved.

"That's enough time."

"Beast." Helena uncoiled herself from the chair and stood up. She stretched languorously, showing a very nice curve of hip and full breast, then fluffed her hair with her fingertips. She looked at him a moment, considering, then shrugged. "You're a great lover, Jase, but there's more to life than sex, even on the cargo-chain."

"Oh?" he asked skeptically.

Helena snorted and stomped into the shower cubicle. Jason sighed his disappointment, but she missed it in the slam of the shower door. He shrugged and blew another smoke ring at the fan.

Even on the cargo-chain, she had said: so the boredom had finally gotten to Helena, too. He smiled sourly at the irony. An endless void in all directions, innumerable stars blazing in all colors, drifting clouds of nearly-invisible gas, the singsong pelting of dust grains on a ceramic ship hull, hundreds of colonists' lives dependent on the ship's safe arrival on time—and Jason sometimes felt as caged as the Alaskan bear he had once seen in the Edinburgh zoo, a massive animal pacing the barrier, toeing heavily on six-inch claws, seeking a way out, somewhere, anywhere.

Like you, you old bear, he thought.

God, old at thirty-five. He drew a deep drag from his cigar.

A much younger Jason had thought cargo-chain the best of all lives. In his lighter moods he still did and wanted nothing else. He had sweated over his EuroCom tests, then had thrown himself into Mars pilot prep as single-mindedly as Helena van Duyn still pursued her own ambitions. How long had the unalloyed joy lasted? Two circuits? Three? How long until he noticed the tedium that filled the long weeks between stars, the nothing-to-do, idiotic bureaucratic rules, the irritating quirks of his shipmates known too well?

Too long. In his darker moods he sometimes felt as if he could tear *Flag* apart with his bare hands, a frustrated Atlas wanting to shot-put the world. Let someone else tote the cargo-tin line to dinkum colonies on the survival edge; surely a Titan had grander things to do.

Yeah, guy. What?

In the beginning of it all, he had read, when lunar colonies were still a pipe dream and PanUnion's NASA still fiddled with its expensive "space trucks," other planners had dreamed of Martian colonies, gas mining at Titan, a massive spaceport on frigid Pluto for the Great Launching Outward. They had peered through their telescopes, lusting after farther worlds in Gemini, a few choice stars in Hercules, the glittering panoply of yellow suns in Sagittarius, busily planning Earth's future star empire, confident of humanity's destiny among the stars. All they needed was a ship drive to take them there. And that was the rub.

At sublight speeds a ship took centuries to cross the immense void between stars. Earth had always had its pioneers and so had found a few takers for that permanent trip into oblivion, with no possibility of return to the Earth they had left behind in distant time. Two generation ships had left for Hercules several decades before; both were still on their way, one a dead hulk riddled by fragments of a comet in the wrong place at the wrong time, the other babbling mad juvenile nonsense at zipsqueal frequencies as the ship faded toward light-speed. None of the consortia had dared to launch another such ship, even if they could have found new idiots to go, not after PanUnion had released the transcripts of what had happened aboard *PanUnion Liberty*. *Liberty*'s feral children had rewritten the book about long-term claustrophobia and the raw power of collective insanity.

Then Leonid Shaukolen had finally found a sleight of hand to bend Einstein's light-speed rule by adapting a quirk of high-speed particle behavior to create a tiny singularity in space, an impossibility in space-time that forced the ship within it to Jump elsewhere. It was a beginning, and for a time the planners resumed their megalomaniac dreams—only to find that Einstein's other rule was a rule even more inexorable in its limits: the faster one went, the more time it took to get there. A new colony needed support, supplies and new people, contact with home. Four or five years, real time, between supply ships promised an extinct colony upon arrival, but Earth lacked the resources to build a thousand ships to fill the need and lacked too, the power technology to accelerate her few ships to Shaukolen's Limit within the necessary parameters. And so Earth had found herself cruelly limited to a sphere of twelve light-years, a planet-poor desert of red dwarfs and three marginal orange stars. Glumly, the planners had finally faced reality and given up the hope of farther stars, obsessing themselves instead with the few marginal habitats Shaukolen had given them.

Humanity had needed its dreams. When the powers that were had given up, star dreaming had become unpopular, a dementia of purposeless behavior, an idiocy of pilot types and fanciful children who didn't know better, a refusal to face the facts of humanity's adulthood. And so the bureaucratic wars had begun as Earth's six consortia squabbled over a limited toy box, doing each other's dirt and publishing their endless rules for the peons who slaved on the company payroll.

Jason drew the redolent smoke deep into his lungs and scowled. So do something else, Jase, he told himself irritably. Grow up: give up the starry-eyed daydreams about Gemini and the other golden stars just out of reach. Shaukolen's coda on relativity was the end of it; all the big brains said so. He stubbed out the cigar in an ashtray, then swung his legs over the edge of the bunk. Go home to Earth? Each time Jason took home leave, Scotland seemed more crowded, with an elbow-jostling, frenetic pace of life he hated. A man could hardly turn around, it seemed, without bumping into something big and shiny or hairy-faced and rude. Mars was worse, with over-crowded bubble domes, constant political wars over territory lines, and an entrenched consortium bureaucracy. And each of the out-system colonies struggled, straitened by survival regs and rationing, cautious of expansion, making do with too little, redlined each year however their directors fiddled with the profit figures. Jason eyed his hairy legs gloomily.

Crap. He could tell it would be one of those days. Lighten up, Roarke; today is not a day to mourn over personal daydreams. So she turned you down on an encore. Did the universe quake?

Helena emerged from her shower and snagged a towel from the nearby rack, then bent and vigorously toweled her hair. Jason watched the jiggle of her breasts, then let his eyes wander downward, his thoughts lustful. Helena had taken the second-pilot berth on *Flag's* last circuit, drifting in and out of an ongoing affair with Jason as she divided her attentions between Jason and *Flag's* captain, Yves Merceau. But somehow sexual attraction had never developed into a genuine love, despite Jason's sometimes vague inclination; he suspected that Helena privately thought him a fool, as she thought almost everybody.

She looked up and raised an eyebrow. "Why are you still sitting there?"

"Admiring the view."

Helena tossed her head impatiently. "Later, Jase—I've got things to do." She picked up her underpants and slid them on, then reached for her blouse.

Her irritated tone flicked hard on Jason's temper. "Right," he snapped back. "So maybe I don't want to be your stud, Helena, your little diversion, your nice sexual exercise." He stamped past her into the shower.

"Jason, I didn't mean . . ."

"Forget it." Jason snapped shut the shower door and wrenched at the faucet, turning the water almost intolerably hot. When he emerged several minutes later, sweating from the steamy shower, Helena had gone. He aimed a bare toe at the metal base of his bunk. From his experience with their previous quarrels, Jason knew she would not be back for a considerable while. One did not criticize Helena van Duyn, not when one expected certain favors.

He knew it all too well. Helena would spend the next several days acting brittle and aloof, delivering sarcastic comments, impressing Jason with his lack of gratitude and charm, starting new quarrels in front of the others, then gradually forgive him. In a few weeks they would go to bed again, nothing resolved, nothing changed between them. Bright as a tack, a smart pilot, ambitious as hell, Helena relished the sass and put-downs, elbowing her way into the limited world of cargo-chain with a perky flash and unbounded confidence. From the beginning they had tossed words back and forth, an easy camaraderie between ship's pilots, until things had gotten a little too personal between them. Now Helena used the words to shove Jason away when he got too close, still equivocating as she played her games with Yves and Jason, wanting both and thinking she could keep it that way.

It was not rational, but it was typical on cargo-chain.

Ceti Transport's shrinks had a name for it, as they sat smugly in their Mars offices busily pasting labels on people, thinking labels solved the problem. They administered their battery of psychological tests to every candidate for cargo-chain, published their voluminous rules of ship's etiquette, loaded the ships with videos and book-tapes and a schedule of amusements, lectured and cajoled and declared, and still, inevitably, every time, people got on each other's nerves. Togetherness had its pinches. Ship tedium was a fact of life on cargo-chain, and each crewman acted off in unique ways, compounding his or her label. On *Flag*, Yves turned prissy, touting his perfect regs and lecturing the others about the superiority of French culture; Helena played sex games beyond reason and planned her career strategy in exquisite detail. Inga and Axel Stromstad, the married Swedes, obsessed themselves with tending ship systems, Inga the biosystems, Axel the engines and computers, endlessly repeating panel checks beyond reason.

And I start fights, Jason thought. He smiled as he opened his closet and pulled on a shirt, remembering a few of the choicer to-dos on earlier ships. Such glorious fights, you sod. He rather missed the turmoil he had made—an insulting eyebrow here, a wide-swinging tirade there, his opponent paling with rage, Jason always giving better than he got: at least it was something to do during the long months from star to star. But after that bar fight on Mars with Rodin, the whiny-faced sod of an engineer on *Ceti Star*, Central had threatened to boot Jason off the cargo-chain and had finally meant it, citing clause this and clause that of his pilot's contract. After Jason had groveled, as much as he could, the ship's director had relented: Ceti Transport needed its prime pilots, and Jason had flair, a natural skill with free-fall piloting and the narrow limits of cargo-tug maneuvering. But Jason had also believed Carson's firm promise if Jason ever tempted Central again.

And so the shrinks had put their pointy heads together

and picked Yves as his new captain, someone to lay down the rules and insist that Jason keep them, calmness to balance Jason's volatility, order to tame his chaos. The chief shrink had actually waxed poetic in that assignment report, the old fart. Sure. It had worked for a while, but only because Jason had decided to behave himself—not that the pointy-heads gave him any credit for that—and only until Stoeffel had transferred downside to that jitney-pilot post on Lalande and Helena had replaced him as second pilot, promptly messing up the shrinks' social diagrams.

And how will you combat ship tedium, Pilot van Duyn? they had asked her, and Helena had said all the right and dutiful things, bright and competent and clear-eyed, then had sashayed aboard the ship, blond hair bobbing, hips swaying, eye winkers batting, determined to exploit the impact of her charms on her captain and senior pilot. She meant well—Helena liked sex and in variety, especially when it might help her career—but it had thrown Central's careful dynamic between Jason and Yves into a cocked hat for a reason the pointy-heads never expected, not from their sedately rational and excellent captain. Yves did not want to share, no, not at all.

Apparently Yves had coldly studied the problem, had measured the lithesome goal in view, and had chosen his tactics well. Not the wide-swinging shouting and devastating put-downs so well versed in Jason's arsenal, but the insinuating war, the niggle war, the constant finding of fault in Jason, however small, the arch of that sardonic Gallic eyebrow, that drawl of the nasal voice, that smug superiority of rank and ultimate rule pushed to the edge, a noble attempt to make Jason revert to form and quarrel himself right out of cargo-chain. Jason saw him doing it, adjusted his calmness index as best he could, and finally went to Inga, as much as it galled him to ask for help. As the ship's medico and psych officer, Inga should have stepped in and stopped it, but she did nothing, even affecting surprise and disbelief that Jason would impute such goings-on to the impeccable and wonderful Captain Yves, everybody's hero.

Later he had sneaked into biosystems and read her report about the conversation. *Paranoia* was a nice word, yes, indeed. So were *disruptive* and *difficult*, *immature* and *unsuitable*, though all her examples were drawn from other ships, not *Flag*. Inga's loyalties were distinct if hardly fair, though she pretended to lofty fairness, a dispassionate equality, as cold and calm in her duties as suited a physician. Games, even from her. The pointed dislike implicit in her report had shaken him: he wasn't used to being disliked. Shouted at, sure; insulted and stamped at and chewed out, always. But not this cold exclusion, the first temblor of the plotted death of a pilot's career. Why? Just because of Yves's sexual jealousy? Where did that fit into Central's social rules?

I'm not good at this, he realized. I can't fight a hidden war, not well, not to win. But try to get either of them to admit anything. Yves had affected surprise at the insult and had stomped off to new niggles; Inga had sighed herself to patience and had lectured him on stability of character. He ground his teeth in frustration.

Cargo-chain. The group dynamic. A five-person crew cooped up in a box of a ship for too many weeks and months, sharpening their knives for the bloodbath when *Flag* got back to Mars, with Jason as victim, Helena as the spoils.

Oh, yeah? he thought defiantly. We'll see about that. I can be adult. I don't *have* to fight: just watch me.

He straightened his collar, finished dressing in trousers and boots, then snapped shut the wardrobe door. He stared for a moment in the small wardrobe mirror, studying himself. Blue eyes, tousled mud-brown hair, square jaw admittedly a bit weak in the chin, what the hell, imposing nose: Scot to the core, what remained of Scots these days. All he needed was kilts and sporran to pipe in the kirk, manfully indifferent to the swirl of cold mountain air sneaking up his kilts like a ghoul's kiss. A claymore to slash and hack in battle over the glens, fighting for the Bruce against any dastardly foe. A battle to win, a sweet wench to bed, his clansman's wild yell to cry . . . He lowered his eyebrows in a fierce scowl.

Cargo-chain, he thought irritably. Where's the drama? Where's the cheering squad when Yves bugs at you and

Helena flounces off? Where's the wider horizon in driving truck for EuroCom? Hip-hoorah for the heroes of cargo-chain.

And anything else would be only half a life, you sod, and you know it.

He reached for his cap and put it on, tugging it down tightly on his head. Only four more days to Wolf. Four more days to the busy activity of shuttling cargo tins to the colony, trading supplies for helium-3 to fill *Flag*'s fuel tanks and a few tins of product for sale back on Mars. Four more days to a temporary reprieve from the boredom—and maybe enough distraction to divert Helena into a variation on her too-predictable revenge. Maybe. Helena was a determined type. Four more days.

Whistling "Bonnie Brae," Jason left his room and headed for his duty watch.

Even without the encore, the early-morning dalliance with Helena had made him late, and he no doubt would spend all the ship's day trying to catch up with himself, ably assisted by snotty reminders of the tardy start from Yves. He yawned and strolled along the inner corridor, looking at his ship with appreciative eyes. If Yves won the war, and he just might, Jason figured he'd better enjoy *Flag* while he could.

Ceti Flag was a Class B design EuroCom freighter towing a double line of cargo tins, braked by the netted magnetic fields of the forward ramscoop and powered by four Shaukolen engines aft. *Flag*'s habitable crew module rotated amidships between the scoop and engines, a hollow-core cylinder supported by a wide rectangular frame. To the crew module's five occupants, *Flag* seemed to be a continuous rising corridor on two levels, with the two tiers connected by ladders every fifty meters and each fronting a series of long rooms. Biosystems, sick bay, the ship's garden, storage, and crew quarters occupied the upward inner ring immediately next to the ship's core; navigation, engineering, and the central control room were sited in the downward outer ring. Only eight years in service, *Ceti Flag* still showed much of her virgin polish.

On the crew module's upper ring near the ship's garden, a former crewman had painted brightly colored murals on the walls, some abstract, some remembered city scenes from Earth, others a remarkably vivid panorama of Mars' Olympus Mons and the bright auroras of Tau Ceti skies. Ceti Central, true to form, had written him up for "defacing company property" and transferred him planetside, then ordered the murals removed, a flimsy Yves had uncharacteristically arranged to misfile somewhere. Near biosystems, Inga had supplemented the garden's oxygen production with thirty feet of trellis roses and climbing ivy, a touch of home that Jason especially liked. So far Central's spies had not noticed the nonregulation roses, a state of affairs Jason hoped might last a while. He paused and counted the new colors Inga had coaxed from her meticulous grafting, peeked in at Inga busy at the biosystems panels, then ambled onward, hands in pockets, comfortably slouched.

Ceti Flag was a pretty ship, nimble and smart and good at her job. He smiled, sniffing at the reconditioned air, his boots tapping a quiet rhythm on the metal floors. At the next ladder he clattered down the metal steps, took a swift left; two dozen strides down the floor and he was at the control room. Jason strolled in, finding Yves on duty at his command station, busily studying printouts.

"Morning, Yves," Jason said.

The Frenchman grunted an acknowledgment but didn't bother to look around. Jason got about four more steps before Yves delivered the rest. "You're late," he growled.

"That's an o-kay," Jason retorted. "So dock me for the ten minutes, I don't care."

"That's obvious," Yves said bitingly.

Zing! Walked into that one. Jason clamped his teeth together to keep back a few choicer words. Yves waited expectantly for a moment, then harrumphed and went back to his printouts.

A handsome dark-haired man in his late thirties, Yves Merceau prided himself on his efficiency, with a bureaucrat's obsession with rules and reports that pleased Central no end. Ceti Transport's captains tended to gather such quirks after a few years of constant nagging by Central, and Yves was a captain of several years' standing, well advanced in the mental disease. Yves had never missed a report due date and rarely varied from routine, making himself yet another of Central's dutiful high-priest captains dutifully chanting regs against the darkness. Sometimes Jason wondered what Yves would do if he ran into a nonreg problem; probably Yves did, too, though he would never admit it. Oh, no. Follow the rules, and the universe was as safe as a toy boat in a bathtub, bobbing happily away. After all, Papa Central said so.

Throughout their three years as shipmates Yves's fastidious habits had always grated on Jason, just as Jason's informality annoyed Yves; their unspoken rivalry over Helena had only tightened the conflict. Neither felt comfortable with the other, both uneasy with a difference of temperament magnified by the long months of nothing to do on *Flag*. Opposites did not always attract, whatever Central thought, and Yves no longer bothered to hide his dislike, an erosion of courtesy Jason reciprocated. Still, they did have to share ship together, and squabbling hardly helped *Flag*'s efficiency. Now that *Flag* was approaching star point, putting an end to the weeks of sitting around, maybe he and Yves could mend some fences. Maybe.

"Do we have signal acquisition with the colony?" Jason asked casually.

"Yes." Yves flipped a page and bent closer to study the data, then punched several figures into his computer.

"Everything on the green at Wolf II?"

Yves turned his head. "Are you going to work today?" he asked unpleasantly. "That would be nice."

"All right, already! I was just making conversation."

"Central doesn't pay you to be a social star, even if I were interested in chatting with you, Jason, which I'm not. Just get to work." Yves swung his chair completely around, presenting his back. End of conversation, Jason thought gloomily. And so much for fences.

So where are the cheers for making an effort? When does *Yves* make an effort? Jason balled his fists in frustration. The hell with Yves and his stupid war; he wasn't in the mood to cajole further. He walked stiffly behind Yves to his own console and sat down in his chair, then quickly scanned the readings on the approach board. The hell with it all.

Flag ran the Lalande route, one of twelve Ceti Transport cargo-chain ships on constant circuit to supply EuroCom's three red dwarf colonies at Wolf 359, Lalande 21185, and Ross 128. By subjective ship time, courtesy of Shaukolen's Drive and Einstein, a cargo-chain circuit took only eight months, though the universe totted the time as three years on its real-time clock. Eight months of mind-numbing routine, of the same four faces known too well, broken by three brief interludes as *Flag* delivered cargo tins to the next colony station, trading supplies for helium-3 pellets and a marginal export in transuranics and rare-earth lanthanides. It had its charm, he told himself.

He keyed up another panel and studied the display. So far few of the approach telltales had lit; Jump itself took only an instant once *Flag* had reached sufficient speed, but the relativistic effects lingered well into *Flag*'s deceleration into Wolf system, a weird quirk of Shaukolen's formulas that nobody understood. The ship had several hours before she reacquired real time and fully rejoined normal space.

In the front screen, bracketed by the power-systems panels, *Flag* seemed to be hurtling down a tunnel of stars, each elongated into a glowing streak of serrated primary colors, a tiny spectrum analogous to the star's true light when red-shifted by a set constant. At the end of the tunnel gleamed a large ruby jewel, growing visibly larger as *Flag* entered Wolf-system. Jason tapped a dial: still over four million kilometers away but on course. Beyond Wolf a small white dot gleamed half a degree above the star's right quadrant, Wolf II in its farside orbit.

Jason brought up other system displays on his screen, cross-entering into Axel's programs to check power levels on the forward braking engines. Now well into Wolf's cometary plane, *Flag* was catching enough dust and gas in her forward ramscoop to brake at full power; she would fight the same dust concentration as she accelerated outward with her four engines, slowly building speed to Shaukolen's Limit and the next Jump. With the red star now conveniently between the ship and Wolf II, *Flag* could brake even faster with a swing-by trajectory, using Wolf's own gravity to slow down. He queried a radar scan of the cargo-tin alignment, double-checking that none of the tins had moved dangerously adrift and that they all still followed *Flag*'s smooth parabolic toward Wolf. On the green. *Flag* would arrive on course and ahead of schedule, with all tins intact.

"Strange," Yves muttered.

"Strange?" Jason echoed.

Yves swiveled his chair and deigned to notice Jason again. Well, it was a start, Jason thought sourly.

"How far to Wolf II?" Yves asked.

Jason craned his head to look back at his screen. "Uh, four-point-six-five million kilometers. Why?"

"I've been scanning the light trace from Wolf. I can't see any sign of flares recently. That's odd."

Jason shrugged. "It seems to me that no flare at Wolf is good news. So what's the problem?"

Yves raised an eyebrow. "Wolf 359," he drawled, "relieves its internal pressure with periodic flares—like a steam kettle, to bring it down to your level." Jason bit back a word, trying to hide his resentment. Yves smiled slightly, seeing it all with those clever eyes. "Without regular flares, the pressure builds to a bigger event. *Not* good news for our colony. Do you understand now?"

"Yeah, Yves. I understand. So?"

"Just commenting," Yves said loftily, and turned back to his control board.

Jason stared at the red star in the wall screen, struggling with his anger. You will not start a fight; he wins when you fight. Calm down, boy.

When do I get better at this? he asked silently.

In screen center Wolf 359 was a wide disk of brilliant red gas in turmoil, ever moving, turbulent, bracketed by the serrated rainbows of the residual warp effect. Even a diminutive star had its grandeur, lessened only by the comparison to other larger stars, not to itself. Many of the red dwarfs lived out a sedate life, as serenely quiescent and benign as Sol, tending their two or three tiny planets with a dim and invariable light too weak to stir random molecules into life. Other red dwarfs, the flare stars, policed their neighborhoods with violent outbursts of gas and particles, ripping apart any biocarbons that wandered into reach, including the intelligent kind who strayed in from Earth. Except for Wolf 359.

No one knew why Wolf lived her double life, too active to be a standard red dwarf, too mild to be a genuine flare star. The star cycled up and down, blitzing the frequencies to unravel her magnetic lines at irregular intervals, never at danger level, with certain colony precautions, but never quite quiet enough to be ignored. Earth telescopes had plotted Wolf's light trace for three centuries; EuroCom had waved around those charts at the colony hearings in Geneva, had pointed beyond Wolf to two other standard red dwarfs, Lalande 21185 and Ross 128, had argued the feasibility of cargo-chain resupply, had stamped their feet and waved their arms and pleaded most beseechingly, and had finally won approval. EuroCom had drilled Wolf Station deep next to a sheltering crater wall, tripled its radiation shields, and set up the flare-watch protocols, then had moved on to Lalande and Ross, the true objects of its corporate lust. The dozen years of success on the Lalande cargo-chain had legitimized a longer cargo-chain to the double red dwarfs of Groombridge 34 and a sister star astronomically nearby; Jason had heard rumors that EuroCom was planning a third route somewhere near Epsilon Indi. EuroCom still ran its expensive starliners to Earth's principal colonies at Alpha Centauri and Tau Ceti, spilling red ink all the way, but cargo-chain worked better, with Wolf 359 as the cornerstone for it all.

As he watched the star, an arc of yellow-tinted gas leapt upward near the ragged edge of a southern starspot, curving gracefully along an invisible magnetic line toward *Flag*, a beauty he never tired of watching at star point. A man could too easily forget the beauty of stars close up, tricked by the illusion of distance to think them nothing but those points of light dusting the sky in every direction; he could forget the reality of the violence, the immense size even of the smallest stars, the blazing light that warmed a tiny pocket of space millions of kilometers across, making life possible within the cold void. Wolf was a prettier star than most, a lady dangerous and wild. He smiled as he watched as the gas plume joined with another from a nearby starspot, leaping upward together into the shimmering corona, twin arcs of brilliant fire. A moment later still another plume of bright yellow gas joined the dance, then another and another . . .

"Yves . . ."

"What?"

Jason half rose from his chair as Wolf's gas plumes suddenly joined into a brilliant wall of gas that flashed from pole to pole, then swept eastward across the face of Wolf toward the limb and the small white dot of Wolf II, a glowing wave accelerating as it built its strength from the star's own substance, suffusing the entire star face with a brilliant yellow light. "Yves!" he shouted.

Yves turned just as the massive flare rolled around the star edge and winked out. "What?" he repeated irritably, glancing suspiciously from Jason to the wall screen. An instant later *Flag's* consoles lit up like a Christmas tree as the attenuated storm of particles and flux swept by and through the ship, quickly over. "What the devil!" Yves exclaimed.

"Thank God for four million klicks and a warp tunnel," Jason breathed. "I think Wolf just blew the lid off her kettle." Appalled, he looked at Yves, then back at the screen. "And that flare was rolling straight around at the colony, too."

Yves hesitated, his dark eyes narrowed with distrust. He flicked another glance at the wall screen, obviously doubting Jason's word.

"I saw a flare, Yves," Jason said firmly.

"Maybe."

"What do you mean, 'maybe'?" Jason asked in outrage. "Run back the tape and look at it yourself!"

Yves set his jaw stubbornly, an expression Jason knew all too well from recent weeks. Shut-out time. What was *wrong* with the man?

"Run back the tape," Jason repeated.

"All right, so you saw a flare," Yves conceded ungraciously. "Wolf is a flare star. Nothing new in that."

"That wasn't a normal flare. Since when do we get flare-storm readings at this distance?" He gestured expansively at *Flag*'s consoles.

Yves shrugged again. "In due time," he said. He showed his teeth.

"If you don't run back that tape, right *now*, I'll log a protest. And if Wolf *has* flared, you can explain to Central why you ignored crew's report."

"Hmmph," Yves grunted, pretending to be unimpressed. He turned back to his console, and Jason saw his shoulders tense suddenly.

"What is it?" Jason asked. He craned his neck to look around Yves.

"The colony's radio signal is gone." Yves quickly ran an acquisition check. Jason rose and joined him, leaning over his shoulder to watch.

"See?" Yves asked, waving his hand at the end display. The com board read zero, little but star noise when it should have been blaring the colony station's recognition signal. The loudest thing in the neighborhood was Wolf's solar wind, a recognizable oscillating wiggle despite the distortion of Jump effect. "Hmmm," Yves said. "A puzzle. Maybe their comsat's broken and due for repair."

"Sure, Yves. Or maybe the flare just took it out."

That got Yves's attention. Jason saw the flash of sudden fear in Yves's dark eyes, stark in that too-controlled face, quickly hidden behind blandness. The Frenchman shrugged.

"Wolf's flares attenuate quickly," he said dismissingly, "even close in, and the comsat's shielded. Not likely." He looked past Jason at the wall screen and flicked his eyes over the navigation panels above and below. "Solar radiation looks normal, slightly high on starspots. Maybe they had a planetquake or a power failure."

"Or maybe a flare," Jason repeated. "Run back the tape."

Yves's dark eyes flashed stubbornly. "Later."

"A flare's gamma flux kills machinery," Jason reminded him. "Like comsats."

"Don't try to teach me fundamentals, Jason. Wolf doesn't flare into risk range."

"Yet, you mean." Jason thumbed over his shoulder at the wall screen. "There's Wolf II. So where's the signal?"

"Wolf has never flared at that level," Yves said stubbornly, then managed another indifferent shrug. "No need for alarm quite yet."

"Excuse me?" Jason knew Yves was a cautious man, but he had not thought it extended to denying an obvious problem merely to count coup on his senior pilot. Why the big deal about running the tape now? Only because Jason had suggested it? He looked at Yves's stubborn face and decided that was exactly why. "What's the drill for a flare incident?" he insisted, pushing.

"*Merde,* I don't know."

"You *should* know."

Yves's face flushed with a genuine anger, than hardened again. "We don't have any colonies at flare stars," he said dismissingly, "for the obvious reasons—except at Wolf. I'll have to ask the computer."

"So ask, Yves."

"Maybe later," Yves said with finality. "We'll keep to standard procedure until we're past swing-by. I'm sure we'll reacquire the signal by then." Yves turned back to his console and ran his slender hands over the keyboard, uploading another systems-check program, hands moving deftly, neatly.

"Yves . . ."

Yves clucked his tongue in approval at the new readings, then keyed in another request. Damned Frenchman! Jason thought, and stamped out of the control room. He turned right and headed automatically for the cargo deck, then stopped, wondering what to do. Anything? If Wolf had flared enough to destroy the colony beacon, what waited for *Flag* on Wolf II? His imagination promptly supplied a number of nasty possibilities. Radiation burn, panic, loss of systems, four hundred colonists at risk . . . And what in the hell could *Flag* do about it?

So maybe the problem was nothing, as Yves hoped; better to be pleasantly surprised than caught with their pants down sitting on the john.

He hesitated, almost turned back for another argument, then decided he needed better help. Helena was off on her snit; no point in looking there. But Yves might listen elsewhere if Inga and Axel could be persuaded. He rattled up the near stairway, one hand lightly on the rail, heading inward toward biosystems.

Chapter 2

Isaiah Kendall glanced upward through the alloyglass dome of his harvester cab, his eyes drawn again to the Wolf star. Above the scarp, the knife-edged towering wall of stone that bisected Tri Ellium crater, the dwarf sun filled a full third of the planet's eastern sky, visibly turbulent, blotched by ragged-edged starspots spreading steadily toward each pole, its ruddy light tingeing the rocks and dust and scarp of Wolf II's surface with a blood-red hue. The Wolf-light flickered uneasily, shifting perceptibly in its strength but so subtly to the eye that it seemed a ghostly illusion, as if alien shades stalked through the emptiness above the white dust, made themselves into sheeted curtains drenched in gore, then vanished from view.

Flare soon, Kendall thought. He frowned uneasily.

In his five years as harvester subchief at the Wolf II colony station, Kendall had never seen Wolf so black with starspots. Usually the star flared every few weeks, righting its magnetic lines with a burst of accelerated particles and gamma flux. The flares, never quite predictable, created temporary havoc with the colony's electrical systems and radio, forcing the station's surface crews underground for a beer or three and making life a scramble for any harvester crew caught out in the dayside craters. Even so, Wolf's mild flares had never tested the design limits of the colony station or its harvesters. Like vacuum suits, bureaucratic idiocy, claustrophobic quar-

21

ters, short rations, and even shorter pay, flare storm was only another nagging fact of a Wolf colonist's life.

His fingers twitched on the controls as his eyes again strayed to the star: it looked diseased. He forced himself to look away and concentrated on his driving.

On his console, the soft ping of the harvester's radar scanned for dust pits ahead that might swallow a harvester whole; the muted light displays on Kendall's sophisticated monitors watched for other dangers in the cold airlessness of Wolf II's surface, an environment more hostile than Earth's moon. Another screen flickered in synch with the variable oviod shape of the magnetic field that enclosed the cab and its trailing dustbin, the bubble's smooth display curve shifting subtly in response to the unsteady pressure of Wolf-light, shielding the cab's two occupants from the sheeting solar wind that bathed the planet's surface between flares. Even with all the safety devices, the sophisticated machinery long tested in vacuum, the experience of twenty years in colony service at Wolf and elsewhere, it paid to stay alert. Here mistakes of a certain kind could kill a man—and his cabmate with him—before he even noticed it happening. Kendall intended to avoid such mistakes.

Beyond his cab to the left, two other harvesters plowed straight lines across the crater floor, scraping up the top few inches of the white dusty soil. With its massive treads, the boxy shape of its control cab, and the long jointed rectangle of its dustbin trailing behind, a bellyloader harvester looked like an ungainly metal caterpillar humping slowly along the crater floor, single-mindedly intent on its feeding. In small craters, the harvester teams used ten-meter tractors adaptable to the four dozen other uses of colony surface transport; in dust-rich craters of Tri Ellium's size—three kilometers wide from scarp to crater wall, smooth as a calm sea, and blessedly free of rocks and the other ancient projectiles of Wolf II's violent birth—the larger belly-loaders could harvest in a single trip forty tons of the helium-enriched dust that coated Wolf II's crater, a needed wealth for a colony on a ragged economic edge. With the helium-3 isotope refined from the dust and used in fusion power plants and ship drives,

Wolf Station paid ship fuel and barter credit to the Ceti Transport cargo-chain freighters that delivered supplies every three months from Mars. The dust silicates became colony building materials, the residual rare earths and transuranics a new money for Sol's infant colonies at a scattering of nearby stars.

In a few hours the station's cargo hauler would return and lift the dust-heavy harvesters back to base, one last haul before the next cargo-chain freighter, *Ceti Flag,* arrived on its circuit outward to Lalande 21185. True, Wolf Station could use the extra barter, but Kendall had argued against this final trip into dayside, quarreling again with Chief van Griff—not that Willem needed much cause to throw another of his black rages. As usual, Director Danforth had taken van Griff's side, more concerned about profit figures than about men's lives. An acceptable risk, Danforth had said, smiling that smug smile of his, shrugging his sad sigh of resignation, patting Kendall paternally on the shoulder as he guided him out of his office, a touch that came a whisker within landing the director of Wolf Station flat on the floor, courtesy of Kendall's fist. Bureaucrats! Kendall glanced again at Wolf's mottled face.

A few hours.

Damn, he swore to himself.

To the left of his cab window the massive scarp lifted its chiseled vertical edge a hundred meters, dividing the small impact crater in a jagged cliff line running from rim to rim. An ancient wrinkle of the planet's coalescence, the scarp had stood nearly unchanged for two billion years, bathed in Wolf's ruddy light, slowly degenerating a few centimeters every million years under the star's solar bombardment. Near its base, reflected light from the high-albedo white dust of the crater floor shed a ragged band of dim twilight unusual in vacuum, shaded from ruddy gray to the impenetrable black in the crevices, visibly shifting in response to Wolf's unsteady glare. Half-embarrassed by his own uneasiness, Kendall steered his harvester into shadow.

"Hey!" Leland squawked behind him. "Where's my line of sight?"

Kendall glanced back at the young scientist who shared his cab that day. Tall and lanky, with a shock of unkempt blond hair brushing his collar, Leland sat near the bin station panel at a jury-rigged telescope, his Wolf-watch equipment piled haphazardly on either side of his chair. Normally Mack Summers rode Kendall's bin chair, monitoring the dust as it steadily filled the massive compartment behind the cab. Today Danforth had thrown Kendall a sop by putting the young Wolf-watch astrophysicist in Kendall's cab, as if that would help anything if Wolf blew. The younger man glared at Kendall in outrage.

"So watch some other star," Kendall said mildly. It wasn't Leland's fault, Kendall reminded himself, that Danforth had ledger paper for brains. "I want to stay in shadow."

"You've ruined two hours of readings . . ." Leland waved a despairing hand at his monitors. "How can we ever get a pattern if you cut off the data in mid—"

"Driver's privilege, kid," Kendall said, cutting it off. He turned back to his controls.

"I'll report this to Danforth," Leland muttered ominously.

"Do that."

One eye on his radar and the shadowed ground ahead, Kendall inspected the dials on the control panel, then edged up the power feed to the magnetic flux surrounding the cab. Even with the half meter of lead shielding in the cab roof and a safety margin of a magnetic bubble, high-energy iron particles could zip through metal and flux, coring out whole cell lines. Kendall planned to have children someday—if he ever found the right woman who would have him—and valued his other cell types almost as much. Behind him, he heard Leland's chair squeak, then the stamp of Leland's booted feet as the other came forward.

"Have a seat," Kendall invited.

"Thanks."

Leland belted himself into the extra chair by the controls, his expression still disgruntled. After several hours of their forced companionship, to his surprise, Kendall had found Leland to be a nice kid, easygoing and enthusiastic, despite his reputed brilliance among the astrophysics big brains. Most of the bright boys had ego quirks to match their brainpower, but Leland seemed to value the lesser sorts of his station fellows, even a lowly harvester driver. It was a refreshing change. Most of Wolf II's fifty scientists seemed to think the station's labor force a suitable repeat of medieval peonage, with the contract language to back them up. The Wolf scientists got the best quarters with the most amenities, the privileges, the exceptions to regs, free access to Sol-bound travel despite the cost and limited bunk space, and the deferent attention of any Ceti Transport official. Labor got the leavings, trapped by low wages, the high cost of transport home, and the fine print in standard contracts. On Wolf the leavings weren't much—enough for a man to live and have a purpose, but one couldn't help but notice the contrast.

"Sorry, Paul," Kendall said. "I don't like the look of Wolf's starspots."

"You're telling me?" Leland said disgustedly. "I've tried to warn Danforth and Dr. Harrod for days, but who listens?"

Kendall grunted back and watched as the younger man bent and rummaged hungrily in the console storage compartment for a chocolate bar. From Kendall's brief observation on this trip, Leland seemed to live solely on chocolate bars; he eyed the young man's gawky seventy kilos and wondered irritably where it all went. After Kendall's last checkup by the doc, he had reluctantly given up even *thinking* about chocolate bars, at least until he dropped the extra ten kilos he had picked up somehow.

"Want one?" Leland asked.

"No thanks," Kendall said virtuously.

"Harvester Three," the radio squawked. "Why are you out of position?"

"Three here," he answered van Griff, keeping his tone carefully level. "I saw a good stretch by the scarp."

"Huh." The radio snapped off. Typical, Kendall thought angrily, staring down at the mike in his hand. The Dutchman enjoyed throwing his weight around; since his promotion last year, he had found all kinds of opportunity with his crews, pushing any quarrel with his sub-chiefs beyond reason. Kendall ground his teeth and thrust the mike back into its prongs.

He waited, fiddling usefully with the bubble controls, until he had his temper back. "Why don't you check the bin dials? We should be about full soon."

"Before Wolf blows?"

Kendall shot him a glance. Leland shrugged.

"Let's say I value good instincts, chief. In my field you learn the worth of a good hunch—half of astrophysical theory is guesswork, anyway. I think Wolf is cycling into something new, but Harrod wants proof—and a gut feeling doesn't translate into data integrals. So I value instinct—even if van Griff doesn't, and wouldn't listen to a warning if you gave it, even if Wolf was black from pole to pole." Leland looked outward at the towering scarp rolling by their cab, a broken wall of cracked stone in deep shadow. "Shadow won't keep it all out, you know, not if Wolf blows a flare on UV Ceti scale. And those guys are in full sunlight."

"Hmmph." Kendall hunched his shoulders and focused on the controls. Leland watched him as the cab bumped over the soil, scraping away.

Kendall reached for the radio. "Harvester One."

"Yeah."

"Chief, I don't like the look of Wolf. It might be good to get into shadow."

Van Griff jeered. "Is that why you're scarp hugging, Kendall? I thought as much. Good stretch, ha!"

"Why don't you let the men make their choice, Willem?"

Van Griff swore bitingly, then snapped off.

"Asshole," Kendall muttered.

"Double asshole," Leland agreed, then tipped his chin, bemused. "Is that a workable curse? Or merely an anatomic oddity?"

"Holy Christ, Paul."

"Anything for levity. I heartily think we'll need it." Leland flipped his candy wrapper over his shoulder, looked as he missed the trash chute by three feet, then reached for another chocolate bar. ''Want one?'' he asked impishly. He waved the foil-wrapped bar in Kendall's direction enticingly, a slow dip and swing, tempting Kendall past endurance.

''Drat you, Leland. Yeah, sure.'' Kendall took the chocolate and made a small ceremony of peeling away the foil, then took a bite. Chocolate. Wonderful stuff. ''Why don't you go check the bin level?'' he suggested again. Maybe it would read full, he wished. Maybe.

''Right.''

As Leland headed back to the bin station, the dim twilight beside the scarp darkened abruptly, then flared into a dazzling yellow, too bright, too quick. Kendall looked upward a moment at the scarp, puzzled, then slammed down the autopilot button and lunged away from the control board.

''Get down!'' he yelled. He threw himself into the rear of the cab, away from the glass dome of the driver station. As Leland turned in surprise, Kendall hit him midbody in a flying tackle. The two men rolled to the rear of the cab, nearly bringing Leland's equipment down on their heads, then landed with a jar against the back wall. Frantically, Kendall tugged Leland underneath him, shielding the younger man with his own body.

An instant later a blazing flash lit the cab's interior, glancing inward from the glass dome of the cab. Kendall lifted his head and squinted against the glare, watching, amazed, as ionized light crawled along the metal of the cab walls, touching every frame and dial rim with a shimmering glow. It slipped down the metal seams of the cab walls, danced idly a moment on the jumble of Leland's Wolf-watch equipment, then flashed into the brighter glare. A moment later a cacophony of alarms blared from the cab's control panel as high-energy particles pierced the magnetic shielding, flooding the enclosed space of the cab with secondary radiation. Another alarm shrieked as the flare's gamma flux flattened the cab's magnetic shield nearly to roof level. Kendall flinched at the sound of the gamma alarm and clutched convulsively at Leland. Even in shadow . . . God! If the gamma flux got through, killed the machinery . . .

He waited, hardly breathing, for the cab to die, for the abrupt end to the alarms when the flux broke through and smashed the electronics, fusing, destroying, killing. He waited, conscious of Leland's fingers digging into his chest, of the young man's violent trembling beneath Kendall's sheltering body. Keep on, he wished at the alarms as they shrieked their warning. Keep on, keep on, keep on . . .

He shuddered with Leland as the deadly light built still higher, one minute, two minutes, three minutes of an ever-brightening brilliance, forcing Kendall at last to hide his eyes from the horrible light.

Oh, Lord, he prayed in his terror, save us from the fire . . .

Wolf II Colony Station, Home Crater, Level 3, Office 15A, 12 days past first dawn.

Thirty meters beneath Wolf II's cold and rocky surface, Colony Director Peter Danforth sat in his private office and struggled with his computer display, jiggling the station's profit-loss numbers, then sighed resignedly. Maybe next quarter, he thought, knowing it a useless hope. With a marginal habitat, limited cargo-chain access, and Ceti Transport's unrealistic expectations of early profit, each quarter's financial report to Central was a frustrating exercise, especially when the company expected its cargo-chain colonies to make up losses elsewhere. As one of the six United Nations consortia that administered Earth's struggling out-system colonies, EuroCom's Ceti Transport shared in the starliner franchise to Alpha Centauri and Tau Ceti, a cutthroat competition that bled needed wealth from corporate coffers, wealth *he* was supposed to replace.

Idiots, he thought disgustedly.

Until Earth discovered the power technology to use Shaukolen's Drive to its full potential, Earth colonization remained limited to its sphere of twelve light-years: a planet-poor space with only three marginally habitable orange stars and a swarm of red dwarfs, most of the latter too violent to colonize. A few space stations orbited in

Sol system, expensive experiments in man-created world-lets, but humanity needed good real estate more, good and workable planet homes to ease the population pressure of a burgeoning humanity on Earth and Mars, planets with breathable air, decent gravity, plowable soil, reliable sunlight, good weather, and raw resources. A place to put the extra millions, not mere thousands; worlds to build, not to warehouse the unemployed of Earth's slums; new science to discover, not a scramble for awkward solutions to environmental limits.

He lit a cigarette and keyed on his wall screen to watch the cargo lander on topside. In the shifting red-grays of morning, a dozen spacesuited men and women stamped around the wide landing struts of the cargo lander outside the main base hangar, readying the slim and nimble ship for harvester retrieval. Other crews worked by the processing sheds and subsidiary hangars near the crater wall; another group struggled with the new telescope for the clifftop observatory, a balky weight even in Wolf II's half-Standard gravity. To the left, low above the bulking shadows of the hangars and dust-processing sheds, Wolf 359 burned redly in an uneasy glare, caught midway in its strange antics at perihelion.

For thirteen days during first dawn Wolf rose a few degrees into the sky, then sank back below the eastern crater rim, only to dawn again a few days later for the four unbroken months of Wolf II's dayside. Danforth had seen first dawn only twice in his three years as colony director, had listened to the astrophysicists' explanations of a tidal-locked planet's rotation and orbital speed, but still marveled at the sight of a sun going backward in the sky. Amazing, truly amazing. At home, Mercury's temperatures precluded any tourist jaunts to watch a similar event; in other circumstances, Wolf Station might have drawn a sightseer crowd big enough to satisfy Central's greedy demands for money. The Double Dawn Hotel. First Dawn Enterprises. The Wolf Resort Inn. He glanced at the spreadsheet on his desktop computer, a lesser marvel he could happily toss into vacuum, then shut off the screen in disgust. Nuts. He puffed at his cigarette, drawing the end into a bright coal.

Another hour and Danforth might squeak through a decision he now regretted; accustomed to manipulating others with ease, as any good colony administrator needed to do, he sometimes had an occasional blindness when others chose to manipulate him. It irked him, especially when it allowed a loudmouth like van Griff to jerk his strings. He should not have sent out the harvesters: he knew that now. *Once I was a fairly decent design engineer,* he thought, angry at himself.

He watched the activity on the surface for several minutes, then found his gaze drawn to the dawning star. During the long four months of nightside, when the station was shielded from the star's antics by the planet's bulk, Danforth could forget about flare safety and focus on the hundred and one other things that plagued an administrator's life. During dayside the flare regs kept the station safe, though inevitably some crewman forgot the rules and killed himself with stupidity. But not from flare damage—Danforth saw to that, haranguing the labor crews during safety meetings, lecturing scientists more interested in experimental data than basic brains, making sure the teachers drilled the precautions into the eighty children who had followed their parents to Wolf or had been born afterward. Not that the children were allowed topside, of course, but a few high-acceleration particles of the larger flares sometimes penetrated to Level 2, enough to be a minor hazard. And so he harangued and nagged and pushed, for his people's sake and for Ceti Transport's need for Wolf Station to supply the cargo-chain. Without Wolf II's processed H-3 and the interim stop, Ceti's freighters could not reach the two newer colonies at Lalande 21185 and Ross 128 farther outward. And so Danforth's actions had implications beyond his own station—as Central lectured *him* whenever it sent an inspector to poke into cupboards and stir up labor with impossible promises and make Danforth's life hell for three months until the next freighter bore him safely away.

Danforth frowned as he puffed at his cigarette, glowering at the sky-wide ruddy face of the star, now half-receded behind the crater wall; he welcomed the return of nightside for the next several days and wished he could

put off second dawn indefinitely, at least until the star
delivered whatever it had planned. For weeks the Wolf-
watch had brought their warnings, steadily more alarmed
by the unusual stresses building inside the star, something about magnetic stresses and variability cycles and
whatall. Young Leland had been the worst, actually shaking his sheaf of data faxes in Danforth's face, the young
twerp. Danforth had shrugged him off, more concerned
about the upcoming quarterly report to Ceti Central. Another blindness—young Leland had brains; perhaps he
should have listened. Should have, shouldn't: how could
a man decide? He stubbed out his cigarette angrily. I'm
getting too old for this job, he thought. For twelve years
the station had weathered Wolf's small flares without
trouble; Danforth saw no reason to expect a change. He
had enough problems already.

Another hour.

He saw the flare actually begin, a brilliant yellow flash
at star edge that spread in an instant across the western
longitudes, a flare bigger than any he had ever seen except in the remote-camera films of UV Ceti, the worst of
the flare stars. A moment later, an instant shorter than a
breath, every flare alarm awoke on his monitors, shriek-
ing downward through the station's levels. After another
moment of startled paralysis, Danforth jumped to his
feet, rocketed his chair against the wall, and ran madly
into the corridor. He flung himself down a low ramp and
skidded around the turn, then lunged at the double doors
of the power room, knowing that the colony's life could
be counted in seconds before the gamma flux burst
through the station's shields.

"Switch to backups!" he shouted at the four techni-
cians inside the room. "Power down the main systems!
Now!"

The men stared at him in astonishment, then quickly
obeyed, typing wildly on their boards. Panting, one hand
pressed to his side, Danforth watched the wall-panel displays change sequence one by one as the techs disconnected the main computer systems, removing the
dangerous electric current that gamma flux would send
into a frenzy of memory-wipe. The backup systems, de-

pendent on an older technology of vacuum chips immune to flux, smoothly took up the load, allowing minimal power, a minimal environment.

They almost made it.

An arcing short circuit leapt between the left control wall panels, then racketed around the room, skipping the darkened main panels, making hash of the still-active memory banks. Appalled, Danforth rocked from foot to foot, watching the damage spreading through the systems.

Just leave me a little power, some fans, he begged the star, something to survive with . . .

The short circuit died, killing the overhead lights. In the sudden darkness, one of the techs screamed, a thin wailing cry.

"That's enough of that," Danforth said harshly. "Restore enviro-controls."

"Limited capacity, sir," a shaken voice answered from the shadows. "Our vacuum-chip systems can handle only twenty percent of normal load."

Danforth peered at him, trying to see his face in the dim greenish light of the few computer wall screens still active. The man looked tense but seemed under control.

"That's enough for lights and air. You're in charge. Begin damage-control procedures. I'll be uplevel."

"Yes, sir."

Danforth took a hand lamp from an emergency capsule outside the power room, then continued his way back upward to Level 2. In the darkness he heard shouts, weeping, the sounds of beginning panic.

"People!" he shouted. "Be calm! We're working on restoring power!"

At the next turning, Mack Summers suddenly loomed out of the darkness and grabbed Danforth's tunic, half lifting him off the floor. "Kendall was right!" he shouted into Danforth's face. "You mealymouthed number pusher!"

Danforth pushed him off angrily. "We've got an emergency, man. Are you going to help or bleat?" They glared at each other.

Summers retreated a step, still simmering. "The harvesters . . ."

"I've got four hundred people at risk here: help me save them first. What about the surface crews? Did anyone get below?"

"Are you kidding?" Summers asked angrily.

Danforth's shoulders sagged; he straightened with an effort, knowing he would get no sympathy from this angry man. People looked to Summers, he knew, and so he had regularly taken Summers off harvester duty to manage the topside crews. Summers had adapted well to the new responsibilities, and Danforth valued him as an asset, well aware of the resentment building in recent months among the labor crews, inflamed by a dozen small insulting choices, a few unpopular orders, and the careless arrogance of the scientists toward the contract laborers who worked with them. Ceti Central had built the simmering resentment into every vacuum colony by recruiting the desperate unemployed in Europe's slums, promising things it knew full well the cargo-chain colonies could not deliver, not yet. That anger threatened them all now, for angry people did not care to listen, even at the cost of their lives. He eyed Summers warily.

"Come with me," he told him.

Danforth marched onward, gathering several other men and women as he passed through the second level, then delegating others as section leaders, following the flare drill he had long dreaded, the drill that had worked itself into his nightmares, whatever Central's smug assurances. In those sweat-tormented dreams he had lived and relived this disaster, planning what he would do, living the part of hero, sometimes coward, seeing all his people die, all survive. He shuddered, then angrily pushed away the memory. This was *now*.

As he reached the first level, the overhead lights flickered and built up to a murky yellow illumination, enough to see by. Danforth snapped off his hand lamp and took his men into the station conference room, where the principal scientists and other labor chiefs were gathered, waiting for him. The air already seemed stuffy and hot as ventilators and heat exchangers labored below optimum. He noted the fact absently. Though surrounded by the deadly airless cold of space, a vacuum colony worried more about discarding its waste heat than about keeping cold out, an irony Danforth knew was now a critical problem.

A half dozen heads turned expectantly as he walked into the room. He saw Victoria Renfrew at the left end of the table and nodded to her. Renfrew had Earthside training in hospital administration, Danforth remembered, his mind clicking smoothly. As chief of biolab, she could coordinate a temporary sick ward when radiation sickness overfilled the base hospital's fifty beds. How many will die? he wondered bleakly, remembering the alarms. Most flare storms rarely penetrated below topside; this flare had gone far deeper, perhaps even as far as Level 4. Thank God, at this hour most of the colony children would have been down in the residential level; the last thing he needed was parents screaming hysterically about their kids. He shoved away that problem, too—later, he would deal with it later—and sat down.

"How long until *Ceti Flag* arrives?" Dr. Renfrew asked, her pale face tense with apprehension. Normally calm, collected, and competent, Renfrew was Danforth's equivalent people-problem asset in science, able to smooth over troubles the aging science chief, Dr. Harrod, could not. He noted that Harrod was not present and wondered irritably why.

"We had comlink acquisition three hours ago," he said briskly. "They're four days out on a swing-by trajectory from the other side of Wolf-system."

"Opposite the flare," Dr. Renfrew stated anxiously.

"Yes," he said, but remembered that the flare wall had rolled around the edge of Wolf—from the other side of the star. Best not to mention that, he decided. "They won't even cross the radiation cone," he lied. "Probably won't even catch on we've had a flare incident at all until they get here." He saw the tension smooth in the faces around the table and smiled confidently at them all. *Incident*, that was the right word. "*Flag* will arrive on time,

Victoria—we just have to get through the next four days until they do.''

"We won't last four days," a voice muttered.

Danforth craned his neck to see the speaker. "So curl up and die, Jenkins," he said cruelly, trying to jar them all. "You know the drill. We've got a chance if we follow the regs, keep down the panic, get through the time until *Flag* arrives. As to what then, I'm open to suggestions. Think about it." He looked around at the faces, waiting for any more challenges. There were none. "Summers, you get down to Level Five and open up the emergency stairwells: those people will be in a panic if the elevators aren't powered. Rodriguez, start a survey of our enviro-systems—see what we've got left. And you, Jenkins," he said, stabbing a finger at the man, "take a crew to the ventilator shed and replace the control chips. Orders, people."

"And then what?" Jenkins asked, his expression ugly.

Danforth stared him down. "We wait for *Ceti Flag*."

Wolf Colony Station, Level 5, near Living Unit 134B, 6 minutes after flare.

On the fifth level the sudden darkness and racheting alarms had caused a panic, fear fueling fear into an unreasonable flight to the elevators. Fifteen-year-old Magda Janozek plunged into the mob of screaming, stamping people in the corridor outside her apartment, struggling to reach the elevator. A man slammed an elbow into her ribs, exploding her breath outward; the girl hit back instantly, connecting hard with his face.

"Out of the way," she shouted at him. "Let me by."

The man snarled at her from a demon's mask and raised a clenched fist; she ducked away behind fat Mrs. Galiano and heard the blow and the louder shriek. Terrified, she pushed vainly at the backs ahead of her, trying to wiggle her adolescent body through the gaps, squirming, pushing, hammering with her fists. "Let me by!"

A gap opened unexpectedly, and she took the chance, getting near enough to see the elevator doors still closed, people pounding vainly on the metal surface, prying with their fingers at the midline crack. They aren't working, she realized with a new heart thump of fear. But the lights are on again . . . She looked around wildly, seeing only fear and panic in the people near her as they pushed and shoved and screamed.

"We can't get out!" a man shouted hoarsely. "We're gonna die!"

A wail from a dozen throats answered him with shouted words in a half dozen languages as the crowd surged forward. Magda saw little Josef Marzek fall beneath the stamping feet and grabbed for him, nearly overbalancing as the mob swayed toward the elevator. She snagged his sleeve and dragged him toward her, only to lose hold as a beefy man lurched into her, pushing roughly. Her feet lifted helplessly from the floor as the crowd carried her away.

"Help!" she cried. "Help, help!" Powerless in the grip of the mob, Magda closed her eyes and screamed, buffeted by the bodies around her, lost in the terror that had caught them all. "Motherrrr . . ."

The crowd surged suddenly down the corridor past the elevators, toward the far corridor turn. Magda struggled to keep her feet, knowing she would be trampled like Josef if she slipped. As she was borne helplessly around the corridor turning, she saw Mack Summers ahead, motioning everyone through the open stairwell door, bellowing orders no one could hear. As she reached him, Summers caught her up and hugged her close.

"Careful now, Magda. Where's your mother?"

"On Level One, I think, helping Dr. Sorenson. I don't remember. Oh, Mr. Mack . . ." She buried her face against his broad chest and sobbed from fright, clinging to him. He patted her awkwardly.

"We'll find her," Summers said. "Don't you worry."

She looked up at him through a glaze of tears. "Not *worry*?" she asked increduously. "Are you *kidding*?"

"So it was a stupid comment," he muttered, and looked away.

"I don't think you're stupid," Magda promptly declared. "Not at all. Neither does Mother."

He smiled down at her then, looking pleased. "That's

nice to know." She smiled back, liking Mr. Mack's smile, his deep voice. Sometimes Magda thought her mother was incredibly dense.

"Everything's all right now," she said confidently, "now that *you're* here."

Summers shuddered at her words, reawakening the girl's fear. She pressed closer to him, anxious. "Mr. Mack?"

The last of the crowd vanished past them into the stairwell. "Listen, I've got to go back up," he said. "You stay close to me, okay?"

Magda nodded and slipped her hand into his. He looks afraid, she realized, and she had never seen Mack Summers afraid of anything.

And angry . . . why is he angry? What has happened?

Bewildered, she followed Summers into the half-lit stairwell. As they climbed upward, following the others, she clung to his hand, comforted by his presence. But why is he afraid?

"What happened, Mr. Mack? Why did the lights go out?"

"Later, sweetie. You just stay close by me until we find your mother. Okay?"

"Okay." It was not okay, not really, but she could tell that he didn't want to say any more. Why? She thought of her mother and began to hurry, suddenly afraid that she knew the reason, why he wouldn't tell her.

"Careful," he warned as she half stumbled on the stair, then steadied her until she had her balance again.

"I'm okay," she said, and tried to smile back at him, tried to be brave like he was, though her heart pounded a dull panicked beat and her palms had turned clammy with sweat. "I'm okay," she assured him. He nodded and led the way upward.

Magda clung to his hand as they entered the corridor on Level 3. She sensed the fear in the air as people rushed by them, jostling her into Mack again and again.

"Stay close," Summers murmured, and tugged her after him. In the dim light it was hard to see far ahead, though Magda had known these corridors most of her life. Somehow everything looked different in the half-light of the emergency lamps.

He led her to one of the large schoolrooms on Level 3. Already some of the adults were shoving the long tables to the walls, folding them into stacks, then folding the chairs on top of the stacked tables. Others brought in foldaway cots and bedding from stores, a bustle of activity Magda found bewildering—but somehow comforting. After the panic of the adults on Level 5, it was good to see order again, the order of busy activity and purpose to which she was accustomed in her home of constant rules. Summers guided her into a corner and set up a cot for a seat.

"Wait here. I'll find your mother."

She grabbed at him anxiously as he turned to leave, then quickly released his arm and tried to smile. "Okay."

She folded her hands in her lap and twisted her slender fingers, then looked around at the busyness in the room; she thought maybe she could help but didn't know who to ask. Cooperation keeps a colony alive: it was one of the maxims of the schoolroom, one Magda saw in operation every day—or had it pointed out to her by Mrs. Green, the ninth-form teacher. She shook blond hair back from her eyes, then began nervously twisting the ends into plaits. She saw her mother the instant she entered the room.

"Mother!" Magda leapt up and ran to her, throwing her arms around her mother's shoulders, hugging her close. "Are you all right?"

Elizabet Janozek smiled as she loosened her daughter's hold, then smoothed back Magda's hair from her face in what had been her special caress for as long as Magda could remember.

"So here you are," her mother said softly. Magda took her hand and led her toward her cot, then sat her down on the narrow bed with a little ceremony, as if only Magda could have delivered her there. It made her mother smile.

In her youth Elizabet Janozek had tramped the hills of Croatia with Magda's father, fighting with the partisans against the repressive New Serb government. The Serbs

had won bloodily and, in their anger, had moved quickly
from village to village with their tanks and soldiery, from
Rijeka to Zagreb to Osijek, decimating whole towns on
mere suspicion of rebellion, killing and killing until the
Peacemaker battalions had swept into Yugoslavia and
forced them to stop. It had been a horrible time, those
brief weeks of slaughter, a time that had scarred her
mother beyond Magda's young understanding. Later, too
late for her father and the thousands who had died, had
come the Peacemaker trials in Geneva and the new exe-
cutions, the elaborate masses for the martyred dead in
all the Catholic cathedrals of Europe, and the reparations
to the Croat survivors, both those who remained in Croatia and those who fled their ancient homeland in anguish, never to return.

In that bitter time, Elizabet had buried her heart with
her husband, refusing all comfort, and had taken the prof-
fered lab posting at the new colony on Wolf II and its
hope for a new life with the other dispossessed of Earth,
far away from memories. Had she found it there? Magda
had never really known. Surreptitiously, she had sought
out the history tape on the Croat rebellion and looked at
the pictures of Croatia in the atlas, trying to imagine her
mother's youth in those hills and river plains, those times.
The pictures perplexed her. She tried to imagine the dis-
tances, things named wind and clouds and mountains,
trying hard to put herself *into* the picture to see the
place—but it eluded her. All her remembered life Magda
had known only the corridors of Wolf Station, the ceiling
lighting, the crowded spaces, the barely perceptible sighing from the ventilators; she couldn't imagine sun and
wind and mountains. It eluded her, that fierce love for a
place and people that had killed her father and forced her
mother into self-exile. Yet the answer was there in the
pictures, just beyond her reach, a tantalizing promise of
a way to understand her mother's grief.

Each year Magda had watched as her mother had grown
more silent, more passive—until recently when Mack
Summers had started courting her. Funny to watch her
mother not notice for the longest time, though that was
very hard on poor Mr. Mack; then, suddenly, her mother

had noticed, and that was funnier still, the way she acted, blushing as she stammered, smiling as she dodged. Magda so hoped . . .

"Mack said he'd found you," her mother said as Magda sat down beside her on the cot. "Are you still frightened?"

"No, Mother."

"Good." Her mother tugged her sleeve gently. "Remember that you are the daughter of the Croat partisan Paul Janozek—and myself, of course. You come from stern stock." The smile deepened, lighting a ghost of a twinkle in her eyes, something new in recent months, something good to see. "Children can be frightened when there is sudden danger, but young women, as you are now, my Magda, must be brave. When I was only a little older than you, I was already married and living in the hills. So long ago." Her hand caressed Magda's face. "I am pleased you are not frightened."

"Well, a little frightened," Magda admitted more truthfully. "Mother, what has happened?"

"We've had a bad flare, far worse than the others. Matters may become desperate—and you must be brave, daughter, whatever happens to you—or to me." Elizabet stopped and bit her lip, and the desolation that suddenly filled her mother's eyes frightened Magda more than ever. Her mother saw the fear, as she always saw everything, and pressed Magda's hand. "You've been sheltered here at Wolf Station, perhaps too much—how I have tried to shelter you from the hardness of living, my child. I've tried to keep you safe—but the hard times have come, as they came for me, and now it's time to grow up quickly, as I did when there was need. Will you try to be braver, for my sake?"

"Yes, Mother."

"Whatever happens? However hard the times?"

"Yes, Mother. I promise."

"Good." Elizabet sighed, then straightened and took a deeper breath. She glanced briskly around the room, then stood up. "Come along, now. There is much to do."

Wolf Harvester A39469, Tri Ellium crater, Mining Sector 17,
9 minutes past flare.

Slowly the flare light faded, shifting from the harsh
brightness of near ultraviolet to Wolf's normal ruddy twilight. Kendall raised his head and looked around the silent cab. A single stub light flashed steadily on the control
board as the cab pursued a mindless path along the scarp,
bumping awkwardly through the broken terrain on autopilot. The electronics had held somehow, for all the good
it might do himself and Leland. If the cargo hauler had
been caught aloft, they couldn't expect rescue soon—if
the colony station had even survived the flare.

He reached toward the radiation badge in his chest
pocket, then skipped it. We're dead, he thought bleakly,
remembering the radiation alarms. Just a little time to
keep on breathing, that's all. He elbowed himself up and
looked down at Leland's pale face, wishing he had had
more time to know this man. More time.

Leland's eyes fluttered open. "Isaiah?" he asked
weakly. "Is it over?"

"Yeah, Paul. It's over."

Leland blinked. "So what do we do now?"

"Now?"

Leland looked at him squarely, their faces only inches
apart. "Yeah, chief. Like in action. Like getting back.
Like in surviving."

"You do beat all." Kendall rolled away and got to his
feet, swaying off balance as he stood. Then he looked
around again, automatically checking the array of lights
on the control board forward, the enviro-panel, the bin
readings. He snorted at himself at the last: a full cargo
of dust was about as relevant as sex to his maiden aunt.
His hand strayed again toward his pocket, but he firmly
put it away. Nuts to that. He'd had enough bad news
already.

He flicked his glance again over the instrument panels,
checking the readings on power, heat exchange, ventilators, air. A few odd readings he would check out, but
everything seemed to be working. The power of prayer,
he decided ironically, amazed, then stepped into the front

of the cab and shut down the autopilot. The harvester
ground to a stop in a convenient spot of darker shadow.
Out on the white dust of the crater floor, the other harvesters stood motionless at the end of long shallow
grooves scraped in the crater soil, Wolf's reddish light
glinting off their hulls. The shades of Wolf-light danced
above them, flickering in their half-seen curtains. Kendall grimaced and turned back to Leland.

"Got any ideas?" he asked.

"Maybe a few."

Kendall walked back and put out a hand to pull Leland
to his feet. "We need them, friend. Start talking."

Chapter 3

Cargo-chain freighter Ceti Flag, *EuroCom registry, crew module inner level, biosystems, 15 minutes past flare.*

Inga Stromstad looked up and smiled as Jason walked in. A regal blonde in a trim blue shipsuit, her braided hair coiled neatly around her head, her expression habitually calm, she sat at her desk in the center of the room behind a welter of printouts and computer tapes. Behind her a dozen wall panels flickered as the biosystems computer monitored *Flag*'s artificial environment; to the left, Inga maintained a small surgery and four-bed sick bay; to the right were several shelves of data tapes. Everything gleamed, polished bright and scrubbed. Biosystems was Inga's domain, as neatly ordered and compulsively serene as her person. She lifted an inquiring eyebrow.

"What do you know about radiation sickness?" he asked.

"Radiation?" Inga stiffened. "I saw the particle readings, but surely . . . Why was anyone outship? Who's been hurt?" She started to rise from her chair.

"No," Jason said hastily, putting out a hand to forestall her. "Not on *Flag*, Inga. Maybe a flare at Wolf."

Inga let out her breath in an audible sigh and relaxed, then shook her head. "Don't worry, Jason," she said, her hands already busy with her papers. "Wolf Station is well shielded—five meters of rock, a magnetic flux field, backup environmental controls—everything. More than enough to shield Wolf's flares."

"How about a big flare, something like UV Ceti?"

"Wolf doesn't—"

"Yet," Jason said decisively.

Inga's blue eyes widened. "Yves thinks Wolf has turned violent?"

Jason tightened his lips; it wasn't really quite a lie if he didn't nod.

Inga looked away from him, her eyes abstracted, and tapped a slender finger. "Well, add another order of magnitude. UV Ceti's particle storms can pierce rock—or ship shielding—for several dozen meters. The real problem is gamma flux: it erases computer systems—and with it, power and biosystems. Without ventilation and heat exchange, the residual atmosphere might support the colony for a day or more, that's all." She shrugged.

Her cold-blooded tone made Jason's skin crawl. She laced her fingers and looked at him calmly.

"What about backups?" he asked hoarsely.

"Oh, the standard vacuum chips, I'm sure, but vac chips haven't the speed or capacity to run all systems—assuming Danforth had the chance to change over. He might not have. A red dwarf flares to full intensity within seconds, quite unlike Sol. If they were in dayside . . ." She shook herself briskly. "I'll get Axel," she said, and rose from her chair. "Crew meeting in ten minutes?"

"Right." Yves would not appreciate a meeting he hadn't called—but he might listen to the Swedes.

"We'll be there." Inga smiled again and left the room, not hurrying, her elegant head carried high. Jason stood in front of her desk for a few moments, looking over the neat order of desk, shelves, surgery. An entire colony might be destroyed, but Inga didn't hurry a step, never that.

What is *wrong* with everybody?

He shook his head, baffled. Each circuit Inga seemed to grow stiffer, calmer, more tightly controlled, finding her own anodyne in enforced serenity. It made her a superb doctor, a perfectionist on biosystems, an ever-calm if distant psychotherapist—but somehow less of a person. Even her roses had been more an experiment in bioteching than a labor of love.

Where is the passion, Inga? he wondered bitterly. Do you ever miss it?

He curled his hands into fists, then flexed his fingers, examining his knuckles with a concentrated attention. Good strong hands, callused in the right places, capable, deft, a wonder at piloting, gentle in lovemaking, vivid in gestures, smart in a needed fistfight, good servants in many causes. And useless against the inertia of cargo-chain and the strange things it did to people.

I don't understand, he thought angrily, I don't understand at all. Maybe I used to, but it's all gone, stolen by the cargo-chain.

He slammed his hands onto the desk, hard enough to make his flesh sting, and stalked out of biosystems.

Jason paged Helena on the ship intercom, then fumed as she chose to not answer. Drat the woman. Cursing under his breath, he clattered down the next ladder to the lower level, heading outward and aft toward the starboard gimbel port to cargo deck. Unlike the crew module's directions of "up" as "in" and "down" as "out," courtesy of its sidewise rotation, the stationary frame and its ship bay were oriented to *Flag*'s vertical axis, with "up" and "down" dependent on *Flag*'s forward momentum. The gimbel port, a complicated tumbler and ladder arrangement, solved the discrepancy, linking the two sections of the ship. At the port, Jason stepped carefully onto the rotating strip and caught a hand rung to steady himself as the strip cycled him ninety degrees.

As he stepped out of the gimbel port, Jason glanced around the cargo deck, then automatically looked up at the cargo tins visible through a wide view band on the aft wall. Dimly visible in Wolf's attenuated illumination, the metal sides of the cargo tins glinted as reddish shadowy blurs against the blackness, two neat boxy lines bracketing the grayish bulk of *Flag*'s engines. *Flag* pulled two lines of cargo tins, twenty in all, each cargo-tin line tethered to an aft corner of the ship frame on a flexible cable assembly continuously monitored by computers on both the ship and each individual tin. The cargo tins added a new dimension to ship maneuvers: half of Jason's and Helena's responsibility on circuit lay in making sure none of the tins went adrift. With smart computers, the newest tether alloys, and a constant awareness of *Flag*'s little ducklings trundling behind their mother, so far none had.

To his right, next to the exterior ship port, the slim two-seater jitney sat in its wall clamps, a pretty little craft useful for quick transport to the surface. The bulkier ship tugs occupied the left half of the bay, their forward robot arms raised in mechanical prayer. He looked at the tugs fondly, liking their ugly lines; in vacuum, both were nimble and efficient, a joy to pilot. Helena was sitting at a systems panel just beyond the farther tug, her back to him as she ostentatiously concentrated on her computer program. He knew she had heard him come in. As he walked up to her, she turned and scowled at him.

"Don't even start," Jason warned her. "We've got an emergency."

"What emergency?" she asked sharply.

"Maybe a flare at Wolf. Everybody's ordered to control deck."

"Flare? Don't be ridiculous—the colony's shielded."

Jason slowly counted to ten to himself, trying to control his temper. It was no use; in this mood, Helena turned his dial to full boil.

"So I told you," he snapped. "So you heard the word. So don't come to control." He stamped back toward the gimbel port.

"Jason!"

Jason was through the gimbel port and well down the corridor when he heard her footsteps hurrying after him.

"Wait up!" she demanded. He kept at exactly the same pace, knowing he was being contrary but likely to tear apart the walls—or her—if he got pushed too hard.

"I said wait up!" Helena grabbed at his sleeve and yanked him to a stop. "You oaf!"

Jason carefully detached her fingers one by one, dropped them, and headed off again. He heard Helena stamp her foot and grinned to himself. Fights: they're wonderful.

She caught up with him by the next ladder, then half skipped to keep up with his long strides. He glanced at her and saw her lips tightened into a firm line, her blond hair bobbing, her breasts jiggling under her tunic. He considered, then shortened his steps slightly.

"Beast!" she muttered as she noticed the change.

"Bitch," he rejoined mildly. "How about a truce?"

"With *you*?" Helena laughed sarcastically, pretending amazement. Games, Jason thought disgustedly. Always games. He lengthened his steps, then added a bit more to set Helena panting as she hurried. They didn't say another word all the way to the control room, although she managed quite nicely to keep up. Helena yielded few battles easily, even the most asinine.

As he had expected when Helena delayed him, Inga and Axel had arrived first; they and Yves had obviously had time to compare notes. Damn, he thought as he saw their faces. Yves glowered at him, one hand idly tapping a pen on his knee, as Jason walked to his chair. Nearby, Axel Stromstad, a squat blond man in his forties, idly swung his chair from side to side, his expression remote and noncommittal; Inga sat quietly beside him, her hands folded in her lap, her lips pressed together in prim disapproval. All three sets of eyes followed him inexorably as he walked toward his own chair, making him feel absurdly self-conscious of his stride, the arc of his arms as they swung, the soft sound of his boots on the tile.

Damn . . . He sat down, his chair creaking as it took his weight.

"What's going on?" Helena asked, alerted by the tension in Yves's face. She looked at Jason, then at Yves. "Yves? Aren't we having a meeting?"

"Apparently," Yves said tightly. "Interesting—I knew nothing about it. Are you the captain now, Jason? Perhaps I missed that flimsy."

"I saw a need, Yves."

"Oh? Since when do your 'needs' have anything to do with authority on this ship?"

"I'm not challenging your authority," Jason said, trying to placate him. "I just think we should discuss—"

Yves threw his pen down on his computer console. "I told you I would act in due time. Loss of radio link could have a number of causes . . ."

"Oh? At a flare star?"

"We don't have radio link?" Helena asked with alarm.

Yves glanced at her resentfully, then tightened his lips. "No. We lost acquisition shortly after Jason says he saw a flare. I doubt there's a connection . . ."

"Oh?" Jason asked sarcastically.

". . . but we'll analyze the tape. If you'll oblige us again, Axel."

So he *had* looked at the tape, Jason thought. Before or after the Stromstads had shown up? Who could tell? The wall screen flickered into grayness as the computer hunted for the requested tape. Silently, *Flag*'s crew watched the firestorm sweep over the star, vanishing abruptly over the star edge.

"Like I said," Jason said irritably, and saw Inga stir warningly, her blue eyes flicking from him to Yves. Warning to whom?

"Wolf is not a typical flare star," Yves snapped back. "During all modern observation, its flares have never exceeded—"

"Yet," Helena said. Jason looked with some sardonic surprise at her; she promptly glared back. "I gather that Jason called this meeting—nice of you to lie about that, Jason—but why? Why did we lose radio link? How bad was that flare?"

"I don't know yet. It takes time . . ." Yves shrugged.

Helena sat down and crossed her arms across her full breasts. "Then a meeting is certainly in order, Captain."

"I don't agree," he snapped.

Helena scowled ferociously, her eyes flashing with resentment at his tone.

"Nor do I appreciate the insubordination on this ship," he went on.

"Insubordination?" Helena asked. "Since when is *Flag* an autocracy, King Yves?"

"That's enough, Helena!"

"No, it's not enough! Just because you don't want to admit Jason might be—"

"I agree with the captain," Axel interrupted smoothly, his tone bland. "This discussion is premature. Even if Wolf did flare past maximum, the colony station was likely in nightside; aside from a mild cascade from the planet's magnetosphere, flare effects would be minimal.''

"Have you confirmed nightside?" Jason asked, his fists bunched on his thighs. "Do we have real-time readings yet?"

Axel cleared his throat and looked sour, his glance flicking to Yves. "Not yet," he admitted reluctantly. "Another hour perhaps. Assuming the standard time slippage, we could compute the planet's approximate dayside from our last access data."

Jason stared at him, waiting. After a moment Axel shrugged and swung his chair to tap at his computer console.

"Wolf II has nearly complete tidal braking, with a spin-orbit coupling of three-two," he said pedantically, reading from his screen. "At our last real-time reading three years ago, Two was fifty-two days past second dawn, which would put it ten days past first dawn now—" He stopped as he realized what he was saying.

"In dayside," Jason said for him.

"At an oblique angle," Axel argued back. "With most of the station sheltered by the cliffside."

"Maybe."

Axel harrumphed. "Right now the station should be entering shadow again, four days from second dawn. The odds the flare hit during full dayside are—"

"A star doesn't pay attention to odds," Jason said impatiently. "Nor does wishful thinking make a missing signal a nonevent. Why don't we have acquisition?"

"Equipment breakdown," Axel rumbled.

"They have backups," Jason reminded him. "Hell, they could even cannibalize a harvester radio if they had to. They know we're due. They know the procedure for ship approach. But maybe everybody's asleep; maybe it's been a hard day."

"Cut the sarcasm, Jason," Yves snapped.

"So *do* something, Yves! What's the protocol for a flare event? How will we make rescue? What are the parameters? How many people might be hurt? How damaged are their station systems? What do we *do* if Wolf has flared?''

''We'll study the problem—''

''Yves,'' Helena interrupted, her face sober, ''I agree with Jason. We don't have time to 'study the problem.' ''

''The odds . . .'' Axel began.

Helena jumped to her feet. ''What is *wrong* with you people?'' She swept the three with an angry glance. ''Jason's right this time! You can't wish it away. So we waste some time planning for an emergency that never happened—big deal! What's the protocol, Yves?''

''Bypass,'' Yves said flatly.

Helena stared at him in shock and slowly sat down again. Jason saw Axel swallow uneasily, then glance at his wife.

''We must refuel at Wolf Station,'' Yves explained. ''If we can't, we can't afford to lose momentum for our next Jump to Lalande. So we accelerate again and bypass. That's the protocol.''

''Bypass! You mean just leave them—''

''*That's* why we study the problem,'' Yves insisted. ''Why attempt a pointless rescue of a dead colony? Besides, if Wolf has entered a bad flare cycle, *Flag* herself would be continually exposed during decel, then at risk every time we moved into dayside orbit. Lalande and Ross need our supplies, too—thus the triage.''

''Why weren't we ever *told* this?'' Helena demanded.

''It wasn't necessary—Wolf doesn't flare into risk range!'' Yves thumped his fist against his thigh. ''And we don't know—yet—if it has! Inga, what are the parameters on a flare at UV Ceti's level?''

''One hundred percent fatality,'' Inga said solemnly. Yves leaned back and spread his hands expressively.

''Half of UV Ceti?'' Jason asked sharply.

''One hundred percent. You see, Jason, once the radiation pierces the shielding, they might as well be in open space—actually, worse. High-energy particles impacting with matter—such as rock shielding—set off a cascade of secondary radiation that can be more lethal than the primary flux. The particle speed drops, you see . . .'' Her voice trailed off.

"One-third."

Inga looked thoughtful. "The lower levels might survive, but radiation sickness would be immediate, with most dosages fatal within several days—assuming the machines survived. As I told you earlier, the major risk is the gamma flux."

"Twenty percent?"

"Some personnel might have nonfatal exposure," she said slowly.

"Ten percent?"

"How do we get them home?" Helena asked, bewildered. "How do we transport four hundred people? Even two hundred?"

"We don't transport," Yves said, shaking his head. "We go on to Lalande. That's the protocol."

"I don't accept that," Jason said furiously.

"Neither do I." Helena glared at Yves. "We have friends there, Yves. Why are you writing them off?"

"I'm not writing them off. I'm just saying that the protocol says—"

"Oh, sure," Helena threw at him. "Big difference. You haven't even measured the flare. What *percent* are we dealing with?" She snarled the word.

"Axel will run the analysis; we will find out." Yves leaned back in his chair and flicked his glance over them all. "I will always listen to crew opinion," he said stiffly. "Axel? Your conclusions?"

Axel glanced at Jason, then hesitated. "I still say the odds are against any significant problem. Otherwise, the protocol seems harsh but—prudent." Inga nodded, her face troubled.

"I agree," Yves said, not bothering to hide a look of triumph at Jason. "Command decision, with note of the majority opinion among the crew. We will wait until we know what *percent*," he threw back at Helena, "we're dealing with. Is that understood?"

Helena surged to her feet and flounced out of the room.

Jason slowly stood up. "We'll be on the cargo-tug deck—if you need us."

Yves nodded curtly, then looked away. After a moment Jason shrugged and walked out.

Helena was waiting in the corridor, still simmering. "What's the matter with him? Can't he *see*?"

"Pipe down. They took a vote—democratic astrophysics, works every time." He pulled her out of earshot. "You know the regs: once the captain makes an official decision, crew doesn't debate it further."

Helena stared at him. "Since when are you so hipped on rules, Jase? You? Since when do we just sit?" She started to boil again.

"So who says just sit?" he retorted. "Come on, pilot."

"So what are you going to do?" Helena asked suspiciously as they cycled through the gimbel port into the cargo deck.

"So how do we transport a few hundred colonists, probably most radiation-sick?" He waved at the line of cargo tins visible through the view window overhead. "So we arrange a place to put them."

"In the cargo tins? Are you *crazy*? Tins don't have that kind of capacity."

"I'm getting tired of hearing everything is impossible. You sound like Yves."

"Don't be insulting."

"Insulting, is it? So you thought the same about that little comedy act upship; I thought so."

She scowled at him, hands on her hips, and said nothing.

He tried to be patient with her. "Look, the colony has environmental equipment, enough to cannibalize; so do we. Okay?"

She nodded.

"So we dump our cargo, adapt several of the tins, and fill up any extra tins with air, water, food—enough to keep resupplying the passenger tins during transit. It won't be comfortable, but most of the trip the tins will be in zero gee."

"Four hundred colonists? You're crazy."

"It won't be four hundred," Jason said bleakly. "You heard Inga. Even if it's half that, we have to try. With flare damage, we're their only chance. The next ship won't get here for three months, time I doubt they'd have.''

Helena frowned, then looked up at the cargo tins, obviously wavering. "But Yves says the protocol is to bypass Wolf."

"We'll see about that," Jason said grimly. "Central has cheese for brains on this one. Triage! I can't believe it!"

"But our fuel . . . And what about the risk to *Flag* during decel?"

"Space has lots of risks."

Helena shook back her hair and puffed her cheeks as she exhaled. "To get the tins ready, we'd have to start now."

"Exactly."

"Against orders? Central would have our skins!"

"So what's more important, Helena? Your career or our friends at Wolf?"

Her face darkened with anger. "That's not fair. Just because you don't care if you never get off the cargo-chain doesn't mean I—"

"So go twiddle and watch the screens with Yves."

Jason turned away and walked to the suit cabinet. He heard Helena's retreating footsteps and scowled. Just once, why couldn't she be reasonable? Yeah, Roarke, and you're the only one with the answers. He stopped in front of the cabinet. If he was wrong, he would lose cargo-chain: fights were one thing, outright insubordination quite another—and he had already been warned. Watching a button in an Earthside factory? Sweating over the innards of executive turbocars on Mars? God, I'd rather be dead, he thought.

But if he was right? Maybe the same result if he pushed Yves too far. Mutiny was a nasty idea.

Are you so sure, smart guy?

He looked through the view window at the stars beyond the cargo tins, a wealth of brilliant diamonds on endless black. The universe went on forever, stretching outward, beckoning, implacable in its dangers, rich in its wonders. Humanity had a start in its exploration, a slender handhold, and he had a place in that beginning, however he chafed at current limits.

Are you so sure?

He reached for the suit cabinet and snapped it open; ten minutes later he cycled through the rear air lock, heading for the nearest cargo tin. He floated easily to the first tins on the starboard line, then checked the dial meters on the H-3 tins, noting the amount of remaining fuel and mentally juggling how much H-3 would have to be salvaged from Wolf to get everybody home. In earlier years cargo-chain ships had carried enough fuel for the entire circuit, an expense quickly economized as the Lalande-route colonies began to manufacture their own H-3. Both tin assemblies were nearly depleted. If Wolf could not provide more fuel, *Flag* would be as surely marooned as the colonists—and just as exposed to sunlight every time she orbited into dayside. The protocol was right about that.

Wonderful, he thought.

He stopped by the fourth tin and slowly floated over the metal surface, then headed down the other side, inspecting the seams and vacuum controls. Possible—it might work. Though only thirty meters in each dimension, the cube-shaped cargo tins came equipped with an air lock, rudimentary atmosphere capacity, heaters for transport of the more delicate supplies, and an adaptable radio link through the on-tin computer. Although technically *Flag* might pack four hundred people into the crew module—the corridors were long enough—the crew module's biosystems were programmed for a crew of five, with prudent no-you-don't safeguards that might take a week to futz around to yes-we-will, assuming Inga wanted to help, another probably. But the tins might work. His mind clicked through the possibilities, testing one problem after another.

It just might work. Roarke, old boy, he told himself, you're an inspiration.

He rotated to look sunward toward Wolf, its disk already visibly larger as *Flag* hurtled deeper into her swing-by trajectory past the star. He could see the dark blurs of multiple starspots across the star's ruddy surface, the flickering of plumes from the curving edge, the brief flash of a small flare near the right quadrant. If Wolf decided to turn nasty at the wrong time and in their direction during swing-by, *Flag* needn't wait for planet orbit to get fried. Another nice thought.

He felt his skin prickle with apprehension. He watched Wolf for several moments, measuring his adversary.

"I start fights," he told the star. "I *always* win." Not exactly accurate, but how would a star know that? He set his jaw determinedly, then remembered his face making at his closet mirror. He smiled ironically. Roarke against the universe, pioneer extraordinary. Sure, guy, he thought. Why are you so sure? Maybe you only want a purpose beyond boring system checks and stupid arguments, something heroic to give meaning to your life, no matter how many have to die to give it to you. Maybe you're a vulture, Jason Roarke. Maybe you just need to believe in disaster as much as Yves needs his regs.

He turned and floated onward.

He had reached Tin 9 when a movement behind him caught his eye. He pivoted gracefully, facing back toward *Flag*. Another spacesuited form floated toward him, linked by a long tether to the crew lock, a second line clasped in one gloved hand. Jason snapped on his suit radio.

"Hello, love," he said softly.

He watched, smiling, as Helena drifted up to him and grabbed a nearby handhold. She bent to snap the extra line on his suit belt, then glared at him.

"You want to get to Lalande the hard way?" she asked. "If you go adrift, it'd only take about forty thousand years."

"Want to come along?"

"I prefer shorter relationships, friend. Besides, I'd miss the sex." She tipped her head and eyed him ruefully. "You're crazy, Jason Roarke. You know that?"

"Of course; it's part of my charm. Let's get to work."

Cargo-chain freighter Ceti Flag, *EuroCom registry, cargo-tin deck, 87 hours to Wolf II.*

"We don't have enough air-converters for the other tins," Helena said three hours later as she leaned over Jason's shoulder, studying the list of *Flag*'s stores on his computer screen. "Thirty colonists would use up the tin's oxygen in a few hours."

"We have the components to build more," Jason replied, frowning. "Extra catalyst screens, the tubing, some smaller generators. Or we could link the cargo tins with supply hoses—a single converter could handle several tins indefinitely."

"And if a hose comes adrift, the tin's occupants suffocate."

"Same result if they don't have an air-converter, love."

Helena shrugged and straightened. "True. What about heat exchange?"

"We can adapt the converter to vent the excess heat." Jason scrolled the screen farther and keyed it to a stop. "Hmmm. Those look like good water jugs."

"In another life those bulbs were called radar reflectors. What about food?"

"That's the rub. We just don't have enough carbohydrates aboard to feed a few hundred people for twelve weeks. The colony will have to contribute their own stores—water, too."

"And air."

"If they've got it, yeah."

"Why are you so sure about the flare, Jason?" she asked curiously.

"What—that Wolf had a bad flare or that somebody's survived if it did?"

"Your pick."

He keyed off the screen and swung his chair toward her. "I guess I take votes the way I like them, too. I just don't believe in sitting around hoping problems won't happen."

She looked away. "Yves is cautious. He's a good captain."

"Hey, I'm not arguing. I just don't understand his resistance—nor why Axel and Inga go along like wimps. I mean, he acts like I made the whole idea up just to bug him—and Axel backs him up.''

''Axel is cautious, too—caution gets ships around the cargo-chain circuit. When you take risks, you get more accidents.''

He looked her over a moment. ''Are you changing your mind?'' he demanded. She shook her blond head. ''No. I've just been thinking about—''

''Your precious career guggling down the drain. Listen, I'll tell the board I ordered all this, first pilot to second pilot. Does that make it better?''

''You don't have to be sarcastic. I've gone along, haven't I? When Yves finds out, my name with him will be mud just like yours. I happen to like Yves, so I'm grieving a little. Okay?''

''My heart is touched.''

She glared at him. ''Sometimes, Jason, you're a total washout as a man.'' She turned and stalked off past the nearer cargo tug.

''Hey, wait!''

Helena turned and looked back, then put one hand on a slender hip and stood hip-slung, shoulders pulled back, chin lifted. Her pose looked magnificent—Helena always did know how to use her body to good effect, Jason thought, especially when she was mad.

''You have a word, you slug?'' she jeered. Nice, he thought irritably. Helena was reaching new heights today.

''Don't quote bad videos,'' he advised her. ''I always liked *Return of the Ant People* better, anyway. 'But, John, you know I never meant to kill it,' '' he piped in a falsetto voice. '' 'Hell, Sheila, these ants might be intelligent! How *could* you, Sheila?' '' The falsetto again: '' 'Oh, John, please forgive me!' ''

''How would you like to be brained with a wrench?'' Helena asked. ''It might improve your personality; I think only a full lobotomy could.''

''No doubt. Hey, I'm sorry. Yves isn't my favorite person right now, okay?''

Helena hesitated, then walked back over to the computer station. "You're a real comic, Jason."

"Humor on the edge of doom, love," he said.

"Hmmph. The real humor will be if you're wrong and what'll happen to you if you are. Now *that* will be funny."

"No doubt." He turned back to the computer and scrolled onward through *Flag*'s stores. "We need to rig the tins with straps for free-fall—hmmm. Those cables padded with insulation might work."

"For four hundred belt sets? That's a lot of assembly."

"That's why we've got a head start, sweetheart." He swung back toward her. "Six and Seventeen are empty—we'll start with those. You can install the link hoses on Five through Eight, start the air cycling; I'll work on the startboard from Seventeen. We can shift cargo up-line to get working room in the other tins; I don't want to jettison until we have to."

Helena looked distinctly uncomfortable. "Uh, Jase . . ."

"Yeah?" he challenged.

"Nothing." She scowled at him.

"Just keep up your enthusiastic support, Sheila."

"You sod." She stalked off again.

Jason chuckled and toggled off the computer, then followed her toward the suits. He had just finished his suit prep and was helping Helena with a balky valve when she suddenly stiffened, looking over his shoulder. Jason turned.

Yves stood in the metal frame of the gimbel port, his face thunderous.

"Hello, Yves," Jason said casually.

"You aren't scheduled for a tin check."

"Pilot's discretion, Captain."

Yves hesitated as he decided whether to push it, then punted. "Postpone that, please. We've finished the analysis of the flare," he said. He chopped his hand down angrily. "Crew meeting *now*!"

"That's an o-kay."

Yves hesitated, then turned inship and vanished back into the gimbel port.

"Do you have to challenge him that way?" Helena

asked, her tone exasperated. "Does everything have to be a war?"

"Hey, I didn't start this war. He did."

"Oh, sure, Jason."

Jason laid his palm over his chest and put on a sincere look. "My heart is pure, Sheila."

Helena hissed and pushed her helmet at him; he caught it just as she dropped it.

"Hey, watch the equipment," he protested. "Central paid a pretty piece for these suits."

"As if you care, I'm sure." She hurried off toward the gimbel port.

Jason watched her go. To mend her fences with Yves? To promise what? Whatever you say, Yves, I'm on your side, Yves, hiss spit that nothing of a man Jason, oh, Yves, bat the eyes, soulful look, Yves.

God. She just might. She hadn't exactly been a stolid rock about this.

Jason looked up at the cargo-tin shadows in the view port. Hey, Helena, lives might be in the balance. Can't you see that, can't anyone see that? Whatever the triage regs about bypass, if anyone on Wolf II had a chance, they *had* to go in, had to. Somehow Jason had to turn it around, make them see past the petty quarrels, the weirdness of cargo-chain. Somehow. He hesitated, then quickly stripped off his spacesuit—best to avoid a visual side issue with Yves—then found his cap and took a deep breath. He wished an appeal to Whomever might be listening, then headed inship.

Chapter 4

Cargo-chain freighter Ceti Flag, *EuroCom registry, control room, 86 hours to Wolf II.*

Jason entered the control room and calmly walked to his chair, then spun to face the others. "So what does the analysis show, Captain?"

Yves frowned and glanced at Axel. "Ambivalent at best," he said reluctantly. "Not as great as UV Ceti, in fact quite a significant minimum—but enough for bad damage to the station. The comsat's out, as you know; likely they lost most of their topside machinery, with heavy radiation penetration into the station levels. Inga estimates fifty to seventy percent casualties."

"Based on what?" Jason glanced at the medico. "Wasn't Wolf Station in half shadow?"

"More or less," Inga agreed. "I hadn't factored that in. Yves asked for a worst-case analysis."

"What about the best-case analysis?" Jason insisted.

"The protocol says," Yves interrupted, "that we should bypass if—"

"Inga?"

Yves glowered.

Take it easy, Jase, Jason told himself. Back off. "Sorry to interrupt, Yves. Inga?"

Inga thought a moment as she tapped a slender finger on the arm of her chair. "Well, assuming everything favorable, maybe two-thirds survival among base personnel. Maybe. My computer program has limited variables. Central never assumed an intermediate flare."

"That's typical. Does Danforth know about our protocol?"

"Damned if I know," Yves said. "What difference does that make?"

"Lots of difference. If he knows you'll bypass, maybe he won't try as hard. Maybe when we get down there, we'll find that everybody gave up—because Central opted out on four hundred people. You want to know what the baseline is, Yves? Money, like it always is with Central. Why risk a million-dollar freighter for dead people? Let's cut the losses and keep the deficit down. Every little bit helps. Only it looks like some people might be alive. What's the value of lives, Yves? Where does that fit into the money equation?"

"*Flag* operates under Ceti Central authority. The regs say—"

"People, Yves. Friends." He glanced at Helena's noncommittal expression, saw no help there—yet. Get off the fence, sweetheart, he wished at her, and tried another tack.

"How does Central set its regs, then? Let's put it in another equation, Captain. What happens to morale at Ross and Lalande when the colonists *there* realize they're expendable, too? What happens to the cargo-chain when we *all* realize we're expendable? So easily expendable—get yourself a big problem and Central doesn't know you anymore. Regs are meant to help people, not write them off."

"The regulations," Yves corrected, "are to ensure against risk, to follow procedure that's been proved again and again . . ."

"Not this reg, Yves. Wolf has never flared into risk range. What happens when Ceti Central has to pay reparations to all those relatives at home? My uncle is the MP for Aberdeen; he rather likes me, and he's a loudmouth, too—runs in the family. If I were in trouble and Central let me die, he'd raise holy hell in Parliament. Danforth has big-shot connections, too; so do a few of the scientists at Wolf Station. We run out on them and Ceti Transport will have problems like they wouldn't believe. You think the other corporations will cry? Hell, they'll join in on the hunt."

He leaned forward earnestly. "The flare protocol assumes a no-win rescue, no chance at all. Get a flare on UV Ceti level and everything's crisped—no question, no doubt. No one would complain. But Wolf Station didn't get a UV Ceti flare. Possible survival throws all of Central's assumptions onto the trash heap. And who is Central going to blame? Not themselves, of course not. They'll blame us."

Helena straightened in her chair, glancing at Jason with alarm. Count on Helena to get jerked by that, Jason thought sourly. He glared at her.

"Listen," Yves protested weakly. "I have friends at Wolf Station, too. I'm not making any kind of economic argument. I'm just saying the regs . . ."

"Okay, let's talk regs. Ship regs say you can solicit crew discussion and vote when the problem's ambiguous. The protocol doesn't fit this flare—and all of us have to live with this choice later. So let us vote—a real vote, for once not based on Axel's knee-jerk loyalty, Inga's disapproval of certain persons on this ship, or Helena's worries about her career. *Or* this upmanship war you've got against me."

"What war?" Yves challenged.

"Ah, shit. Forget that, then. Put it to a real vote, of people for people—and see where it comes out. That's all I ask."

Yves studied him, looking for the catch and not finding it. Jason just hoped the catch was there. He needed only two of the crew to vote his way, just two. Yves thought about it a minute, then glanced at Axel.

"That reg is designed for unforeseen problems," Axel admitted. "Jason has a point."

"I'd like to vote," Helena declared.

"I don't see a need," Inga sniffed. "This is a captain's decision."

Yves cleared his throat. "If the vote goes against you, Jason, will you accept it? Stand with *Flag*'s crew all the way? No press conferences back on Mars? No talking to your machine-driver friends on Lalande? No protest of any kind—ever!"

"You've been listening too much to Inga. I do stand with this crew; I always have."

"Sure, Jason. I really believe that." Yves shrugged elaborately, not caring about Jason's protests. "Will you accept it?"

"You'll put it to a vote?"

"Yes—if you'll accept the vote. Will you accept?"

Jason closed his eyes and counted three breaths as he looked at the idiocy of this vote, of playing with people's lives like this. "Yes. Will *you* accept it?"

"Yes." Yves glanced around at the faces. "All right. This is the situation. We have probable bad flare damage at Wolf Station, with possible casualties up to seventy-two percent. Flare protocol orders us to bypass Wolf to preserve *Ceti Flag* and continue onward to Lalande. I do *not*, by the way, accept Jason's threats about reparations or corporate scandal or damage to our respective careers—this is strictly a question of proportionate risk. So . . . if Wolf flares again on bypass, there's a risk we'll suffer irreversible ship damage. If we descend to Wolf and the H-3 plant is damaged, we may not be able to refuel."

"And if we do bypass safely," Jason amended quickly, "and Wolf Station does have H-3, we can make rescue."

"How?" Yves protested.

"I have some ideas. Get to the vote."

Yves scowled at him, then turned to Axel. "Do we bypass, Axel?" he asked.

Axel looked uncertain, his eyes darting from Jason to Yves, then focused on Yves's face. "What will you decide, Captain?" he temporized.

"A *real* vote," Jason said irritably. "No cheating."

Axel glared at him, his broad face flushing with anger. Jason quickly made a conciliatory gesture.

"Sorry, Axel. I was out of line. I apologize, but I do ask that you vote for your own reasons, not his."

Axel harrumphed, then nodded.

"If the choice was yours," Jason said, "what would you do? That's the vote."

Axel let out a big breath and looked distractedly around the control room, his brow furrowed. "My reasons?

First, I doubt if Wolf will flare during bypass. That kind of flare takes time to build again; risk favors a safe passage by the star to Wolf II. Secondly, if the topside facilities are ruined, we have equipment we could use to salvage the H-3; the chemical itself wouldn't be affected by radiation—it's too simplistic in its structure. I therefore expect we can refuel, whatever awaits us at Wolf II.'' Yves's face had darkened as Axel disposed neatly of his objections; Axel answered the look with a slight defiance. ''I am offering my considered opinion, Captain. Whoever wrote that protocol didn't ask the engineers. They just assumed.''

''But Wolf *could* flare during bypass,'' Yves said.

''Assuming a sufficiently unpredictable cycle, something completely new, yes.''

''And the damage at the station *could* be too great to refuel.''

''Also true. I am only citing probabilities. If Jason has a way to rescue the Wolf colonists—though I can't imagine what it is—we should not bypass.'' He looked at Yves stubbornly. ''There is risk, but there is also a chance.''

Yves tightened his lips but nodded. ''Inga?''

''I have seen what radiation damage does to people— I was in the EuroCom medical crew that examined the Mare Australe reactor accident. Even if we rescue them, most will die within weeks.'' She shot a glance at Jason. ''You can juggle the figures with wall shadow and shielding, but that kind of radiation kills. I think the effort would be useless. A physician learns to accept triage.''

She shook back her shoulders and stared levelly at Yves. ''Jason asks for an honest opinion. I believe in options free of emotion, that look at a situation as it is— and I believe Wolf Station has been lost. That is my opinion. Ceti Central has established the protocol; we shouldn't second-guess it.'' Her face spasmed, then stilled. ''That is my opinion,'' she repeated faintly. Axel reached for her hand and squeezed it, his expression stolid. Inga bowed her head, refusing to look at anyone.

''Thank you, Inga,'' Jason said softly, offering respect for the honesty. She ignored him carefully.

''Helena?'' Yves asked.

"So I make the choice for *Flag*, Yves?" Helena twisted her hands in her lap, then shot a glance at Yves. "Is that how it turns out? Jason and Axel vote yes, Inga votes no—you vote no, I make the choice." Yves clamped his lips together. Helena took a deep breath and shook back her hair. "I vote for life, for the people on Wolf Station. We make rescue."

"How do you know I would have voted for bypass?" Yves asked her quietly, as if he were alone with her in the room. "Why do you think that?"

She gave him a bitter smile, not liking the burden. "Because it's Jason's idea, that's why. All you do is react to Jason. If he says no, you say yes. If he says yes, you say no. Why don't you wake up, Yves? It makes me sick, the way you act." She stood up and dramatically marched out of the room.

"Christ," Jason muttered as he saw Yves's face. "She's out of line, Yves. This was a real choice, remember?"

"I don't need your comfort, Jason," Yves said. He tightened his lips, struggling for self-control. "All right! We ignore the protocol. We'll at least check at Wolf Station before we go on."

Jason stared at him in dismay. "We'll *rescue* them, Yves! That was the vote!"

"It was not," Yves said, nicely rearranging reality. "We were voting on ignoring the protocol, not committing ourselves to rescue. Isn't that right, Inga? Axel?" The Swedes hesitated and looked at each other in confusion.

"Wasn't it . . ." Inga began, then lifted her chin. "Yes. That was the vote."

"You can't just leave them if they're alive!" Jason protested.

"If?" Yves asked. "So you admit some doubt? What if they're all dying, Jason? What if rescue only means transporting corpses back to Mars? Listen, I understand your concern about the colonists—I share it, of course— but I have to think about this ship and its purpose. It's my responsibility. I'm the captain." He hammered his fist on his thigh. "And I *will* make the decision when it comes. I'm not committing *Flag* to a useless gesture. Is that understood?"

Jason looked at Axel's troubled face, at the faint air of triumph in Inga's cold expression. So much for a real vote; Yves had his dodge, courtesy of the Swedes. "Oh, yeah, Yves, I understand. I understand everything."

"Good. You said you have some idea for rescuing the colonists. What's this brilliant idea?"

"We use the cargo tins."

He saw Yves immediately resist the suggestion, then think about it, clicking through the same possibilities that Jason had. Yves conceded reluctantly with a shrug. "Possible. *D'accord.* You and Helena adapt the tins, Jason; you might as well continue the work you've started. Do you really think I didn't know about that?"

"I didn't think anything, Captain."

"That's obvious," Yves said dismissively. "Inga, I want you to run the parameters on the expected radiation injuries. What's the standard treatment?"

"Limited."

"But there is treatment," Yves insisted. "What kind?"

"T-cell boosters and plasmids to help repair the cell damage; they work if the radiation damage isn't too severe. Some prophylactics to help the immune system recover, pain pills, sedatives. Wolf Station will exhaust its supplies quickly."

"See what we have to supplement. Set up a plan for treatment after transport, if we transport. I'll at least keep an open mind," he added loftily. "Axel, I need a better trajectory past Wolf, something farther out. Let's get a safety range as best we can."

"Yes, sir."

Yves looked at Jason. "Are you waiting for something, pilot?"

"No, sir. I was leaving right now."

"Good."

Jason stood up and went.

Later that evening Jason hesitated in front of Yves's cabin door. The ship had entered night cycle, the air sighing softly through the ventilators, the corridor lights dimmed. At "night" on *Flag*, everything seemed strangely hushed, as if the senses quickened with the simulated darkness, a forgotten memory of cool evenings under a mother planet's single large moon, the vegetation nearby rustling with the movements of other creatures that relished the night. He lifted his hand and touched the door chime, requesting entry.

"Who is it?" Yves's voice came muffled through the door, tense but expectant. Sorry to disappoint you, Yves, Jason thought wryly, guessing too well that the captain expected someone else, a certain someone else.

"It's Jason."

He heard the thud of feet on the floor and a padding toward the door. The door panel hissed open, revealing Yves in rumpled pajamas, a vid-tape canister in his hand. His dark eyes simmered, wary, at guard.

"Yes, Jason?"

"I'd like to talk to you—in private. May I come in?"

Yves hesitated, his eyes bright with suspicion, then moved aside ungraciously. "As you wish."

"What are you watching?" Jason asked, motioning at the vid-tape.

"Why should you care?"

"Come off it, Yves! I'm just being polite."

"Fake interest is a politeness I can do without." Yves turned and stamped back to his bunk, then sat down resentfully. "So sit. What's so important that you need a private conversation?"

Jason lowered himself into the bedroom chair. "We have to stop this," he said earnestly. "We don't have time to spare, the energy to spare, not in this kind of crisis."

"What are you talking about?"

"Yves! Stop playing games! You know what I'm talking about!"

"I'm sure I don't."

"Listen, I apologize for every insult I've given you. I apologize for everything, whether I did it or not. Hell, I apologize for existing. We've got to stop fighting, especially like this, so table it, Yves. I'm asking."

Yves shook his head and laughed, his voice heavy with amazed disbelief. "I honestly don't know what you're talking about. What fighting? Have you talked to Inga about these delusions?"

"Oh, sure. Talking to Inga really helps. What has she been telling you?"

"Nothing. You're paranoid, Jason. I'm not fighting with you. You just can't take orders. It's that simple." Yves tossed the vid-tape on the mattress beside him and leaned back, cupping his hands behind his head. "But tell me more about your delusions. Tell me why you think I'm winning. Isn't that why you're here?" He smiled sardonically.

"Hell." Jason stood up. "Listen, I tried, but you want to play games." He stabbed a finger at Yves accusingly. "Well, we'll see about games when you get to Wolf Station and face all those people. We'll see if you tell them about triage, how you're going to leave them all behind. We'll see who wins then." He slammed his palm on the door's key panel and stalked out.

He turned toward his own door and halted abruptly as he saw Inga watching nearby. The medico stood in the doorway of her own room, arms crossed, her lips drawn down in disapproval. Behind her, he could hear Axel's unmistakable snore. Jason sidled up to her in fake menace, making her retreat a step inward.

"Stuff it in your file, Inga," he hissed. Then he swept onward, heading downship for cargo deck, his boot heels resounding on the metal floor of the corridor. Hell, he would sleep on cargo deck if he had to. The hell with all of them. He had tried.

Halfway there, he changed his mind and went downlevel to the control room. In the darkened room the bulking shapes of the monitor desks flickered with the multicolored lights of *Flag*'s active systems. Beyond the consoles in the forward wall screen, Wolf 359 blazed in crimson glory, filling half the screen, the warp-effect halo completely gone. For better or worse, *Flag* was committed to running the gauntlet, fully exposed in real time. At least he'd gotten the gauntlet. He would get more, he promised himself that.

"I always win," he muttered savagely at the star, and sat down at his monitor station. He asked the ship's computer for the flare tape and ran it in his side viewer, watching it several times. The golden firestorm swept across the star again and again, a dance of destruction, a torrent of beauty that caught at his throat. After the fifth replay Jason heard the creak of a chair behind him and turned, startled, toward the noise. Yves crossed his arms and leaned back in his chair, staring at Jason across the darkness.

"Go away, Yves," Jason said tiredly, and turned back to the side screen. "Just go away."

"You think I *want* to leave them behind, don't you?" Yves asked. "Why don't you try to understand *my* position just for once? Eh? Why do you assume you have to be right?"

"Because I *am* right," Jason said, not looking around. "And you know it, too."

"No, I don't know it. We have a responsibility to Lalande and Ross. *I* have a responsibility to Ceti Central for this ship. It's not your responsibility, Jason; it's mine."

"That works for Axel and Inga; it doesn't work for me." Jason swiveled toward the captain. "Some choices a man has to make for himself, and I say you're wrong, Yves. You're flat wrong."

Yves' shadowed face hardened. "We shall see."

"Yeah. We'll see."

"D'accord." Yves waited a moment, then stood up and padded out of the control room.

Was it a truce? Jason doubted it. He leaned his arms on his console, then let his head sink downward until his face rested on the cool metal. Why do I believe you'll try to leave them, Yves? Why do I think you'll try no matter what we find there? Tell me that, Yves, if you're done playing games. Tell me.

Cargo-chain freighter Ceti Flag, *EuroCom registry, cargo
deck, 42 hours to Wolf II.*

Two days later Jason and Helena had finished the initial
rigging of the spare cargo tins. When Helena balked about
jettisoning some of the stores that wouldn't juggle neatly
into crannies elsewhere, Jason compromised and helped
her shift the awkward parts of *Flag*'s delivery goods into
Flag itself. It wasted time, time they might not have to
spare, but Jason admitted that she was right: jettisoning
good cargo for no reason—if it ended up no reason—
would be a poor career move. He countered by suggest-
ing Helena's personal quarters for some of the three-meter
pointy-wand radar sets destined for Ross 128; she ri-
posted with a few boxes of a special-order smelly cheese
for some Lalande bigshot. They called it a draw and hid
both in one of the cargo deck's emptier storerooms.

Ideal economics decreed that each cargo-chain freighter
leave Mars with all tins full, but even three colonies did
not need everything every three months; *Flag* had de-
parted with two empty tins and two others only half-full.
It gave them a starting point for rigging some empty space
to park colonists, first by installing the air-converters and
other environmental equipment to supplement the machinery already inside each tin, then by shifting cargo around
to give them room for rigging the free-fall belts in the
nearby tins. They concentrated on the two tins following
the empty at Tin 16 starboard and the tins bracketing Tin
9 portside; if necessary, they could rig other tins in each
series after *Flag* had a chance to download cargo at Wolf
Station. After some more thought, Jason had decided he
agreed with Helena about jettison; Central would *not* take
that kindly, no matter what had crisped Wolf II. Bureaucrats had bottom-line minds. Fortunately for the compro-
mise, most of the tin cargo was packaged for easy handling
in free-fall so long as one was careful about the foot-
pounds vested in a particular delicate shove.

Now they sat together on the cargo-tug deck, rigging
the free-fall belts. Helena was in a good mood. The day
before she had mended her fences with Yves, apparently

to their mutual satisfaction. Jason had overheard part of the pretty apology and seen the tears and had slipped away unnoticed as Helena went on to seal the breach with the expectable invitation. Yves had turned smug again, the vulnerability on the darkened bridge wiped out. He made sure that Jason saw them together; he chortled and joked in the dining room, showing his possessiveness while Helena giggled girlishly, one of her best acts around Yves. As usual, the yang of the giggle yin was an especially bitchy attitude toward Jason. She was still mad about the sexual stud crack, as she had belatedly remembered and now chose to act out. Life as usual on the cargo-chain, repeating itself in all its weary detail.

"What's the matter, Jason?" Helena asked archly as he bent over a belt. "You're awfully quiet today."

"Just leave it alone, Helena. I'm not in the mood."

"I just want to know why."

"So who has to tell you? You don't owe me, Sheila. Hand me that socket wrench."

She tossed it over and then shook her head irritably. "Stop calling me Sheila. I'm helping, aren't I?"

"And bitching all the way—Sheila."

She put down her own wrench and leaned her elbows on her knees to stare at him, then shook back her hair. Jason had studied that gesture for its warning potential, but it suited too many outcomes. If she had a predictable system, he hadn't figured it out yet; he eyed her warily.

"I'm a good bitch," she said reflectively. "It takes a certain art."

"Not just good—superb," Jason grunted. "If you could bottle it, you'd be rich. Think of all the husbands who still aren't henpecked; the women would line up in droves to buy what you've got."

"Is that what you feel like, Jason? Married?" She grinned at him, thinking she had just won a point.

"Hardly. You're more the type of a captain's wife, the way you chase after perks."

"Ooh, rough. Ever thought of getting married?"

"No," Jason said flatly. Did the games ever stop? He looked at her with real distaste.

She missed it completely and wrinkled her nose fetchingly. "I pity your poor wife if you ever do."

"I'll let her know. She can call you up and complain. Are you going to just sit or finish that belt?"

"Yes, Daddy." Helena picked up her wrench and flipped the belt ends together with a neat motion, then reached for a bolt. She smiled to herself as she worked. Jason watched her from the corner of his eye, then gave a mental shrug. Helena was Helena, what the hell. When Helena decided to be a friend, she was a good friend—the problem was, she wasn't always deciding.

"How's Yves?" he asked.

"What do you mean?" she retorted defensively.

"I'm not asking about your sex life, Helena. Spare me that, please. He just seems tense to me, more than usual."

"Do you blame him? You won the vote, Jason. I couldn't believe that Axel came down on your side like that; I'm surprised you're not rubbing that in more than you are."

"You really are a bitch."

"Thank you. I try."

"I didn't do this for 'sides,' okay? Put that in your pea brain and cook it, Sheila."

Helena glared at him. "Stop calling me that!"

"Then stop playing games, okay?" Jason tossed the belt in his hands on the pile near him, then levered himself off the floor with a groan. Free-fall or not, he felt the effect of too much physical activity after sitting around for weeks dodging the ship's gym. He had to walk around a few steps to get blood reestablished in his legs, then bent for his pile of belts. Maybe I'm just getting old, he thought, disgruntled—they say the arthritis starts setting in around thirty-five. It's all downhill from now, Jase—keep it in mind. "I'm going outship to Tin Sixteen," he informed Helena.

"You're the boss," Helena said archly.

"Yeah. I've noticed that."

He dumped the belts into a carrysack and suited up, then climbed up the wall ladder to the crew port and its access to outside. He clipped the carrysack to his belt as the lock cycled, then floated into the open blackness beyond. A few meters from the crew port he moved out of the crew module's bulky shadow into sunlight and stopped himself with a tug on his safety line, mesmerized by the vast expanse of star face barely a quarter million kilometers away, still slightly forward of *Flag*. Smart to come out in the middle of swing-by, he told himself, then quickly pulled himself back up his line to get back into shadow. Not, of course, that metal between him and Wolf would make much difference if the star shot a flare strong enough to get through *Flag*'s magnetic shields. He edged out again, fascinated by the vista of turbulent plumes of roiling gas, the reds in a dozen shades, the endless depths of black in the starspots, a star that blotted out nearly half the sky. God, the size of it! he marveled.

A towering plume of plasma leapt upward from the surface near the western limb, steadily ascending an invisible magnetic curve, then fragmenting into glowing arcs as it plunged downward into the eddying gases beneath it. More plasma jetted and roiled near the edges of the starspots on both sides of the star's equator, a vivid contrast of blacks and oranges and reds thousands of kilometers across. Another plasma jet burst upward, tracing a fiery arc, then another, wreathing the star in a dance of fiery violence. Jason had seen the really close-up films of stars, had even idly watched Wolf through the ship's cameras on a previous flyby, but pictures could not catch the reality, not this close and not this naked to a living star, small as it was.

Small? God, I should be so small, he thought. Magnificent!

And dangerous as hell, too, he reminded himself. For every plasma jet he could see, about several billion particles he couldn't see no doubt zipped in his direction. Even a quiet flare would be damned dangerous this close. He preferred the safety margin he had in hiding behind the ship's metal, whatever the view. He pulled himself back into shadow and detoured along the inside edge of the ship frame and under the aft throat of the ship's tubular core and the ramscoop. During deceleration, the ramscoop's magnetic cone was closed, allowing braking power from the impact of dust and particles caught by the scoop; when the ship left orbit, the same dust and solar particles would act as a catalyst for the H-3 that fed the engines. It was a neat system, one well proven for a dozen years. At the starboard end of the ship frame he pulled himself along one of the tethers running down the sides of the tins and moved hand over hand down the tin line to Tin 16. He cycled himself through the tin's small air lock, then snapped the switch on the single overhead light.

Empty, the thirty-meter tin resembled a vast, windowless room, harshly lit into stark shadows by the fluorescent light. On one wall near the flat oblong shape of the tin's interior computer module he and Helena had rigged a panel box for one of *Flag*'s spare heat-converters and a jury-made air-converter scavenged from parts; access hoses would supply the four tins following Tin 16. A small food processor and water tank had been bolted to the wall near the air assembly; a portable toilet behind a privacy screen occupied the nearby corner. He floated past the air assembly to the next tin wall and toed himself to a stop with his boot magnets, then opened his carrysack.

Each wall had a grid pattern of padeyes for securing cargo inside the tin; he used those connections for securing the acceleration belts, ten sets about a meter apart on each of the remaining three walls near the "floor" of the tin. Other padeyes up the wall could suit for tying personal goods, blankets, and food supplies; later he and Helena would rig more lights along the ceiling. Though *Flag* could pack more than thirty people in the largish tin, Jason had decided against automatic claustrophobia; people needed more than three square meters for their individual space. With the uploading of cargo into *Flag* and other offloading at the base or jettisoning into open space, they had the extra tins to make the colonists' three-month trip back to Mars more tolerable. He looked around the tin for a moment, imagining three months inside this can. Less intolerable, maybe. Maybe they could bring some people upship on rotation, just to help.

He felt the tin wall shift slightly under his boots as the computer adjusted the catch basket at the front of the tin. The catch basket was another modification that worked well in practice. During acceleration, the tins followed *Flag* docilely on their tethers, neat beads on a triple string; when the ship slowed, the tin tethers slackened, threatening imminent collision as the tins tried to climb aboard the crew module. With the catch basket's system of ward-off lines and the spider-frame assembly between each tin and the next, *Flag*'s computers then balanced the tins like a juggler with plates on a pole, a delicate business during the usual curved trajectories of decel. He felt the wall shift again and detached his boots, wary of adding his own mass to the computer's problems, then inverted to float facedown by the lower wall. Tin design had become a perfected art among Central's system designers; perhaps that art might end up doing more than transport and save some lives on Wolf II. Maybe. He attached the assembled belts in his carryall, working with the ease of long practice in free-fall. When his carrysack was empty, he clicked it on his suit belt and left the tin.

Outside the tin he checked the hose connections to Tin 17, entered Tin 18 briefly to check the interior air vents, and then made his way back to *Flag*. After over forty hours of hard work, Jason could see a steady progress—but would they be in time? If the work would even be necessary. He paused by the crew lock and pivoted to inspect the alignment of the tin lines by eye, then edged out of shadow to watch Wolf again.

Beyond Wolf, to the far right, the star's second planet was now a visible disk a half degree in diameter, a small white circle just discernibly shadowed by its rough cratered surface. In one of those craters near the dawn limb four hundred people were at risk, maybe dying, maybe already lost.

Maybe Yves is right, he thought bleakly. Maybe it's a useless try. God, how to know. Maybe.

Maybe you're a fool, Roarke. Maybe Helena has the right idea in hiding behind her games, pretending nothing is wrong, that everything's ordinary. When you're hiding, you don't have to look at what's coming right at you. You don't have maybes to tear at you, wondering if your captain will take your dare and find it possible in himself to abandon hundreds of people, chanting his perfect regs all the way—with nothing you can do about it, nothing.

Maybe on that, too. But what? What *could* he do?

With a curse, he swung himself back into shadow and went inship to rig more belts for the tins.

Chapter 5

Wolf Colony Station, Home Crater, Level 3, Temporary Dormitory 2, 6 hours past flare.

"But I don't see *why*," the fat woman complained loudly.

She stood in the middle of the Level 3 storeroom doorway, clinging resentfully to the mountain of possessions in her arms. Magda squeezed by her, nearly dropping her own load of spare clothing and a few vid-tapes; Mrs. Galiano gave her a chilly glance as Magda bumped her. Magda returned the look, even though it wasn't polite at all; she had always thought Mrs. Galiano was a twit, the way she borrowed rations and never paid them back and let her kids run wild through the residential level, breaking just about *every* rule no matter who complained. "It's more dangerous closer to the surface," Mrs. Galiano declaimed loudly. "What if there's another flare? Why can't we stay on Level Five?"

Elizabet straightened from making up a pair of cots and gave her a level stare. "We're in shadow now, Maria. Director Danforth wants to conserve the air in the lower levels, and so we're moving up here. Why don't you choose where you want to sleep and stop blocking the doorway."

Mrs. Galiano flushed and stood her ground as one of Magda's ninth-form classmates squeezed by her, his lanky arms full of sheets and pillows. "I'll do what I please, Elizabet Janozek, whatever your snooty airs! You can't order me around!"

Ramon rolled his eyes expressively at Magda as he

passed, then jerked his eyebrows in a flawless imitation of the angry woman in the doorway. Magda giggled.

Her mother took the clothes from Magda's arms, then laid them neatly on the mattress. "Magda," she said quietly, "could you go find Dr. Renfrew and ask her to come here?"

The threat lay on the air for a moment. Mrs. Galiano gave Elizabet a venomous look and waddled forward, then stamped toward the cots on the far wall, pointedly as far away from their cots as possible. Her mother watched her go, disapproval plain on her face.

"Mrs. Galiano is a twit," Magda murmured.

"Be polite, dear. Adults are not 'twits.' "

"Oh?"

Her mother chuckled, then tried to change to a reproving frown before the smile came back. "Well . . . we'll let that pass this time. Put the clothes in that locker at the foot of the cot. Must you bring every vid-tape you own?"

"I only brought five." Magda clutched the vid-tapes to her chest, guarding them.

"I didn't have *any* vid-tapes in the hills."

"Golly, Mother, that's awful." Magda goggled dramatically. "I don't know *how* you got on." Elizabet made a move on the vid-tapes, and Magda danced out of reach, laughing.

"Put them in the footlocker, twerp."

"Yes, Mother."

Her mother put a finishing touch on the blanket, then straightened again and suddenly pressed her palm to her forehead. She swayed a little, her face very white. A fine sheen of sweat coated her face, and she seemed to swallow painfully. Magda dropped the vid-tapes into the open locker, alarmed.

"Are you all right, Mother?" she asked, her voice high.

Elizabet dropped her hand and hesitated, then smiled reassuringly. "Yes, dear. Perhaps it's nothing. Why don't you go help Mrs. Tertak? Her boy just toddled away into the corridor."

"Sure." Magda waved at Mrs. Tertak, whose alarmed

expression showed that she had just realized she was missing one, and bounded into the corridor to fetch Aloys. The two-year-old had made his determined way half down the corridor toward the stairs, intending God knew what. He squawked in protest as she scooped him up. She promptly upended him, dangling him by his legs and jouncing him until she heard him chuckle. Aloys was a sweet child, full of mischief and easy affection; he and Magda had always gotten along when she baby-sat him. She juggled him upright and gave him a kiss. "Where you going, little man?"

Aloys smiled placidly, keeping his secrets, and twined the fingers of one hand in her long hair, then stuck a chubby thumb in his mouth. She carried him back into the dormitory to Mrs. Tertak. Her mother had gone over to Mrs. Tertak to talk; when Magda appeared, the two women looked up, both looking upset. "Here he is, Mrs. Tertak," she called out reassuringly. "He's okay."

Mrs. Tertak smiled and took Aloys but did not seem reassured at all.

"He's okay," Magda repeated.

"Yes, dear. Thank you." Mrs. Tertak turned to her mother. "Be at peace, Elizabet. I'll watch over her."

"There may be many of us, Sereni. Half the colonists were on Level Two or higher; Dr. Renfrew is very concerned."

"When *Ceti Flag* gets here . . ."

"Some things even *Flag* cannot help, not now—and the ship won't arrive for another three days, anyway." Elizabet looked around the dormitory sadly. "All this effort now, all this striving that will be needed, and for too many the battle was lost in the first three minutes. I just can't believe Danforth wasn't more prepared than this."

Mrs. Tertak snorted. "That one," she said in a bitter tone Magda had never before heard from her. "Marcos says that Danforth had Wolf-watch warnings for days and just ignored them. He'll be brought to account, I'm sure."

"Maybe. Sometimes justice is far away—or comes too late, much too late. How well I know that." Elizabet pressed Mrs. Tertak's arm. "You're a good friend, Sereni. I could almost think you have Croat blood; it's not that far to the Hungarian border, you know. After all, Croatia and Hungary once shared a nation together. Surely—"

Mrs. Tertak snorted. "Never! I'm Magyar to the heart, and I'll never change. Croat blood!" She pretended to shudder. "Who'd want it?" They both laughed.

"Come along, Magda." As her mother led her away, Magda looked back and saw tears in Mrs. Tertak's eyes. Then she looked at her mother, suddenly understanding. Fear clutched at her heart, making it hard to breathe, as everything she had learned about flare storm and radiation clicked into horrible understanding. She had thought the alarm she had felt on the stairs with Mr. Mack had been nothing, wiped away when her mother appeared shortly afterward, healthy and unharmed, a nightmare that had never happened. She had thought it because the alternative was too awful to think about, too awful . . .

"Mother!" she cried.

"Let's make up your cot, Magda. You'll need a blanket." Calmly, Elizabet unfolded a sheet and laid it smoothly over the mattress. "Though perhaps not—it seems the heat exchangers aren't doing too well." Her mother lifted her calm eyes to Magda's face, silently challenging her daughter's fear. "Help me now," she asked quietly.

Magda hesitated, wanting her mother to say it wasn't true, needing that reassurance desperately. Her mother looked at her calmly, waiting for her obedience, refusing her.

Magda's shoulders sagged. "Yes, Mother." She bent to the cot, smoothing the sheet corner as her mother worked on the other side.

Wolf Colony Station, Home Crater, Level 3, Temporary Dormitory 2, 12 hours past flare.

"This is Karlovac," Elizabet said, "a river town on the Kupa River. Your grandfather lived there for many years. He was a shoemaker."

Magda nestled close to her mother as they sat comfortably together between their cots, looking at Magda's vid-tape of Yugoslavia. The dormitory lights were dimmed as mothers put their children to bed, then gathered in groups to talk quietly or left for night duty elsewhere in the station. The air was noticeably hot and stuffy, but it was cooler near the floor. Magda watched her mother's face in the half-light, then looked obediently at the old town in the vid-screen.

"I remember him very well," her mother continued, her voice soft with memory. "He was a wiry and crochety old man—your father was born when he was in his fifties—with this white shock of hair that stuck up in all directions, these gnarled old hands that had a magic in them when working leather. He didn't approve of me as Paul's wife—he was eyeing someone else for his last son, some witch with a better figure and some money—but we got along in time, he and I. Then you were born, and I could do no wrong after that. He doted on you, Magda, making people listen and nod as he carried you around the neighborhood and bragged about you, watching you while he worked in his shop. He even tried to teach you about leather, you being all of eighteen months old. Paul and I had joined the partisans by then, and you were too young to be with us, so he took care of you, that old man who had so disapproved of me. See this street? His house was just beyond that row of houses on the end."

Magda took the vid-tape and clicked forward to one of her favorite pictures. "Do you remember this place, Mother?"

"Ah, yes. Those are the mountains near Brinje. We lived in these hills for two years while the Serbs hunted us; sometimes we would go into Brinje at night for supplies. There weren't many of us in our band; the partisans operated in small groups scattered across Croatia, the better military tactic for guerrillas. See this mountain? We had a permanent camp right under this ridge in a large cave; the Serbs never did find it. There were wildflowers in the meadows nearby; your father would weave sunflower diadems for my hair and call me his sunflower. We were very much in love." She smiled. "He was such a romantic, far more than I was. When you're a romantic, you can ignore hardship and setbacks, however harsh they are. All you see is the shining goal ahead, and belief is enough for everything." She lifted her hand and caressed Magda's hair. "It is one kind of bravery, my child, one of the best kinds, to be a romantic."

"What does wind feel like?" Magda asked. "And sunlight?"

Elizabet sighed. "Aliveness. Warmth. A peace that . . ." She fell silent for a moment. "I have often wondered if I did the right thing, bringing you here to this sterile place. I'm sorry, Magda. I'm sorry I robbed you of your homeland, running away like I did." She let the vid-tape sink onto her knees and bowed her head.

"You don't have to be sorry for *anything*, Mother," Magda said fiercely. "I won't let you."

Her mother didn't seem to hear. "Before I left Yugoslavia, I wished for vengeance," she said, talking more to herself than to Magda. "I wanted to murder and destroy, to obliterate as they obliterated Paul. Justice! I cried. Where is justice? Your grandfather asked me to wait, to see what the Peacemakers would do to the Serbs. And they did kill him, that colonel who ordered Paul shot with the others in Brinje—not because he killed your father but because he crossed their judicious line on his killing. Kill dozens or hundreds, and they forgot you, shrugged it away; kill thousands, and you got your place in the trials, paraded out as a butcher, one of the select players in the show trials. But Paul was still dead—and they didn't kill the colonel because he killed Paul. Oh, no, never that."

She curled her fingers into a fist. "I should have killed him myself, that Serb colonel. I had the chance, that day on the street in Brinje as he passed by in his autocar, bright with his ribbons and boot leather. I should have taken my vengeance. Would that have been bravery? I have always wondered." She closed her eyes and swallowed convulsively, her face pale and shiny with sweat. "I'm going to be very sick, Magda. You must be brave."

"I don't believe it!" Magda cried. "You're fine, Mother. You *have* to be well."

"Child, I was on Level One during the flare. Some

facts cannot be escaped.'' Elizabet's pale face became
stern and inexorable. "Face them.''

"I *won't* believe it!'' Magda lunged away and jumped
to her feet; all around the room heads turned. "I won't
believe it!'' she shouted at her mother angrily. "Don't
say those things!''

"Magda . . .''

Magda covered her face with her hands and began to
cry.

"I'm sorry, Magda,'' her mother said weakly, her
voice hoarse with a pain and regret that tore even deeper
at Magda. "I'm sorry.''

The regret in her mother's voice haunted Magda for
the days afterward as her mother steadily weakened and
finally collapsed while on duty watch, joining the few,
then the dozens in Dr. Renfrew's temporary wards. Magda's fear compressed to a hard knot in her gut as she
helped in the hospital, running errands, helping tend the
sick, keeping busy as her mother asked. She watched
Aloys and his sister, Taran, when Mrs. Tertak left for
duty watch in Enviro-control, as if all things were normal, just like before the flare. Desperately, Magda clung
to that normality as her mother rapidly worsened, as the
radiation deaths began in Wolf Station, emptying the hospital beds one by one by one.

"You are a good child,'' her mother said the second
night. "Be brave, my Magda.''

"How?'' Magda leaned close and squeezed her mother's hand desperately.

Her mother sighed and did not answer.

*Wolf Harvester A39469, Tri Ellium Crater, Mining Sector 17,
62 hours past flare.*

Kendall had parked their damaged harvester in deep
shadow between the walls of a crevice in the rock wall,
maneuvering carefully backward into the cleft to give
them a clear view of the crater plain. Deeper shadow
might not help much in another flare, but he wanted
whatever safety margin it might give the harvester. Most
of the machinery had survived but with damage, and sev-

eral critical systems had crashed in the hours immediately after the flare. By scavenging for spare parts from nonessential equipment, he and Leland had managed to keep power and some heat exchangers, then had tinkered with a balky air-converter for nearly a day to recondition what atmosphere they had left. He stood in the front half of the cab, bone-weary, and watched the enviro-panels warily for several minutes, daring them to announce another crisis. A harvester's internal environment could maintain two men for up to a week, assuming nondamaged equipment; he and Leland had managed nearly half that time, though with no guarantees it would last much longer.

He checked his watch and walked back into the cab to wake Leland. The younger man was sleeping on a pallet they had wrestled out of stores, snoring noisily on his back. In the dim light of the harvester lamps, Leland's face looked pale and drawn, its muscles tightened in pain. Neither man had slept well, their unceasing anxiety about the integrity of the cab disturbing their dreams into nightmares. Kendall bent with an involuntary groan as his back muscles knotted and shook Leland's shoulder.

"Rise and shine, Paul," he said cheerfully. "Comsat's coming up again."

Leland muttered and slapped at his hand, then turned away onto his side. Kendall edged his boot under Leland's exposed back and wiggled his toes, irritating Leland into waking up. The younger man groaned and threw an arm over his eyes.

"Go away," he grumbled sleepily.

Kendall wiggled his toes more vigorously. "I'd do it myself," he said, "but my arm's about two meters too short. Wake up." He backed up hastily as Leland suddenly rolled over and surged to his feet; then he caught the scientist's arm to steady him as he swayed off balance. Leland blinked at him, trying to focus.

"Good morning," Kendall said.

"Go to hell," Leland replied.

Kendall had decided from experience that Leland was not a morning person. "Are you conscious?" he asked pointedly.

Leland wiped his sleeve over his mouth and straightened into something less than a forty-degree lean. "Yeah—I guess so. Comsat check?"

"Righto." Kendall turned and stomped forward to the cab's control panels, then made a few final adjustments on the microwave com-panel. Tri Ellium lay only a thousand kilometers south of the colony station, well within range of a microwave bounce signal off Wolf II's communications satellite. Normally the comsat caught and stored any signal impacting on its radio dish, neatly resending the message at the proper angle back to base. That function, of course, presumed working machinery inside the comsat, an unlikely proposition if the comsat had been in dayside orbit during the flare. Kendall had tried a standard acquisition signal, had gotten nothing back, and so had assumed the worst. On the comsat's last four passes the two men had attempted radio-signal billiards, hoping that at least part of the signal made it to base *and* that the base had a working microwave receiver. The comsat's current space-junk condition argued against the latter, at least for the colony's surface receivers, but maybe Danforth had improvised since the flare to contact *Ceti Flag*. Maybe.

We've got too many maybes, Kendall thought irritably. He looked back at Leland. "Ready?"

Leland sat down lumpily in the aft chair, then shook the rest of the cobwebs out of his brain with a vigorous yawn. "Yeah. Who the hell designed this com-system, anyway?" He squinted into an eyepiece and manipulated the cab's robot arm for a better grip on the cab's antenna.

"Somebody who thinks comsats always work. Why bother with pointing when the comsat always talks first?"

"I'd like to meet that man. Uh, I've got it at forty degrees from plane, sighted four arc-seconds south of Delta Aquarius."

"Check. Comsat approach in thirty-eight seconds. Loading the zip-squeal signal, power up. On the mark, thirty, twenty-nine . . ." Kendall counted off the seconds from the clock on the panel, his finger poised over the sending button. "Here she comes, Paul!" he warned. "Four . . . three . . . two . . . one!" He stabbed at the button. Leland moved a lever in a smooth arc, his body tense with concentration.

"Pass completed," Kendall announced. "Did you track it?"

"God only knows." Leland disengaged the robot arm and grimaced uncomfortably as he shifted in his chair. Both men had had loose bowels, with Leland having the worst of it. A sheen of sweat gleamed on the younger man's face, partially masking his pallor. He pushed his hair out of his eyes and scowled. "Look," he said, swinging his chair toward Kendall, "a cargo lander would be here by now if this worked. Right?"

"Maybe. All I want is a recognizable man-made signal to hit the colony. Maybe we've managed that." Kendall snapped the radio switch to receive.

"If anybody's listening," Leland said sourly.

Kendall shrugged, conceding the point. "All the world to call and maybe no one to hear, but we've got to try. You feeling sick again?"

"Yeah."

"We seem to be trading off on that—that's a good sign."

"It is?" Leland swallowed uneasily, his eyes vague. Both men had shown signs of radiation sickness, but neither seemed badly off—yet. Kendall had not liked the exposure range on their badges, not at all, even if it wasn't as bad as he had expected; even so, without medical treatment soon, things might get iffy. Though Kendall's body had shielded Leland during the flare, Leland seemed the worse off, probably because of his lower body weight. Kendall stood up and got him a tumbler of water from the cab's small sink.

"Here, drink this."

"Thanks."

"Hey, cheer up, Paul. I'm sure somebody survived at base. Wolf Station is built deep, and Danforth isn't a fool all the time."

"Yeah? If he's so smart, why are we stuck in Tri Ellium?"

"I said not all the time. Hell, I've had my quarrels with him, but he's a good director. He'd be prepared for something like this, whatever Central snoots about probabilities.''

''We could debate that point for a few hours—it'd use up some time.''

Kendall squatted by his chair and looked up into Leland's face. ''Time we've got—for a while yet. Listen, buddy, I'm not the better cheerleader—that's your job. I'm too old and cynical, seen too much. You're younger, and young men have a gift for ignoring reality that I wish I still had. So tell me why we're in great shape. I could use the reassurance.''

Leland smiled at him wanly. ''You're something else, chief. Why did you ever come to a place like Wolf?''

''Why did you? You've been here—what, eight months? A bright guy like you belongs in an Earthside university, using up grant money on new cyclotrons and such.''

''I asked you first.''

Kendall shrugged. ''I don't really remember; it's been too long since I went starside. I went to Mars first and then spent a bunch of years at Centauri servicing terrain rovers. Been here five years, expect I'll retire here—assuming I live that long.'' He grimaced. ''That assumes some facts, of course, like getting out of Tri Ellium back to base, if there'll be a base later. After this, they may have to shut down the Wolf colony.''

''Might be a smart idea. Something's happening to Wolf, I think, some cycle we didn't anticipate. Do flare stars wake up? Wolf might be doing that.'' Leland frowned. ''We could move the base to Wolf I—it's got full tidal lock and a permanent nightside.''

''Not enough gravity. Centrifuges go only so far, and kids need weight to grow bones properly.''

''True.'' Leland shrugged. ''Lord, Isaiah, how we need an enhanced drive. We fuss and putter and fight against limits just because we don't have the range we need to get to better stars. Twelve light-years isn't enough, not with what we've got in our neighborhood. Centauri has skewed biochains we can't eat, Tau Ceti's planet orbits are too eccentric for a tolerable climate, red dwarf planets never have atmospheres, and so on. Vacuum colonies just aren't feasible, not in the long term.

You want to know why I came to Wolf? Because I want to find that enhanced drive.''

Kendall sat back on his heels in surprise. "Here? Besides, I've heard there isn't any such drive; the formulas can't go that far.''

"Yeah, I've heard that, too. I don't believe it. Listen, Shaukolen dumped relativity on its ear with his new formulas; before him, faster-than-light travel was impossible, period. You want to know why Shaukolen thought different? Because he got interested in UV Ceti. That nasty little star apparently pushes flare particles past light-speed in a second or two, something it's not supposed to be able to do. Shaukolen thought half of UV Ceti's solar wind might be tachyons, faster-than-light particles we can't see. Maybe it comes from some new quantum mechanics we haven't discovered; maybe it's a side blow of plasma physics. Matter does strange things to itself inside a star. But if UV Ceti can accelerate matter into tachyons, we can, too—if we can figure out how it's done.'' He shrugged. "Oh, I tried to get some funding Earthside for some computer studies, but who believes a kid with crazy ideas? Everybody knows the drive can't be enhanced. Wolf is the only flare star we've colonized, so I came here.''

"And got stuck in a harvester with me.''

"I'm not complaining.'' Leland smiled. "The heat exchanger is clanking again. Want a chocolate bar before we go see why?''

Kendall hesitated, looking at Leland's mocking face. "Yeah, sure. Why not? After all, you gotta believe.''

"That's the spirit, chief.''

"Stuff it, Paul. I'm too old to believe in young men's dreams. Enhanced drive!''

"I'll bet you two thousand chocolate bars I'm right.''

"That's a deal.''

*Wolf Colony Station, Level 2, Room 27B, temporary
hospital unit, 74 hours past flare.*

In the half-light of the sick ward Magda pressed her
forehead against the hard wood of the cot frame, only
vaguely aware of the hushed voices, low moans of delir-
ium, and soft movements elsewhere in the room. Desperately, ignoring all else, she focused on the remaining
warmth in her mother's hand, holding tightly to those
fingers as slowly the hand cooled into death, unrespon-
sive and slack and cold.

"Magda." Someone touched her shoulder, and she
flinched, not wanting any other touch than her mother's.
Inexorably, Dr. Renfrew bent over her and gently pried
apart her fingers. She resisted a moment, then dully allowed her hand to be pulled away. "It's over, Magda,"
Dr. Renfrew said.

Magda opened her eyes and looked at the body on the
cot, seeing a face she had known with love all her life,
now pale and quiet after a full day of helpless vomiting
and pain, of uncontrollable hemorrhage that bled crimson blotches into sheets and bandages, of loosened hair
that had parted from the scalp in clumpish wisps. Elizabet Janozek had died a hard death, one of too many
among the newly dead. Magda didn't care about the others, she told herself. She didn't care, not in the unimag-
inable disaster of her mother's own death.

Her head pounded with the effects of the sedative Dr.
Renfrew had insisted she take as her mother became ex-
tremis; sound seemed strangely hollow, sending wave after wave of vertigo sweeping through her body. Dr.
Renfrew had sedated all the children as the deaths came
and many of the adults, too, keeping away panic and
hysteria as the horror mounted, following regs Magda
had not even known existed. She swallowed uneasily and
tightened her fingers on the cot frame, holding to that
frail anchor.

Come back, she pleaded to the still body. She seized
the limp hand again and squeezed hard on the fingers.
Come back.

"Magda."

Magda pushed the woman away. "Leave me alone."

Dr. Renfrew made an exasperated sound, then turned away. For three days since the flare Magda had returned whenever possible to her mother's cot, sleeping at its foot, watching desperately through the hours for a sign of returning wellness in her mother's face. She felt the flick of guilt the other intended as Dr. Renfrew willed her help elsewhere; she clung stubbornly to her mother's cot. As long as she refused to accept this, the world would not be filled with a terrible and strange emptiness; as long as she willed her mother back to life, death could not be. Come back, come back, she pleaded to the still face. Don't leave me. I can be brave, so very brave, Mother, but not without you.

Her mother did not move, and her fingers had become icy cold. Magda watched her mother's face earnestly, willing her back to life, *believing* . . . but nothing happened, nothing at all.

"Mother," she whispered in despair, and pressed her face hard against the cot frame, blotting out the world. "Mother."

With a sudden flush of hot anger Magda hated the time she had lost away from her mother's bedside—such precious time while her mother still lived, could still see her daughter's face, still spoke and moved and needed Magda. She hated the pain and bleeding, the strange distortion of the writhing body, the shocked grief in other faces over other deaths that had terrified her with their foreboding for herself. Dr. Renfrew had moved calmly from cot to cot, working efficiently, carefully detached, competent, white-faced with fatigue. In other wards nearby, others died, each hour bringing a new soft tramp of feet as the morgue detail carried bodies to storage elsewhere. Why? Why had this happened?

She hated it, she hated it all. She began to shake violently.

All her life she had been the gentle child, the happy child, confident and careless, puzzling without understanding why her mother had grieved, untouched, blindly innocent. Now her childhood had been forcibly stripped from her within a few short days, leaving only a rage that shuddered through her body, convulsing her.

"Motherrrr . . ." she wailed aloud. Footsteps moved

quickly, hands touched her. She fought them instantly, violently, striking out as she cried out her anguished denial. Hands forced her roughly to the floor; she felt the sharp prick of another hypodermic and fought even that.

"Magda!" Dr. Renfrew said to her sharply, struggling with her. "Stop this!"

"No! No, no, no . . ."

"Magda! Get control of yourself!"

A child nearby shrieked in distress at the commotion. A babble of voices arose in the room, sharp with panic. Dr. Renfrew's eyes blazed at her, angry now for the disturbance, not caring why, not caring at all.

"Motherrr . . ." Magda panted as she fought them, struggling against their hard grasp as they pinned her to the floor and dragged her from the cot; she fought as the drug moved into her and leached the strength from her body. "Let me go!"

"Put her in another bed," Dr. Renfrew told the others. "We can't have this. Tie her down if you have to." Helplessly, Magda felt herself lifted upward and carried away from her mother. Already men had appeared in the doorway, bearing a stretcher to take her mother to lie stiffening and cold among the other dead.

"No!" Her vision blurred as she weakened, unable to fight any longer, unable to push away the hands as they laid her down on a cot. "Motherrr . . ."

She awoke later, chilled and sick, her thoughts sluggish. As she moved her body slightly, she felt a hand take hers, holding it warmly. She shifted her fingers in that tight grasp and opened her eyes.

"Mr. Mack," she whispered.

Mack Summers smiled wanly at her, his tanned face tired and drawn. He was not a handsome man, but he had a nice smile that lighted the eyes, a rumbling chuckle that invited a shared laughter, a silence sometimes when he was thinking hard. In her daydreams, Mack Summers had begun to replace the shadowy image of the father she could not remember. If they had only had time, time for her mother to see a future with this man. Now Summers looked rumpled, his hair dirty and disordered, his eyes bleak as he looked down on her. In his face she saw the grief she had seen in too many faces, and suddenly she hated him for it, hated them all.

"How do you feel, sweetie?" he asked gently.

She turned her face away, refusing his comfort. "Empty."

Summers pressed her hand tighter. "I'm sorry," he said awkwardly. "I'm so sorry."

"Yeah." She closed her eyes, hating.

She heard a rustle and the tread of a foot near her bed, then felt a slight pull on her fingers as Summers turned toward the visitor. "I see the sedative has worn off," came Dr. Renfrew's voice. "That's good."

"She seems so pale," Summers said worriedly. "Is that normal?"

"Quite normal. I was surprised at her hysteria; Magda has always been a quiet child, but stress does strange things to us. We'll keep her on a mild sedative until she has time to work out her grief."

Magda clenched her teeth as they talked about her as if she were not even there.

"It's not radiation sickness, her being so pale?" Summers's voice echoed unpleasantly in her ears. She squeezed her eyes tighter as the darkness moved uneasily in shuddering waves, lifting her up and down, pressing on her body.

"No, not at all. The radiation damage didn't get past Level Two; we've established that by now. She'll be fine."

Summers let out a deep breath. "It's hard on her, Doctor. She and Elizabet were very close."

"It's hard on all of us."

Magda heard the rustle of Dr. Renfrew's clothing as she turned away, then the sound of their retreating footsteps. The soft sounds of the sickroom returned, quiet rustlings, moans of pain, the quick step of people tending others on the cots. Magda listened to the emptiness in the room, that empty place where her mother had been, an aching emptiness that belonged to the roiling darkness that billowed over her.

Mother . . .

They let her get up a few hours later to return to the labor of bathing sweated faces, holding the bandage bas-

ket, changing soiled sheets, and running errands to supply. For every cot emptied by death, new sickness brought
another tormented body to be tended. Many of the faces
Magda knew, adults who worked on the upper levels like
her mother, cursed to be on duty when the star struck at
the colony station. Magda watched them coldly, her grief
compressed to a hard chill knot of rage. She saw Dr. Renfrew watching her and behaved most carefully, accepting
the sedatives, even smiling at times, though the effort
pulled painfully at her lips and hurt something deep inside
her. What did Dr. Renfrew care? she thought resentfully.
What did anybody care?

In the corridors, as she ran errands, Magda heard
whispered rumors of one hundred already dead, of others
dying, of rads and gamma flux damage and *Ceti Flag*.
She saw Director Danforth hurry past her, a data disk
clutched in one hand, and saw the resentful glances that
followed him, heard the angry murmuring. Is it his fault?
she wondered suddenly as she watched him disappear
into a conference room; she clenched her fist, wishing
for the first time in her life that she owned a weapon, a
way to stab and slash and punish. A scientist flapped by
in his white coat, then beckoned curtly to several of the
men standing nearby. Is it *his* fault? she thought. Who
has done this to us? Who?

All her life she had been taught the importance of the
emergency drills, the survival rules, the hundred and one
things to remember. Why hadn't anyone prepared for
this? Why? Why was her mother dead?

I should have killed the colonel, her mother had said,
her voice hoarse with regret at a chance missed, a justice
denied. Would it have been bravery?

She looked at Director Danforth and dug her nails into
her palm, her head pounding with the medication that
Dr. Renfrew still insisted on giving her. It was hard to
think, her head pounded so.

"Magda!"

She turned toward Dr. Renfrew's voice and gave her a
tight, gut-wrenching smile, then followed the older
woman back to the dying and newly dead.

Chapter 6

Magda leaned wearily against the corridor wall and stared dazedly at her shoes. She just couldn't walk anymore. An hour before, Dr. Renfrew had released her from hospital duty and told her to get some dinner and go to bed. The thought of food made Magda feel queasy, so instead she had wandered the main corridor of Level 2, hugging the walls, until her legs ached with fatigue. With everybody moved upward from the lowest two levels to conserve power and air, Level 2 seemed more crowded than ever, especially with the bustle of the sickrooms in the eastern end of the corridor. In the western wing Director Danforth conducted endless meetings in which Magda had no interest. Talk, talk, talk—what good did it do? It didn't stop the dying.

"Magda!"

Her head jerked up. Dr. Renfrew was standing in front of her, hands on hips, mouth drawn down with displeasure.

The older woman tapped her foot sternly. "I told you to go to bed. How can you help efficiently if you don't rest?"

Magda involuntarily lifted her head, wanting to reach out to the woman, then let her hand drop. What she wanted lay stiffening in a dark storage room on Level 5. She looked away.

"I'm not sleepy," she said sullenly.

She jumped as a hand touched her cheek. The hand

caressed her long hair, ending with a light tug at the ends as it fell away. She looked up, bewildered, into a face that had softened, exhaustion written plainly in the lines around the beautiful eyes and the elegant mouth.

"Child, I know it's hard," Dr. Renfrew said softly. "It's hard for all of us, but try to hope. When the young despair, the heart is gone from us, truly gone." She brushed an errant strand of Magda's hair back into place, then smiled, all hard edges gone, her voice soft. "Now go to bed, sweet child. You need the rest."

Then, as if ashamed of her lapse, Dr. Renfrew turned abruptly and moved away, her steps quickening smartly as she vanished among the milling people in the corridor. Magda stared after her in confusion, too tired to be comforted by the wrong touch, the wrong voice. Was no one the same anymore? she wondered. Nothing was as it had been. Nothing.

Dizzily, she pushed herself off the wall and obediently headed for her dormitory on Level 3. She clumped down the stairs in the stairwell, her feet jarring her body on each tread, then walked slowly onward past the soft noises coming through the open doorways. Formerly storerooms and the gymnasium, the six larger rooms in this wing now housed all the colonists still able to care for themselves. She turned into a middle room on the left and picked her way through the rows of cots and mattresses, trying not to see certain faces pale with radiation sickness. A few struggled to conceal the symptoms, talking loudly with wide gestures, until neighbors looked their irritation and shushed; others wept quietly or cradled their limp-bodied children or simply lay inert on their cots, staring at nothing. The close air of the room resonated with despair, too warm with the gathered bodies, stuffy and oppressive. She felt a lump gather in her throat.

Will I die, too? she wondered sadly. It would be good to die, she thought, testing the idea. It would be good to have an end.

She noticed a group of several men in the far corner of the long room, talking heatedly in low voices, their hands punctuating the air with angry gestures. Magda had seen many such groups of men gather in the hours since the flare, quickly dispersing when a crew chief came by, then regathering again to talk among themselves. On impulse, she veered toward them and approached quietly, pretending she belonged in that section of the room, then edged into the gap between two occupied cots. She slid to the floor and pulled up her knees, grateful for the hard support against her back.

"Hell, they had full warning, Mitch," one man said loudly. Magda peeked up over the cot, trying to see his face. "They knew it was coming. Didn't you hear what Alvarez said?"

"Alvarez couldn't read a dial on a pressure gauge," a tall man said contemptuously, glancing at a dark-haired Latino in the group. "I should know: he's been on my topside crew. What does he know about Wolf-watch?"

Alvarez glared at Mitch with angry black eyes. "I only tell you what I heard them say," he said. "They say they had warnings, warnings for a long time. They say Danforth made business as usual, ignored the warnings. They knew . . ."

"Knew what?" Mitch demanded. "Wolf has never flared into risk range—never! Why should this time be different?"

"They knew," Alvarez repeated stubbornly. "Danforth, all the scientists. And made sure they were all safe below when the *fiero* came, too."

"Nuts. I just put Dr. Sorenson in the morgue—and he's not the only one." Mitch stepped closer to Alvarez, menacing him. "You watch your dangerous talk, Alvarez. I'm tired of your troublemaking."

"So go tell Danforth," Alvarez taunted. "Go bleat and whine, saying 'please sir' so maybe he'll wipe your butt for you if you ask special nice." He thumbed a cigarette from his chest pocket and lit it, then sauntered away. Mitch, fists clenched, watched him go.

"He's not the only one thinking like that," the first man muttered, glancing at the others. "Can't say I don't myself." Two other men murmured in agreement.

"You can't just talk it away, Mitch," one of them said. "You can't cover over the facts. Danforth knew."

"You guys are crazy. And that kind of talk doesn't help us now." Mitch looked from face to face for a moment, then turned and stamped toward the door. Magda scooted down a little, hiding herself behind the cot, as the other men scattered in twos or threes, some following after Mitch, others moving off to new talk, as possessed with talking as the other adults on the level above.

Magda studied her thin hands and picked at a shred of flesh by a thumbnail, indifferent to the pain as she tore it too deeply.

Danforth.

She wrapped her arms around her knees, then let her head drop forward until her face rested on her kneecaps. She began to rock on her buttocks, shifting back and forth, conscious of the tickle of her swinging hair on her shins, the snores of the man beside her, the other soft sounds in the room, the despair and uselessness and pain. Magda began to weep quietly as she rocked, her sobs lost beneath the sound of the sleeping man's snores, weeping for the dead, the lost, the emptiness that could never be refilled, never again, wept until her chest hurt to breathe with the effort to be quiet, to disappear, to have an ending.

Danforth.

No, not yet. She wouldn't die yet.

Would it be bravery? her mother had wondered, regretting her missed chance, forever empty by having missed it.

She wiped her eyes and took a deep breath, then another. Then, determinedly, she stretched out on the floor between the cots. She would sleep and build her strength, guarding her vengeance—she knew the name now. She would be strong. She would be brave, as her mother had asked. She would be steel as Dr. Renfrew was steel, yet unmarred by the weakness the other had shown in the corridor. She would be strong and cold and clear in her purpose.

She closed her eyes and willed herself into sleep, her body trembling with rage.

* * *

Magda awoke several hours later. She sat up and rubbed her back awkwardly, then levered herself upward on the wall. The man still snored beside her, one arm thrown loosely across his eyes. She glanced at the sleeper on the other cot, a woman she knew vaguely, then swayed as a wave of dizziness swept down her body, making the room tilt oddly and the half-light of the overhead panels turn suddenly harsh. She swallowed against a sudden spurt of fear, her heart pounding, but waited for the room to steady. Not yet, she promised herself. I won't be sick yet. It's just the sedatives, anyway.

She pushed herself away from the wall and wobbled forward, then found her stride, stepping wider to stretch her muscles. Gingerly, she retraced her steps among the lines of beds and decided she needed breakfast. She had not eaten at all the previous day—had she eaten the day before? She couldn't remember. The day before, Magda had still been a child and her mother had been alive; perhaps she had eaten. She walked down the corridor to the cafeteria and stood patiently in line, watching the people at the nearby tables without interest.

She would need a weapon. As the line hitched forward one place, she tried to think of a good choice. The colony should have pistols and other guns, though maybe not, but she didn't know where they were kept and doubted she could get close enough to take one unseen. She took a tray and reached for silverware, then turned the table knife over in her hand, considering. It lacked a proper edge and would need more strength than she had to make a lethal blow. She would have only one quick chance before they dragged her away; she must be sure of her strike.

She took a carton of milk from a shelf, then accepted a plate of steaming food from the woman behind the counter. Beyond the woman's head she saw an array of carving knives on pegs over the broad stove, neatly arranged among copper pots and other large utensils. Two other women worked briskly at the stove, hands moving deftly as they flipped pancakes and eggs, put bread in the toasters, and chopped fruit from the colony farm. Magda hesitated, looking at the knives.

"Anything else, honey?" the counterwoman asked as Magda failed to move on.

Magda shifted her gaze to the woman. "Need help in the kitchen?" she asked hoarsely.

The woman smiled, her tired face lighting with relief. "Don't we always? Lots of people to feed. Do you want to help?"

"Sure." Magda bent her lips upward, copying the other's smile, playing the game.

"You'll be welcome, surely. Eat your breakfast and I'll get you an apron."

"Okay."

Magda sat down at a table where she could see the knives and studied them as she ate. They looked sharp enough, long enough. She imagined the weight of the knife in her hand, the swinging slash at Danforth's throat, the spurting blood. Or perhaps she should stab him in the chest—the heart was on the left side, wasn't it? She fingered her own ribs, feeling for the dull thump of her heart, measuring the spaces between the bones. She would have only one chance; she had to be sure. She felt herself tremble with her need.

When she finished eating, Magda carried her tray to the disposal window and stacked it with the others, vaguely conscious of movement in the room beyond the kitchen as others worked, then approached the woman behind the counter.

"I'm ready," she said.

"Good. Here's an apron now. You ask Marcia what to do." She pointed at one of the woman behind the stove. Magda walked around the far end of the counter, then approached Marcia, her body taut and halting as she neared the array of knives. She forced herself to relax, refusing to look at the beckoning knives, and touched Marcia's shoulder.

"I'm here to help, Marcia."

"Good! That's a dear." Marcia stretched and took a long carving knife off the wall, then handed Magda the knife and a large bowl of apples. "Cut those up for me, will you? That's a good girl."

Magda moved several feet to a clear counter space, her

fingers tightly gripping the heavy knife and bowl. She looked quickly around, then looked down at the knife, weighing it in her hand. It had a sharp edge, a long blade, a good weight. It would do.

Calmly, she reached for an apple and slashed it into exact halves.

Wolf Colony Station, Home Crater, Level 2, Conference Room 2C, 86 hours past flare.

Danforth surveyed the tired faces around the table and cleared his throat. The past three days had been hard, but, he told himself optimistically, he had preserved the necessary minimum, a feasible holding pattern as the colony waited out the hours until *Ceti Flag*'s arrival. How the cargo-chain freighter could help, he didn't know, and he tried not to think about the one hundred dead for whom *Flag* would arrive too late. He had learned the art of imposing his will on balky difficulties and unpleasant facts, he told himself; this newest crisis was only a matter of degree.

In his deepest mind, his sense of innate decency rebelled against the complacent arrogance of that thought, but he pushed it away. He didn't have the time.

"Your reports?" He looked around the table expectantly.

To his left sat the chief of science, Dr. Harrod, a slightly-built elderly man with a shock of disordered white hair and distracted eyes. Since the flare Harrod had seemed overwhelmed by the crisis; only by prodding had Danforth forced him to take responsibility in organizing his section. Harrod had been a different man, Danforth remembered, when he had smugly shrugged off young Leland's anxiety about Wolf. Danforth tried to hide his resentment: he needed Harrod, as weak as he was.

Next to Dr. Harrod at table center sat the downside and topside crew chiefs, Rodriguez and Summers. Danforth had delegated the liaison on enviro-controls to Rodriguez, a sturdy middle-aged family man well liked by both the labor crews and the science team. Summers had taken charge of the crews working on the ruined surface

facilities. To Summers's right, Victoria Renfrew sat quietly, eyes closed, her chin leaning into her cupped palm,
exhaustion written plainly in the pallor of her face. John
Wilson of supply and computer tech Natalie Desart completed their group, both sagging in their chairs. He nodded
first at Rodriguez.

"What do you want to know?" Rodriguez asked truc-
ulently, obviously under strain. He looked disheveled,
his longish black hair unwashed, his overalls stained and
wrinkled; he squinted uncomfortably against the soft
overhead lights. "Why is this meeting necessary? Is more
talk going to stop the garden from dying or repair ventilator machinery that can't be repaired?"

"I just want to know our status," Danforth said pla-
catingly. "We need to coordinate, compare ideas." He
leaned forward and laced his fingers on the table. "We're
on the edge—we must work together or all our efforts will
be wasted. Don't you agree?"

"Reports won't help the garden," Rodriguez said, un-
moved by Danforth's appeal. "We've had seventy percent vegetation loss since the flare, just like the rest of
our Level One casualties. We don't have enough workable air-converters to make up the loss; most of that
equipment was stored topside. Smart, Danforth: we put
all our air potential on the level closest to our little flare
star just because Central didn't want to drill a sixth level.
Who in the hell decided these things?" He hammered
his fist on the table.

"How long until we run out of breathable air?" Desart
asked with alarm. "I thought we salvaged air from Levels Four and Five."

"We did—but we've got three hundred people in this
base, all of them breathing in and out twenty times a
minute. The carbon dioxide levels are well above rec-
ommended standard, and I don't have any way to bring
it down. We've got problems with the heat exchangers,
too, as you may have noticed from the temperature in
here. It's coming unglued, Danforth—we just had too
much damage. We can't hold it together much longer."

"We'll have to keep trying," Danforth insisted, trying
to impose his will on the man, on everyone.

"How?" Rodriguez barked in frustration.

"How *much* time on our air?" Desart insisted.

Rodriguez shrugged. "Maybe thirty hours, maybe twenty more if we go on air-conservation drill, and I mean right *now*. No unnecessary movement, no talking, all nonessential personnel on sleep drugs, the rest on tranquilizers. Or did Central forget to stock enough no-worry pills, too?"

"We have enough," Dr. Renfrew said quietly. "Long-term sedation must be monitored, of course, but the side effects are limited and known."

"Well, okay. I expect the garden to fail completely within twelve hours; without its help for the air-converters we've got working, the carbon dioxide levels will shoot sky-high. That's my report." Rodriguez sat back and crossed his arms, glowering at Danforth.

"What side effects?" Summers asked Renfrew.

She shrugged. "In certain drug-sensitive individuals, mild tremors or tics, occasional internal bleeding, sometimes even temporary psychosis. Any drug has its risks. The spectrum we use has been well tested in clinical trials on both Earth and Mars. I anticipate no serious difficulty."

"Thank you, Doctor," Danforth said firmly. "Dr. Harrod?" The chief of science jerked his head up, then looked around in bewilderment, as if he hadn't a clue to place and time. God, Danforth thought disgustedly, what a support in a high wind. "Dr. Harrod," he said again, trying to get Harrod's attention. To his dismay, he saw Harrod's old eyes fill with tears. "Wake up, man," Danforth said impatiently.

"I . . ." Harrod's mouth flapped impotently.

"This is crap," Summers said. He shifted his chair closer to Harrod and patted him on the shoulder. "Take it easy, Chet," he murmured kindly. "You don't have to report right now; it's okay." He glared at Danforth. "Like I said, crap. You're treating this like a nothing-different staff meeting. Don't you hear José? We're running out of *air*, Colony Director. All your bullshit meetings aren't going to change that."

"When *Ceti Flag* gets here . . ."

"And does what? What, Danforth? A four-engine freighter with two dozen boxy cargo tins and no fuel. By the time *Flag* can get back to Mars and bring back a starliner, we'll all be long dead. So tell me what *Ceti Flag* can do for us."

Danforth stared back at Summers's angry face. He considered his response a moment and decided on frankness, even though it exposed some vulnerability, might undermine some of Danforth's control: Summers would respond to bluntness, would back off. "I don't have an answer for that, Mack," Danforth said, making his tone softly earnest. "All I can do is offer the answers I do have—what potentials we have left, what time we have left, the people we have to mobilize. How is your work progressing on the radio array?"

That diverted Summers. "Nowhere. We salvaged some equipment from the lower levels, but every few hours we get a random burst of microwave readings, God knows why. Jenkins is breaking down the set again to trace the defect."

Danforth frowned. "What kind of readings? From *Flag*?" For a moment his hope soared that the freighter might be a full day early.

"No," Summers said deflatingly. "The pulses are too scrambled, and the comsat isn't working, anyway, so it can't be from there. It's got to be an internal defect, something in the chips."

"So we *still* don't have a working transmitter to talk to *Flag*," Rodriguez said, throwing up his hands. "Great."

"*Flag* doesn't need our help to enter orbit," Danforth reminded him.

"How did Central manage that oversight?" Rodriguez asked sarcastically. "How did this happen, anyway, Danforth? I've got talk going on in my crews, bad talk. Why didn't Wolf-watch warn us?" He shot an angry glance at Dr. Harrod, who flinched and looked down in agony at his folded hands. Damn his incompetence, Danforth thought angrily, too angry to give the old man any sympathy. Once again Danforth wished science had put its labs on a lower level—over half of the science personnel were already dead, like Leland out in the lost harvesters. He didn't have anyone else with enough rank to run the labs—just Harrod. God, he wished Leland were there, young as he was.

"Why weren't we prepared?" Rodriguez demanded. "Why?"

Danforth jerked his attention back to the angry chief and dodged. "What kind of bad talk?" he asked sharply.

"This is news?" Summers asked sarcastically. "Where have you been lately? I've got talk, too, and maybe more than talk soon. Second dawn is coming up, and some of my people may refuse to stay topside."

"Refuse? They can't do that. We need topside repaired!"

"Oh? Just watch them." Summers leaned forward and tapped the table. "You got personnel problems with labor you wouldn't believe, courtesy of a few stupid maneuvers in recent months. And everybody's got someone in the hospital by now, many of them dead." His face spasmed with sudden pain, but he plowed onward. "My crews are angry and confused—and they blame you, Director. Can't say I disagree, either."

"*That* opinion you've made known already," Danforth said angrily.

"I got a right to my opinions, just like Isaiah did. But we know what happened to him, don't we?"

"That's enough!" Danforth struggled to control himself. "Just get the H-3 processor fixed so *Flag* can refuel thirty hours from now. When that's ready, we'll power down topside and bring all crews below. Dr. Renfrew, we go on air-conserve immediately. All nonessential persons will go to sleep—decide how many you need for a skeleton hospital staff. Same for the other sections." He spread his hands. "We've got to do what we *can* do. Is that agreed?" He looked around at the skeptical faces, then received a reluctant nod from Rodriguez. He saw Summers glance at his fellow chief, disappointed.

"Only fifty hours on air," Desart muttered. "It'll be close."

"I want to finish repairs on the cargo lander," Summers said. "The guys at Tri Ellium deserve at least a look-see."

"You focus on the H-3 shed. That's an order."

"You can't just leave them out there!"

"While I'm director of this colony, you will focus on the H-3 shed. And we *will* leave them out there. Is that understood?"

Summers flushed. "You're a bastard, Danforth."

"*Is* that understood?"

Summers hesitated, then looked for support in other faces. Seeing none, which Danforth noted in satisfaction, Summers reluctantly nodded. "Yeah."

"Orders, people," Danforth said coldly. He rose from his chair, signaling the end of the meeting. He waited for a nod from each, then dismissed them.

Wolf Colony Station, Home Crater, Level 2, near Conference Room 2C, 87 hours past flare.

Magda waited in the corridor by the main conference room, trying to make herself inconspicuous against the wall. She could hear Danforth's voice among the other voices behind the half-closed door; she watched the passing faces, trying to avoid catching anyone's eye, and hoped Dr. Renfrew didn't come looking for her. Probably the doctor would look through Level 3 first, thinking Magda had gone to bed or to an early meal. Magda had counted on that in her planning.

She slipped her hand under her tunic and fingered the hilt of the long knife she held pressed between her arm and ribs. She would have to raise it high, then stab downward at Danforth's chest with all her strength—maybe a two-handed grip would be best. Or perhaps slip behind and shove the point deep into the back. Or perhaps slash at his throat too deeply for the doctors to save him. She couldn't decide. She imagined the shock of impact through her arm, the cascading blood, the screams and confusion as they dragged her away. But the chest or the throat? From the front, so he could see her face as she killed him, or from the back, to be sure of the strike? She closed her eyes and swallowed uneasily, trembling.

She had hunted Danforth for the past two hours, ever since she had slipped away from the cafeteria duty. At first she couldn't find him and didn't dare ask, worried that she might arouse suspicions. A lab assistant's teenage daughter had no business with the colony director, not when she belonged elsewhere helping in the hospital. Then Danforth had appeared suddenly on Level 2 by the elevators, striding past her in the company of a Latino crew chief and Mr. Mack; Summers winked at her as he passed but didn't stop. She cautiously followed them, her heart beginning to pound frantically as she reached under her tunic for the waiting knife. Then she hurried, deciding in a rush—*now*. She was only two strides away when the men abruptly turned and disappeared into a conference room, leaving Magda to linger impotently outside.

And so she had waited, her thoughts filled with images of blood and retribution.

I'll do it, she promised herself. I'll do it.

She tensed as chairs scraped inside the conference room and voices moved toward the door. She wrapped her fingers around the knife hilt and quickly crossed the corridor to stand beside the conference room doorway, her every sense focused on that half-open door. The door swung open, and she pressed back against the wall as a young woman emerged and turned right, hurrying away down the corridor. Two other men crowded behind her, one a white-haired older man, the other the Latino chief she had seen earlier. The chief eyed her curiously, then walked onward.

"Why, Magda—what are you doing here?" Mack Summers stopped short in front of her, blocking her view of the doorway. She craned her head to see around him, then tried to sidestep as Danforth came into view behind him.

"Hey, hey," Summers said, catching her arm. "What's the matter? Magda?"

"Let me go . . . please." Magda grimaced at him and tried to shake free, then wrenched away as Danforth walked unconcernedly after the others. Summers's grip jostled her knife, and it came loose from her hand, dropping to the floor with a faint clang. As she bent quickly for it, he promptly stepped on the blade, then kicked it against the wall out of her reach.

"No, Magda," Summers said in an anguished voice. "Sweet Jesus." He caught her as she lunged for the knife and pinned her arms; she struggled against his grip, panting. "Magda!"

"What's happening here?" a woman's voice asked irritably. "Summers? What is this?" Dr. Renfrew had stopped in the room doorway and now looked at them in surprise. "Magda? Why aren't you working in the sickrooms?"

Summers bore down hard on Magda's forearm with his fingers, making her gasp with the pain. "A little bit of hysterics," he said to Dr. Renfrew, his tone light. "I'll take care of her."

"Oh. Well, we'll put her down early, then." Dr. Renfrew looked irritated, already thinking of something else. "Dormitory Three, isn't it, Magda? I'll be there shortly." She turned on her heel and left them.

"You're hurting my arm," Magda protested, prying frantically at his fingers with her other hand.

Summers pulled her a few steps farther down the hall, away from the adults exiting the conference room. He looked down sternly at Magda. "If I let up, will you give up on getting the knife?"

Magda nodded. "It's too late, anyway," she said dully. Summers released her arm, and she rubbed it, her head hung low. "What does she mean, 'put me down'?" she asked rebelliously, furious at him for stopping her.

"We're low on air, so you and most folks are going to sleep until *Flag* gets here."

"No!" Magda threw up her chin and glared at him. "I don't want to sleep."

"Why?" he asked pointedly. "So you can have another chance at Danforth? This isn't Yugoslavia, Magda. You don't solve things that way here."

"He killed Mother!"

"Hush! Do you want everybody to hear you? Dear one, he didn't kill your mother—your mother died from radiation sickness."

"He could have stopped it. Everybody says so!"

"That's a lot of stupid talk that goes farther than it should." Summers bent down and picked up the knife, then slipped it through his belt. "I'm surprised at you, Magda, really surprised. Whatever your mother thought later about it, she did the right thing in not killing that colonel. They would have shot her, too, right there on the street. Where would that have left you, all alone and orphaned? Would that have brought your father back, committing suicide like that? Are you listening to me?"

Magda clenched her teeth and refused to look at him. He hesitated, then tried to pat her shoulder, but she flinched away from his touch.

"Leave me alone!"

"All right, then!" Summers said angrily. "*Don't* listen to me. Come on—I'll take you to Dr. Renfrew."

"No! Please, Mr. Mack," she pleaded, clutching at him desperately. "I don't want to sleep. I'll never wake up."

"Don't be silly. Of course you will."

She shook her head solemnly. "I won't. Can't I stay with you? I'll behave, I promise I'll behave right. I won't go anywhere near Director Danforth, I promise!"

Summers stared down at her. "Promise?"

"Yes!"

He hesitated, then scowled ferociously. "All right. I'll think about it. You go help in the hospital like you're supposed to. I've got something to do right now—I'll come get you later. You tell Dr. Renfrew I want to talk to her first when she tries to sedate you. Okay?"

"Okay. Thank you, Mr. Mack."

Summers looked at her uncertainly, then walked away, shaking his head. Magda waited until he vanished into the crowd, then hurried toward the stairs. The Level 3 cafeteria was only a few paces from its lower landing. Confidently, Magda walked behind the service counter and touched Marcia on the arm.

"Hi! Can I help some more?"

Marcia smiled broadly, gabbing something Magda didn't bother to hear. Smiling as broadly as the other, Magda waited patiently as the older woman bustled for a bowl and something to chop, then looked with great affection at the new knife that had appeared in her hand.

It would do quite nicely. Yes, indeed.

An hour later, as soon as she could safely get away, Magda hurried down to her dormitory to hide the knife beneath her bed. She couldn't trust Mr. Mack to believe her—and so should be prudent. She couldn't trust anyone, not until she had accomplished her purpose. I will be strong, she chanted to herself, and slid the long knife beneath her mattress. There, she thought, patting the mattress. You wait there until it's time.

"There you are, Magda," a voice said behind her. Magda whirled and looked up at Dr. Renfrew, then focused with horror on the hypodermic in her hand. Behind her, she saw Mack Summers, his face troubled but determined.

"No!"

Dr. Renfrew looked at her sternly. "Do I have to call for someone to hold you down again?" she asked, her voice edged. "Do I?"

Magda looked wildly around and cringed back against the bed.

"Magda?" Dr. Renfrew insisted.

"Why?" she asked Summers in anguish. "You said . . ."

"I'm sorry, sweetie," Summers said gently. "I'm really sorry."

Dr. Renfrew took Magda's unresisting arm and injected the drug. "Now lie down and sleep. You'll feel much better later. That's a good girl." She helped Magda lie down on her bed, pulled up a blanket and tucked in the ends, then walked away.

Magda looked up at Mack Summers, accusing.

"I'm sorry," he said again, his expression stubborn. "I know how your mother thought, all those partisan stories she told you. You don't solve things that way, Magda."

"The Serbs did," Magda hissed at him. "They solved lots of people, all of them Croats."

"That was a long time ago and another place. I said I was sorry, but I obviously can't trust you when I'm not here to watch you. And I can't be all the time, not until *Flag* arrives. Don't you understand?''

"No, I don't! It's not fair!" Magda turned her face away from him, dizzy with the first rush of the sleep drug. He shuffled his feet uncomfortably as he looked down at her. Then she heard his footsteps move away, echoing with an eerie overtone to the blood pounding in her ears. She clenched her fists, trying to fight the drug, but fell toward a deep roiling blackness, falling, falling . . .

Her thoughts scattered into fragments, lost in the darkness. Mother . . .

Chapter 7

Cargo-chain freighter Ceti Flag, *EuroCom registry, control room, 2 hours to Wolf II.*

"Calling Wolf II Colony Station. Calling Wolf II Colony Station."

Jason watched as Yves intoned his appeal into the microwave transmitter. Across the room Axel sat before the power systems panels, his head turning slowly as he systematically monitored the colored wave curves and other schematics of the ship's final deceleration into orbit around Wolf II. Above Axel's head the Wolf star glared redly in a secondary wall screen showing *Flag*'s rearward view over the tin lines. The probabilities had held—only who knew what Wolf was saving up for later by being polite while *Flag* zipped by.

He put the thought away and focused on the cargo-tin alignment. His board would ring a dozen noisy bells if any tin dared to shift off-line with *Flag*'s smooth flight curve. Tins adrift during orbit insertion could crash ships if simply everything went wrong; and, past a certain margin on the catch baskets, the tin lines could choose a divergent trajectory not convenient to ship integrity. Once a PanUnion ship had managed to pull herself into pieces, courtesy of a half dozen little things in the wrong combination. The PanUnion crew had survived to push factory buttons on Earth, but it was not a fate he wished to repeat with *Flag*. So he kept an eye out, as always, sometimes from the auxiliary console on cargo deck, more often from the control room where *Flag*'s crew tended to gather during transition. He checked over his schematics again,

110

mindful that any big problem on the tin line always started small.

Lots of problems started small, so small that one hardly noticed. They started with a mild argument about proper tin delivery schedules, an hour taken for a beer with the cargo shed crew, getting chewed out in front of the others, of watching Helena play take your choice with bedrooms. Then they got bigger, and one began to wonder sort of what to do. Sometimes the problems got way out of hand—like a war with one's captain that wouldn't end, like certain smug assurances about a flare star made by pointy-heads on Mars. Or like what radiation did to human bodies, or bad air or too much heat, or no air and vacuum cold, or the claustrophobia that murdered the hopeful promise of a starship. That's when one started to really worry.

He listened to Yves's futile efforts at the transmitter. After each sending Yves paused for fifteen seconds for a response, allowing time for any comsat return to earlier sendings. Even microwaves took some appreciable time to cross twenty thousand kilometers, though the distance was steadily shortening as *Flag* descended into orbit around Wolf II. In the forward wall screen a dish-sized planet gleamed dimly in the reddish illumination of its primary, a whitish globe of dusty craters and shadowed scarps. In one of those craters, just short of the dawn limb, lay the colony station that still had not answered their hail.

Yves finally snapped off the radio and leaned back, scowling. "Well, they aren't yet in line of sight."

"Line of sight?" Jason asked. "Hell, Yves."

"I concede that the comsat isn't working," Yves said irritably. "We knew that four days ago." He checked the clock on his console, then keyed the time into the navcom computer. "They've had plenty of time to erect another transmitter; maybe we'll pick it up when we pass over Wolf Station. We'll try then. If we get a signal, we'll go downplanet."

"And if you don't get a signal?" Jason asked.

"We'll consider other options," Yves said stubbornly.

"Yves . . ." At the captain's black look, Jason tightened his lips, his temper rising again. "Crew opinion," he said, "is not insubordination, in case you're thinking of filing a flimsy against me."

"*When* opinion is invited," Yves snapped. "I'm not inviting."

"Oh? You should." Jason turned around to his own control board and called up his cargo-tin program again.

"Shut up! I've had about enough of your—"

"My what? Captain, I am *not* your problem." Jason pointed at the rearward wall screen and the angry red star that flickered behind them. "*That's* your problem. If you're so sure no one's alive, why even go into orbit? Haven't we been over that already? You managed a fancy little side step on the vote and got the Stromstads to back you up. Is this another one? What do I have to do, call for another vote?"

"One was enough."

"Apparently not."

The two men glared at each other again. Stalemate. Yves could not condemn him on the spot—after all, Jason might be right—but the breach of authority could not be ignored, either. Jason saw the conflict in Yves's face and felt a brief pang of compassion; if regs and Helena had not come between them, they might have become friends. Axel looked toward them, and Jason saw him exchange a glance with Yves, then quirk an eyebrow.

"What would you do?" Yves asked Jason reluctantly, and forever changed their relationship. It diminished the other man, and they both knew it—in time Yves would hate Jason for what he had done today, if he didn't already. That Axel had witnessed it only made it worse. Jason bit his lip, regretting the loss.

"Yeah. We should take the jitney down now to see, signal or no signal. You should go; I'd like to go, too."

Yves shrugged. "All right. You have command, Axel." He stood up abruptly, his chair rebounding violently on its pivot, then stalked out. Jason sat a moment, watching the chair rock back and forth.

"Christ, Axel," he muttered.

"It could have been done better," Axel rumbled, his face showing his disapproval.

"Yeah? You were a big help."

The big Swede stiffened. "It's the captain's decision. I state my opinion when needed."

"So do I," Jason reminded him. "Like I said, you were a big help." He looked at the planet swelling in the wall screen and wished suddenly, for new reasons, that he had found another way. How had it turned into this? You win or I win? He kicked his chair and left the control room.

He hurried after Yves, the magnetic insets of his boots clicking as he walked. Now that *Flag* had quickly lost momentum in the dust-heavy vicinity of the star, cargo deck had begun to shift into free-fall, making magnet boots necessary for traction. It didn't help the captain's mood that Jason had to remind him of that before entering cargo deck. Yves got his boots from the nearby locker and sat down to put them on, scowling ferociously, then preceded Jason through the gimbel port.

For the next half hour Yves stomped stickily around cargo deck, inspecting panels and the jitney's fuel tanks, then insisted on performing the ship prep himself. Jason watched him resignedly as the jitney, a two-seater intended for quick transport from ship to planet, slid outward on its slender tracks from its storage position on the portside wall, then moved smoothly at right angles toward the launching rail into the larger ship port. When the ship's undercarriage had attached itself to the rail, Yves keyed open the gull-wing hatch and hauled himself across the padded bench seat into the far set of acceleration belts. Jason joined him, buckling his own restraints as Yves began the final checklist with calm efficiency.

I already knew you could do this, Jason commented silently. I know you were a pilot once, years ago, just like me. I can do it, too. As Yves checked off the last item, Jason keyed his control board into the cargo-deck computer.

"Preparing to launch," Jason said.

"Proceed," Yves said brusquely.

Jason punched in the launch sequence, and the automatic controls responded immediately, sliding the jitney forward into the exterior ship port. As the lock cycled them through, he pressurized the cabin and put the jitney on internal air, then watched patiently as the telltales shifted through a multicolored sequence. The outer hatch irised open; Jason lifted the jitney on her belly jets and eased her forward. Clear of the port, the tiny ship shot forward and down, falling gracefully ahead of *Flag*'s course toward the planet.

As they banked left beneath the starboard cargo-tin line, Jason called for a grid readout of their trajectory to Wolf II, then checked the course and let the computer autopilot take over. In open space the computer could usually react and dodge faster than a human pilot, so long as the human kept a wary eye out for things not in the computer's mental universe. The truly unpredictable was a major problem in automated tin delivery, short of using a cyborg, of course— and that particular nasty idea of disembodied brains had yet to get past EuroCom and the Geneva Protocol, even for R&D. Hey, he told himself sardonically, if I'm wrong about this, maybe I can volunteer to be the first Mecho-Man. You always wanted to be a pioneer, Jase ol' boy; there's your chance. Ho ho. He settled back, adjusted his shoulders more comfortably into the seat back, and glanced at Yves. The captain stared straight forward, his lips set tightly.

"Yves . . ." Jason began.

Yves set his jaw tighter and deliberately looked out the port window, ignoring him.

"Hell, man, I didn't arrange this. I've always thought you were a good captain, never said otherwise."

"Oh?" Yves asked bitingly. "Then why do you always challenge my orders?"

"Always? I do not. When Helena acts up and calls you names, you don't complain. Even Inga can say a flat no to you when she gets on her medical high horse. Why am I different?"

Yves turned toward him, his face shadowed in the dim light of the jitney's control panel. "Always. I can see it in your face every time. 'That's wrong, Captain.' 'That's stupid, Captain.' You always think you can do better."

"That's not so!"

"*Merde,*" Yves said. "I know you, Jason Roarke. I know what you've done on other ships, stirring things up, making trouble, pushing and pushing and pushing. It never

stops, even after Central warned you.'' His voice trembled
with rage. ''That's the difference between you and me,
Jason. I'm reliable. I can make the hard choices. If you
don't like a directive, you ignore it, no matter who pays.''

''I do not. When?''

Yves ignored the question. ''And that's why you'll never
be captain on cargo-chain. Central needs captains who can
face the hard choices and make them, who follow policy
about designated risks. You're not capable of looking the
Wolf colonists in the face and enforcing triage.''

''And you are.''

''Yes! And I will. If they have extensive topside damage, heavy casualties, limited environment, we go on.
We follow the protocol and leave them behind. Is that
understood? I am captain of *Flag*, and it's my decision,
no matter how you maneuver with crew votes and pretty
appeals to Axel. Give it up, Jason. But you just can't
leave anything alone, not even Helena—'' Yves stopped
himself abruptly and looked out the window.

''Helena makes her own choices,'' Jason said quietly.
''You think I've liked sharing her with you?''

''She was mine first—until you moved in.''

''Helena isn't anybody's, Yves. Is that what this is really about? All she cares about is her career. Don't you
know that? Everything else is just games.''

''That's not true!'' Yves said hotly.

''Shit, if you feel that way, why don't you tell her?''

''I did. I told her I loved her; I told her everything.
She seemed . . . pleased. We had everything planned.
But you kept pushing and pushing, tempting her—'' He
broke off, his hands clenched in his lap.

''I didn't know, Yves.'' *I'm grieving a little,* Helena
had said when she had chosen sides against Yves. God.
''She never told me.''

''Oh, sure. I really believe that, Jason. I'm letting you
know that you can't have my ship, too! It's mine!''

''Yves . . .''

''No! Shut up! Leave me alone!'' Yves chopped decisively at the air with his hand, his dark eyes gleaming
malevolently. ''Not one more word!''

Jason nodded numbly, and Yves turned back to the side

window, shutting Jason out, his body tense with fury. Jason swallowed uneasily and looked out forward at the white face of Wolf II. You're really aware, Roarke, he told himself disgustedly. You really clue into things. "Yves . . ."

Yves's hands curled into fists as he swung toward Jason, ready to lunge. Jason warded him off hastily, wary of the controls only inches away.

"Hold it, man! We're in flight! Yves!"

Yves controlled himself with an effort. "You . . ."

"I told you I didn't know. Helena never told me. *You* never told me. And I'm not after command of *Flag*. This is about Wolf, not *Flag*!"

"I don't believe you," Yves said coldly.

"Fine. That's just great." Jason threw up his hands in surrender. "Well, you better get hold of yourself, Captain. We have a probable crisis, and you can't wish it away by blaming it on me!"

"Go fuck yourself." Yves turned his shoulder and stared out the window.

"Yeah, I just might," Jason muttered. "Nothing else to do right now."

Yves said nothing.

The jitney fell steadily toward the planet, racing ahead of *Flag*'s own approach. Jason watched their progress glumly, not knowing what else to say. The little ship made quick progress, though the minutes stretched like hours with Yves's angry presence seated next to him. Jason silently sang himself sad songs for a while, then decided he didn't deserve *all* the fault—so he thought about Helena's nicer moods, thought about the Stromstads and some disrespectful speculations about those two cold fish in bed with each other, thought about *Flag* and her familiar spaces, remembered some women he had known, some friends he would like to see again, some rumors he had heard on Mars about the current bureaucratic wars that might affect cargo-chain. It used up time, time he would rather not thinking about Wolf II and what might wait for them there, what Yves obviously intended to do. He would find that out soon enough.

As they at last fell into orbit around Wolf II, he keyed the jitney's transponder to search for the base beacon, a

steady atomic clock that emitted a short-distance signal
for the cargo handlers. The control board flashed a recognition—at least the beacon still worked, God knew why.
The beacon was buried on the side of a mountaintop west
of Home Crater; likely it had escaped the worst of the
flare. If the beacon had survived, so might other machinery—like the computers that allowed Wolf Station ventilation and power and heat exchange. The little ship
swooped downward over an area of dayside sun-white and
shadowed terrain and headed toward an insignificant crater
near the dawn limb, rushing over the dusty surface at
multi-Mach speed, scarps and craters a blur beneath them.

A hundred kilometers from the base Jason switched the
controls to manual, his hands fitting comfortably into the
grips, the jitney humming deep in her small engines, a
palpable vibration beneath his seat. He lifted the prow
slightly as they passed over a wide mountain range bisected by the ever-present scarps, then ducked over the
limb into nightside, approaching the base in a wide curve
from the west. A ruddy glow spread across the eastern
horizon ahead, the presage of Wolf's second dawn, still
a few days off. Beneath the ship the craters and stony
rills still flowed in the blur of their speed, a flickering of
shadow and deeper shadow now faintly tinged with the
first darkest reds of dayside.

As the jitney approached Wolf Station, Jason activated
the baffle jets and slowed their descent, then waited vainly
for flight-nav acquisition with the base computer in the
topside hangars. By now he should have had a comlink
with the computer's network grid of sensors, allowing a
steady stream of data to perfect their approach. Nothing.
He read off his onboard instruments carefully, mentally
compensating for the lack of groundside data, then powered down still further as they entered final descent.
Guided by Jason's deft hands, the jitney slowed smoothly
into a wide curve and arrowed over the last scarp, beginning its descent into the darkness of Home Crater.

Jason strained forward in his seat as they crossed the
crater wall, searching for the base lights near the farther
rim wall. Nothing, not even the field lights for the cargo
landers or any other topside readylights that were always

lit, even in dayside. Why didn't they have power? Where *was* everybody? Anxiety snaked down his spine, raising the hackles on the nape of his neck. Vacuum put survival on the razor edge, a fact too easily forgotten when humans assumed themselves gods of creation, as they always did. Two-thirds fatality, Inga had said, worst case. Where *are* the lights? he wondered, and gripped the jitney's controls tighter.

As the jitney swept across the crater basin, rapidly closing the distance to the base, Jason could pick out a few huddled shapes nestled by the eastern cliff, vaguely distinguishable in the dim glow of the approaching dawn. To the left and center, several ship hangars and repair facilities spread in a semicircle beneath the cliffside, a curved wing centered on the towered topside access to the five underground levels of the base below ground. To the right, the low rectangle of the cargo-lander service shed loomed gray-red in the shadows; behind it, nestled against a cliff-high rock outcropping, the massive H-3 processing plant spread its array of cubes and boxy distillation towers. High above on the cliff top the dawn light silhouetted the spiderwork girders of the half-constructed new observatory. Nothing moved on topside, as if Wolf Station stood frozen in an instant of time, a technician's sketch of a colony base, without color, without motion, without life. He glanced at Yves, then chose a landing site four hundred meters from the main hangar, bumping down on the rough crater soil with a tooth-rattling jar and a cloud of dust behind them.

As they taxied toward the hangar, both men saw the several spacesuited bodies collapsed near a waiting cargo lander, awkward broken dolls sprawled in the dust. ''God in heaven,'' Jason breathed, and heard a single echoing curse from Yves.

The jitney bumped over the rough rubble of the base outskirts, then rolled easily onto concrete as they rolled up to the hangar. Jason signaled to the door locks and waited vainly for a response.

''Vacuum suits,'' he said, then stretched behind him to toggle the suit compartment. Yves looked out the window bleakly, his eyes still riveted on the bodies by the cargo lander. Jason tugged down the suits, jostling Yves's shoulder; Yves roused himself enough to glare.

"Is that necessary?" he asked, eyeing the suit-paks with distaste.

"What do you suggest? Just take off and go back to *Flag*?"

Yves hesitated as if that were exactly what he wanted to do. Likely he did. "No, I suppose not," he said reluctantly. He took a suit-pak, and the two men maneuvered awkwardly in the small cabin, careful not to touch one another as they tugged on the suits. Finally Jason snapped down his helmet to the neck ring and checked his air dial. The jitney's vacuum suits held forty minutes of air—enough to get into the hangar and explore downward a little, not much more.

"Radio check," Yves said, his voice tinny over the suit-band channel.

"You've got a check. We'll take this, too," Jason added, and stretched to get a pistol from the overhead compartment. "We might have some desperate people." He hoped—desperate people were alive.

Yves grunted noncommittally and pressed the evac button. They waited as the jitney recaptured most of the cabin air into the aft tanks, then Yves pushed open the gull-wing hatch and climbed down the handholds into the soft puffing dust that had silted from the crater onto the asphalt. Jason jumped down after Yves and let him take the lead toward the main hangar and its elevators leading downward; their steps made odd gingerly progress until they caught the rhythm of Wolf II's half-Standard gravity. They stopped at the hangar air lock, a small port access to the right of the wide hangar doors, now firmly shut, and pushed vainly at the buttons. Nothing.

"We'll have to take the outside elevator," Jason suggested.

"Where is it?"

"Come on." Jason headed for the exterior elevator shed at the other end of the hangar, a small elevator used for direct vacuum access that bypassed the pressurized hangars—and, if he remembered Isaiah's casual instructions on a previous surface expedition, a gravity-powered mechanism not dependent on station power. He inspected the emergency elevator's control panel, then pushed the access button. An instant later the elevator door swooshed open, scattering dust with a blast of contained air. The two men hastily stepped inside and closed the outer door with the interior level wheel, stopping the air bleed from the elevator shaft.

"Atmosphere below," Jason commented. Yves did not bother to reply, again off in his distant spaces. Together they watched the button lights shift as the elevator descended to Level 3, the administrative level. If Director Danforth had survived, they could expect to find him there. A minute later the elevator door opened, revealing an empty access corridor dimly lit by panels overhead.

They do have power, Jason marveled, and felt his suppressed tension lift with a shock almost as keen as pain. Air, lights—could somebody really still be alive? They advanced cautiously down the short hallway toward the turning onto the main corridor.

In the dim light of the main hallway Jason saw a man slumped against the wall. As their boots scraped on the floor, the man lifted his head blearily and focused on them. He stared at them a moment, dazed, then surged to his feet.

"*Flag!*" he cried, his voice ringing triumphantly down the corridor. "*Flag* is here!" His voice rang with jubilation.

"Mack . . ." Jason said, taking a step toward him. He heard the echoing murmur of Summers's shout as the news swept through the level, then a chorus of ragged cheers in the distance. "*Flag! Ceti Flag* is here! *Flag!*"

Summers bounded over to them and grabbed Yves's arm, then Jason's, pressing hard through the fabric of their suits. He grinned at them rather insanely, Jason thought. Though it seemed rather justified, too. He found himself grinning back as maniacally.

"Merceau! Roarke! Oh, God, it's good to see you!"

Jason released his helmet from the neck ring and pulled it off, then gave Summers a shake back. "What happened, Mack?"

"Bad flare, really bad. We've been waiting on power down for two days, hoping you'd get here in time. Nothing works topside—you noticed, I'm sure—but we've repaired a few things, just haven't powered up, working on others. Things aren't good, guys. Come, Director Danforth will want to see you right away. What are your plans? Can you help us?''

Yves looked at him blankly, his expression frozen. He had not responded to Mack's jubilant welcome, had not smiled, had not moved. As Summers looked at him expectantly, Yves opened his mouth, then shut it impotently and looked despairingly past Summers at the darkened corridor beyond him. Several people were hurrying toward them, half skipping in their haste to reach them, their faces split by smiles as wide as Mack's.

"Uh . . .'' Yves said.

"Wake up, man,'' Summers said impatiently. "Surely this isn't a surprise to you—or don't you bother with radio checks anymore?''

Yves flinched at Summers's taunt and found enough spirit to glare. "I'll take it under advisement,'' he said stiffly.

That was definitely the wrong thing to say. Summers dropped his grip on Yves's arm and flushed in dismay— and a rising anger. How long had Mack been waiting the minutes, the hours, for *Flag*? Jason wondered, understanding the anger. Shit, Yves.

"Advisement?'' Summers asked incredulously. "Are you joking? Christ, man! We've got a crisis here—and you're still 'under advisement'?'' His voice rose to a near shout.

"Easy, Mack,'' Jason said, conscious of the other people hurrying toward them. The two in front slowed and hesitated, their faces confused by Summers's shouting. Like it or not, Yves now had an audience of more than one angry man. Jason tried to catch Summers's sleeve, tried to warn him, looked an appeal at Yves. Summers shook him off angrily. "Take it easy,'' Jason repeated.

Summers threw Jason a disgusted look. "Oh, sure. Come on, *Flag*—I'm sure Danforth wants your *advice*.''

He stamped off, pushing his way through the crowd that still gathered in the corridor. Jason glanced at Yves, but the captain wasn't interested. They followed Summers down the hall to an open doorway. At a table in the center of the room, Peter Danforth sat in a chair, hands clasped in front of him on the plastic table surface, stiffly erect, poised with tension. As the two *Flag* officers appeared, as he saw them, Danforth took a deep shuddering breath and abruptly looked down at his entwined fingers. When he lifted his head a moment later, Jason saw that his eyes had filled with tears.

"Flag," Danforth whispered.

God, he's aged, Jason thought. He had always thought Danforth one of the invulnerable ones, so exquisite a bureaucrat that nothing touched him, nothing mattered to him except figures on paper.

"Flag," Danforth whispered again, then stood up shakily and walked around the table. "You're here. You're actually here." He pumped Yves's hand, shaking the captain until he jounced like a trembling leaf in autumn. Yves pulled away and stared at him. Then he looked at the other people at the room, the ceiling, the floor, even turned to look behind him, seeing the faces, the hope, the need.

"I . . ." he began.

Danforth glanced uncertainly at Jason. Jason guessed that Danforth had held on until this moment, and now, after offering too many answers against hope since the flare, expected others to have answers. Yves scanned the conference room again, his struggle apparent in his face. As the silence lengthened, the people in the room began to shift uneasily from foot to foot, looking at each other with quiet alarm. Then Yves's mouth opened and shut uselessly again as he faced the choice he had dared himself to make, was too decent a man to make.

"How many survivors?" Jason asked quietly.

Danforth turned to him eagerly. "Almost three hundred," he replied.

Jason winced, totting the body count down from four.

"We had heavy casualties topside and on the upper two levels—radiation sickness, burns, some from flash fires and electric shock. Others are sick and getting worse. Can you transport us?"

That jarred Yves. "Transport? To where?"

"Mars, of course! Where else? We can't stay here, and Lalande doesn't have the facilities. Hell, our survivors outnumber their entire base personnel. You must take us back to Mars!'' Danforth cried, all his usual smooth demeanor gone. "You must!''

This, then, was the hope Danforth had given them—Jason saw it in the faces in the room and the corridor outside. One desperate hope, that a mere cargo-chain freighter could take aboard hundreds of people, get them back home, to safety.

Yves began to shake, his face in turmoil. "I . . .''

Christ, Yves, Jason thought. Damn Central and its protocol! Damn the pointy-heads who sit behind their desks and shuffle lives like playing cards, expecting their captains to tear out their guts to bid the suit. Christ. He looked at the dismay in the faces, at his captain in his agony.

"Can you ride in cargo tins?'' Jason asked, projecting his voice to everyone. As he spoke up, Yves jerked and shot him a look of pure hatred. It gave Jason a sudden chill of foreboding. Yves had called the play, set the match, made the war—and both had lost, Yves in his proud dare to himself, Jason in the only life he had ever wanted. Yves would never forgive him, not this.

Danforth's breath gusted out in a sigh of relief. "I had hoped you'd have a plan. Bless you.''

Yves turned angrily toward Jason. "I haven't authorized that!''

"This is not the time,'' Jason murmured. "Not now, Yves.''

"I am the captain of *Flag*—'' Yves's voice cracked in outrage. Willingly, he turned on Jason for the blame, as he had from the start.

"Yes, you are,'' Jason reassured him, and tried to touch him, to get him to control himself.

Yves shook him off. "I'm not a child! Leave me alone!''

Danforth's eyes flicked between the two men. "What's going on here?'' he asked sharply. "Do you have capacity or not?''

"Ask Jason,'' Yves snapped.

"But you're captain . . .''

"Oh? Am I?''

Danforth lost his patience as he finally caught the gist.

"Good God, man—we have a crisis and you're worried about rank."

"Not rank—mutiny." Yves swung toward Jason, who was suddenly glad he had the jitney sidearm on his belt. He backed away involuntarily at the physical threat in Yves's furious face. Had Jason not obviously had the advantage of weight and strength, Yves might have flung himself on him right there.

"Easy, Yves!" he protested.

Yves actually shook his fist, his face contorted with rage. "You mark my words, Jason Roarke," he shouted. "Your career on cargo-chain is over! I promise you that!" Then he turned on his heel and stamped brusquely out of the room.

Yves's angry footsteps retreated down the hall, then faded into the distance as the colonists looked at each other in silent confusion.

"Where's he going?" Danforth asked.

"Hell if I know." Jason sighed. "You'd better go after him, Danforth, and calm him down. He's not listening to me."

Danforth nodded. "I'll make him listen," he said confidently, then turned to a Latino man nearby. "Rodriguez? You've got the authority on coordinating the evacuation. Get everybody in the dormitories awake, ready to go. Talk to Dr. Renfrew about moving the sick. Summers? Where is he?" He craned his neck and spotted Mack behind Jason. "Oh, there you are. You're in charge of the crews topside on the H-3 tanks. You go with him, Roarke, coordinate things you'll need to get our personnel up to *Flag*. I'll be back in a few hours." Again the competent bureaucrat, well accustomed to maneuvering, Danforth bustled out of the room. Jason decided he liked the other man better, the man he had glimpsed who hoped against hope, but wished both men luck with Yves.

On the far wall, the empty wall screen gave Jason a perfect analogue to his future career. Out of ships, he thought bleakly. How do you survive, Jase? How do you pay all the rest of your life for this one need?

He looked at the people near him, their exhausted and desperate faces lit with hope as they talked excitedly to each other, making the room a babble of noise. Does it really matter that much?

Maybe, in what really mattered, being out of ships was a good price to pay.

Mack Summers unleaned from the wall and crooked a finger at Jason. "Come with me," he announced. "You and I are going places."

"What places?" Jason asked mildly.

"Never mind. Come along." Jason obediently followed Summers up to Level 1, where Summers pulled a vacuum suit from a storage closet. "Put your helmet on, Roarke," he said impatiently, and donned his own suit, then ran a radio check with Jason's helmet frequency. He thumped his finger on Jason's chest. "You and I are going to Tri Ellium. We've got some harvester crews to retrieve."

"What about the H-3 tanks?"

"Hell, they're ready, have been for two days while you took your sweet time getting here. I told you we had made repairs—just hadn't powered up. What kind of topside chief d'you think I am?"

"Okay." Jason had not been aware of Summers's promotion, but a lot always happened in the three-year gap between *Flag*'s visits. It explained the edge to Summers's anger: people responsible for other people often felt it more—except for smug turtles like Danforth. "Isaiah?" he asked, guessing suddenly at a further reason. Summers and Kendall were close friends, longtime cabmates on the harvesters ever since Isaiah had transferred to Wolf II.

"Yeah, he's out there—maybe dead, maybe not." Summers swore angrily. "Danforth sent them out to die, wouldn't authorize cargo-lander repairs to go check it out. So I worked on a jitney in a side bay, nothing big but enough to get out there, anyway. Now that Danforth's not here to say no, you and I will go see." He looked Jason up and down. "Or are you as mealymouthed and yellow as your captain?"

Jason winced.

"We saw that little byplay—all of us did."

"We'll get you back to Mars, friend."

"Oh, sure." Summers jabbed his finger at Jason again.

"First we get Isaiah—then we'll see about the other, *Flag*."

"Lead the way," Jason said.

Mack stared at him for a moment, then snorted and stamped into the emergency elevator.

They rode upward in silence. This was one angry man. Summers had always had a short fuse, but Jason had never seen this depth of rage in him—or in the others here. Bitching, sure, occasional fistfights and pushing, but not this simmering rage that consumed a man. And how would you feel, Jase, he asked himself, if you finally had something to be *really* mad about? Not just poor-me boredom, not just tiffs with Helena to pass the time? Summers's anger made him feel intensely uncomfortable; he didn't like the light it cast on his own anger.

Tough. And you were so proud of all those fights you started, too, you trivial sod.

On topside Summers headed determinedly for a small bay door set into a subsidiary hangar, then signaled Jason to wait. He wrestled with a door lever, then vanished inside. Jason looked around and saw that *Flag*'s own jitney had already left—he caught a wink of metal above the far crater wall, a flash quickly lost in the background stars. Danforth was nowhere to be seen, so he guessed that he had made it aboard. Yves moved fast, but obviously not fast enough. When pushed, Peter Danforth could outmuscle anybody about turf, a necessary survival tactic in the bureaucratic wars. A gift, Jason supposed, though not one he missed in himself that much.

I've got enough trouble already, he thought.

A few minutes later the hangar door receded into its slot, revealing the middle-range surface vehicle kept there. Barely twenty meters long, the ship was not much larger than *Flag*'s jitney and was probably used for the same limited purpose. Summers taxied the ship through the bay door and stopped it with a lurch; Jason hauled himself up the side ladder into the small cabin. Behind the front seats, a small cargo space three meters square took up the rest of the interior. Stored against the back wall were two oxygen canisters and a bulky med-kit.

"I'm an optimist," Summers muttered as he noticed

Jason's look back. ''Belt up. You can read the beacons for me.''

''How far to Tri Ellium?''

''A thousand kilometers. While we go, you can tell me how *Flag* thinks it's going to solve this mess.''

''Sure.''

Mack glanced at him angrily. ''Doesn't anything touch you, Roarke? You're unbelievable.''

''I'm just accommodating an angry man, Mack, somebody who used to be a friend and thought I was a good guy to know—one of Isaiah's other friends, his many friends.'' Jason belted himself into the other seat and stretched his legs. ''Right now, you've got enough anger for both of us—and I think Isaiah is dead, just like you do, like a lot of people will be dead before this is over. Let's say we see more eye to eye than you think.'' He bent forward and powered up the radar scans on his side of the console, then stretched an arm to key the dial on cabin integrity.

''Merceau is afraid,'' he continued quietly, knowing that Summers was listening now, ''so he plays indignant captain. Danforth isn't afraid; he's too busy being director-hero.'' He looked into Mack's resentful eyes and saw the pain, something more than even losing Isaiah. Who had he lost to put that kind of pain in his eyes?

''Pilots and machine drivers,'' Jason said, ''learn to live with fear, my friend, especially out here. We don't need games.''

Mack thought about that as he put the jitney into motion, then shook his head ruefully. He raised his gloved hand, palm out. ''Okay: truce. We're on the same side.''

Jason nodded. ''We always were. Let's get this heap off the ground, machine driver.''

Chapter 8

Isaiah swore and slammed his wrench against the metal shield of the ventilator cabinet. His muscles ached from his cramped position in the cranny access, an ache in symphony with his dizzy head and queasy stomach. High CO_2, radiation sickness, too many hours without sleep as he and Leland struggled to keep damaged equipment alive—what did the body matter now? He drove himself onward, unwilling to accept defeat, knowing that defeat lay only a few hours away. The two survivors aboard Harvester A39469 had finally run out of luck.

He straightened his back with a groan and wiped sweat from his eyes. Already the temperature was rising inside the cab, courtesy of the ventilator's heat exchanger futzing out for the third time. Whatever the vacuum-cold temperatures outside the cab, human bodies and machinery generated heat with nowhere to go unless vented outside. He glared at the ventilator and hit the cabinet again with a thunderous clang.

"Goddammit!" he shouted.

"No go?" Leland asked weakly behind him. Isaiah turned awkwardly in the cramped space. The boy looked even worse than before, well into the nausea and weakness of advanced radiation sickness. He saw Leland copy his gesture of wiping sweat from his face. "Hot in here," Leland said. He took a sip from the water glass in his hand.

"Yeah." Isaiah maneuvered himself backward and

128

stood up, swaying dizzily, then tossed the wrench on the instrument console. "Third time's the charm. It's out for good."

"It was a good try, Isaiah." Leland looked around at the interior of the cab, a metal tomb littered with tools and scrap, a few half-eaten meals, instrument covers wrenched off their tracks and stacked untidily near the bin station. "What a mess—looks like my lab desk."

"How do you feel?" Isaiah asked with concern.

"Weak. To be expected, I suppose. I had accumulated rads from observatory duty, more than I should have. It builds up." He lifted his hand and studied its lean bones and pale skin, then closed his fist over its trembling. "Too many rads."

"We'll get out of here," Isaiah said encouragingly. "Somebody will come."

Leland gave him a crooked grin. "You're a good man, Isaiah. Glad to have you here the last four days. But we both know how it'll end. Truth."

Kendall bent over the tool bin and rummaged for some spare wire. "Ain't truth until it happens, Paul. After all, you gotta believe."

"True." Leland chuckled.

A few seconds later Kendall triumphantly held up a length of wire and stamped back to the console for his wrench.

"When are you going to give up?" Leland asked curiously.

"Won't." Isaiah levered himself back into the cranny and faced the ventilator again. "Father Thomsen says we'll see paradise after this life, but it's not an idea I care to test before I have to." He opened the ventilator side panel and peered into its innards. "I object to dying—never did think it was one of God's better ideas—so He'll have to haul me off kicking. Told Him that years ago, so He can't be particularly surprised."

"You're religious?" Leland asked dubiously.

"Out here, lad, it gets a bit rough if you don't keep at least an open mind. Yeah, I suppose so. You're not?"

Leland did not answer. After a few moments Kendall

turned to look at him. Leland was leaning forward, every muscle taut, as he stared the cab window into the crater.

"Paul?" Isaiah asked, alarmed by the other's strange tension. "What's the matter?"

"I thought I saw a flash over the crater wall," Leland said in a choked voice, then abruptly lunged forward in his seat, craning to see. An instant later he surged to his feet, his glass bounding across the floor beside him, water splashing everywhere. "There it is again! Isaiah, come look! Oh, come look!"

Kendall scrambled out of the ventilator cranny and joined him at the window. He peered outward. "I don't see anything."

"There! Above that crag on the far crater wall." Leland pointed. "See? A few degrees right of Beta Aquarius. Don't you see it?"

Kendall looked obediently, wondering if Leland's illness had turned delusional, then saw the tiny ship shape flicker above the crater wall an instant before it vanished behind the crag. He strained forward, too, watching the far side of the crag until the flicker shape appeared again, larger now, circling wide for a landing on the crater floor. He turned toward Leland.

"Suit up—" Kendall began, but got no further as Leland threw his arms around him and dragged him sideways into an awkward dance around the cab floor, stepping all over Kendall's shoes.

"A ship! A ship!" Leland chanted ecstatically as they danced, then abruptly sagged to a stop, gasping for breath.

"Hey, take it easy. You haven't got the strength," Kendall said, then grinned back at Leland's joyous smile. "Celebrations later, Paul."

"Oh, yes. Celebrations." Leland swayed and caught himself on the console, still breathing heavily. He swallowed uneasily and closed his eyes. "Celebrations forever. Paradise."

"Come, I'll help you," Kendall said, alarmed by Leland's pallor. "We'll make it. I promise."

Several minutes later Kendall cracked open the cab door and jumped out, impelled outward by the gush of

atmosphere escaping with them, and bounced lightly on
the crater dust. Leland jumped down behind him, and
together they bounded onward, moving easily in the low
gravity, waving their arms in abandon at the tiny silver
ship swooping low across the crater floor. As the two
men emerged from the shadow of the cleft and ran into
full sunlight, the ship veered toward them, slowing fast
for landing.

Halfway to the ship Leland stumbled on a rock and
fell, raising a cloud of finely sifted particles that engulfed
him in a swirl of dust. Kendall went back for him and
waved futilely at the cloud as he hunted, then found Leland's leg. He tugged Leland into a shoulder carry and
turned back toward the ship. It taxied toward them, raising twin runnels of dust behind its engines.

Kendall heard his helmet radio click on, then the sound
of Mack Summers's voice over the base frequency. "Isaiah?"

"Mack!" Kendall cried. He bounded toward the ship,
too aware of the ruddy sunlight beating down upon them
and the tiny silver ship, the flickering over their heads as
sheeted curtains danced. Behind them the Wolf star filled
the eastern sky, turbulent and blotched with spreading
starspots. Kendall spared the star one anxious look,
then broke into a staggering run. Just a few minutes, he
thought, an hour to get to base—hold off that long! He
tightened his grip on Leland's legs, feeling the younger
man's helmet bounce loosely against his back. Time
for Paul, Lord, time for me, for all of us. Give us the
time . . .

*Wolf Jitney G39281, control cabin, on ground at Tri Ellium
crater.*

Summers swore vividly as he braked the ship to a full
stop, then turned to Jason. "Get ready to open the outer
door."

Beyond him, through the ship's side window, Jason
saw the other two harvesters a few hundred meters away,
each stopped still at the end of long straight lines scoured

across the crater floor. "What about them?" he asked, gesturing. Summers looked.

"Christ, Roarke, they're in full sunlight." Summers's face twisted a moment behind his suit's faceplate. "But you're right . . . we'll have to check."

"I'll go," Jason said.

Summers shook his head. "My job—I'm harvester crew."

"I'll go," Jason repeated firmly. "You take care of Isaiah and the other man." He unbuckled his shoulder belts and twisted himself around his seat into the cargo space behind.

"Thanks, Jason," Summers said quietly.

"Sure. Opening the door."

Jason thumbed through the open sequence on the door panel, then extruded the ladder downward, though the one-meter drop to the surface and Wolf II's light gravity made jumping as convenient. He grabbed the door frame with both hands and swung himself outward, then let go, landing in a puff of dust by the ship's starboard wheel. Fifty meters away Kendall had slowed to a rough jog, his companion flopping on his shoulder. Jason took several steps toward him, then waited as Kendall crossed the remaining distance.

"Hey, Jason," Kendall panted as he saw Jason's face. "*Flag* is here, huh? Yay." Kendall stopped and leaned on the ship's hull with a gloved hand, his knees visibly sagging. "Get Leland, will you. I don't want to drop him."

Jason grabbed one of Leland's arms, then lifted the man onto his own shoulder. "You okay, Isaiah?" he asked, peering into the other's faceplate.

Kendall laughed. "Okay? Man, oh, man, are you good to see! Yeah, I'm great, boyo. Hey, Mack!" He waved at Summers in the ship's doorway. "Long time, no see, Mack! What took you so damn long, you Limey bastard?" Kendall stamped toward the ship, cursing Mack cheerfully as he stormed up the ladder. Jason followed more sedately, grinning as broadly as Mack, then lifted Leland up to the two men above.

"Save your go-juice, Isaiah," Jason advised. "Somehow I don't think you've got much in reserve to waste."

"Crash your jets, Jase," Isaiah retorted, and disappeared inside the ship.

"Ten minutes, Jason," Summers called down to him.

Jason waved and set off toward the other harvesters. He trudged across the crater dust, raising small puffs with each step, his breathing loud inside his helmet. As he came near the first harvester, his steps slowed, weighed down by his reluctance to witness what Wolf had done to these crews. Despite ten years in space, Jason had rarely seen a corpse, though cargo-chain had its occasional deaths, some from natural causes, some from accident. In each case the dead were quickly whisked away to storage and later burial on Mars. Who would bury these men? Annoyed at his own dread, Jason approached their metal tombs.

He blinked irritably against the salty sting of sweat trickling into his eyes. Hey, hero, he sneered at himself. Can't you take it? *Pilots and machine drivers learn to live with fear, Mack,* he had said. His fatuous words taunted him now. Easy when you don't see it coming; easy when you can't bear backing off in front of your shipmates. But who in the hell wrote the rule that bravery means looking at dead men? He forced his feet to move faster, ashamed of his pounding heartbeat and the sour smell of his fear.

At the base of the first harvester he reached up and pounded on the air-lock door without response, then studied the lock control panel beneath the door. Assuming flux-damaged electronics, he couldn't count on the inner-lock door to cycle properly even if the lock panel still worked; he might open the cab interior to vacuum. He circled the cab, looking for a way up to a window. The harvester had two side windows toward the rear, neither reachable, and the curving band window of its front hull; a flexible robot arm, half-extended, and a cable toggle gave him a first foothold. He grabbed for a cab-light housing, then stretched and caught the other cab light, dangling spread-eagled against the hull. He lifted his feet, scrabbling slightly with his boots until their magnetic

soles caught on the metal hull. He tested their hold on
the hull by cautiously shifting his weight upward, then
straightened his legs to bring his head past window level.

One glance inside answered any question about survivors: four days of decay in atmosphere had made the
bodies a grisly ruin, further blackened by the smoke of
instrument fires set off by the flux. In the driver's chair,
what was left of Willem van Griff stared sightlessly at
Jason, his eyes bulging obscenely from their sockets, his
tunic swollen and split by the internal gases that had ruptured his body. Jason loosed his grip on the cab and fell
two meters to the crater floor, then fought against dry
heaves as his stomach reacted.

He bent forward, clutching at his middle and breathing
heavily, and tasted the sharp bitterness of vomit in his
mouth. Do *not* throw up inside your suit, he told himself.
Not a smart move, Jase. Don't do it, man. Keep it under
control, Jase. Don't, Jason. After a few anguished minutes he managed to straighten up and take a deep breath.
Then he swore with the vilest language he knew at Ceti
Transport, Danforth, and the Wolf star burning malevolently overhead. Nobody deserved to die like that. Nobody.

He stamped toward the other harvester, his fear burned
clear by his anger. He repeated his climb to the front cab
window, said a single biting word, and dropped back to
the ground. He turned toward the jitney and clicked on
his suit radio.

"Mack? They're all dead."

"Couldn't expect otherwise," Summers said dully.
"Move your feet, Jason. I want to get these two men
back to base quick."

"Coming fast, Mack."

Jason bounded around the ship's landing assembly and
pulled himself up the ladder, then shut the door behind
him. Summers was bending over Leland, checking the
monitor dials on his suit. Isaiah waved at Jason, his face
split by a wide smile.

"Yo, Jason," he said jauntily. Jason could see a sheen
of sweat on his face through the faceplate; Isaiah did not

look well. Apparently his companion was worse—but they were alive.

"Bet you never expected to see us, friend," Jason said, smiling back.

"Hell, no—never doubted you. After all, ya gotta believe. How's the colony?"

"Not good—but most are still alive. We're taking everybody back in the cargo tins."

Isaiah stared at him a moment. "The cargo tins? You're crazy, Jason."

"So I've heard lately," Jason answered sourly. Isaiah looked puzzled at his tone, but Jason turned away. Worth it, he thought. He maneuvered himself around Summers and Leland and slipped back into his forward seat, then touched on the radar display. Summers joined him a few seconds later and powered up the controls.

"Let's go," he said brusquely. "Leland needs professional attention, more than I can give."

"I have to get to *Flag*, Mack. Can I borrow your jitney?"

"You might get there a little short of fuel, Jason," Summers warned. "This ship's strictly a planet hopper."

"Nice thing about free-fall; you can always coast."

Summers gave a short bark of laughter. "Okay. Take the ship and start bringing down the cargo tins. From what I've seen, you're the only guy on *Flag* who's got his wits. Down here I'm not even sure about me. And tell Danforth to haul his ass back down here."

"I'll do that."

Wolf Colony Station, Wolf II, Level 3, Temporary Dormitory 2, 35 hours before second dawn.

Magda stirred, then blinked at the face above her bed. Dr. Renfrew smiled, then moved away to the next cot. What? Magda thought blurrily, then sorted together the place and time. She heard voices nearby, stirrings as blankets were thrown off, yawnings and stretchings, a sharp thud of feet on the floor. She closed her eyes and drifted, preferring the darkness, oblivion, the not remembering.

"Get up, Magda," Dr. Renfrew ordered as she breezed past the end of Magda's cot. "Get up now."

Magda opened her eyes unwillingly and looked around, then began to move. Her arms seemed weighted, her body still asleep. With a groan, she swung her legs over the edge of the cot and sat up, then held her head in her hands. What?

She remembered then that Mr. Mack had betrayed her, that she had failed at what she had promised to do. It wrenched at her gut in a sudden pain, then shifted to a quick nausea. She swallowed convulsively and nearly threw up, then opened her eyes to distract her from the malaise that swept upward from her feet up her body, making the room tip alarmingly. Move, she ordered herself. Get up. But her body would not obey her; it felt sluggish and distant. Get up.

She tried, then wisely sank back on the cot, waiting for her body to return to her. What is happening? she thought in confusion, looking around her. Why did they wake everybody up? The question seemed remote and without importance, overwhelmed by the fact of her failure. She let it go, not caring for an answer.

She saw Mr. Mack come through the door; his face lit up as he saw her sitting up, a smile that nudged at her deep inside. She scowled irritably. Summers strode toward her, then suddenly grabbed at the sleeve of a man who hurried past him into the room. "Hey, Jenkins," he said. "What in the hell are you doing here? I told you to take those enviro-units topside."

The ferret-faced man shook him off. "And go out into another flare? No thanks. God, chief, it's almost second dawn."

"It ain't any second dawn yet. You get back to work."

Jenkins edged away, his eyes hollow with fear. Why is he afraid? Magda wondered suddenly, then looked for the fear in the other faces nearby. It still goes on. Why doesn't it *end*? Why isn't it *over*? She clenched her fists in her lap, the hatred rising again like an acid bubbling in her gut. *Why?*

"No way, chief," Jenkins said defiantly. Summers

grabbed him and shoved him against the wall, then shook him hard enough to rattle his teeth.

"I've had enough of your bitching, Jenkins," he growled. "Subchief or not, if you won't earn your air, you can go topside and vent your suit. I don't need any slackers. You got that?"

Will he shake me, too? Magda wondered sadly, then remembered that she no longer cared. Daydreams had died with her mother, ending all things except one last task, one thing left to do.

"But chief . . ." The man's voice jangled in her ears and she bowed forward, hugging herself.

"You got that?" Summers shouted at the man. Voices started murmuring around the room, questioning, comparing opinions, complaining, a babble that rose and fell as each and every person in the room started talking and talking. Always talking; it never stopped. *Stop it,* she wished at them all. Oh, just stop. She heard a scuffle of feet as Mr. Mack jerked the man away from the wall, then sent him staggering a few steps as he let him go. "Get moving."

Jenkins scuttled out of the room. Mr. Mack glared after him a moment, walked over to her cot.

"Hi, sweetie," he said, smiling down at her. "How're you feeling?"

She stared at him, saying nothing.

"Now, Magda, don't be that way," he pleaded. "Don't you feel better now? You had a long sleep—and *Flag* is here. We're all going to be rescued."

"Not Mother," Magda said bitterly.

"That's true," he said slowly. "Her and a lot of other people."

Someone called to Mr. Mack from the doorway.

"Just a minute!" he called back. "I have to go, but we'll settle this later. I don't want you feeling this way, Magda. Listen, when we get back to Mars, I'll see you have the best of everything, I promise that. I'll make it up to you, Magda."

"But it wasn't your fault."

"It wasn't Danforth's, either," he said sternly. The voice at the door called again, more urgently.

"So you say," she told him, unconvinced.

Summers sighed and hit his leg with his fist in frustration. "Save me from stubborn women! You and your mother, what a pair! Get your head on one idea and never let it go, never! Magda, sweetie . . ."

"*Mack!*"

"Oh, hell. Keep your drawers on, Sergei! I'm coming!" He bent to caress Magda's hair, a tentative touch she could barely feel, then awkwardly took back his hand. "We'll work it out, I promise. Now you pack up a few things, get ready for evac. I'll be back later."

Magda watched him walk away from her and waited until he was clearly gone, then eased herself off the cot to her knees and pushed her hand under the mattress. Her fingers touched the cold steel, and she looked around carefully, then slipped it under her tunic. *There,* she told the knife. *You just wait there until you're needed. There.* She smiled to herself, comforted by the flat shape of the knife against her ribs. *There.*

Cargo-chain freighter Ceti Flag, *EuroCom registry, control room, third orbit at Wolf II.*

Danforth glanced at *Flag*'s walls screen as if the planet unrolling below might grant him some help in dealing with the ship's angry captain. For the past hour, during the jitney flight and now on the ship, Merceau had ranted at the absent Jason Roarke, his tirade growing more and more frantic as Danforth tried to reason with him. From his ravings, Danforth had picked up the nasty little surprise about Central's protocol, blast their idiot ledger minds, and had guessed more about the crew crisis that had been brewing aboard *Flag* between Merceau and Roarke. How had it gotten so far? Where had the medico been during it all? Danforth didn't dare leave the ship, not while Merceau still controlled the *Flag*. The captain might do anything, even take *Flag* out of orbit, dooming them all.

The ship's engineer had been worse than useless in helping Danforth calm Merceau down; Danforth looked resentfully at the phlegmatic man as the other sat stolidly in his chair, his eyes moving from Merceau to Danforth and back again. The medico had kept herself in biolab, claiming essential work, refusing to deal with the problem. What was *wrong* with these people? On Wolf II, Danforth could have ordered Merceau off duty for a medical check, even thrown him into confinement if necessary; on *Flag*, he had to sit uselessly without authority, trying to talk sense into a raging man.

A chime on his board diverted Stromstad's attention. "Jitney approaching," he announced quietly. "Must be a Wolf Station ship."

Merceau whirled toward him. "Who's aboard? Jason? Tell him to report to control—*now!*" he shouted.

"Cancel that," Danforth promptly countered. "Not until you calm down, Merceau."

Stromstad looked at Danforth without interest, then turned to his control board to start the hail. Danforth crossed the deck between them in a few strides and caught his arm.

"I said cancel that."

"You have no authority here, sir," Stromstad said, shaking him off.

"I am assuming authority." The engineer hesitated, then looked an appeal at Merceau.

"Carry out my order," Merceau hissed.

"Roarke won't come," Danforth said. "Isn't that the gist of the complaints I've been hearing? He's decided to deal with the crisis—you won't. Apparently you aren't going to, either."

"I'll see that he obeys," Merceau snarled, and whirled toward another control panel.

"What are you going to do?" Danforth asked in alarm.

"You just wait. Axel, give me power to the laser array."

"What?" Stromstad asked in alarm.

"The lasers! Power up the lasers! I'll stop him once and for all."

Danforth slammed his hand on the intercom button on Stromstad's board. "Medico, to the control room. Emergency!" The call stopped Merceau from whatever he planned at that other board.

"Cancel that order!" Merceau shouted at Stromstad, raging at them.

Danforth bent over and thumped a finger hard into Stromstad's chest. "You had better make a choice, right now, engineer. And I'll let you choose only one way, because my colony *will* be rescued. We *will* have this one chance! Do you understand me?"

Stromstad nodded jerkily, overwhelmed by Danforth's rage. Danforth whirled toward Merceau.

"I am relieving you of command, sir. You are on sick call."

Inga Stromstad hurried into the room, nearly breathless with her haste, and halted short as she caught the tableau of the three men.

Danforth pointed to Merceau. "This man is hysterical. I want him confined to quarters and sedated. That's an order."

She looked confusedly at Merceau, then at her husband.

"Isn't it?" Danforth shouted at Stromstad.

"Yes," he muttered.

"Louder!"

"Yes!" Stromstad looked at Merceau, his broad face twisted with anguish. "Can't you see he's right, Yves? Firing the lasers at—You're not yourself, sir."

"You traitor," Merceau said in contempt. "You're finished on cargo-chain, Axel. You and Roarke both." As the medico moved toward him, he darted around the control station and faced her defiantly. "Stay away!"

"We'll do this by force if we have to," Danforth said. "Or you can accept it peaceably. But it *will* be."

"I'm captain of the *Flag*!"

"You *were* captain. Perhaps you might be again, but at this moment you are *not* captain. My people will have their chance!" Danforth glared at Merceau, then signed to the medico to move ahead.

Merceau looked wildly around, then darted around her and rushed for the door. Danforth threw himself after him and caught him in the corridor. They wrestled for several moments, until Merceau's better conditioning gave him the edge to shove Danforth back. Danforth stumbled off balance and fell heavily on the metal floor, then thrust out a leg to trip Merceau and pounced on him as he fell. Merceau squirmed like an eel and struck out, connecting hard with Danforth's chin. Danforth felt the crack of bone breaking, then reeled as the shaft of excruciating pain shot up his face. He tried to retreat, stunned by the agony in his jaw, but Merceau followed him and hit again, his mouth contorted with fury as he smashed his fist squarely into Danforth's face. Then Stromstad was there, lifting Merceau and controlling him easily as the lighter man cursed and threatened.

"Sedate him, Inga," Stromstad ordered calmly, then held Merceau mercilessly to the floor as the medico administered a hypo. Merceau shouted incoherently, his struggles weakening as the drug quickly took effect. Stromstad kept hold of him, watching vigilantly for any return of resistance, until Merceau's head sagged backward into unconsciousness. Then, with a grunt of effort, Stromstad lifted him. "See to Danforth, Inga."

"Put him in Bed Three in sick bay," Inga said. Stromstad nodded acknowledgment and stalked off toward the nearest ladder, Merceau's body flopping loosely in his arms.

Inga knelt by Danforth and gently tipped back his head to examine his jaw. The answering pain made him groan in agony, and he nearly blacked out. As she reached for another hypo, he caught her hand quickly.

"No," he protested. "I have to stay awake. Somebody has to keep it going." Each word made his jaw lance in agony; he wasn't sure if she understood his garbled plea. He strengthened his appeal by crushing her fingers in his. "No."

"Something for pain, then," she said, her beautiful face rigidly calm. He watched her select another hypo and wondered if he could trust her. Easy to put him out, too, then rouse Merceau and give *Flag* back to him, keeping Danforth in unknowing oblivion as Merceau exacted his revenge on Roarke. Danforth had done the same during sleep-down, knowing control of rebellion had been as essential as control of the air supply, an unspoken fact he had not mentioned to the others. A fitting irony, that, and so easy for her.

"Must stay awake," he mumbled in a last plea, and submitted to her hypo. As the blackness moved in moments later, scattering his thoughts, a bitter laughter welled up from deep in his mind, deep down near the few shreds of genuine honesty he still had within him. End of you, Danforth: you get yours at last for killing your people. They've got you now. End of you, you miserable, fatuous bastard.

Cargo-chain freighter Ceti Flag, *EuroCom registry, cargo-tin deck, third orbit at Wolf II.*

Docking the Wolf jitney into *Flag* gave Jason some busy moments; Summers had been right about fuel capacity, and a dead-stick ship was a balky beast. When he managed to match ship with the help of a cable thrown from *Flag*, he jumped across the intervening hundred meters and entered the ship through the crew lock. Helena was waiting on the cargo-tug deck, her eyes apprehensive. Beyond her, *Flag*'s own jitney still sat in the recovery bay, its gull hatch gaping open.

"Danforth's here?" Jason asked.

Helena jerked her head toward the gimbel port. "He and Yves are 'in conference' with Axel."

"About what? Deciding who gets to decide the decor in Tin Twelve?"

"There's been another flare," she said somberly. "Axel called down a while ago to tell me."

"*When?*"

"*Twenty minutes ago. We caught the particle flash off the comsat. Thank God Flag* was in nightside orbit at the time, or it'd be all over right now. If you'd taken a dayside orbit instead of powering straight up to us, you'd have been caught in it, too." Helena stepped closer to him, then turned away abruptly as Jason responded automatically by reaching for her. "They're deciding what to do."

"Do? What's to decide? What about the cargo tins?"

"All ready—but Yves won't give me permission to take them downside. Wants to 'study the problem.' "

"Oh, Christ," Jason said tiredly. They looked at each other in baffled frustration.

"What's wrong with him, Jase?" Helena asked. "We just don't have the time anymore. And it's not just the colonists at risk, either; at the next flare, *Flag* might not be in convenient shadow. We could *all* die, every one of us."

"This is news? He wants to leave orbit, get on with the bypass."

She scowled at him. "I can't believe that, not Yves. He wouldn't do that. You *are* a bastard, Jason Roarke."

"Then why did he storm back up here? Why hasn't he told us to start transport?"

Helena shrugged. "I don't know. I haven't heard a peep from control since Axel's message. The tugs are prepped. Your move, Jason."

Jason took a deep breath. "Okay. Let's start the tins downside. Summers and Rodriguez are in charge; they're expecting us."

"Right." Helena turned on her heel and headed toward her cargo tug. Jason followed, hoping earnestly that *Flag* would still be there when they came back.

Ten minutes later both tugs slid neatly into their launch racks, then drifted into open space.

"I'll take the starboard line," Jason radioed to Helena.

"Roger."

Jason maneuvered his tug down the cargo-tin line to Tin 16 and hovered over the tin. He extended the tug's manipulator arm sockets, waited for the tin's computer to acknowledge the contact, then ordered disconnect from the line. As the line connection blasted free with a small puff of vapor, the slight differential in momentum between the tin and the line caused it to surge upward at several foot-seconds; Jason promptly corrected the drift and backed away from the line, the tin firmly attached to the tug's grapple arms. When he was clear, he rotated the tug neatly ninety degrees, then keyed the prow downward, beginning the long fall to Wolf II.

The two tugs descended in a long spiraling orbit straight down from *Flag* to the base, approaching the colony station from the west. At high altitude, Wolf had already dawned, but the terrain below still lay in nightside. As Jason skimmed over the mountain range west of the base, the ruddy glare of Wolf struck into the cab windows over the wide metal top of the cargo tin, striking flashes from the metal brackets and the chrome rim of the windows. Jason flinched despite himself and ducked quickly down into shadow into a low glide path across the foothills. The tug swept past the small series of craters that stair-stepped to Wolf Station. As he passed over the last scarp, he throttled back speed.

"Helena?"

"Right behind you."

"I'll land and taxi into the primary hangar. It should hold both tugs."

"Tight fit. Why not use two of the secondary hangars?"

"Simpler for loading. Follow me in."

"Right."

Jason activated his landing gear and elevated the cargo tin above the level of the wheels, blocking his view out the forward window, then glanced automatically at his VFR approach controls. "Blast," he muttered as the screen stayed blank. Apparently Summers still hadn't powered up topside, assuming the VFR had even been repaired. He snapped on his side cameras mounted on each engine housing; a pair of small monitor screens lighted overhead, restoring his view of the surface.

"No VFR," Helena warned a minute later.

"Got that. Use your side cameras."

"Okay."

Jason's tug swept still lower, the crater floor a blur of gray and black. As he descended to ten meters, he cut back power still more and touched down smoothly, then braced as the retro-jets cut in to brake the tug's speed. The tug bounced roughly over the crater floor, then slid onto the smoother ground of the base field. As Jason taxied toward the main hangar, two spacesuited figures waved at him, backlit by the illuminated interior of the hangar. At least Summers had rigged some lights. It was a start. One man bounced lightly to the side wall, getting out of the way, while the other guided Jason by hand signals onto the cement apron of the hangar and within. As he rolled past the hangar door, Jason turned the tug to the right and taxied toward the far wall, the cargo tin held high in the tug's arms. As Helena had said, it would be a tight fit.

He maneuvered the tug sideways against the far wall and lowered the tin to the concrete floor, then powered down the tug. Helena rolled in after him a few minutes later. As the hangarmen closed the outer doors and began pressurizing the hangar, Jason ran a swift check of his tug controls, then left the tug. Subchief Jenkins, a whiner on topside crew Jason had never cared for, was standing by the tug's wheel, staring at the cargo tin.

"We're supposed to fly out of here in *that*?" he demanded angrily.

"That's the idea," Summers said as he walked up. "Shut up, Jenkins."

"I got a right to have an opinion, don't I? This is crazy!"

Summers checked the exterior pressure dial on his wrist, then opened his helmet. "So don't come," he said placidly. "Sun will come up in a while, ready for stir-fry on Jenkins cho luk. It'll be a blast for sure." Jenkins threw him an angry glare and stamped off toward the elevator.

"Lot of that down below?" Jason asked as Helena came up to join them.

Summers nodded. "This is one angry colony. Jenkins is the worst, but most folks have it under control now that *Flag*'s here. Jenkins got a lot of attention he didn't deserve while we were waiting, wondering if you guys would show up. How many people can one of those hold?" He pointed at the nearest cargo tin.

"We've rigged acceleration straps for thirty," Helena answered. "It'll be crowded."

Summers grunted. "And you've got how many tins?"

"Eight, not counting the fuel tins, plus Inga has room in sick bay and the corridor nearby for maybe sixty more, assuming *Flag*'s biosystems can handle the extra bodies. We'll have to ask her about that.''

Summers squinted, calculating the numbers in his head. ''Barely enough, considering our casualties. And a lot of the sick may still die—a ghoulish advantage. As claustrophobia gets to the survivors, the dead conveniently make more room for tolerating it.'' He surveyed the two tins, fatigue etched deeply into his face. ''This *is* crazy. Come on.''

Jason and Helena followed Summers to the elevator, then exited with him on Level 2, where Dr. Renfrew was waiting anxiously for them by the elevator door. Apparently the news of their arrival had spread fast.

''The tins are ready?'' she asked the moment Summers appeared. Then she saw *Flag*'s two pilots behind him. ''Good. Everyone's awake now, and we've been preparing the injured for transport. I'll check on the stretcher detail.'' As she turned away, Summers caught her sleeve.

''Doctor . . . wait.'' She looked at him, annoyed by the delay. ''Hospital goes last. We have to save the healthy first.''

Dr. Renfrew hesitated, then nodded. ''Of course. How stupid of me. I've been so wrapped up in caring for the sick, I've actually forgotten the healthy.'' Her lips quirked in self-mockery, oddly bitter. Her face was pale and drawn with strain, marked by too many hours of hospital duty.

''A doctor's preoccupation, Victoria,'' Mack said, smiling at her. ''Understandable, quite right for noble physicians.''

The bitterness faded from her face as she looked up at him, then eased into a genuine smile. ''Thanks, chief.''

''Any time. I need the first sixty told off right away. Please make the announcements.''

''Right away.'' She hurried off.

''She's done a great job,'' Mack said, looking after her.

''You've done well, too, Mack,'' Helena said quietly, ''keeping order here. I wonder how many people could.'' She looked around the half-lit corridor.

Summers flushed, then shook away the compliment with a toss of his head. "As long as it lasts, that is. Listen, what kind of instructions do they need?"

"Not much," Jason said. "Mostly standard survival regs. The tins have acceleration straps, the basics in air, water, power, a chemical toilet, a radio link to the tug. Put a good man or woman in each to keep order; we'll sort out the rest after everybody's at *Flag*."

"Okay. Helena, I'd like you to go back topside, supervise things as the first group comes up. We'll try to get them to you in ten minutes."

"Right." She flicked a glance at Jason, then left for the elevator.

"Come on, Jason."

Summers turned into a nearby stairwell and clattered down the stairs to Level 3, Jason following closely behind.

"What do you want me to do?" Jason asked.

"Tell them what to expect, give them some hope." Summers ran his fingers through his hair in a quick, anxious motion. "God, Jason, what happens to the tins if Wolf flares?"

"The same that happens to *Flag*. Lucky we were in planet shadow for the last one."

Summers stopped short on the stairwell landing and stared at him. "Last one? You mean Wolf flared again?"

"Yeah. Didn't you know?"

"No, I didn't know," Summers said, sounding irritated. "Well, it'll give us a little time before she winds up again—but Wolf-watch said the cycle was getting more active before the flare blasted out their instruments. Let's get the first group up, then take it one step at a time.

The two men stepped into the Level 3 corridor. Jason heard a growing babble down the corridor, punctuated by loud voices as people tried to shout down others.

"Come on," Summers said. "It sounds like people just got the news."

Jason followed Summers toward the open door several meters away, then entered a wide dormitory. As they appeared, the noise hushed as every eye focused on them, some tearful, some afraid, some resentful. Summers raised his arms.

"The first two tins are down. You know Jason Roarke, first pilot of the *Flag*. Jason?"

Jason cleared his throat self-consciously, then looked around at the faces. "The tins are equipped with low-gee straps—it'll be crowded. Bring a minimum of belongings—a change of clothes, a few mementos, your ID. No more."

A thin balding man to his left, dressed in the ubiquitous lab coat of the scientist, immediately objected. "I have equipment I must bring, experiments that are crucial!" He stopped uncertainly as a chorus of scornful catcalls rose up from the people near him.

"Experiments when people are dying!" one woman shrieked in outrage. "What kind of ghoul are you?"

"Why don't you stay planetside with your precious equipment?" a man suggested bitterly. "Let Wolf flare you both into ashes!"

"Quiet!" Jason commanded. "I'm sorry, nothing but the bare minimum. We have lots of people to fit into *Flag* but room for everybody." He swept the room with his glance, trying to show a confidence he didn't feel, but saw a response in several faces. "First sixty to the topside hangar."

A woman bustled into the room and gave Summers a sheaf of computer fan paper. He spent a moment arranging the pages, then lifted his head. "Families first, starting with West Level Five apartment numbers. Francois Aury! Wife Madelon, daughter Lucienne. You're in charge inside the tin, Francois—come see me before you go topside. Marcos Tertak! Wife Sereni, children Aloys, Taran." He looked at a blond girl on a cot nearby. "Magda, you go with the Tertaks. They'll watch over you."

The girl half rose from her seat on a cot, her hand clutching convulsively at her tunic. "I'd rather go later, Mr. Mack," she said in a quavering voice.

"This tin, sweetie," Summers said with a gentleness that caught Jason's attention. He looked at the girl more closely, then revised his first assumption about the new relationship: daughter, not wife, at that age. He had wondered if Mack Summers would ever find someone special—a man got too busy working his trade, too comfortable in all-male company. Matchmatcher uncle, that's me, he told himself, but felt pleased for Mack. A good man.

"But Mr. Mack . . ."

"That's an order," Summers said.

The girl's face spasmed as if in pain, but she nodded. As Summers looked away from her, Jason saw a strange gleam pass through her eyes, an odd expression for a frightened child. Child? That glance did not fit a child. Something there, something more than the grief or anger he had seen in other faces. Did Mack know? He watched the girl pick up a small case of belongings and walk after the Tertaks, head low, her blond hair concealing her face. Jason half turned as she passed him, puzzled. He didn't know the girl; maybe the look was just his imagination.

Summers continued calling out names until the sixty had been called, then began naming the next group. Jason left him to it and followed the tag end of the people moving toward the elevator, then rode up with the last of the group. On topside, Helena was busy shepherding people into the open hatches of the tins. The loading proceeded smoothly, with the people perhaps too numbed to make trouble. Quietly they filed into the tins, climbing upward by the handholds to the next set of acceleration straps, mothers belting in their children and whispering encouragement, their men settling nearby. When everyone was in place, Jason and Helena made one last check of both tins, then toggled home the hatches.

"Here we go," he said.

"It'll be a rough ride inside the tins," she answered dubiously.

"Yeah. Let's go, pilot."

Chapter 9

Wolf II Colony Station, topside main hangar, 34 hours before second dawn.

Magda fingered the long knife under her tunic as she waited in line behind Mrs. Tertak in the topside hangar. She felt a little crazy with her need but refused to give up the one goal that gave everything a meaning, a reason for the emptiness, the end of things. She clutched her knife more tightly. The mist of her induced sleep had finally cleared; she felt strong and alert, ready for her next chance.

Chance? How could she reach Danforth if they put her in that boxy thing? She studied the two huge metal cubes on the floor of the hangar, each grasped in the metal claws of a squat and ugly jitney, then looked at the men scurrying about, at the tall *Flag* pilot who seemed so confident. A blond woman in a spacesuit was there, too, wearing the same shoulder patches as the tall man, trim and efficient despite her suit's bulky folds, instructing the front of the line with quick gestures. Magda wondered at their confidence; they seemed as if they really thought they could save people. Amazing.

In front of Mrs. Tertak, four-year-old Taran clung to her father's belt, rocking back and forth in random motion, her long hair swinging. Her father reached back absently to pat her; Taran dodged, giggling, making a new game. Mrs. Tertak shushed her and turned to smile at Magda, little Aloys tucked in a crook of one sturdy arm. Ahead of them the line started to move as the *Flag* pilots finally motioned people into the tins.

Mrs. Tertak smiled at Magda, a kind smile that wrenched at some part of Magda she no longer wanted to know. She looked away at the small boy in his mother's arms and suddenly hated him because his mother still lived to hold him close.

The line hitched closer to the cargo tin, and then it was Magda's turn to climb through the open door and strap herself into the belts next to Mrs. Tertak. She looked around at the people in the tin, a narrow enclosed space lit by lamps on the ceiling. The light made shadows of the faces, giving them strange expressions that shifted as the heads moved. Magda felt disconnected, not quite tuned to reality. Everything was so different now; strange expressions seemed quite natural. Next the heads would look at her and snarl their insults, then perhaps leap on her, tearing her to shreds. Beside her, Mrs. Tertak began singing to little Aloys in a soft voice, caressing his hair as she sang. Magda ground her teeth.

The blond woman from the *Flag* put her head into the open doorway and took a quick check, then waved and shut the door. The metal squealed as the door shut, sealing them off from the hangar, leaving them alone in the confinement of the tin. A few minutes later Magda felt the tin move slightly and quickly grabbed on to the straps across her chest, swallowing convulsively. The tin swayed more vigorously as they moved definitely backward. She bit her lip hard. She would not be afraid. She would wait. She would be strong.

"Magda, honey," Mrs. Tertak said quietly, "don't be afraid. We'll be all right."

Magda ignored her, ashamed that the older woman had seen her fear. I will be strong. She thought the words as a litany, steeling herself as the tug swung around and the bumping increased to a tooth-jarring rattling. Her body surged forward against her straps as the tug built up speed, pressing her young breasts painfully against the tough webbing. She fought against the acceleration, arching backward toward the steady wall behind her. Aloys whimpered, a sound quickly lost in the growing roar of vibration that shuddered through the walls. How long would it go on, that roaring? she thought, her heart thudding frantically. It sounded like monsters roaring. Monsters, there were monsters outside the tin, she thought, her heart pounding with fear. She listened to the roars of frustration outside the tin walls, felt the monsters shake the tin with their evil talons, demanding flesh to tear and bloody and devour. She closed her eyes, knowing she could not defend against them, not with a single knife. She would use her teeth and fingernails, too, make them pay for killing her.

Her body surged into the straps as the tug leapt into the air, and Magda stifled an involuntary scream. She felt the tug sideslip alarmingly as it left the ground, then surge sharply upward. She dug her fingers into her palms, fighting against a sudden nausea. Aside from a single flight with Mack Summers on a cargo-lander run over the nearby craters, Magda had never left groundside. She imagined the dizzying space beneath the tug, the hurtling upward, as the monsters pulled them upward to their lair deep within the nearby star. There they would apply devices to open the tin, bright orange flames to melt the edges, to crack the seams, eating inward to the soft trembling meat within. She fought down a surge of terror. *I will be strong,* she promised herself desperately as the tug altered vector, rotating as it moved upward. *I will be strong.*

"How long till we get to *Flag*, Francois?" a man nearby asked calmly, as if nothing were happening at all. She looked at him incredulously. Didn't he know about the monsters? Maybe he didn't. She looked around at the other faces. Was she the only one who knew? The thought terrified her.

"Maybe forty, fifty minutes," Mr. Aury answered. "Depends on where they match orbits."

"Fifty minutes? And we're loading only sixty colonists at a time? It'll take hours."

"Not much way around orbit mechanics, Ray. It'll take what it takes. Mrs. Tertak, I suggest you put a flightsick bag on that boy of yours—all of the mothers here. We'll reach free-fall shortly. You others, too—and I mean everybody. We don't need the problems if any of you throws up." Mr. Aury smiled at little Aloys and held up a small polyethylene bag. "And that means me, too, youngster. Won't we all look funny with bags on our nose?" He fitted the sick bag straps around his ears and winked. Aloys stared wide-eyed at the man, then giggled.

Magda found her own sick bag in a bracket by her left strap. It was a small polyethylene bag with straps and some kind of suction valve to draw the vomit into the bag and keep it from floating back into the face and eyes. She turned it over and over in her hand, confused. He knew just what to say, she thought, distracted from her terrors by the insight. Everybody's afraid, including me, but he knew just what to say. How did he know that? She had watched several adults keep order since the flare, each in a different way. Dr. Renfrew acted impatient and matter-of-fact, Mr. Mack talked quietly and gave people things to do, Danforth held endless meetings. It could have been much different, a larger version of the panic in the fifth-level corridor that had killed Josef Marzek. But they had kept order, kept people alive.

After Danforth had killed so many, she reminded herself. Would they forget that when they had their show trials, as they forgot the Serb lieutenants who killed hundreds, not thousands? I should have taken my vengeance, her mother whispered. You must take yours. Magda felt the cold weight of the knife in her side pocket, a long narrow shape pressing alongside her ribs, easing now that the acceleration dropped off. She noticed the change in movement, distracted again, and noticed that her body seemed strangely light, lighter than anything on Wolf II. She raised her hand and let it float in front of her body, fascinated. I'm floating. I could swim through the air, like a fish in water. She had learned about free-fall in school but had not really believed it happened, not really. She waved her fingers, letting each float separately. I am part of the air.

She glanced across the narrow tin at the other faces and saw tension, unhappiness, fatigue, resignation, a lingering terror in a child's eyes, but not delight, not wonder. Nobody cared about floating right then, and Magda felt apart from everyone, connected to no one, an oddity people would stare at when they finally saw her among them. She pushed away the feeling of shame and waved her fingers again, smiling behind the cloth bag covering her face. *I don't care. This is wonderful.*

Her fright ebbed away as she focused on the sensations of no weight. She forgot about monsters and thought instead of angels on wide gossamer wings, lifting the tin in their pearl-white hands, flashing their golden wings as they rose upward to heaven. A brief surge as the tug changed attitude returned a temporary gravity, sending her sideways into her straps, but not painfully, not scarily like before. She sensed vaguely being quite upside down, like the fish in Dr. Sorenson's biolab when they played at swimming, waving their fins at each other as they sported.

I am a space fish. She waggled her finger-fins, imagining long finny draperies of blue and gold trailing behind her, more colorful and graceful than the swaying fins of the starey-eyed fish in biolab, their round mouths gaping as they puffed fishily and watched Magda back. *Oh!* she realized suddenly. *They won't be bringing the fish! Or any of the animals? They'll all die.* Her elation swept away like a cloth over a slate, and she closed her eyes against the hot pricking of tears. *No, I won't cry, not anymore. I've cried all I'm going to cry—until he's been punished. And I will punish him for everyone who has died because of him.* She pressed her arm against the comforting shape of the knife in her pocket, feeling its strength. *I will.*

She watched the faces near her, listening without interest to the quiet conversations. Mrs. Tertak was patting her son, who had thrown up as expected. Magda smelled the sharp odor of vomit and fought an uneasy surge of her own stomach, then heard the sound of other retching. The next several minutes became a private desperate war against her own interior, not helped by another mild surge of the tug, then another. *Why are they moving around so much? Is something wrong?* She grabbed at the distraction to calm her queasy stomach. *Were they at Flag?* She had seen pictures of the cargo-chain ships in school and suddenly wished she could see it with her own eyes. She wanted to see everything for herself, things in the school tapes that had been only pictures, things remotely otherwise, not real, not real the way the colony station was real, her mother was real, Mr. Mack was real.

A crackling of static echoed through the narrow space of the cargo tin, followed by a man's voice through a speaker to Magda's right. She recognized the voice as the *Flag* pilot who had stood beside Mr. Mack in the dormitory. Calmly, as if everything were perfectly normal, he told them what to expect at *Ceti Flag*, how they would be connected to the cargo-chain tether, that they should make themselves comfortable. Someone would visit the tin after transport had been completed. He sounded calm, reassuring, confident. Magda felt another tiny surge of acceleration, then nothing but the floating.

"When we get there," Mr. Aury said, "everybody stay in straps unless you need to use the can. That's that cubicle over there." He pointed. "It's a bit of a puzzle to use if you haven't used a weightless toilet before, but the instructions are on the toilet back. We'll break out some food later; if you're thirsty, we have water packets. Raoul, you're nearest the food containers—why don't you be chef? Madelon, you be water tender." Calmly, without fuss, Mr. Aury organized them.

"How long will we have to be in here?" a woman asked.

"All the way home, I expect."

"In here?" she asked incredulously. "Packed like sardines? That's ridiculous. I thought we were being taken up to the ship."

Fish, Magda thought, and nodded her agreement. No one paid her any attention. She floated her fins, ignoring them back.

"We *will* be at the ship," Rodriguez said patiently. "*Flag* doesn't have the biosystems for three hundred extra people, so most of us are riding home in tins. It won't be easy, people. It'll be cramped and smelly, but we have air, food, water for now, with more available from *Flag*'s stores and the supplies they'll bring up from base. Chief Summers briefed me as tin chief before we left." He smiled at his silly title, inviting answering smiles from everyone. "We'll make it."

"But I don't want to stay in here," the woman said frantically. "I don't like free-fall. What about my child? What if he gets sick? What if Wolf flares again? We don't have any protection. We can't *do* this."

"Quiet!" Aury commanded, his voice ringing. "You'll have to do this. We don't have any choice, so everyone listen up! We have to be smart and under control, all of us. We don't have any latitude for being stupid or scared—not if we want to get home. So shape up!" He glared at the woman, cowering her. "I'm not accepting any nonsense from anybody—and that's a warning. I want to get home. I want my family to survive."

"But we'll be in here for weeks!" the woman argued. Magda looked away, wishing she would shut up.

"And we'll take it one day at a time." Aury shouted her down. "I told you—no nonsense! We will stay in this tin, and we will survive. There aren't any alternatives. None! You understand that?"

The woman muttered and looked away from him. "I don't like it."

"Neither do I," Aury said more gently. "Believe me, madame, Ceti Transport is going to pay through the nose for putting us through this if I have to buttonhole every Mars senator from pole to pole. They'll pay."

An angry murmur of agreement swept around the tin, starting another angry discussion about the flare. Magda tuned it out, tired of hearing the same things she had heard for six days. She knew what she needed to know, knew whom to punish. But Danforth was on *Flag*—if she couldn't get out of the tin, how could she kill him? As the conversation moved around her, she hung loosely in her straps, floating, and cudgeled her brain for ideas.

She had to get to *Flag*—the woman was right about that. But how? She hugged the flat cold shape of her knife to her ribs, trying to think. She would find a way.

Maybe I've gone crazy, she thought suddenly. I want to kill a man, and it seems right to want it; it never was before. She thought about that, trying to think back to when it had begun, when she had heard the men talking. It still felt right: it *was* right. Danforth had to be punished. Maybe I'm crazy, and that's why Mr. Mack has been so patient and quiet with me. He knows I'm crazy. Crazy people aren't responsible. Will they lock me up for being crazy? She looked around the small tin and decided they already had. Maybe everybody else here is crazy, too. How do I get out of here?

She lifted her hands and floated her fins for a while, imagining herself a fish. Crazy, crazy, everybody's crazy. Somehow it didn't seem very important. I am a fish, she told herself proudly. Out of the corner of her eye she saw Mrs. Tertak look at her strangely, but that didn't matter, either. Fish, fish, fish.

Magda smiled broadly as she watched her bobbing hands.

Cargo-chain freighter Ceti Flag, *EuroCom registry, crew module, sick bay, sixth orbit at Wolf II.*

Danforth awoke in sick bay. He came back to consciousness slowly, aware first of the crisp coolness of the bed linen, the sigh of air on his bare skin, then the dull aching pain that stretched from his chin to his ear. His face felt frozen, a mask without expression. He raised his hand and weakly fingered his jaw, then opened his eyes and squinted against the bright ceiling light. He tried to remember where he was, who he was. What was this place? He heard soft footsteps approach his bed, then blinked as the medico's face suddenly appeared above him.

"How do you feel, Director?" she asked soothingly.

"Waa happ'd?" he mumbled, and winced as the jaw movement sent a lancing pain up his face.

"You passed out from pain and shock. I've wired your jaw and numbed it—it was a clean break through the mandible. Your nose is broken, too; you'll need surgery later, after the swelling has subsided." She smiled faintly. "Your eyes are purpling nicely."

"Merceau?" he asked urgently.

"Sedated, as you ordered. He's over there in Bed Three." She nodded toward the left and behind him. A thin line of distress appeared between her brows. "It's not a decision we like, as you can understand. You haven't any authority over *Flag*, not to do what you've done, but Axel decided to keep the status quo until you woke up.'' She settled one hip on the side of his mattress and looked pensive, an expression Danforth promptly suspected as an act. He didn't know Inga Stromstad well—she and her husband had usually stayed on ship during *Flag*'s previous visits—but he sensed the opening gambit. He eyed her warily.

''Where is this going to go, Director?'' she asked calmly. ''You'll have to answer for what you've done today.''

He considered his options, then countered with a resigned sigh, smoking her out. ''Nothing else to do,'' he said, making his voice dull.

''We need to discuss your decision, Director, consider its implications.'' She smiled at him gently, the sympathetic medico accepting of the weaknesses of others. Danforth wondered briefly if Stromstad had put her up to this or if she was acting on her own. He wished he knew her better, enough to sort the playacting. What did she want?

''What do you think I should do?'' he asked weakly, squinting at her.

''Yves is the rightful captain of *Flag*, Director,'' she said earnestly. ''We need a single authority, not this division where everyone does as they please. This won't work.''

Ah.

''Have to,'' he said, shaking his head. Inga frowned and opened her mouth to say something else. He forestalled her, abruptly tired of the games. ''No other choice. Where's Axel?'' The attempt to speak had made the pain settle in his jaw, a shooting pain along the injured nerve that burned like a current of fire. He tried to move his jaw to a more comfortable position; the pain moved with it.

''In the control room, monitoring the tin delivery.''

''How's that going?''

''They've left surface with the first two. Director . . .'' She leaned forward.

"No other way," he said firmly, ending the game. "Want up."

She hesitated and glanced behind him at Merceau's bed. He determinedly pushed aside the bedcovers and rolled away from her, getting his feet tangled in the sheet. Inga obligingly pulled the sheet free and walked around the bed to steady him as he stood up. Danforth awkwardly rebuttoned his tunic, then pushed past her.

"Be with Axel," he muttered, and walked unsteadily toward the door.

As he reached the doorway, he turned and looked back at her for a moment. Merceau's sheeted body lay on another of the beds, slack and quiet in the grip of the sedative. Would she wake him? Would anything else he might say give an extra margin against it? He tried to consider, distracted by the throbbing in his jaw. Danforth could not risk Merceau loose on the ship, not now, not until his people were safely in orbit with *Flag*. And perhaps not even then. Did she understand at all? Inga looked back calmly, saying nothing, her hands folded together in front of her. Danforth left her to it and wobbled into the corridor.

He walked the empty corridor of *Flag*'s upper level, his footsteps echoing hollowly in a silence broken only by the faint sibilance of the ventilators and the distant click of machinery. Over his head the twin rows of fluorescent light panels paced him with their soft light, flickering slowly like a highway median line; he could hear their low hum wax and wane as he passed beneath them. He looked around almost nervously, unaccustomed to such silence—and emptiness. Wolf Station had enough excavated space to house its population with reasonable comfort, but one never escaped the incessant murmur of people nearby, perhaps not in view but a background noise that comforted and consoled. Danforth had not sought out solitude for years and had finally lost the need of it. It made the silences of *Flag* seem unnatural.

What is it like, he wondered, to live most of your life with only four other people in all this space? He had never thought of that before, had never wondered about

the cargo-chain and its crews. He had merely accepted
their service, expected it as part of the colony plan he
administered, as he accepted the service of other neces-
sities. How did a man cope with such silence? He walked
on, circling the upper level, then slowed as he neared the
crew quarters.

In this part of the ship someone had painted murals on
the walls, wonderful pictures of Mars and Tau Ceti. He
stopped in front of the mural of Olympus Mons, the massive volcano near Mars's equator, impressed by the ar-
tist's skill. Beyond the Mars panoply the artwork gave
way to brilliant flashes of color over Tau Ceti's single
marginal world, then an abstract painting of golds and
blues against the whorl of the Milky Way, with other
murals beyond. How many hours had the man—
woman?—labored with his sketches and paints? Days,
perhaps months. The colors filled the enclosed space,
simulating windows upon realities elsewhere, denying the
sameness of metal walls, of humanity's limited environ-
ments, of the tedious hours on cargo-chain.

He stood transfixed for several minutes. All my life I
never saw what was out here, he thought in wonder, then
turned in a half circle to take them in all at once. I just
never bothered to look, too obsessed with details. He
stepped closer and touched the mural of Tau Ceti, caressing the uneven grooves of the paint that curved and
whorled in incandescent curtains above a dark cratered
plain. Does it really look like that? he marveled. He felt
a sudden desire to see those places himself, to watch
transfixed as the curtains of light danced in a blue-black
sky, to fly the Great Rift below Olympus Mons at break-
neck speed, daring the canyon walls, to fling himself between the never-ending streams of stars, to look and look
and never tire of the looking. Is this what the silence is
for, to see this chance for all of us?

He drew back his hand and closed it into a fist. Perhaps if I had seen, I would have done better. He remembered his bitter thought as Inga had sedated him, plunging
him into the unforgiving darkness, when he had, for once,
admitted his own fault, free of the self-satisfied excuses
and the fatuous pride in his manipulations. Because of

him, a hundred people had died; because of him, more might die. He trembled at the abyss beneath his feet, if he failed again.

I promise, he thought, not knowing to whom he promised—perhaps the dead, perhaps the living—I promise to be different. I promise to remember this, to give up the games, to find another way. He lingered beside the murals for several more minutes, drinking in the beauty of the otherwhere places, then turned away reluctantly. He hurried toward the downlevel ladder, hastening to preserve what he could, while there was still time.

He burst into the control room, startling Axel Stromstad badly. Slightly embarrassed, Danforth stooped to pick up the clipboard the other man had dropped in his startlement and handed it to him. Stromstad peered around him curiously, obviously looking for the cause of Danforth's abrupt arrival. Danforth shrugged and lowered himself into the nearby chair.

"Merceau's under sedation," he said challengingly.

"I know. You have a point?"

When Danforth did not reply, Stromstad turned back to his control panel and made a notation on his clipboard, then touched up another display on the screen without hurry, moving sedately through his routine, whatever it was. Danforth looked at the curving lines on the screen, recognizing only a few scattered symbols. A younger Danforth had once thought of switching fields to ship design and had even been offered an entry position in Luna's New London shipyards. He tried to remember that younger man, seeking in the memory a way to connect with Stromstad, to keep his loyalty, to make him *see*.

"Axel . . ."

The engineer looked at him calmly, his face devoid of expression. "Yes?"

Danforth winced and touched his jaw deliberately, reminding the other man of his injury. A shadow of concern touched Stromstad's face—reluctantly, but enough to show Danforth he could be reached . . . and controlled.

"You are hurt," Stromstad rumbled, stating the obvious. Stromstad was an obvious man. Ah.

"What has happened here?" Danforth asked, trying to articulate clearly around the lancing pain in his face. "Why does Captain Merceau hate Jason Roarke?"

"Yves doesn't hate him," Stromstad demurred. "He just objects to Jason's insubordination. Jason never has bothered to fit himself in." He waved his clipboard at the screen. "Now he's out there being a hero, saving the colony."

"Somebody had to," Danforth muttered despite himself.

Stromstad shrugged. "There are other ways."

"What ways?"

"Ways. Director, this is ship's business; it's not your affair." Stromstad deliberately turned his shoulder to Danforth as he looked at another screen. "I've consented temporarily to your demand for authority, at least until we've moved farther into the colonist transfer, but I am still considering my options. This isn't your ship—nor is it Jason Roarke's." He ground his stylus into the paper on the clipboard, writing vigorously.

Leaning back and studying him, Danforth decided he understood a little more about Roarke, too. On Mars, Danforth had fought his wars with the lower-echelon cabals, had seen this blind devotion to authority and the rightness of the regs. At Wolf, he had exploited it in his own underlings—but at Wolf, regs meant survival. At Wolf, men did not have the freedom to deny a crisis, did not have a ship to carry them away to safety. For a moment he felt a flash of hot rage at Stromstad for that safety but shoved it away. Not now.

He looked past the other man at the main wall screen, watching the scarps and craters of Wolf II move slowly underneath the ship. Stromstad continued writing, resistance written in every stiff line of his chunky body, his jaw unconsciously slung forward. Danforth ignored him, letting the silence build, and watched the Wolf star light the horizon curving around the upper edge of the screen, bringing *Flag* again into dayside and its peril. An obvious man believed what he heard, he thought, if it fit his assumptions—perhaps he could pretend disapproval while keeping Roarke firmly in control of the evacuation. Or he could champion Roarke, beating down on Stromstad to face facts and so threaten the engineer's loyalty to Merceau—and maybe force him into the counteraction of releasing the captain from his drugged sleep. Too risky—he wasn't sure he could win an open confrontation. Or . . . what else? Perhaps a side step between the horns, something ambiguous to trouble an obvious man. He weighed his options, not sure what to do, and so committed to nothing.

He saw a moving speck against the dim whiteness of the planet, then saw the other tug below it as both flashed redly into direct sunlight. The tugs rose gracefully in shallow arcs toward the ship, falling upward to link two more tins to *Flag*'s cargo-tin line. He made his choice and leaned forward suddenly to tap on Stromstad's shoulder. He would go with ambiguity, keep Stromstad off balance, cautious of matters as they were.

"I want to talk to Roarke."

"Why?"

"Just do it, Stromstad," Danforth said impatiently, irritated at the difficulty of clear speech with a wired jaw. His slurring made him sound drunk, not an idea he wanted to give Roarke, not without some private explanations first. "How do we make radio contact?"

"With the radio, of course. The control panel's over there." Stromstad turned back to the display screens, dismissing him.

Danforth thought of forcing him to help, then decided to check the panel controls himself; perhaps he could still run a radio—after all, he had been an engineer himself once. He walked over to the communications panel and studied the display windows and lever bars, then pushed the power bar. A crackle of static promptly rewarded him for the effort. He leaned toward the small microphone disk and moved his jaw experimentally. The pain shot through his face, making him dizzy for a moment. He paused a moment, then forced it to work. "*Flag* to cargo tugs. This is Danforth."

"Roarke here."

"Roarke, can you bring up some of my Wolf-watch team and deliver them to *Flag*'s crew module? I want their experience in watching for flares."

"How will a Wolf-watch help?" Roarke asked sarcastically. "Orbit is orbit, Director, whatever Wolf flares. Look at the dayside on your screen."

"It might time your tin deliveries a little smarter."

"Well, true. Who do you want?"

"Sanchez, Van Leeuk, and Leland. Uh, cancel that last," he added hastily, remembering belatedly that he had sent Leland out with the harvesters. It wasn't a reminder he wanted.

"Leland's in the hospital, but I'll check on him."

"Say that again?"

"I said Leland's in the hospital—he and Kendall got some radiation exposure, Leland the worst, but the doctor is working on them. Summers and I went out and got them, Danforth. When the cat's away, the mice do what they want." Roarke sounded quiet unrepentant, even jaunty. Danforth stifled his surge of irritation, then wondered what else Roarke and Summers were doing against orders.

"Uh, good," he said to Roarke. "Bring Leland if he's able. How're things at the base?"

"In good order," Roarke said briskly. "We're bringing up the first and second tins now; Summers and Rodriguez are organizing the rest of the base personnel. We can make three more trips before we have to refuel the tugs, enough to bring up almost everyone, so I'd rather not waste time coming inship twice."

"I'd like to see you as soon as possible," Danforth insisted.

"Two trips after next *is* soon as possible," Roarke said stubbornly. "Take it easy, Director. I'll have Isaiah bring your Wolf-watch over to you in spacesuits next trip. How're things on *Flag*? Where's the captain?" Danforth heard Roarke's unspoken question about his own delay aboard *Flag*. Roarke had good antennae—or shared the same worries. He glanced uneasily at Stromstad. The engineer pretended to ignore their conversation, feigning disinterest. Danforth couldn't leave, not while matters aboard *Flag* were still in flux. He tapped his fingers irritably on his thigh, knowing that Stromstad would mistake his irritation for anger at Roarke.

"Uh, the captain's sleeping. Things are moving along," he added vaguely. "You'll come aboard on two trips after next, then?"

"Yeah." Roarke paused, alerted by Danforth's tone. "I'll meet you on cargo deck in six hours."

"Roger."

Danforth clicked off and watched the tugs grow larger in the wall screen. He laid his palm along his puffy jaw, pressing at the pain that jumped and flashed along the injured nerve, willing it away. Not now, not when he needed to think clearly, to plan. He could see the shadowed outline of the tins held firmly in each tug's robot arms, boxy shapes that held people, his people. The two cargo tugs moved slowly across the screen and drifted out of sight as they rounded the ship, curving neatly around the fragile web of the ramscoop dimly visible against the white plains of Wolf II. Danforth looked around at the ship's control panels, wishing he knew how to operate the screens to watch the tugs further, and thought of asking Stromstad. Then, accepting that idea as useless, he sat back to wait, wishing briefly that he dared leave to go look at the murals again. Maybe later, he promised himself, and looked around again at the flickering panels, the neat array of counters and screens, and the window onto space that filled one wall, listening to the silence of *Ceti Flag*, a waiting silence.

Everything hold together, he commanded all sternly, determined that it would. He would see to that.

He hesitated, remembering his promise by the murals to become a more honest man. He scowled and put the thought away. Later, when he had more control of the crisis, he could try a better honesty. Maybe. Anyway, later. He crossed his arms and settled down to wait for Roarke, his mind ticking smoothly as he weighed his strategies.

Chapter 10

Cargo Tug 1, descending into Home Crater, 21 hours to second dawn.

As Jason and Helena descended to Wolf Station for the fifth time, the Wolf star had already spread a dim reddish glow across the eastern horizon, the harbinger of second dawn only twenty-one hours away. Jason watched the approaching dawn uneasily, half his attention on his tug, half on the implications of a base fully exposed again to dayside. They needed the H-3 and supplies still at Wolf Station, needed the topside power systems to take them upship. In the best of better situations, Jason would have delayed transporting some of the colonists to bring up *Flag*'s fuel and other supplies—at least the fuel—but air was air, after all, especially when it was running out. At *Flag*, the colonists again had a working environment inside the tins, limited in space, true, but no longer with bad deadlines on breathing.

Should we have taken up the fuel first? he worried, shifting uneasily in his flight seat. I'm not qualified to make these choices, don't have the training; good as they are, neither do Rodriguez and Summers, as hard as they're trying. Danforth and his other admin chair-weights do. This isn't a job for machine drivers only.

Why was Danforth still aboard *Flag*? Every time Jason talked to Danforth by radio, the director played word games, hinting at trouble, raising subtle alarms with his voice tone and silences, then giving blithe assurances that everything was fine. What game was the man playing? Danforth should be planetside organizing the evaculation—it was his *job*, after all—but instead he had stayed on *Flag*, asking for status reports, reporting on the tin line, as if *he* had the authority, *he* had the worry over *Flag*. Where the hell was Yves? Jason hadn't heard a peep out of him ever since he had stormed upship from Wolf Station.

God, maybe Yves was drunk, he thought. That would be just lovely.

What if we make a wrong judgment? he fretted. What if we kill everybody with a wrong choice? Rodriguez was good at handling people; he was keeping down the panic and had already started a systematic survey of the station's salvageable supplies. No complaints there. Summers was just as good in finally rigging the rest of the power to the hangars topside; Roarke could see the array of lights far ahead across the crater. Now Summers was up at *Flag* supervising his spacesuited crew in the final rigging of the last two tins and setting some intraship radio links. Good people—one never really knew how good until they came through like this. Everything seemed to be moving along well, yet Jason felt deeply uneasy, as if they had missed something or should know something they didn't. But what?

Maybe, he thought, Yves was flat on his back, snoring away like a Gallic teakettle while Inga's biosystems worked overtime getting rid of his personal cloud of alcohol fumes. Or maybe Yves had piled into the jitney and taken off for parts unknown, denying *everything* as he waved his cultured fingers to his tapes of Debussy and Ravel, chortling happily that he, Yves Merceau, was French, too, just like them.

Crap, he thought disgustedly. How's a man to know? And I thought I knew everything important already. He snorted at his own pretensions.

On this next trip the tugs would finally bring up Dr. Renfrew's hospital, the last sixty or so colonists who needed special handling in the transport. Except for Rodriguez and his skeleton crew of thirty men, *Flag*'s tugs had successfully evacuated the entire base personnel to *Flag*. Every dayside orbit, of course, they risked another flare—but everybody had air to breathe. What a trade, he thought, but vacuum made some things more imperative, even over the risk of getting crisped. And, as *Flag* moved out-system, accelerating slowly toward Shaukolen's Limit, Wolf could throw anything she wanted at their retreating backside. Something there, niggling at his mind, something he should think about. But what?

Maybe we should have tried something else, he worried again, looking at the safety of the shadows along the cliffside. Maybe moved the base far into nightside—though dayside would have come everywhere to Wolf II again before *Flag* could bring help back from Mars. Maybe we could have held out until the next cargo-chain ship arrived in three months. Maybe. But how could a flare-wrecked station and a single freighter transport enough air, enough food, enough power to an unprepared cliffside? For three hundred people? Make that three hundred and five. *He* wouldn't have stayed in orbit for three months, thumbing his nose at Wolf every time *Flag* whirled into dayside. It's never a smart move to walk under a flyswatter when you're a fly.

"Helena?"

"Yes, Jason?"

"Why do you think Danforth's still on *Flag*?"

"Is that important?" Helena sounded puzzled by his question. "Maybe he thinks he can coordinate better from there with Yves."

"What Yves? And without radio contact with the base? Come on."

"Danforth does what he wants, Jase." She sounded tired, her voice edged. "It's part of being a big shot."

"You're a big help, Sheila."

"What?"

He snapped off radio contact, feeling the fatigue in his own muscles, the tightness in his neck. Five trips—they had been piloting continuously for nearly thirteen hours. Jason calculated the trips left—the hospital, then the four H-3 tins, then tins of extra supplies—and wondered how he would manage to stay awake long enough to keep from crashing himself into permanent oblivion.

So get some more pilots, he told himself. You think you're so special because you can fly a cargo tug? But he shuddered at the idea of an inexperienced pilot coming too close to *Flag* and her cargo-tin lines. Any good pilot could land a tug and take her back up again to *Flag*—handling the tin line was something else. He tried to make his tired mind think better. Ideas, Roarke, get some ideas.

He lifted the tug's nose slightly and swooped over the last mountain peaks, then descended swiftly into the base crater, skimming across the white-dusted crater floor toward Wolf Station. Summers had managed to activate most of the field lights, too, but the open bay of the main hangar was an adequate beacon for the two tugs. He felt the slight shock of his wheels touching down, then gritted his teeth as the tug bumped roughly over the ground. Five minutes later both tugs were again inside the hangar, ready to load the last group of evacuees.

Dr. Renfrew awaited them by the elevators, still helmeted after the hangar had been fully pressurized. As Jason reached her, the telltales above the elevator winked green and Rodriguez stepped out. He nodded, a look of exhaustion around the eyes, a slowness to his muscles. Rodriguez was tired, too—they were all tired. Dr. Renfrew struggled with her helmet a moment, then pulled it off. "The hospital is ready," she said.

"We have to unload the cargo in these tins first, then rig some air and the straps," Jason told her. She frowned, displeased. "It'll be an extra hour or so, Doctor," he said. "Sorry. Danforth says Inga has sick bay all ready to receive them. We'll have to stack them in the corridors until your assistants can empty a storeroom, but you'll have a good place for them."

"You talked to Danforth again?" Rodriguez asked. "Why the hell isn't he back here?"

"I don't know, José. I figure he has a reason." Jason decided to give the director the benefit of the doubt. Why, he didn't know, but his mind was too wasted to play detective. "He didn't say. I wish I knew what's going on up there."

"*Madre de Dios.*" Rodriguez blew out a breath and scowled, then looked around the hangar at the busy activity as his crew began unloading the new tins. "It's not moving fast enough, Jason; at this rate we'll still be load-ing base supplies at second dawn.''

"We're going as fast as we can.''

"Yeah, I suppose so. Sorry. God, I wish we had more ships down here, anything to carry up cargo, but Mack scavenged everything usable for that jitney you took to Tri Ellium. Everything else topside is so much scrap.''

"Jitneys can't carry much, not to be worthwhile.''

"Yeah,'' Rodriguez said again. His crew already had one of the cargo tins open. A man rode a powered forklift menacingly toward the tin, engine whining, mechanical arms at point. Helena jumped hastily out of the way and threw the driver a rude gesture as the forklift whizzed by. The driver returned the compliment over his shoulder and looked back to grin, which only made her stomp around harder. Jason chuckled.

"Watch it!'' she bellowed at the forklift. Helena had a good set of lungs, he noted.

"What's in the tins?'' Rodriguez asked curiously.

"Computer equipment for Ross, some new technology their director just has to have. Some other stuff for chem lab, catalysts and acids, some plutonium. I'd advise your crew not to drop anything this time.''

Rodriguez snorted. "Broken labware doesn't bother me, Jason, but I see your point. I'll let them know. When do you want to load H-3? That'll release half of my top-side detail.''

"Next trip, okay?''

"We'll be ready.''

Jason descended to Level 2 with Dr. Renfrew. He tugged at her elbow, pulling her out of the way as a stretcher team stamped toward them. Dr. Renfrew stopped them and sent them back down the hall.

"Danforth asked again for Sanchez,'' Jason said.

"He died an hour ago,'' she said, sounding tired and defeated. "All the Wolf-watch team except Leland are dead. Accumulated rads, you see, even for those below Level Two.'' She shook her head. "So many dead.''

"And so many alive, because of you, Doctor.''

She smiled tiredly. "And others. Will we make it home?''

"Maybe. No promises."

"I appreciate the honesty. Will you help me with something while we're waiting? I need some medical supplies taken up with us, and I'm not sure how to package them for the tins."

"Sure." She smiled at him again, a tired woman with tired eyes, the age lines around her mouth and eyes deepened with strain. Beautiful eyes, ones that accepted far more of life than Jason ever had. He touched his helmet in a sketched salute.

"*Salut*, Victoria," he said, giving her the respect.

Her smile turned bitter. "Yes, *salut* to all of us. *Salut* for maybe surviving our own stupidity, for thinking we can live in such places safely, for killing our children by bringing them to such bitter hells as this . . ." Her mouth twisted, and she turned away, hiding her face from him. "If we get home, Jason, it's the end for me. I don't want this heartbreak again, never again, don't want to see people killed by vacuum, by starlight, by the wrong gravity, the wrong pressure, by the lightless places. We don't belong out here. It's not right for us."

"You're just tired, Doctor." He realized that it sounded condescending the moment he said it.

She glanced at him, irritated. "No. Just wiser." She walked away, her stride long and quick, as if she had rejected what he symbolized, pilot of the *Flag*, the creature of the agency that had killed her people. Jason felt her condemnation and resented it, then sighed. Maybe she's right, after all, he thought, about me and everything. I don't know anymore. I just don't know. He looked down at his feet and studied the padded boots of his spacesuit.

And if I've made a mistake, overlooked something, made a wrong choice, I'll kill more of them. God. How will we live with that, me and Mack and Rodriguez and everyone with the choices? How do you live, Jase, if you get back and so many others don't?

Hero. Forget the hero bit. It's not a burden I want—not that I have any choice about it now, of course. Maybe all the heroes just get caught up in it before they know it, before they can stop it. You're pickled now, Jase old boy, so pick up your feet and get on with it. He picked up his feet and followed Dr. Renfrew past the lighted rooms of the hospital, nearly the last to go now.

Cargo-chain freighter Ceti Flag, *EuroCom registry, cargo-tin deck, nineteenth orbit at Wolf II.*

Two hours later Jason maneuvered his cargo tug carrying nearly the last of Wolf's personnel into the wide ship lock of *Flag*. He helped Helena open the tins and then directed the orderlies toward the gimbel port, giving them directions to Inga's sick bay. A moment later Inga herself appeared on cargo deck and went into immediate consultation with Dr. Renfrew. Then Mack Summers and four of his outside crew came in *Flag*'s crew port, maneuvering effortlessly in free-fall like seals. *Flag* was getting crowded; on cargo deck the fishbowl description was not that far off. Jason ducked as one of Summers's crewmen dived at him, skimming inches over his head.

"Cute, Philippe," he growled. Philippe called out something in French as he floated away, probably something disgustingly rude, knowing Philippe, then sported onward. Jason waved Summers over, then bent again to attach the chemical-fuel line to the tug's fuel assembly.

"Yo, Jason," Mack said as he floated up.

"How's it going?"

"All hooked. Not everybody's happy, of course—Tin Six thinks Tin Seventeen has a better radio than they do, and Mrs. Gilinsky is aflutter about her boy's fainting spells. Todd's been fainting for attention for years, so that's nothing alarming. It looks like everybody that's going to get sick has—no new cases of radiation sickness, at least not bad ones."

"That's good news."

"I was wondering when it was going to stop. You look tired, man. Want a breather?"

Jason straightened and studied him a moment. "Think you could pilot a tug? Not at the tin line, maybe, but enough to get down to the base and back again?"

Summers looked up appraisingly at the tug. "Sure."

Jason nodded. "I'm getting too groggy, could use some

sleep. We could keep the delivery going if you could spell me or Helena each trip.''

''That's a deal, Jason. Let me go check on a few things with my crew and I'll be right back.''

Jason saw Danforth emerge from the gimbel port and head toward him. As the director came closer, Jason straightened and stared at him. ''What happened to you?'' he asked incredulously. Danforth's face was a livid bruise, one eye nearly swollen shut and painful-looking stitches along the jaw.

Danforth shrugged and looked around the cargo deck. ''Where's Sanchez?''

''He died,'' Jason said curtly. ''All you've got is Leland. Sorry.''

''Oh.'' Danforth focused on him blearily. Jason could guess at the awkward meeting when Leland had come aboard, especially with Isaiah to push it all over the deck—as Isaiah would. Jason had heard all about the argument about Tri Ellium on the trip back to base, and he thought Summers just might have found the time to chip in his four cents, too. Danforth's demand for Sanchez had come shortly afterward. Suits you, he thought, and bent again to the fuel toggles. Everyone's working their tails off at Wolf Station, and you just sit up here, acting important, like you really care. His dislike for the man settled into a hard certainty. Danforth meant well, probably, but he could never be trusted. At least Helena kept her games out in the open, sort of.

''What happened to your face?'' he repeated, wondering if Isaiah had gone *that* far and what had happened to him when he had. He knew his usually peaceable friend was mad enough to get extreme, like lots of people right now.

Helena strolled up and stopped a few steps away to inspect Danforth herself. ''Run into a door, Director?'' she asked.

Danforth didn't spare her a glance, and Helena started to boil. Ain't we got fun? Jason thought. For a supposedly smart man, Danforth sure didn't understand women, especially women pilots. Women pilots actually thought they were *better* than men—and sometimes they were right. Given much more, Helena might just flay him alive.

"How long until you can bring up the H-3?" Danforth asked.

Jason straightened and looked at him, irritated by his tone. He decided he did *not* like Danforth's take-charge mode. "Next trip. Your face?" he asked pointedly.

"I had a dispute with Captain Merceau," Danforth said. "He's under sedation in sick bay. I've assumed command of *Flag*," he added casually.

The first and second pilots of *Ceti Flag* stared at him in amazement. Helena woke up first.

"You've *what*?" she blurted. "Who do you think you are?"

"Calm down, van Duyn," Danforth said. "He's all right. He's under sedation in sick bay, like I said. He got hysterical, lost it. That's what I wanted to talk to you about, Roarke. Stromstad isn't reliable to keep the status quo; I'd like you to keep yourself available to take over if necessary."

"Take over what?"

"Command of the *Flag*, of course." Danforth looked irritated at Jason's denseness. "You're the only officer on *Flag* who has his wits together."

"Thank you very much, Director," Helena said angrily. "Was Yves hurt?"

Danforth ignored her again. "If this rescue is to continue," he said in his snotty voice, still smiling suavely, "I need someone reliable in command. And if we get back to Mars, I'll see that you have *Flag* permanently." He gestured modestly and bent his puffed lips into a smile. "I have some influence with the board, and you'll be able to write your ticket after this, believe me."

"No, thanks," Jason replied coldly.

"I should say not," Helena said. "Who *do* you think you are, Danforth? You don't have any authority over *Flag*!"

Danforth looked at her, unimpressed. "Necessity gives me the authority. Captain Merceau is not dealing with the crisis. Roarke is. And you're out of line, pilot."

"You, you—"

"Helena," Jason said, stopping a further outburst. To his disgust, he saw the satisfied look in Danforth's eyes as Helena immediately shut up. Let him think what he likes, he thought. He might just end up surprised. "Helena, why don't you go upship to sick bay and check on Yves? You say he's all right, Danforth? Does he have visible damage like you?"

"He'd better not!" Helena glared at Danforth and headed toward the port.

Danforth waited until she had moved out of earshot. "Good, Roarke," he said approvingly. "Nicely handled. We'll work together and get through this crisis with—"

"Save me the pep talk, you bastard." Jason thumped a finger on Danforth's chest. "You may think you know me and can push my buttons at will, but you've made a big mistake. I don't want command of the *Flag*; that's not why I went around Yves. So stop insulting me with your little payoff promises."

Danforth smiled suavely. "Well, of course you have to say that. I understand."

"You want me to close your other eye?"

Danforth looked at him warily. "Well, perhaps I was a little crude, Roarke; perhaps I am mistaken. But surely you agree that Merceau can't be allowed to prevent the evacuation."

"Does he want to?"

"I don't know. He won't do anything; all he does is rant about you. Listen, I've got my people to get up here and away from Wolf before everybody loses, including *Flag*. If Merceau's in the way, he has to be pushed aside."

"A successful rescue would salvage your own career, too. I wouldn't think much of your board connections when Mars hears that Wolf Station got crisped."

"Is that what you're worrying about? Be at ease, Roarke. I—" He broke off as Jason stepped toward him, his fists clenched. Danforth hurriedly backed off. "Calm down, Jason."

"It's Roarke to you, Danforth." Jason took a deep breath. "We've got the hospital aboard now—that's everybody except Rodriguez's crew. The next trip I'm bringing up half our H-3; there'll be two, maybe three trips after that to transfer the rest of our fuel and the salvaged supplies. Okay? *Then* we'll talk about who is captain of the *Flag*, and it ain't going to be the answer you think, Danforth, you got that?''

"I got it."

But Jason doubted he did. "So get upship and ask Helena to come back soon. I need her to back the tin assembly out of the line for Mack—he'll relieve her this trip. And one little point, Danforth: If you get smug at Helena and offer more little bribes to her, she'll probably take your arm off and shove it down your throat. She and Yves are close."

"Ah." Danforth nodded, understanding now. "I was wondering why she overreacted."

"Overreacted?" Jason stared at him. The man was incredible.

Danforth smiled and touched his hand to his temple in a smart salute. "Good luck downside!" he said jauntily. He floated off.

Later, Jason decided, after he and Helena got Yves back in command, he would let Helena decide what *Flag* would do to Danforth for this. Like maybe flaying him with a dull knife borrowed from Inga. Or maybe they could put Danforth in a spacesuit between the aft core and the engines and dust him to death. Helena had an ingenious mind, with a reason to get especially fiendish. She would know what to do.

Thirty minutes later Helena and Jason nosed their tugs back out into open space and detached the H-3 tin assemblies from the front of the cargo-tin lines. Constructed as a unit, each specially adapted tin assembly of fuel tin and feeder lines could be separated easily with the proper computer commands, but Jason watched the engine-line separations with special care. He didn't want any damage to the connections, not now. Careless was for other times. He waited as Helena traded places with Mack in the other tug, then watched her float gracefully back to the crew port. One more trip yourself, Jase, and you can get some sleep, too. Sleep beckoned with sexy fingers, a willowy siren of the blank spaces and the ease of a soft mattress. One more trip, guy. Don't crash it.

As his tug fell away from *Flag*, Jason ran a quick radar scan of the ramscoop fields ahead of the ship, checking for smooth field integrity. Although the fusion engines could maintain blast with ramscoop damage, the system was designed with both the H-3 and dust fuel components in mind, crucial for Jump. The scoop seemed all right despite the prolonged stay in the dust-heavy vicinity around Wolf II, but Axel's more sophisticated checks with the onboard computers would say for sure. Stop worrying about *his* job, pilot, he told himself. Just do yours.

"Jason?" Helena radioed on his tug's private frequency.

"Yeah. Where are you?"

"Cargo deck. What's the penalty for justifiable homicide? I'm thinking about wasting Danforth."

"Already ahead of you, love. Death is too good for him; torture is better. I'll handle the rack; you use the tongs."

"I wondered that you weren't tempted by his offer."

Jason flushed, surprised by his flash of hurt at her remark. "Give me a break, Sheila. I'm not you." He heard her gasp and promptly wished he hadn't said it. It was his day for idiot comments. "I'm sorry, Helena; that wasn't called for," he said hastily, but she had clicked off. He keyed his radio to open the channel again.

"Yes?" she said coldly.

"I'm sorry. I shouldn't have said that. How was Yves?"

"Why should you care?"

"All right already! I said I was sorry."

"Sorry doesn't cut it, friend." She clicked off again.

Yeah, Helena, he thought angrily, and where's your apology for calling *me* names? Didn't she understand? Did she really think he had gone against orders to undermine Yves? What was *wrong* with everybody? He checked alignment with Mack on their course downward, then set the tug on automatic flight. The computer smoothly took control of the screens, and he settled back for the ride.

Maybe she did think that, he thought gloomily. Danforth certainly did. Maybe everybody did. And Ceti Central would shrug and shake his hand in congratulation, giving him *Flag* if he wanted, talking up necessity with a casual wink and nod, then put Yves in permanent limbo behind some desk on Mars. He felt his neck going cold, knowing how it could go, how opportunity could make a man betray his captain.

Would you want it that way? he asked himself. Would you take a ship by any way it came? With a wash of shame, he realized that he honestly didn't know. God, command of a ship. He had never even thought of it, not with his discipline record on cargo-chain. But they just might offer him a ship if he pulled this off, or—his breath caught in his throat—maybe even third captain on a starliner, the elite of the elite, contract-guaranteed to have his own command in time, his own starliner. The starliners were the cream of interstellar transport, their captains toadied to by stockholder and board alike. A starliner captain had first-line responsibilities, access to corporate shares that guaranteed eventual wealth, a place in the forefront of the Centauri colonies, distinction . . .

He pressed his hands together in a sudden yearning for something he had not even known he wanted—had not even seen in himself.

Would he take it? Who wouldn't?

That was the rub. He knew the Central bureaucrats too well—none of the fat cats who sat in their Mars offices, scheming and wanting and *needing* their ambitions, would ever pass up such a plum as this, would wonder why he even hesitated. If he said no, they would wonder other things about him—and they would never give him another chance. The strange could not be trusted, not with Central's precious starliners, the lifeblood of Ceti Transport's richer colonies.

He looked out the side window at the black nothingness dusted with stars and remembered that only a few days before he had felt bored beyond belief, racheting around his cabin, thinking himself an old bear inside a cage. Boredom had a certain charm now. Christ.

"Helena?"

His hail was answered only by the sharp click as she broke contact again. Women, he thought disgustedly.

A starliner captain had his choice of women, he reminded himself. Like bees to honey, he had heard, though probably more like wolves to a feast, swarming in a pack whenever the new Captain Wonderful appeared, their ample bustlines panting with desire. Probably fought each other like panthers for any snippet of him, a flash of those perfect white teeth, a quirk of that manly eyebrow, a lazy smile of come-hither. Ah, the come-hither. Welcome, ladies all.

Too bad there was only one of wonderful himself, as he felt sure those bosomy ladies would agree.

Starliner pilots had posting authority, too, he remembered. None of this second-guessing that Yves had to endure on cargo-chain, that had put Jason on *Flag* no matter what Yves wanted. As a starliner captain, he could pick and choose. When he had his starliner, he would post Helena to last-ranked pilot and let her watch the other women swarm over him.

Yes, indeedy. He just might.

Would he? he wondered. That was the rub. What was the penalty for grabbing the golden ring?

Cargo-chain freighter Ceti Flag, *EuroCom registry, port tin line, twenty-third orbit at Wolf II.*

As Mack drifted Helena's tug above the tin lines, Jason snuggled his own tug close to the starboard line to attach the H-3 assembly, then ran a quick computer check of the fuel lines snaking along the frame to the fusion engines. They now had enough fuel to get out of orbit, a relief to his tired mind. One more trip and *Flag* could get out-system, too. One more trip. He swiveled his tug neatly in the space above the engines to inspect the tin lines streaming behind *Flag*. Of the eighteen tins following the fuel tanks, eight were full with Wolf's colonists, waiting anxiously, subjected to fate and whatever amend-

ments the *Flag* crew would arrange. As *Flag* swept back
into nightside, the red light of Wolf 359 glinted off the
tins—as it would glint throughout their departure out-
system. The worry that had troubled him earlier suddenly
crystallized, the something he had missed. The ramscoop
was on the wrong end of the ship.

Throughout their trajectory outward, the tins—and
Flag's crew module, for that matter—would be exposed
to Wolf's flares, *behind* the ramscoop and its protective
net, not in front of it. Oh, dandy, he thought. This is just
great. On the *Libertad*, Leland had told him on the way
up to *Flag*, two crewmen had fused to their control boards
when their ship had lost her race with UV Ceti, both
tossed across the panels by the flare impact and melted
into it, flesh to metal. The evac team had given up trying
to pry them off and had buried them with their control
boards. God.

One step at a time is great, he told himself sourly, but
you can still walk into potholes.

He let the tug drift idly as he studied the configuration,
absently noting that Helena was maneuvering the other
tin assembly into place on portside. Could they turn *Flag*
around and back out? The ship's fusion engines had some
reverse capability, but it was very limited, intended only
for maneuvering and then at a slip angle. Besides, even
if they could remount the engines, direct reverse would
put a few too many neutrons into the crew module, not
a healthy move. Use the ramscoop as a light sail? A light
sail was an interesting idea, well exploited by the rich
Earth yachtsman who had all year to get somewhere,
borne along by the gentle pressure of Sol's solar wind,
cocktail-partying all the way. But for three million kilometers? They didn't have the time for party speeds.

He needed Yves's knowledge of the *Flag*—what was
possible, what would work within the ship's design limits. And he needed Axel.

"Helena, start the next trip down," he radioed.
"Coming over, Mack?"

"On my way."

Jason floated down the tin line and detached another

cargo tin, then backed off the line and waited for Summers to swarm aboard.

"Get some rest, friend," Mack told him as he took the tug controls.

"I will. See you soon."

Back inside *Flag*, Jason hurried uplevel to sick bay. As Dr. Renfrew's crew cleared out a storeroom, several dozen temporary beds lined the corridor walls, each occupied with someone sick. Two looked dead. Jason set his jaw and strode through the door into sick bay. As he entered the room, Inga looked up from her desk, surprised, then scowled. H'lo to you, too, Inga. Jason spotted Yves's unconscious body among the other sheeted forms on the four sick-bay beds and marched over to his bedside. Inga got up and hurried over to them, thinking God knew what.

"Wake him up, Inga," Jason said.

"What?" Inga looked surprised again, and he wondered what else Danforth had been hinting around the ship, pressuring Jason by boxing him in.

He gestured at her impatiently and looked down at Yves. He slept peacefully, all strain eased from his face, his cheek nestled into the pillow. Sorry, Yves, he thought. Sorry to wake you up to a problem you don't want, one you can't win in all the ways. "Wake him up."

"But Danforth said . . ." She glanced over at Dr. Renfrew bending over another bedside and lowered her voice. Several people bustled in and out of the room, carrying linen and medical supplies, conferring briefly as they passed, still involved in organizing the makeshift hospital aboard *Flag*. "Danforth said—"

"Danforth runs—used to run—Wolf Station; he doesn't run *Flag*. I don't know what led to this—though I saw one result on Danforth—but Yves is captain and Yves will stay captain, even if it puts us all down the toilet. Wake him up."

Inga let out a deep breath, then smiled at him with the first genuine approval he had ever seen on her cold face. She bustled over to the cabinets and prepared a hypodermic, then injected Yves's arm. They watched Yves together, not speaking further until the captain began to stir. Yves threw his arm back across his face and shifted his legs, then yawned abruptly.

"Where's Danforth?" Jason asked Inga as they waited.

"In the control room with Axel. Leland and Kendall are monitoring the Wolf-watch; Danforth is supervising them, or so he says. Axel didn't like this." She gestured at Yves.

"I don't blame him."

Yves yawned again and opened his eyes, then blinked groggily at them. Jason hooked his thumbs in his belt and looked back at him, waiting for Yves's confusion to clear. When Yves looked more alert—enough for the anger to reignite in his eyes—Jason quirked him a rueful smile. "Welcome back, Captain."

Yves stared back at him, saying nothing. Shut-out time, even now.

"Well, I guess we need an interpreter," Jason said. "Inga, tell him that I told you to wake him up. Tell him, too, that Danforth tried to bribe me with *Flag* if I agreed to *not* wake him up. Then tell him that I will keep him woken up, period. It may kill us all, but that's the deal." He looked across the bed at Inga expectantly.

"Very funny," Yves growled, and tried to sit up. His eyes went vacant a moment as he tried to track on an obviously spinning room. He looked around at the bustle, the extra people. "What is going on here?" he demanded indignantly.

"Take it easy, Captain," Inga warned. "Everything's all right."

Yves sank back on the pillow with a groan. Jason waited until Yves's eyes cleared again.

"What's 'funny,' Yves? The interpreter bit or the message?"

"Your nobility is funny. Give me back the *Flag*—how polite of you, how magnanimous."

"I didn't take *Flag*," Jason said, trying to control his irritation. If he needed his wits once in his life, this was it. No fights, he warned himself. Do not fight. "Danforth took it. But you are captain of the *Flag*; you are needed, Yves."

"Why? You can't do everything yourself? I'm stunned."

"I *don't* want your ship!" Jason shouted, forgetting all his good intentions. Heads turned all over the room, but he no longer cared who heard. "What's wrong with you, Yves? What do you want of me? Do you want an apology for sleeping with Helena? I gave you that. Do you want me to step aside so you can run the show? I offered—and you did nothing. You just stormed out of Wolf Station and ran back to *Flag*, where you ranted and raved and started a fistfight with Danforth. You've done nothing but bitch and whine ever since I proved we had a problem."

Yves turned his face away, his jaw working.

"And you're still running away," Jason added flatly. "What do you want? What's the price of your cooperation? Tell me."

"My price? I want you off *Flag*." Yves elbowed himself up and glared at him. "I want you out of Ceti Transport. I don't want you anywhere near my life. But it's not going to be that way, not now. Because you're the hero, not me; they'll give you *Flag* if you want it. You think Helena will follow me to some desk job on Mars? So you'll have Helena, too. Everything that I have—" His voice broke, and he fell back on the pillow, his fists clenched. "I wanted to study the problem, make the prudent choice—be cautious, be prudent, that's what makes a good captain on the cargo-chain, Jason. But I couldn't enforce the protocol. I admit it—there! I couldn't do it—and then I lost it in front of Danforth. Danforth will tell Central—oh, I can just imagine that snide turn of phrase, the smug superiority . . . I'm wrong once, just once, lose control just once, and it's all gone, everything, because of you."

"I didn't create the flare, Yves."

Yves turned his face away and studied the wall.

"We need your help," Jason said, insistently. "We have to turn *Flag* to protect the tins. I need your expertise."

"Ask Axel."

"Axel knows power systems—you're the expert on ship

design. And I can just guess how much help I'll get from Axel without you. You know what *Flag* can take and what she can't. I know the tin line; Helena's the specialist on ship maintenance. It's called division of labor, why *Flag* has a multiple crew. We need you.''

"No."

Jason looked an appeal at Inga. "Tell him, Inga."

Inga shook her head. "If I do that, I support you against him," she said quietly. "It'll only make things worse. There's a divided authority on this ship, Jason. You didn't create all of it, but Danforth finished it." She crossed her arms. "It's probably the stupid choice, but I've shared ship with Yves for eight years. I stand with him."

"To do nothing?"

"Loyalty isn't meant to be logical—or even wise. It just is. You've fought all of us ever since you came on board. You never really wanted to fit in. I know you've wondered why the crew always splits three to two—or four to one when Helena chooses the other side. You just don't give the loyalty. You've been on too many ships, Jason, to even know what it is." She flushed slightly and looked down at her clasped hands. "By the way, if you tell me to sedate him again, I won't." She looked up again, her eyes defiant.

"Why would I ask that?"

"I don't know. I don't know why you came up here. What was your plan, Jason? I'm sure we'd both like to know."

"I wanted to ask Yves how to turn the ship. Nothing more."

Inga smiled skeptically.

Jason looked at the two resistant faces, one stubborn, the other flushed with satisfaction. It went down his throat badly, but probably Inga had a point. You're so proud of your fights, he reminded himself. One mistake, Yves said, and everything's gone—like your mistake, maybe, just maybe, all these years. Here's the reward, Roarke. And it's not just you that pays for it. He took a deep breath.

"I'll make you a deal, Yves."

"No deals." Yves studied the opposite wall again, shutting him out.

"Wait until you hear the bargain," Jason said bitterly. "You'll like it. You help me turn the ship, help me—us—get the colonists back to Mars, and I'll resign my commission." He saw Yves's body tense. Inga looked at Jason incredulously. He shrugged back, though it took an effort against the anguish welling inside him. Had he lost his mind? "I'll quit Ceti Transport, like you want. Hell, if you want, I'll go back to Earth and push a button until retirement. How's that for a deal?"

"You'd do that?" Yves asked slowly.

"If Inga can doom us all for loyalty's sake, I can doom me, too. Let's just say I'm packing it all in one offer—a trade, Yves. You save everybody else, and I'll let you destroy me."

Yves's head turned slowly on the pillow, and he examined Jason with his dark eyes for several moments. "You won't be destroyed. You can't be."

"The important part will. We're more alike than you'll ever admit. And the fighting wasn't all one way, Inga—you never let me in, none of you. When Helena joined the ship, you welcomed her—but never me. I'll get off cargo-chain, but I'm not taking all the disloyalty crap with me. Loyalty cuts both ways." He stared down at Yves. "Do we have a deal?"

Yves tightened his mouth. "Am I supposed to feel guilty, poor outcast Jason, and let you off the hook? Is that the game?"

"No games. Just the deal. If you want, cancel the refusal on all the blame. You're right all the way. You can have it all." He turned away.

"If I agree, I *will* take it all."

"Fine."

"D'accord." Yves sat up, then shook his head dizzily. "Can you give me a stimulant, Inga? Help me shake off the rest of this."

"It'll wear off in another twenty minutes."

"I need those twenty minutes," he said briskly. "How many tins left to transport, Jason?" He looked around curiously at the bodies in the nearby beds and watched the renewed bustle of the hospital personnel. "Do we have everyone up to the ship?"

"Almost," Jason said. "Rodriguez kept a crew of thirty planetside. Another trip for H-3 and then the base supplies—say another six hours."

"You look exhausted. After you bring up the rest of the H-3, get some sleep, both you and Helena. That's an order. Axel and I will need time to study and program the maneuver, anyway, once we've decided how to do it. Turn the ship?"

"Yes, sir."

Yves's eyes got distracted for a moment as he calculated. Like a spaniel shedding water, he seemed now to shake off his fear, his sense of authority returning to the positioning of his body, the tilt of his head. He seemed to mutate before Jason's eyes, becoming the man he should have been all along, the captain he had been before the war, before he saw his ship slipping away in his loss of the authority he felt he *had* to have. But I never intended any of that, Jason thought. I just wanted some relief from the sameness of cargo-chain, some sparks to liven up things. I didn't want to put him in a box. Did I diminish him that much?

What's the penalty for that kind of blindness? Somehow, Jason knew that he had probably arranged a suitable punishment. He pushed the thought away, not wanting to think yet of losing cargo-chain, of the nothingness without cargo-chain.

He watched as Yves pushed off the sheet and swung his feet over the edge of the bed. Yves waited as Inga returned with another hypo, then winced as she injected it into his arm. But he flexed his arm briskly, then stretched for his cap on a nearby chair. "Come on, Jason. Let's go evict Danforth out of my control room."

"He'll be along in a minute," Inga said, forestalling them. "I'd like to talk to Jason privately."

Yves looked at her, his suspicions returning for an instant—then he relaxed, confident in her. He nodded. "I'll wait outside."

After Yves left, Inga stared at Jason. "Why are you doing this?" she demanded.

"Is that all you want? Going to write an article for the *Ceti Shrink Review*?"

Inga flushed angrily. "I don't appreciate your sarcasm, Jason. I never have."

"I don't like you, either, my dear. That's a starting point. You're a cold fish, Inga—you're the psychological officer, but you've never lifted a finger to stop the conflict between me and Yves. You just let it go on and on."

"I thought you were giving it all up," she commented icily.

"To Yves. Not to you."

"Thank you for making that clear."

"Any time, Doctor. Any time at all." He pushed past her and stalked out of sick bay. As Jason entered the corridor, Yves turned to look at him, his expression unreadable, then headed off. Jason followed him past the sickbeds, noting the briskness in Yves's step and the drag in his own. The king is dead, long live the king, Jason thought ruefully. He thought about Helena, now falling smoothly down to Wolf Station, and knew how she would choose when she found out. Helena always did have her priorities firmly straight.

But she might have picked you, Yves, without any of this, he thought. And now you'll never know for sure. It's how we arrange our little disasters, how we all do.

Worth it, he told himself as he followed Yves down-level, but the thought was an ache that struck deep and did not convince him, not anymore.

Chapter 11

Cargo-chain freighter Ceti Flag, *EuroCom registry, crew module, control room, twenty-fourth orbit at Wolf II.*

Danforth sat at Captain Merceau's console, watching the control room activity with a careful eye. Leland sat absorbed at the Wolf-watch panel, with Kendall lounging nearby, his face carefully noncommittal. When Danforth happened to look at him, Kendall stared back impudently, daring Danforth to say something, anything at all. Danforth punted each time, though he still was fuming about Kendall's insolence: Kendall had made sure Stromstad was there as a witness, not caring what he ruined by smarting off. A director had to make the unpleasant decisions—didn't Kendall know that? Who did he think he was? Danforth tightened his fingers on the chair arms, trying to ignore the throbbing pain in his jaw. Hard to think with a jackhammer in your jawbone. Kendall would get his—Danforth promised himself that—when *Flag* got back to Mars.

Across the room, Axel Stromstad sat at the power-system screens, his broad back turned fully to the others, resistance in the stiff set of his shoulders. Danforth could tell the man was weakening, could hear it in the lengthening silences, the curtness of any reply, those lengthening seconds between Danforth's next question and Stromstad's decision to answer. Thank God Roarke would be upship soon. Roarke apparently had enough authority to help, judging from van Duyn's jump-to-it when he nixed her mouth on cargo deck. Hell, Danforth would let Roarke take titular control of *Flag* if necessary, with himself giving the real orders, of course. Anything to hold it together.

Roarke would come around. Danforth would see to that.

He heard the scrape of a boot heel on the metal door-sill and turned idly toward the noise. Yves Merceau stood in the doorway, his thumbs hooked in his belt, staring at him. Roarke stepped into view behind him, his face impassive. With that sight, all Danforth's careful plans came unhinged; he gawked at Roarke, amazed at the treachery.

"What's the meaning of this?" he demanded angrily. To his left, Stromstad turned and lit up at the sight of Merceau, then glanced in smug satisfaction at Danforth.

"Roarke?" Danforth asked angrily.

"There's the man to ask," Roarke said, nodding at Yves. "I told you you'd be surprised."

Yves moved smoothly into the control room and walked to Danforth, then waited for him to vacate his chair. Danforth looked up at him stubbornly, not moving.

"Axel?" Yves said. "Your assistance, please." As Stromstad stood up, Danforth yielded the chair with poor grace. Yves sat down and crossed a leg over his knee, smiling slightly.

"You've killed us all," Danforth snapped at Roarke.

"Can it, Director." Roarke passed behind him to the cargo-tin chair, then twirled the seat around to face Danforth.

"This man is not in control of himself," Danforth complained. "I gave an order, and I want it obeyed."

Roarke raised an eyebrow, then looked pointedly to Merceau.

"What's the status on Wolf-watch?" Merceau asked.

Leland looked uncertainly at Danforth, then caught Kendall's nod. They were in it together, Danforth fumed. Him and Roarke. He just knew it.

"Well," Leland said, "we're still looking for an over-all pattern. As long as Wolf continues this pattern of frequent small flares, I think we're okay. The problem is any gap in the flares: it just means the blow-off is that much bigger when it blows. As we found—Wolf didn't flare for nearly three weeks prior to the big one."

"So it'll take three weeks to put us in a similar danger?" Merceau sounded eager for that, still refusing to face facts.

"Not necessarily," Leland said. "Wolf is cycling upward, something different than we've seen before. Its flare intensity and heavy particles simply don't match anymore." He waved toward the analysis screens. "If I can read your instrumentation right, Wolf is now mutating toward a UV Ceti pattern—and that is not good news. It could blow another big one anytime."

"I see. Thank you. Jason, I want the entire tin line reassembled in six hours."

"Yes, sir." The respect was not lost on Danforth. He gave Roarke a disgusted look. Roarke smiled as he headed toward the door.

"And Jason," Merceau called after him, "ask Helena to come upship for a few minutes when she gets back on this trip. I'll need to coordinate with her on turning the ship." Danforth saw Roarke jerk and look back. Then Merceau smiled at Roarke, not a nice smile at all. Roarke hesitated, obviously dismayed by something, then nodded.

Danforth relaxed abruptly and lounged by the console, for once content with the battered face that could hide his expressions. A chink, Merceau, letting me see that: you're an infant in this. He let Roarke walk out of the control room and studied Merceau as the man asked more questions of Stromstad, pretending he had control, ignoring Danforth like furniture. You think so? Danforth thought. You really think it's this easy?

At last Merceau turned to him. "That face looks bad, Director. Why don't you let Inga look at it again? Maybe some sedatives to help you sleep." The captain smiled snottily, reeking with his little triumph.

"That's a good idea," Danforth agreed. "Nice to see you in control of yourself, Captain." He strolled past Merceau's chair, catching the captain's suspicious look as he passed, then ambled out of the room. Once he was out of sight, his footsteps quickened as he set out to look for Roarke.

Merceau just might be surprised yet, yes, indeed.

Jason had just drifted into sleep when his door chime pinged insistently. The sound worked itself into a weird dream about a rude button in a sterile box of a factory, then woke him up. "Whazzaaa . . ." he said eloquently. The door hissed open, and Danforth barged in.

"I thought we had a deal."

"Go to hell, Director." Jason turned on his side to face the wall.

"That man will kill us all!"

Jason heard the genuine fear in Danforth's voice; for once the man seemed not to be pretending. Hell, who could tell? He sighed and turned over again onto his back. "Director," he said patiently, "quite aside from the right of it—you were way out of line in disranking Yves—we need him. I don't have the expertise to create new ship maneuvers that'll work; I just balance the tin line and drive a tug. We need Axel, and you wouldn't have had Axel much longer. The Stromstads have shared ship with him since *Flag* was launched; they put him first, always first, even in a crisis like this. You get me?"

"That's ridiculous!"

"No, it's not," Jason said. He looked at Danforth shrewdly. "You'd expect the same of your own admin staff, wouldn't you? Absolute bedrock loyalty, though you'll never get it, not in the bureaucratic wars. It's different on cargo-chain. To their thinking, captain's authority holds the ship together as much as her hull fittings—and losing it risks everything, literally everything. People die when the captain's not in charge. You can't argue with it, you can't trick them out of it, you can't manipulate them into not believing it. It just is, especially on *Flag*."

"So you won't do anything?" Danforth stared at him, incredulous. "I don't believe it!" His tone sounded false to Jason; Danforth was back to manipulating again, faking outrage, pulling at his strings. Jason elbowed himself up and glared at him.

"Christ, Director, I've been *doing* ever since we failed radio hookup with Wolf II. I got your people up to *Flag*; we'll get the H-3 and supplies up, too. And I got Yves to cooperate again; I won't tell you how—it's *Flag*'s business, not yours. So back off, just once. Let Yves do it. He can—and now he will."

Danforth seemed to waver. "Well, all right," he said reluctantly, and Jason didn't believe a word of it. "We'll see." He turned and barged out again, Dauntless Danforth to the rescue. Dusting was too good for him.

God save me from bureaucrats, Jason thought wearily, and pulled his pillow over his face. God save us all.

Cargo-chain freighter Ceti Flag, *EuroCom registry, twenty-fifth orbit at Wolf II.*

"Come on, Paul," Kendall said. "You need some food. Maybe you'll keep it down better this time."

Leland looked up at him blearily, not tracking on Kendall's voice, then dazedly looked back at his screens. Kendall lifted him by an elbow and marched him out of the control room. The pursuit of science was one thing, Leland's health another. The Wolf-watch would keep for twenty minutes.

They walked down the corridor past the navigation room to the crew's dining room, where some of Dr. Renfrew's helpers had started a kitchen with extra tables and chairs. Kendall guided Leland to an end table, then went off to the processor to get some soup and coffee. He snagged some packaged crackers off a tray walking by and set up the meal on their small table, spreading it ceremoniously before his friend.

"You don't have to do this, you know," Leland said wryly. "I'm not that bad off. I can get my own food."

"Sez you. Dr. Renfrew says you belong in bed."

Leland bent over his soup and took a spoonful. "Bed sounds good, but not the way Wolf is behaving right now. You know, I probably survived because I was out with you in the harvester. Everyone else on the Wolf-watch team is dead, too many hours on Wolf-watch and too busy in Level One labs when Wolf flared. My white cell count is way down, but I'm still alive.''

"Yeah." Kendall smiled at him and got a ghost of a smile back. "You think this backing-out idea will work?" He blew on his own soup to cool it.

Leland shrugged. "It's a reasonable precaution. Of course, we can't Jump until we get some room to accelerate back over Wolf; that's why Merceau's trajectory plot is backing us up and outward rather than straight out.''

"Why can't we Jump? I thought that's why we were leaving orbit.''

Leland looked at him quizzically, as if he were perplexed that Kendall had even asked the question. For the first time in Leland's company, Kendall felt reminded of his comparative ignorance, of Leland as the big brain and himself only a machine driver. He flushed with embarrassment and looked down at his soup, then made an elaborate chore of crumbling crackers into his bowl.

Leland chuckled softly. "Stop that, Isaiah. Did I blush and squirm when you had to point out which dial meant what on the harvester? Be reasonable. Why can't we Jump? Basically, the ramscoop collects charged particles to excite the Shaukolen field. It can't collect particles going backward, so no Jump. Once we can accelerate forward, though, especially with Wolf so active, the ramscoop ought to get a lot of heavy particles even way above the ecliptic. You see,'' he added, motioning with his hands, "the heavier particles, like iron and some muons, spiral down the ramscoop and through the hollow core of the ship, then hit the exciter screens in the engine assembly. Some of them rebound back up the core, where they spiral down the scoop field again, gathering more energy with every loop. It sets up a standing wave down *Flag*'s axis, what we big brains call a Shaukolen field.'' He grinned at Kendall's expression. "Oh, yeah, I've heard your name for us.''

"You're a different sort of big brain, Paul.''

"I think that's a compliment. I'll look at it later and decide for sure. Anyway, the more particles that enter the wave, the higher the total energy. Eventually the energy load hits Shaukolen's Limit, and we turn into a sin-

gularity that can't exist where we are—and so we Jump.
Control your standing wave within certain parameters and
you Jump in a controlled direction—sort of. Accuracy
doesn't matter much as long as you fall a little short of
the starpoint. Then you just curve in on decel.''

''We become impossible.'' Kendall was not sure he
liked the idea. When he had Jumped to Wolf five years
ago, he had happened to be asleep at the time. Ignorance
had its bliss, he told himself, especially in the sack.

Leland smiled. ''Something like that. By adjusting the
exciter screens and our acceleration, we can control—
roughly—how far we jump, too. We have the screen technology to jump forty-five lights, maybe more, but the
ship has to accelerate so long toward light-speed to collect energy that a round trip takes decades our time, a
year or more ship time. It's just not feasible for supplying
a colony.''

''Why do you think flare stars are the answer?''

''Particles,'' Leland said simply. ''Actually, a special
kind of heavy particle.''

''Your ta—tak—what did you call them?''

''Tachyons. Not those—tachyons have no mass or
charge. Tachyons really aren't there, you see, just like
the little man in the refrigerator who turns the light on
and off. You never quite see him, but you know he has
to be there somewhere. Tachyons are like that. What I'm
looking for is the particle right *before* it becomes a tach-
yon, a charged particle that zooms nearly to infinite
mass—for an instant—right before it singularizes. Tachyons are particles that have already Jumped, Isaiah, and
post-Jump doesn't help us; the energy's not available
anymore. But put enough of the pretachyon widgets in
your scoop and you can hit Shaukolen's Limit within
minutes after ignition, not days. And if these particles
really exist, we can find a way to make them ourselves,
not have to borrow them from a flare star. I'm sure of
it.''

''Your enhanced drive.''

''Yeah. I tried to talk Danforth into letting me send
some robot probes toward Wolf to catch some widgets—
if they're there—but he wouldn't authorize the project.

Current drive theory doesn't believe in them, so the feasibility study axed the cost. Harrod's doing.'' He looked glum. ''I've been scanning through *Flag*'s Wolf-watch records, such as they are, but they didn't catch our flare and missed the second. All I got was some random flash off the comsat, scrambled data that doesn't mean much. Wolf plays billiards, too, it seems.''

''About as effectively. Mack says they tore down the microwave set four times looking for the gremlin that was us.''

Leland saluted him with his coffee cup and grinned. ''Here's to gremlins. I'm surprised we even hit the base.''

''You're a mean shot at pool, big brain.''

''Thanks. Anyway, I think Wolf's flares might have widgets in them, even the smaller flares, but Wolf's normal-size flares attenuate so quickly that you can't catch them. All you've got this far out is little men in the refrigerator. It's frustrating. The big flare blew the machinery and made our watch records into so many melted circuits, and *Flag* was in darkside—thankfully—on the second one. So I still don't have any proof.''

''But when the star blows a big flare . . .''

''Virgin widgets—if there are widgets, that is—even out here. But maybe pretachyons don't ever get outside the star; maybe everything converts to tachyons deep down in the gas layers. Aside from a solar expedition—wear your lead pants for that—all you can do is set up your catchers and hope for widgets.'' He raised an eyebrow. ''And I mean *hope*, chief. Roarke had a good idea about using our scoop as a shield, but *Flag*'s ramscoop is only a factor of five over Wolf Station's magnetic bubble. And the big flare smashed through our shields like so much tissue paper. If all we get is tachyons, Wolf will smash us, too, scoop or no scoop.''

''And if we get widgets?''

Leland grinned. ''We go on the wildest ride you've ever seen. Enhanced Jump, right over Wolf. Eight light-years, just like that.'' He snapped his fingers. ''How's that for a grant specification? Make it work and you're famous forever; find out you're wrong and you croak.

Puts a little oomph into the experiment, don't you think?''

''Hell,'' Isaiah said disgustedly. ''And I thought we were saved when Mack got us out of Tri Ellium. Have you told Merceau this?''

''No, and I'm not going to.'' Leland looked stubborn, as if daring Kendall to disagree.

''I'm not arguing,'' Kendall said mildly, and sipped at his coffee. ''I wouldn't, either, considering.'' They exchanged a look. ''I always thought Merceau was on the beam—a little precious on regs and dignity, but he always knew his stuff. I just don't understand it. I'd have expected Danforth to come unglued if I had to choose, not Merceau.''

''Is your friend Roarke going to come out of this okay? I've heard rumors that Merceau's after him bad.''

''He'd better not get him. Merceau would still be wringing his hands up here if it weren't for Jason.'' Kendall took time to look over Leland's face. ''You're looking better, I think. That must be good soup.''

''Great soup.'' Leland stacked his coffee cup in his bowl, then slid it across the table until it clinked against Isaiah's cup. He looked around distractedly, his mind obviously already on his schematics back in the control room. ''I've got to get back to Wolf-watch. Who knows? A widget might zip by and I might not be there to see. I'd hate that.''

''So would we all, Paul, considering.''

''You're so right.''

Cargo Tug 1, in transit to Wolf II, 5 hours to second dawn.

Six hours later Jason's tug caught up with Helena's on the next trip downward; she didn't bother to radio any greeting, still playing her indignation game. Jason passed on Yves' message but kept it short; she did not bother to acknowledge. In all his tiffs with Helena, he had never run into this kind of sustained silence—Helena *always* had something to say. She also had exquisite personal radar for the main chance. Perhaps it had started in anger about Danforth's action against Yves, but she had subliminal judgments that unerringly led her to the best side for Helena van Duyn. Somehow it drew from the instincts they shared as pilots; perhaps part came from the feminine way of knowing things men never knew.

I'll miss her, he realized.

But he found that Helena still had the capacity to surprise him, just when he thought he had her figured out. Halfway down to the base after *Flag* had slipped over the horizon, he heard the radio click on.

"Jason?"

He decided to be difficult. That would show her—what, he didn't know, but it would show her something. "Someone on Tin Eight said their air smells funny," he informed her. "Mack's crew ought to check it out, I guess."

"If you say so," she answered impatiently. "Jason, talk to me. *Why?*"

"Why what?"

"Don't be a bastard, Roarke. How could you give up your career? Let Yves blackmail you?"

"Who told you that?" he puffed.

"Danforth. He says Yves demanded you resign."

That man has the ears of an elephant, Jason thought sourly. Or likely he got Inga to brag by pretending outrage or God knows what. "What a rumor!" he declared. "Danforth doesn't know anything. Don't listen to him."

"I can put two and two together."

"So can I. It's called addition."

"Damn you, Jason! What if Yves goes back to nothing doing again? What if he starts declaring everything impossible and sits on his hands? You saw what he did before. Danforth thinks you're making a big mistake. So do I."

"Make up your mind, Helena! First you frost me for Danforth's plan that I take over the *Flag*—note that it was Danforth's idea, not mine, a little point you decided to ignore. Now you think it's a great idea."

"It's blackmail! Yves doesn't have the right . . ."

"Isn't blackmail if I made the suggestion, love. Hard for you to imagine, isn't it? Hard for you to imagine any kind of sacrifice."

"That isn't fair!" she declared.

"What's not fair? That Yves had to be bargained into cooperating or that you always put Helena van Duyn first? Hell, Sheila, you got everything you wanted now. You don't have to choose between me and Yves now; you just ride along with the tide. Easy for you. He wins all the way."

"Jason!"

"Leave me alone, Helena—just for once, leave me alone."

"You're an idiot, Jason Roarke! A blind idiot!" The radio snapped off.

"Okay, okay," he muttered. "I'm an idiot." How did he get into these situations?

He gave himself to the art of flying, treasuring the few hours left to him in the cargo tug. The little ship was nimble, ugly as hell with its pincher arms and top-heavy lock, but it was his still, for a while. He landed it neatly at the station field and took on the first of Rodriguez's cached supplies. All routine. Sure. He counted the few last times remaining in the tug, tasting the loss, then pushed it away. I don't want to think about it, he told himself, not now, not yet.

Wolf Colony Station, Wolf II, main topside hangar, 3 hours to second dawn.

On the next trip down, as his tug again sped over the mountains west of the base, Jason watched the horizon above Home Crater, blazing with the first reddish rays of second dawn. Above the crater floor, the Wolf-light flickered in an odd illusion of bright shadow curtains, some kind of auroras connected to Wolf's light pattern. Intrigued by the phenomenon, Jason watched the curtains dance around his tug. He had seen it before on prior circuits, not really noticing—lots of things he had never really noticed about this place. The dawnlight had spread across nearly all of Home Crater, nosing into shadows, flashing off silicates in the crater dust, creeping steadily backward toward the deep shadow along the eastern crater wall that still shielded Wolf Station. It would be close.

He set the tug down smartly and taxied toward the hangar.

Helena had deliberately wasted time on the tin line for this trip and had started her descent thirty minutes late, as if even sharing the same hangar with a blind idiot annoyed her sensibilities. Nuts to her, he thought. Rodriguez stood in the open bay door and waved at him, then signaled at one of his crew to close the doors after Jason had rolled inside. When the hangar again held pressure, Jason climbed out of the tug and walked over to Rodriguez.

"How's it going?" Jason asked. "I see you brought more supplies topside." An array of bulky storage cartons stood along the far wall.

"Air, some distillation equipment, some food supplies, everything we could salvage."

"We can use most anything of the essentials."

"You got it. Where's the other tug?" Rodriguez asked, concerned.

"Delayed a little, that's all."

"Okay." Rodriguez gave him a thumbs-up and headed toward the forklift maneuvering into Jason's open tin. As Jason watched, the forklift driver snagged a transport package marked with Ross 248's ID symbols and backed out carefully. *Flag* had dumped all its cargo here, matériel that the Lalande and Ross colonies would miss, maybe even desperately. Not everything in *Flag*'s cargo tins was smelly cheese, but there was nothing to do about that. Stupid, he supposed, to put people at risk on such a fragile lifeline as the cargo-chain, a ship every three months, a half year to make do somehow if something happened to a ship on its way. Nothing to do about that, either—the only other choice was to not try colonies out here at all. Suits. Jason watched the crew continue the unloading, moving easily under Rodriguez's firm direction.

Rodriguez, Summers, Dr. Renfrew, a few other chiefs—of all the personnel on Wolf Station, only a few had taken the leadership, made survival possible. Rodriguez was one of them.

And me, too, he thought. I suppose I can be proud of

that while I'm pushing my button. Hell, I *will* be proud of it. It's about the only useful thing you've done in your entire life, Roarke. Let Yves have his little triumphs; I can last it out. He felt the ache recede a little into the beginnings of some acceptance. He would hate losing cargo-chain, hate it more than he probably knew now, but he would do it. He would keep the bargain.

While Rodriguez's crew started to load his tug, he thought about returning to Earth, imagining better jobs than button pushing, maybe meeting someone and settling down, having the standard 1.4 kids, playing the rest of the typical citizen routine on an overcrowded planet. Aberdeen had changed, but he supposed he could get used to the changes. Scotland still had a few pockets of forest and glen, carefully preserved as parks, though each generation found a facile reason to nibble away a few thousand acres. Maybe he could take up bird-watching, teach his kids about the way things used to be. Maybe.

He daydreamed as the tug moved from sunlight to shadow, from shadow to sunlight, chasing *Ceti Flag* in orbit. On the next and final trip up with the last of Wolf Station's supply tins, Rodriguez shared Jason's cab. The chief looked tired, as did they all, and knew as well as Jason that both had another day to get through before each could finally relax. Jason hoped Rodriguez could get a little sleep.

"Sorry to leave Wolf II," Rodriguez said reflectively as the tug lifted over the walls of Home Crater. "Huhh! Never thought I'd say that after what we've been through."

"Home is where you find it, José."

"True. Damn place. Best to melt it down into slag, I suppose. Does Leland still think Wolf is cycling up to UV Ceti intensity?"

"Yeah. Whatever colony we had here is over with."

"Or else we drill the station levels a lot deeper."

"Come on, José," Jason protested.

"I am a stubborn man, Jason. I don't like losing."

"Yeah."

Cargo-chain freighter Ceti Flag, EuroCom registry, cargo-tug deck, thirty-eighth orbit at Wolf II.

Jason eased the cargo tin into place at the end of the port line, then took the tug inside *Flag*. Rodriguez detached his boots from the deck and did a slow stretch and somersault in free-fall, then touched down with a click of his magnets. "Hey, no gravity's okay," he said, smiling. "I got to do comsat repairs from time to time, loved the work. Got me away from my desk on envirosystems." He patted his belt. "Get chair spread along with the brain rot if that goes on too long."

"You'll have the chance again, José."

"Yeah? I doubt it. Likely Central will sweep all this under the rug, pretending it never happened, just like they pretended Wolf could never, ever, flare into risk range. Bastards. Maybe they'll give me a job filing flimsies in some Mars warehouse. What a thrill."

"Let's hope Danforth's in the next chair. He's not going to come out of this untouched, whatever he thinks, not with Central big shots pointing fingers everywhere. And Yves will go after him, too, now that he's back in charge of *Flag*. Captains' Board won't think much of assault on a freighter captain, even if Yves started it. I think Danforth knows that—thus the sneaking around and tsk-tsking with his aides."

Rodriguez grimaced. "Yeah. But if I know the report wars, friend, and I do, it'll end up a draw. Winning still goes by rank, and neither of those two outranks the other."

"Even if Danforth says Yves flipped out?"

Rodriguez's eyes widened. "Depends on the witnesses. Who were they?"

"Axel and Inga. Everybody else is only by hearsay, with the rumors all over the ship. Isaiah's been listening."

"That changes things. Psych Board outranks everybody." Rodriguez scowled. "If he could wave around an instability charge, it'd shift the advantage to him. Shit. I'd hate for Danforth to win."

"So call the media and bitch," Jason suggested casually. They looked at each other for a moment or two, then both smiled wolfishly at the same time. "Hell, do you think it'd work?" Jason asked.

"Worth a try. Do you think the *Herald* would be interested?"

"Sure. They hate the companies and love scandal. Why not?"

"Yeah, why not?" Rodriguez said. "Hell, it'd do Central good to blush—and the *Herald* is rough enough to see that they do, in spades. Probably won't save Merceau, but it might keep Danforth off another colony posting. Hmmm. Good idea, Jason. Damn good idea."

"I've got lots of great ideas. Ask me for some more sometime; they're all free."

"That's a deal."

They both turned as Mack Summers and his crew came crowding through the crew port. Summers waved his crew toward the gimbel port and floated over.

" 'Funny air,' " Mack said disgustedly. "There was nothing wrong with the air, nothing at all."

"Could be worse complaints," Rodriguez grunted.

"And I've heard a bunch of them in the last four hours. First it's the toilet in Tin Eight, then a sick food processor in Tin Seventeen, then weird radio crackles in Tin Twenty. I feel like a Ping-Pong ball, Jason."

"Almost over now—for a while. Why don't you guys get some rest for an hour or so? You can sack out uplevel in our crew quarters. I'll show you where they are."

"Thanks."

As they stomped past sick bay on the inner level, heading for *Flag*'s crew quarters, a voice called after them. "Chief Summers!" The three men stopped and looked back. Dr. Renfrew hurried over, looking a little more refreshed herself. It probably helped to finally have an adequate sick bay and the assistance of competent hands. She looked ten years younger—but Jason doubted it made any difference in her opinion about vacuum colonies. She focused on Mack. "Do you think you could help in bringing a few people upship from the tins? Your little friend, Magda, is creating more problems, and I have a few more cases of delayed radiation sickness.'' She looked annoyed.

"What's wrong with Magda?" Summers asked with sudden concern.

"Oh, just some disconnected behavior. The tin chief has asked that we move her into the hospital for observation. She's in Tin Sixteen. I'll get you a list of the others.''

"I'll take care of it," Summers said. He turned back to Jason and attempted a smile. "Well, so much for rest for the brave. José, you go roust out Philippe and Klaus again. Knowing those two, they're probably snoring already.''

"Helena's suit might fit your girl," Jason offered. "It's in the suit cabinet on the aft cargo-deck wall, marked with two orange slashes and a circle.''

"Thanks.'' Summers headed back the way they had come.

"Are you two going to the meeting?" Dr. Renfrew asked Jason. Inga had already bustled by them, heading toward the downlevel ladder, Mrs. Efficiency.

"Meeting? Uh, never mind. Sure.'' He glanced at Rodriguez and got an impressive twitch of the Latino's brows, then ambled after Dr. Renfrew, Rodriguez plodding heavily along beside him. Their footsteps echoed hollowly on the corridor floors.

"I haven't been aboard a cargo-chain ship before,'' Dr. Renfrew commented, looking around with interest. "Lots of room here. Maybe we could bring more of the people upship.''

"Low biosystems,'' Jason explained. "We'd have to download Inga's computers.'' They caught up with Inga on the outer level. She had overheard the suggestion.

"It might be an option later,'' she told Dr. Renfrew. "It's merely a matter of adequate time to reprogram. We have the basic equipment to adapt, especially with the extra converters out on the tin line.''

"What are the parameters?'' The two women fell into a technical discussion as the four approached the control room and continued to talk after they stepped though the door. Yves was seated at his console studying a schematic; Axel was leaning over him, just as intent in his concentration. Helena lounged nearby, looking bored. To the left, Danforth sat petulantly, his long face drawn down in displeasure. Probably fake, like everything else about Danforth, Jason thought. As the four walked in, Danforth looked up alertly, pressuring Jason again with a quick flash of hope aborning in despair. What a lackbrain, Jason reflected as he gave a high sign to Isaiah by Leland's chair and got a grin back. A few other people were sitting or lounging by the walls; apparently Danforth had fetched some admin people from the tins, still thinking a ship got run by counting votes. Only sometimes, Director, and you're not a voter. Jason crossed behind Yves to his own chair, then waved Dr. Renfrew to another nearby. Inga sat down beside her.

Yves swung his chair toward them. "So Inga found you, Jason. Nice of you to show up."

"Can't come if I'm not told, Captain."

Yves scowled, then let it go. "Your expertise, please. If we back out of Wolf-system, can the catch-basket assembly stand the strain?"

"It's designed for deceleration down from Jump; I don't see why not. Our problem is turning the lines."

"Well, it'll be slow, of course. We have a choice on reverse power: we can take ten hours to remount one of the engines, or we can use the tugs. I prefer the latter. With both tugs pushing the ship and our current orbital momentum, we can get above the ecliptic well past Wolf II's orbit in about a week. Leland thinks that's out of flare-risk range. Then we can start accelerating over the system." He glanced at Helena. "Helena says you have the greater expertise on monitoring the tin line," he said briskly, "and so she'll defer to you, after all; you will coordinate with Axel on power systems as we leave orbit."

Nice of her to say so, Jason thought. I've only got about eight years of seniority on her. Greater expertise!

"Yes, sir," he said, not giving Helena the satisfaction of his resentment.

Helena gave him a cool look, an exchange not lost on Yves. He looked smug. Little did he know, Jason thought, remembering her doubts about Yves, her suggestion that he disrank Yves himself, but maybe Helena's protest about blackmail was as fake as Danforth's pinning his hopes. Who could tell? Maybe Helena didn't know herself. Games always.

Well, you promised the price, Jason told himself. You could have guessed she'd pick her best choice. He looked down at his hands. "Sounds like a good plan," he said.

"We're going backward?" Inga asked dubiously.

Yves nodded.

"Are you sure it will work?" she asked.

Axel turned and smiled confidently. "Nothing is certain, wife. But yes, we think it will work."

"When do you plan to leave orbit, Captain?" Dr. Renfrew asked.

"As soon as possible."

"Give us an hour, please," she said. "We'd like to transfer a few more colonists from the tins and sedate some of the sick."

"I can only give you half that, Doctor. Sorry." Yves gestured toward Leland. "Leland has been delivering warnings ever since he sat down on Wolf-watch. We can't risk much more dayside orbit, not with the ship lateral to the star on each pass. We have to move now."

"All right." She shrugged. "Just start slowly so we can get our hospital in better order."

"Oh, it'll be slow. If you'll go down to cargo deck and take your station, Jason?" Yves said, offering an elaborate courtesy. "We leave orbit in thirty minutes. Once we get proper trajectory, you and Helena will go outship into the tugs." His dark eyes glinted.

"Yes, sir." Jason stood up and walked out, struggling for control. You will not stamp your feet, Roarke. You will not stomp out on him. You will walk carefully and casually, like it doesn't mean anything. He heard Helena's footsteps behind him, but she didn't hurry to catch up. At the moment he'd rather not talk to her, anyway.

Chapter 12

Cargo-chain freighter Ceti Flag, *EuroCom Registry, Tin 16, star-board tin line, thirty-eighth orbit at Wolf II.*

In the cargo tins the lights overhead were always lit, depriving the passengers of the safe darkness. Magda let her head float loosely, trying to sleep, to gather her strength. She ignored the way the walls moved in a few inches when they thought she wasn't looking, ignored the murmuring voices of the dark angels outside the tin as they plotted death and emptiness, the end of everything. Now they applied their machines to squeeze in the walls, moving them in steadily, secretly, while no one noticed until it was too late. Magda waited for the ending, not caring how it ended, only that it ended at last.

"Magda," Mrs. Tertak murmured to her.

Magda ignored her, her head bobbing. Easier to float, waiting for the scaled belly to turn upward, the fins to close, the gills to stop working. Easy.

"She's been like this for hours, chief. She doesn't respond at all. Before that it was some wild talk and laughing about fish and demon angels—I'm worried about her."

"She's had a hard time," a man's voice rumbled. A hand touched her hair and pushed its floating strands back from her face, then lifted her chin. "Magda? It's Mack. I've come to take you inside *Flag*. Can you open your eyes and look at me?" From a far distance, Magda heard the gentleness in his voice and responded to it vaguely by opening her eyes. Summers floated in front of her dressed in a spacesuit, with another suit under his arm.

206

"Do you think you can get into this?" he asked, still gently, and held up the spacesuit. "That's the girl."

He unbuckled her accel belts and eased her out of them, then guided her feet and arms into the suit. She let him move her body, staring over his head at the lights. The lights never went out, but it wouldn't stop the dark angels from their plan. Nothing could. Summers pulled up her helmet and settled it over her head, then checked connections on her suit. "Come along, sweetie. That's a good girl."

He pulled her after him toward the tin's small exit port, then held her against him as the lock cycled. As she realized they were leaving the tin, she began to struggle against him, terrified of the opening door. "Easy, easy!" Summers said in a choked voice. "Easy, Magda. Take it easy. Magda!" The outer door opened into blackness and the sparkling of stars. As he tugged on her suit belt and pulled her out of the lock, she looked around wildly for the dark angels. But there was nothing. No dread machines, no dark feathered shapes with darker eyes, nothing except the boxy metal surface of the tin and other half-visible boxy shapes beyond.

"Where are the angels?" she asked in surprise.

"What, honey?"

"The angels outside the tin. Where are they?"

"I don't know what you mean, sweetie. Angels?" Summers put his arm around her waist and hooked a long tether to his belt, then pulled on it hard. They sailed over the tin toward other shapes up ahead, something moving around and around, lights in a long row, and a shimmering net against the stars.

Magda looked around confusedly. "Where *are* we?"

"At *Ceti Flag*," Summers said patiently. "Where do you think you are?"

"No angels?" Magda couldn't take it in.

"Only you, angel." Mr. Mack turned his head and looked at her through his helmet faceplate, his dark eyes smiling. "Everything's okay, Magda. Everything's going to be all right. I promise."

They floated over the boxy tins and reached a marked doorway near the line of lights. Mack poked at the key display, then moved her inside. She floated, one hand on a rung grip, as he pulled in the tether behind him. Then he closed the door. When the inside door opened, he pulled her after him again through a lighted space. Magda saw the two tugs nearby, bolted to the deck, then an array of instruments along the other wall. High overhead another little plane was hanging in its brackets. It was such a big room. What is this place? she wondered, looking around her, then followed Mr. Mack docilely toward another doorway across the room.

"Step on that strip," he told her, pointing at the floor inside the doorway, "and hang on. That's the girl."

Magda watched as the strip turned her half-around, then felt weight again, downward through her boots. She smiled delightedly at the wonder of it.

Mack took off his helmet, then helped her with hers, his answering smile filled with relief. "Fun?"

She nodded.

"You'll be okay, sweetie," he told her, as if he were reassuring himself, too. Why was Mr. Mack worried? What had happened?

She followed him down a long corridor that curved at both ends, then started as Dr. Renfrew suddenly appeared in front of her. "Here she is," Mr. Mack said. "She's looking more alert already."

"Hello, Magda," Dr. Renfrew said, and smiled at her, then leaned forward to look at the displays on Magda's suit. "Well, temp's normal, other functions look okay. Convenient to have her suited. Let's get her into bed." Dr. Renfrew slipped her fingers around Magda's wrist and pulled at her gently. "Come along, dear. You'll do just fine."

"Sereni Tertak says she's been very withdrawn, not making sense," Mr. Mack said. He sounded worried again, and Magda looked around for the reason, mildly alarmed. All she saw were people moving around quietly, and other people lying down in beds in the hospital, just like before. Why were they back at Wolf Station? she wondered, looking around.

"She was talking about angels as I brought her in," Mr. Mack said.

Obediently, Magda looked around for the dark angels and wondered if they were hiding inside the walls, working their machines with feverish intensity.

"The sedatives sometimes cause a temporary psychosis," Dr. Renfrew said to the angels. "Not often, but frequently enough to be a documented side effect. Magda was sedated several times, if I remember correctly, the last time for nearly two days. So I'm not that surprised. That and a little claustrophobia might account for it. Magda, dear? Lie down on this bed."

Magda let herself be pushed down on the mattress, then watched Dr. Renfrew slip off her boots and take them away, hiding them out of sight, leaving Magda defenseless. As the doctor turned away for a moment, Magda quickly slipped her knife from her tunic and hid it beside her leg.

"Lie down, now." Dr. Renfrew pulled up a blanket and covered her, then patted her shoulder. "I'll be back later."

"Don't you have any medication that can help?" Summers asked anxiously.

"I'd rather not put more drugs into her system, not with this sensitivity to the earlier medication, but perhaps I can find a mild counteragent. The disorientation should wear off in time." She looked down at Magda and smiled with pointed fangs, her dark wings moving idly behind her. "I'll watch over her. Are you bringing in the others we requested?"

"Philippe and Klaus are working on it now." Mr. Mack hesitated and looked at Magda. "I guess I'd better go help. I'll be back later, sweetie. You rest."

Magda smiled at him and watched him walk away. She waited patiently, listening to the angels mutter to each other in the walls, waiting for her time to strike at the angel named Danforth, the evil angel who led all the dark angels in their destruction. She curled her fingers around her knife and smiled hard at the ceiling, waiting for her time. As she waited, her breathing quieted, each breath smoothly taken, lifting her chest in a slow rise, matching the slow, measured pounding of her heart. She relaxed into the softness of the mattress and closed her eyes, pretending to sleep. Soon Dr. Renfrew would stop watching her. Soon no one would notice as she slipped out of her bed and into the corridor beyond. Soon.

Cargo-chain freighter Ceti Flag *EuroCom registry, cargo-tug deck, thirty-ninth orbit at Wolf II.*

Jason cycled through the gimbel port and clicked his boots down on the wall by the port, then jumped hard enough to detach his boots and arrow across the cargo deck. Halfway across the room he somersaulted over the cargo tugs and landed neatly, boots down, on the far wall by the tin-monitor consoles. Rodriguez had a point: free-fall cleared the fog quite nicely.

"Cute, Jason," Helena said behind him. Well, he thought, you can't impress everybody all the time. He hauled himself into the tin-monitor seat and buckled in; during momentum changes, the entire console swiveled on its gyros to match the "up" and "down" of the room, much like the companion cargo-tug panels in midwall. Helena seated herself more sedately at the other console, although Jason would be the prime operator on the tin monitors. He glanced over at her and saw her shake back her drifting hair, then key up her own program.

Everybody's got to prove something, he thought, trying to excuse Helena. He thought they had shared something in their nearly two years on *Flag*: some fights, true, a lot of chaffing back and forth, but some good times, some meaning for each other. Now he was disposable, he supposed, no longer useful to Pilot Helena van Duyn. He wondered if she was already anticipating her rank as senior pilot of *Flag*; with Yves's power of promotion and his affection in Helena's pocket, she could get the posting. This is the pits, he thought, but people chase what they chase.

And what will you chase, Roarke, when you're back on Earth? He keyed up his own board and displayed the computer schematics of the tin lines that bore their fragile human cargo, the supplies to keep them alive during the next three months, and the essential H-3 to give them the chance. He widened the display to include *Flag* her-

self: the turning crew module, the delicate net of the
ramscoop, the four bulky engines bracketed by the
ghostly radar shapes of the tin lines. The computer over-
laid vector lines, spider-script boxes on stresses and balance, an ambient shimmer for the particle wind caressing
Flag. Solar wind had dropped, he noted—which had
seemed to make Leland nervous. He saw the ready light
wink and turned on the intercom.

"Cargo deck ready, Captain."

"Acknowledged. We'll enter darkside in three minutes, Jason. The schedule is engine blast at five minutes,
then ignition of the portside lateral jet at eight minutes
to start the turn. By the time we leave planet shadow at
thirty-eight minutes, we should have completed 180 degrees. You will monitor the tin lines as we turn; I'll try
to keep it at a smooth transition from tethers to catch
basket."

"Got it, Captain."

"Helena will back you up."

Jason shot a startled glance at Helena, who looked
smug. The intercom snapped off.

"So we've already got the credit lined up, huh?" he
asked her furiously. " 'With the faultless assistance of
Second Pilot Helena van Duyn, Roarke managed to keep
the tin lines from wandering away.' I can see the company fax sheet now."

"Just watch the tins, Jason," she said in a bored tone.

"Once we were friends, you and I."

Helena looked at him haughtily. "We were never
friends."

That did it. "Right, Sheila," he snapped. "Friends
don't act like hyenas, snarling over the carcass." He
watched her start to sputter, then added a rude gesture
he saved for terminal occasions. "One too many word
games, Helena—you just couldn't resist that, could you?
Well, you're right," he said contemptuously. "We sure
weren't friends, not when you're capable of that. Watch
your screens, pilot. I'll key you in if I need you, which
I doubt."

"Jason . . ." she began.

"Shut up."

Calmly, Jason turned back to his console and keyed up other schematics on his screen and arranged them neatly from left to right across the top of the screen, then reduced Yves's trajectory plot to a small box on the bottom corner to add his overrides. Never friends. He cleared his mind of her, like a cloth across a slate, and concentrated on the monitor. This would be tricky, very tricky. It was just like Helena to be more interested in that final shot than in keeping it shut, delivering the final blow right before he needed all his concentration, his every skill on the tin line. He glanced over at the aft window, matching a visual inspection with the schematics on his screens, orienting himself.

"Jason."

"*Shut up!*"

"I'm sorry," she said in a small voice. "I didn't mean that. Really I didn't."

"I don't have the time now, Sheila." He keyed up other programs and put them in reserve under access buttons, then studied the tin alignment on his screens in finer detail. Taking manual control of the tin lines was extremely risky—the human mind just did not have the capacity to run the million calculations necessary to balance the line—but the computers allowed an overview, a chance to see a problem developing. Jason would have to depend on *Flag* and all her wonders in thinkum-dinkums as she took herself beyond program into uncharted territory. The cargo-chain freighters had reverse capacity for dockside maneuvers, but such movements were short term and at minimal speed.

"Jason . . ."

"Goddammit, Helena. Save it for later, will you?"

"I love you, Jason." He looked over at her, startled, and saw the tears on her face. Then she spoiled it with a soulful look, the sleeve across her wet face, the tremulous smile. It was an act, all an act. Helena never cried about anything. He knew her too well, knew when she was playing games—as she was now with the trembling lip and the fake tears. Why this, he didn't know. Why the act? It felt obscene.

"I'm sorry, too, Helena," he said gently, his good-bye to her. "I don't believe it."

His console pinged for attention, jerking him back. He saw the engine signal light on his displays; a moment later he felt a palpable vibration through his chair as the engines ignited. As the ignition pulled on his body, his console pivoted to the new orientation, swinging him left toward the crew module. A quick glance behind him at the window showed all four engines blazing in an incandescent fury; the window immediately shifted polarity to cut down the glare. On either side of the engines the cargo tins followed in neat order, protected by a narrow distance from the shimmering backwash of the engines. Should have put the colonists' tins farther forward, he thought. If the tin line swings into the backwash . . .

He clenched his fist, cursing his own limitations. He should have known he would forget something out of all the things to remember; he had forgotten to change his assumptions from standard forward departure. In all the hurry since his bargain with Yves, he had forgotten that he had put half the colonists' tins at the end of a tin line, in dangerous proximity to the backwash if the tin line swung too far inward. He turned quickly back to his console, his heart pounding as he concentrated fully on the figures racing across the screen. He cleared his mind of everything, of Helena, of Yves, of losing cargo-chain. Not now.

Personal hero time, Roarke, he told himself. What you do now lets them live or die—your doing all the way. Don't screw it up.

An upper display on his screen showed *Flag*'s orbital curve straighten subtly from its ellipse around Wolf II, then lengthen into a smooth parabola, heading outward into the planet's shadow. As the side jet blasted, beginning a slow counterforce to turn the ship, Jason saw the tin lines drift perceptibly to the right. He held back on the override, though the tin line's sway tempted him into that rashness, then bit his lip as the end of the starboard line slipped closer to the engine backwash. Come on, come on, he wished at the computers. Catch it now. The screen flickered with a frenzy of new readings, then steadied as the tin computers and *Flag* adjusted the tether housings to compensate for the drift. The tin lines became a segmented curve, a connect-the-dots configuration but somewhat straighter, then began to bow right again as *Flag* continued to turn. Jason clicked on the intercom.

"Axel! Back off on the starboard power! The computer's losing it."

"Throttling back twenty percent," Axel replied calmly. "I can throttle back a few percent more if you need it."

"Don't need it yet. Let's see how this helps." Jason watched the tin lines with full concentration but didn't see any more distortion of their curves as *Flag* continued to turn. The end tin of the starboard tin line hovered just outside the safety margin from the backwash. Jason keyed up a screen of sensors to monitor the danger zone more carefully. Last thing those people need is more radiation, he thought grimly. As *Flag* settled into her smooth turn, the tin lines steadied in a complementary arc, turning smoothly with the ship. On the green. Jason relaxed a little, saving some of his focus for the next danger point.

Ten minutes later *Flag*'s slow turn approached ninety degrees. The catch-basket assembly tuned in, sharing strength with the tethers, but the tin lines hesitated. Oh, shit, now it's the other one, Jason thought as the port tin line edged dangerously inward toward the engine backwash.

"Power down," Yves announced as *Flag* edged past ninety. The engine vibration ceased as the engines flickered out. Jason watched the port line swing inward, his hand again poised over the override.

"Come on, come on, come on," he chanted. "Axel, give me a blast on the starboard side jet, quick!"

"How long a blast?"

"Just do it! A few seconds. I've got drift in the starboard line."

"Ignition, counting one, two, three, four . . . power down." The tin line hesitated again, then eased outward slightly as the tins rocked down smoothly into their catch baskets. The port line looked fine. Starboard line ditto.

Flag was now going backward, balancing its plates on poles. Jason sat back and gusted a deep breath.

"Christ almighty!" he muttered. He'd take boredom any day now.

"First-rate, Jason," Helena said, maybe with a little real admiration. He ignored her.

"I agree," another voice said behind him. He turned and saw Mack Summers floating a few meters away. He hadn't even been aware of his approach. "Some machine driver, man," Mack said, and winked. "I just had to watch. My, oh my."

"Thanks, brother."

Jason stretched out his legs and noticed that cargo deck had some gravity again—not a lot, but something. "Well, we got some speed."

"Not much. Isaiah says Merceau is gnashing about it." Mack leaned across Jason's chair and snapped off the intercom light, then glanced at Helena in the far chair. "Before you go jockey that tug of yours, I want to talk to you."

"Sure." Jason looked up at Summers expectantly.

"Elsewhere." Mack glanced at Helena again. "Come along—it won't take a minute."

"Where are you going, Jason?" Helena promptly demanded as Jason followed Summers away.

"Back in a sec."

Summers took him completely out of cargo deck through the gimbel port, then tugged him next to a ladder. He looked around quickly, then stared at Jason a moment. "What is going on between you and Merceau? I don't like what I've been hearing of hints dropped."

"I made a bargain."

"Since when does *Flag*'s pilot have to bribe *Flag*'s captain to deal with a crisis?" Summers demanded indignantly.

"Since Wolf blew up and made everything nonreg. Listen, Mack—it was all I could do. I appreciate the staunch defense, but it's no use. Worth it," he said firmly.

"Oh, yeah? Well, a few of us from Wolf II might have some other ideas . . ."

"Don't." Jason raised his hand in warning. "Really,

don't. My career's down the tubes, anyway: I defied a direct order to start prepping the tins before we confirmed the flare. That's all Yves needs—the outcome's the same.''

"If you hadn't . . ."

Jason smiled. "Forget all that. This whole situation's a tinderbox; we *need* Yves. As long as he's cooperating, we have a chance. Whatever I think about him personally, he turned the ship. Not many captains in Ceti Transport could do that, not under this kind of pressure. We just might make it—if he cooperates, *leads* like he's supposed to." He shrugged. "He's a good man, Mack. Some of it I brought on myself."

Summers looked at him quizzically. "This is a different Jason. I hadn't gathered you're the type for self-sacrifice." He meant it as friendly, but the comment bit deep.

Jason shrugged again. "Most of everything Isaiah's told you about me is right, man. Yeah, I know that, too. Maybe once I've decided to act like an adult. Doesn't nobility fit me well?" He struck a pose, chin out, profile left.

"Uncomfortably—definitely uncomfortably." Summers looked away and blew out a breath. "So you want us to just let it go?"

"Yeah. I made a deal. I'll keep the bargain."

"Well, I'll think about it. I don't like it."

"Thanks, Mack. Thanks for everything."

Jason heard angry footfalls coming down the corridor and turned. Helena walked toward him, her hair bouncing, a look of distinct displeasure on her face. As she opened her mouth, Jason knuckled Summers's shoulder and detoured around her, headed in the other direction.

"Jason!" She turned on her heel and hurried after him.

Jason remembered a happier time when he had put Helena in catch-up; it sat badly on his mind now. He had thought more of her, he told himself, but decided he really wasn't surprised. Maybe it was time to get out. He didn't believe it, but he told himself it was the truth. Helena caught up and strode alongside him; uncon-

sciously, he eased away from her, accepting the separa-
tion she had obviously chosen.

He said nothing to her as they powered up the tugs and
left cargo deck. She wasn't interested in talk, either, it
seemed. Make an effort, Helena, he thought angrily. You
started this. As the tug drifted over the cargo-tin lines
and pivoted forward, he keyed his hand mike. "Radio
check. Do you read me, control?"

"We read," Yves answered. Jason heard a muttered
discussion with Axel. Apparently they were debating
where the tugs should push. As the discussion went on,
Jason peered out his small tug window, trying to pick out
the ship ahead of him in shadow. A few seconds later the
movement of the crew module gave him most of it; beyond it, a faint shimmer against the background stars
outlined the ramscoop net against the shadowed whites
and grays of Wolf II's nightside, dimly lit around the
planet's edges with a faint reddish glow that widened as
he watched it. Slow—it was slow. God, too slow.

"Jason?"

"Yes, Axel."

"Go inboard of the ship frame, then hook on at the
forward port corner. There should be room between the
frame and the lower edge of the ramscoop."

"Not much room," Jason argued. "The scoop sags
with light pressure."

"I *know* that, pilot," Axel said irritably. "Just go
where I told you. Helena, you take the starboard. Syn-
chronize with our current speed and do not increase
power until I give the word."

"That's okay," Helena said.

Jason detached his robot arm from its perch on the
frame and powered the tug downward at a slow glide.
He caught a dim flash off Helena's tug as both craft moved
under the crew module; they must be nearing the end of
shadow. A few moments later Jason's window filled with
a ruby light. Jason pivoted the tug under the ship frame
and eased upward against the ramscoop to clamp his tug
to the frame. We need some speed, baby, he told the
Flag. Don't let us down now.

"Contact," Jason radioed.

"About to hook on," Helena said several seconds later. "Contact and synchronized."

"Begin increments of increased power by single percents," Axel warned. "Let's do this slow and easy."

"That's okay." Jason edged up his power, all too conscious of the ruddy starlight that gleamed on the ship frame, striking backward into his window. "How's the Wolf-watch?" he asked nervously.

"Not your concern," Yves said rudely. "Just concentrate on that smooth increase."

Jason bit back his automatic retort. Bargain, Jase. Be an adult. Concentrate on smooth increase. He edged up power again, increasing the tug's push on the ship. It wouldn't add much, but a few days won at the other end of their escape from Wolf-system might count as they approached Mars. If they approached Mars. He watched the power meter carefully, following Axel's timed schedule, hoping that Helena wouldn't get too far behind or ahead—too great a differential on the frame would set the tins swinging again. He edged up the dial a little more.

Sneaky, sneaky, goes the thief . . . The childhood rhyme circled through his head idiotically. Bonky, bonky, make it brief . . . Steadily he inched up the tug's power, percent by percent, until they approached maximum. Sneaky, sneaky, comes the law, catch the thief, ha-ha-ha. Christ, he thought. My nerves can't take this.

The steady red light of Wolf intensified as *Flag* left the twilight behind them. Jason hazarded a look in his rear screens, then bit his lip. It was too slow, even with the tugs helping. Yves's estimate of a week would not be that far off. His power dial read full; he watched the control board for several minutes, waiting for Axel to order the cutoff.

"Cut power on the mark," Axel said at last. "One, two, three, mark!"

Jason powered down, then ran a quick check on all systems. He heard another muttered discussion over the radio.

"We'll ride on this momentum for a few hours," Axel announced, "then check the trajectory before we send you back out. Return inship."

"Coming inship," Jason radioed. "Powered down."

"Acknowledged," Helena sang out. "Coming inship." Jason cycled out of the tug lock and pulled himself along the frame, careful not to lose contact with the handholds. He moved quickly along the outside of the frame, then moved inboard between the frame and the rotating crew module to a set of ladder rungs used for frame maintenance. From his vantage he couldn't see the tin lines beyond the aft frame—a good sign, at least for vertical drift. He hurried, anxious to get back to the tin monitors. With a spaceman's superstition, he knew it was going too easily. When the other shoe dropped, he wanted to be in a position to do something about it—if he could.

Jason pulled himself quickly around the bottom of the frame, checked the tin lines quickly by eye, then pulled himself into the crew lock. He waited, holding the lock cycle on pause for Helena. "Move it, Helena!" he called irritably.

"I'm coming!" she shouted back. He heard her curse as she bumped against something and apparently stopped to get herself free.

"Helena!"

"Damn it. I'm coming."

Chapter 13

Cargo-chain freighter Ceti Flag, *EuroCom registry, control room, 48 minutes after departing orbit at Wolf II.*

Kendall watched Leland anxiously, aware that the young scientist did not like what he saw on his Wolf-watch screen. Danforth drifted over, pretending he had the supervision; Kendall eyed him disdainfully, and Leland saw him not at all. Danforth drifted off again, looking unhappy.

Tough, Isaiah thought.

Elsewhere in the control room, while Danforth sat, Merceau was a bustle of controlled activity. To Isaiah's sour surprise, Merceau was functioning smoothly as captain, making decisions right and left while Danforth lolled nearby, the latter's swollen face mute testimony to the conflicts aboard *Flag*. Kendall watched him surreptitiously, wondering what Danforth had planned, if anything. He had seen the quiet conferences with his admin team, had heard rumors of other maneuverings. So far Danforth had left Merceau and Stromstad alone, aside from a few sparks now and then, probably hoping for another fit of Merceau's paralysis. Then Peter Danforth to the rescue—only Merceau wasn't cooperating and Danforth's career kept on guggling down the drain. Central had a nasty habit of blaming convenient administrators for its own faults.

He wondered idly what Mars and Earth would make of this. Push it under the rug? He had heard of a few colony accidents played down to minimum, but nothing as massive as this. It would be more grist for the mill for the politicos who hated the money drain by the colonies, and it would alter some career tracks in several departments. Kendall looked over at Danforth again, wondering, then smiled to himself. *Me worrying about corporate politics, the future of colonial space—me! And where do you go now, Kendall?*

He watched Leland smoothly key through totally incomprehensible schematics, oblivious to everything behind him. *Maybe I could learn astrophysics. Now that's a thought.*

"Getting anything?" he asked when Leland seemed to come up for air. The boy turned toward him, his face haggard with the strain of too many rads and too many hours hunched at Chief Stromstad's little board.

"Good equipment!" Leland said admiringly. Kendall regarded him with genuine affection. *Ah, to be that young,* he thought.

"If only we could have had some of this at Wolf Station," the boy went on.

"Central does pamper its cargo-chain. What is it telling you?"

"Hell, it gives me the whole pattern. I thought I saw some signs weeks ago, but nobody believed me. But there it is—all we needed was the amplified data." He waved at the squiggles on his screen.

"Pattern of what?" Kendall asked patiently.

Leland looked abashed. "Sorry, Isaiah. Wolf is waking up: I've got changes across the spectrum, including Shaukolen markers. I don't think she'll turn into another UV Ceti, but this area of space won't be very habitable in a few weeks. You were right—we'll have to write off the colony—at least until we come up with a better idea."

"Dreamer," Isaiah snorted—*but you never knew,* he thought. He glanced over at Jason's empty station. *Three hundred people in cargo tins, alive, with a chance now. Who would have thought it? Courtesy of you, my friend. Three hundred lives.*

"You betcha." Leland ran his hands over his board again. "I'm trying now to get predictors that can warn us of the next major flare—I've got a clue it's coming soon, but about the same magnitude as early earthquake prediction. Can't get much warning yet." He fiddled with his board and then watched the results wink up on the screen. "Hmmmph."

"Like when?"

"Oh, maybe in a few minutes or sometime next month," Leland said disgustedly. "*Flag* has wonderful eyes but could use a bit more brains, though it would take a Cray Nine to catch all the data." He inserted a disk-sized record cassette and punched at the board. "At least I can save what I've got. Mars Authority has a Cray—I think, after this, assuming we get back, they'll let me in to use it." He smiled.

"Bright boy comes to amaze."

"Something like that. In fact, I just might—" Leland stopped and stared at his screen.

Kendall automatically craned his neck to see what had caught his attention, then looked at Leland in inquiry. He waited a few moments, then shifted forward. "Paul . . ."

Leland suddenly swung his chair around to face the room. The sudden movement caught everyone's attention. "Rig for flare," Leland said urgently. "You've got maybe two minutes."

Merceau hit the all-ship circuit. "Batten down! Wolf's about to blow again! Helena, get inside the ship—fast!"

"Damn it. I'm coming!"

Jason's voice cut in. "Move it, sweetheart! I've got the lock open!"

Kendall tightened his grip on his chair and looked at the star in the forward screen, its image faintly obscured by the shimmer of the ramscoop. His heart started to pound. I believe in widgets, he vowed. I really, really do. Honest, Lord.

"Widgets," Leland murmured fervently.

"Chocolate bars," Kendall added, and heard Leland laugh. "Well, the extra charm can't hurt. Magic's where you find it."

"That's the truth."

Cargo-chain freighter Ceti Flag, *EuroCom registry, cargo-deck crew lock, 50 minutes after departing orbit at Wolf II.*

Jason grabbed for a nearby hand rung and peered out of the open air-lock door. He heard Helena's quickened breathing over his radio circuit but could not tell her distance away. "Come on, Helena!"

"I'm coming! Believe me, I'm coming."

Jason caught his breath as nearby space seemed to darken into luminous velvet as the flare lit up the microscopic dust surrounding them—what? he wondered. A breath later, the flare seemed to ignite nearby space, blinding the eyes. He flinched backward involuntarily, then blinked furiously against the dazzled shapes of his vision. Dimly, through the blinding glow, he saw Helena's dark shape appear in the hatch doorway. He reached for her urgently. Then, beyond her, *Flag*'s engines suddenly ignited with a flash.

"Yves!" he shouted. "No!" He lunged for Helena and grabbed her arm, then surged against the wall beside the open hatchway as the acceleration hit them. He clung to the handhold behind him, strained between his anchor and Helena on the other arm. Helena screamed as she lost hold of the doorway sill and swung her free hand wildly, reaching for him. Jason tried to pull her toward him, conscious of the open void behind her and her endless fall into nothingness if he lost her, of the building speed that tore at the muscles in his shoulders. He gritted his teeth as he felt muscle fibers separate into a blinding sheet of pain across his back. Then, to his amazement, he felt the ship Jump.

Four dozen times Jason had experienced the momentary dizziness of Jump, the inside out, a sudden not-here, the calm instant after the ship reached over-there. The crew had weeks to prepare for the shift as the ship edged closer and closer to Shaukolen's Limit, not that it seemed much afterward. A bit of dizziness, a sense of disorientation that lingered a few hours, a turning point in the voyage of halfway-there. Deep-space crews accepted Jump as one of the interesting tidbits of cargo-chain life, given to a few. He felt his vision gray out and fought it.

"Jump . . ." Helena gasped.

"I've got you, love." A moment later the sensation reversed, as if he and ship had plunked into a new socket, though he still felt acceleration pulling at him and Helena as the engines continued to blast. He took the chance and planted a foot on the opposite doorsill, then grabbed at her arm with his other hand. "I've got you."

"Jase . . ." She connected with her other hand and pulled on him. Jason clenched his teeth against the agony in his back, then helped her get hold of the doorsill. She fumbled inside for another hand rung, then groaned as she pulled herself up and over him. When she was safely inside the lock, he moved his foot and slammed on the door release. The lock door slid shut. Jason sagged against the lock wall, then watched Helena slide backward, bumping up against the closed door.

"Fast . . ."

"We Jumped. Careful, now—she's still accelerating." But as he spoke, he felt the subtle shift in the ship's speed, the lessening of pressure that held him against the lock wall. Helena turned her helmet toward him, and he saw her white face, her eyes dark pools in the shadows of the crew lock. She seemed to shake herself and sat up straighter.

"What in the *hell* happened?" she demanded.

"Beats me. Are you all right?"

Helena glanced up at the panel above his head, then slid over to him. "Air's up. Take off your helmet," she said imperiously. As he complied, she removed her own helmet, then grabbed him, planting a thoroughly satisfactory kiss on his mouth. She backed off a little and looked at him, grinning. "Hey, friend. Thanks!"

"Glad you're back, Sheila."

"You sod." She pushed him roughly. "You're a poor excuse for a man, Jason Roarke." But she was still smiling.

Jason levered himself to his feet, moving gingerly against the lancing pain in his shoulder muscles, then reached down a hand.

"Race you inside." He laughed, amazed at being alive, that *she* was alive, then winced as the laugh twinged his back. Helena was already at the inner doorway, pressing the entry cycle. As the door slid open, she barreled through onto the wall ladder and half fell several feet to cargo deck. Jason followed more prudently, wary of the heaviness that still lingered in cargo deck. It might have hit five gees.

He moved urgently toward the tin-monitor station, but Helena forestalled him with a quick look down through the aft window. "A tin is gone!"

Jason looked down at the tin lines and saw the empty space at the end of the port line.

"Oh, God!" Helena's hands flew to her throat.

Jason chuckled. "Well, that's one tin of supplies for any aliens that flit by. Let's hope it's the ant people—after what we did to them in that movie, it's all we can do. Calm down, Helena—the colonist tins are at the end of the other line. Remember?" She stuck out her jaw at him, angry at her mistake.

He walked over to the tin monitors and keyed on the radio link. "Tin Seventeen? Check in, please."

A shaken voice answered him. "We're here, but we had some loss of air pressure. Got it under control. What happened?"

"Roger, Seventeen. I'll let you know when I find out. Tin Eighteen? Your status?"

"What in the *hell* happened?" a man demanded angrily. Behind his voice Jason could hear a babble of excitement and terror.

"Damned if I know, Eighteen. Hold tight. Nineteen?" Jason took the tally from the two remaining tins, then called the port tin line. Everyone was shaken up but mostly all right.

"Any hope that Ten might be not far behind?" Helena asked. "It could have come along, just separated at some point."

"Depends on when it dropped off. I think the tether couldn't take the strain." Sometimes God rolled the dice in the right combination. They could get by without the tin. He keyed up the aft radar and sent some useless pings, getting back nothing but dust echo.

"Cargo deck!" Yves called.

"Roarke here."

"Did Helena get inside?" Yves asked urgently.

"She's safe. Matter of fact, she's standing right here scowling at me. We lost a tin, Yves. Tin Ten—supplies."

Yves was silent a moment. "Anything on radar?"

"No."

Yves sighed. "Well, we're lucky we didn't lose more than that. Get upship, you two. Leland says we just discovered a new ship drive." His voice faded as he turned away from the mike. "Will you two quit dancing around?" he shouted at somebody. "This is a control room, for Christ's sake."

Jason clicked off, then turned to Helena. "Care to dance?"

"He's been under a lot of strain."

"We've *all* been under a lot of strain, sweetheart. And that's the man you pick over me." He stamped by her toward the ladder to the gimbel port. Helena hurried after him.

"You never let on you *wanted* to be picked, Jason."

"You never let on you *intended* to pick, Sheila."

"*Stop* calling me that!"

Jason stopped and looked at her. "Don't you ever get tired of the zingy word games?"

"No. It's the only thing that keeps you in your place, Jason Roarke!" She swept by him up the ladder, back in her snit. Jason looked down at the tin lines visible through the ceiling window. Hooray, he thought to no one in particular.

Chapter 14

Cargo-chain freighter Ceti Flag, EuroCom *registry, control room, 55 minutes after departing orbit at Wolf II.*

The first thing Jason noticed when he walked into the control room was Leland and Isaiah in a waltz. He grinned, knowing that Isaiah was prolonging the display just to get Yves's goat. In the far corner Mack Summers chipped in by directing the music with his fingers, his face split by a wide smile. Yves's face was thunderous. As he spotted Helena, however, he rose suddenly and walked to her, then pulled her into a fervent embrace. She laughed up at him in delight and patted him; maybe it was real, Jason thought. As they murmured nothings to each other, Jason stalked by to his own chair. Isaiah promptly broke off his dance and pounced on him.

"Did you see the engines? Did you feel the instant Jump? Hey, boyo, you gotta believe!" Leland came up behind him, grinning from ear to ear. He looked very young. Suddenly Jason felt old again, a nasty old bear pacing his cage—only now the cage might be permanent.

"Yeah," he said, knowing it had nothing to do with him, not now. "Where are we?" He looked at the wall screen and saw only stars, points of light on a black background.

"Right outside Sol's Oort cloud," Isaiah declared, and pulled Jason's arms into a sit-down tango. "Luck of the Irish, you Scottish warthog—we got widgets!"

"Who?" Jason asked, confused.

"Another three weeks and we'll be home!" Leland pulled Isaiah off into another waltz. "Way to go!"

227

Who were widgets? Jason wondered.

"Probabilities, Mr. Roarke," Leland added as they pirouetted by again. "Too much bad luck disturbs the cosmos, makes a singularity that inevitably implodes into luck of the Irish."

"Is that the latest in astrophysics?" Jason asked, amused.

"Why not?"

Danforth stood up. "This is all very entertaining, but we still have to organize this ship. Have you checked on the tins, Roarke?"

Yves turned around immediately and stared at him, his arm still firmly around Helena's waist.

"Director," Jason said softly, "that's not your prerogative. In fact, I don't think you have any prerogative—consultant, maybe. This is the *Ceti Flag*." He pointed at Yves. "On *Flag*, the captain has authority."

"I appreciate the support, Jason," Yves said sarcastically. "Maybe it's half-sincere."

"Oh, shit, Yves! Won't you *ever* let it go?" Jason stood up. "I'm going uplevel," he announced. "If you want to talk to your people in the tins, Director, come along."

"Come along, Summers," Danforth said officiously. "I need you to collect your crew."

Summers dropped his hands from his conducting and stood up, then winked at Isaiah as he passed by. Isaiah bowed with a flourish and made sure Danforth caught it. The three men exited the control room, heading downlevel. Jason dropped to a stroll to let Danforth get ahead of them.

"Did you get your little girl—what's her name?—upship to Inga?"

"Magda. Yeah. She just needed some closer attention, I think. This whole experience has been hard on her. Her mother died, you see." Mack's face tightened around the eyes.

"Special lady?" Jason asked.

"I had hopes." He shrugged wistfully. "Never got very far—Elizabet was still grieving for the one and only she'd married. You'd think after twelve years . . . Well, anyway, Magda is much like her. I'm worried about how she's been acting ever since Elizabet died—I wish I knew what was going on in her head, *really* knew." He glanced at Danforth striding along ahead of them, then lowered his voice. "She blames Danforth, you see, heard too much loose talk among the crews." He shook his head sadly. "I don't know what else to do, Jason. Just don't know. I'm not good with kids, especially the ones almost grown."

"Once we get back to Mars, you'll have the time to make it right."

Summer brightened. "Yeah, I hope so."

Jason heard a clatter of footsteps behind them and looked around. "Oh, Lord, here comes Helena!"

"Special lady?" Summers asked.

"Not mine, boyo. Danforth!" Jason called irritably. "Will you wait up?"

Danforth was already to the next ladder and about to ascend. He stopped and looked back impatiently, then reluctantly walked back toward them. "What is it?"

"Just wait a little for some tired bones, okay? What's the hurry?"

"I don't like your tone, Roarke," Danforth said stiffly, but he waited.

"Stuff it up your ass," Summers advised him, and smiled. It was not a nice smile. Danforth glared back.

"Yves says I'm to observe," Helena announced as she caught up with them. She looked at Jason defiantly and shook back her hair.

"Naturally," Jason snorted.

Cargo-chain freighter Ceti Flag, *EuroCom registry, crew module, outer corridor, 1 hour after departing orbit at Wolf II.*

Magda stiffened as she heard voices on the level below approaching the ladder, then strained to hear Danforth's voice again. She was sure it was him—had to be him. She looked right and left, checking that she was not seen, and worried about someone coming up the bend from sick bay. It was too close nearby, too close to be sure.

She had not yet felt easy in this place. The floors curved strangely, and the ceilings seemed to press down on her, as in the cargo tin. It had a wrongness in the spaces, filled where it should be empty, empty where it should be filled, wrongness. She pulled her knife from underneath her tunic, aware of the whisper-soft sound of its drawing. This time she wouldn't fail. This time—and then she could have an end to everything, an end to dreams with strange happenings, with pursuit and loss, with emptiness and self-destruction. An end to remembering, to acting, the chance to lie down and stop forever, to make everything stop.

The footsteps sounded louder. She crouched next to the wall, watching the opening of the ladder entry, hardly breathing as she wished him to use *this* ladder. The footsteps passed the ladder and moved onward. On tiptoe she raced to the next ladder a dozen meters away and crouched against the wall again, her eyes fixed on the opening. *This* ladder, she wished fiercely. A shoe clanged on the bottom rung. Magda leaned forward in her crouch, one hand steadying herself, the other hand tight on her knife, as the steps moved upward slowly, changing pitch with each step on the metal stairs.

A head, vaguely familiar to her, appeared in the opening. She quickly concealed her knife behind her back in case the man looked and saw her, then slipped it forward just a little to be sure it was ready. The man stepped onto the upper level and turned away from her, then turned back to look down at the next man behind him—and saw her. He froze, his eyes widening in surprise.

"Mack?" he called, his voice strange. "Get up here. No, Helena, stay put. Let Mack by."

"What the hell?" a woman's voice asked in irritation. "Get out of the way, Jason. You're blocking the ladder."

"Roarke, I've had about enough of this," another voice said beneath her, a voice that set Magda's heart pounding. She rose slowly from her crouch and circled the ladder railing, her eyes fixed on Jason's face.

"Let me by," she warned him.

"You stay put," he ordered, pointing a finger at her. She smiled, showing her teeth. "You stay right there."

"I want him."

"Who?" He looked confused.

"Danforth!" She rushed at him, making him flinch backward, then whirled into the stairway. He grabbed at her sleeve and missed. With a yell, Magda threw herself down the ladder into the people below, colliding hard with the woman, then bouncing off her into the railing, heading for Danforth. Danforth stared at her, at the naked knife, then turned and ran up the corridor. As Magda leapt down the last two stairs, she slipped and fell to one knee, then gathered herself to catch him, to catch him at last. Then two arms wrapped themselves around her, pinning her to the floor.

"Let me go!" she shouted.

Ahead of her, Danforth looked over his shoulder, his face white with horror, then disappeared up the bend. Magda hit out at the arms confining her and heard a cry of pain as her knife slashed. The arms loosened and fell away. She squirmed out of their reach, only to be caught again by other arms a step later. "Let me go!" she shouted again, struggling.

"She's knifed Mack!" the woman cried, and grunted with effort to keep hold of Magda. "Jason! Help!"

At her cry, Magda abruptly stopped, her breath coming in great gasps, then turned her head to look behind her. Mack lay on the floor, clutching at his shoulder as his blood pumped out in a reddish stream that curved and wound along the metal corridor floor. He looked up at her in anguish, his face contorted with pain. At that look, the knife fell from Magda's nerveless fingers as everything . . . did . . . stop.

"Magda . . ." Mack said, then turned his face away from her. Magda's blood pounded in her ears as her treacherous heart continued to beat, sustaining her life. She covered her eyes and collapsed in the woman's arms.

"Christ," Jason muttered as he bent over Summers. Magda raised her head and bit hard on her lip, wounding herself.

"Is she crazy?" the woman asked, her voice resounding harshly in Magda's ears, echoing against the metal that confined them in every direction. "Why was she after Danforth?'' Magda felt the woman's body shift as she turned to look up the corridor.

"No, it's all right," Mack said hurriedly. "She's just been under strain—Dr. Renfrew said a bad reaction to the sleep drugs, that's all. Don't say anything, don't.'' Magda heard his voice plead for her, overborne by the rush of dark wings.

"That's ridiculous. This has to be reported. She tried to murder the director!"

Jason swiveled on one heel and looked at her. "No, it won't get reported. You hear me?''

"You don't have that kind of authority, Jason,'' the woman said coldly. "Don't you understand that *yet*?''

"Let's put it in other terms, sweetheart. If you tell Danforth it was Magda, I'll tell Central about your game playing with Yves's orders ever since the flare. I'll tell them about you helping me with the tins against orders, about you taking Danforth's side on waking Yves up. You haven't been a rock of loyalty to Yves, you know. And if I tell Central, you'll never get your captaincy. Central doesn't think much of rogue crewmen.'' He smiled unpleasantly. "I should know.'' The woman's fingers tightened painfully on Magda's arms, gouging into the muscle. She winced.

"You bastard.''

Magda heard a murmur of voices down the corridor, coming fast. Jason quickly stood up, then looked around. "Where's the knife? All right, Mack, you fell on the knife as it fell out of your pocket when Magda bumped into you on the stairwell. Got it?''

"Got it,'' Mack said weakly.

"Helena will take you to sick bay.'' The voices were louder, coming fast. "I'll go stash Magda somewhere.''

"You can't expect to put it over,'' the woman protested. "Danforth saw her coming at *him*.''

"Danforth is under strain. He imagined it.'' Jason stared over Magda into the woman's face, challenging her. "Didn't he, Helena? The three of us against him, and he's the one who assaulted *Flag*'s captain, after all. He got unglued, accused this innocent girl of attempted murder. Now, who's Central going to believe?''

"It'll destroy his career!"

"No—just even things up a bit. Danforth can say Yves is crazy, and *Flag* can say Danforth is crazy. It'll be a tie. Poetic justice, don't you think?" Jason pulled Magda to her feet and pushed her up the stairs in front of him.

"Got the story?" Jason shouted at Helena over his shoulder.

"I got it! I hate you, Jason!"

"Appreciate the sentiment, love. Come on, Magda, move your feet."

Chapter 15

Cargo-chain freighter Ceti Flag, *EuroCom registry, crew quarters, 65 minutes after departing orbit at Wolf II.*

"In you go." Jason pushed Magda into a room on the upper level. She caught a brief glance of a bunk and chair, shelves.

She staggered a few steps, then whirled to look at him. "They'll believe Danforth," she said defiantly. "I'll tell them what I did."

"Now, that would be very stupid, Magda," he said, then studied her a moment. "You think your mother was all you had? Doesn't Mack count?"

"What about him?" she said resistantly.

"Is that all you can say? You put a knife in his shoulder and you just shrug? Just like you wanted to put a knife in Danforth. That's stupid, Magda, and you don't strike me as a stupid girl. Killing Danforth won't bring your mother back—all it will do is ruin your own life."

"I don't care!"

"Well, I do. Your mother died because Danforth was stupid when he believed other stupid people who think the universe is a safe place. It's stupid to think that vacuum is safe, that a colony by a flare star is safe, that we can stroll around being careless. That's stupid, and now a lot of people have died because of it." He stared at her until she looked away. "I've been stupid all my life, little girl, thinking fighting and making trouble were the answer for certain disappointments—and now I'm going to lose everything I really wanted, just because I was stupid. This vendetta against Danforth is the same kind of stupid, the kind that closes doors forever.''

''But Mother's dead!''

''That's true. So?''

''Somebody has to pay!''

''Why? Does that erase death? Will it make you feel better? Isn't that the core of it? You wreck your life—and Mack's, too, by the way—but you'll feel just fine, won't you?''

''I hate you,'' she said, and looked away from his implacable face.

He sighed. ''That's okay,'' he said gently. ''It's all right to hate me. You can hate the whole universe if you want. Go ahead: turn into a vicious bitch who hates everything. They'll come after you because some folks aren't as forgiving; they think everybody should be happy and chuckling or it ruins *their* illusions, and that isn't allowed. But they won't convert you; you can put all that willpower of yours on track and hate everything forever. I'm sure your mother would have wanted that.''

He stepped back through the doorway. ''Mack loves you, you know. You're the daughter he never had; everybody has his daydreams. Guess he's stupid, loving you, stupid just like the rest of us.'' The door hissed shut after him, leaving her alone.

Her head jerked up as she heard the musical tone sequence of the door lock. She jumped to her feet and rushed at the door, then stopped herself from crying out at him. She heard his footsteps recede—then silence. At the left side she saw the lock panel, a box of six numbers to push. She squatted down in front of it and started systematically to find the combination, two numbers or three or five, she didn't know. She would start at the beginning. She punched one, then one-one, then one-one-one, then one-one-one-one, then . . .

Her hand hesitated over the panel. This is stupid, she thought. A six-number panel has thousands of possibilities—it could take hours to find the combination. And what then? Why am I doing this?

She sat back on her heels and stared at the lock panel. Stupid. She tried to think back to when it had begun, when she had overheard the men talking about Danforth. Then the angels had come. She lifted her chin and listened for the dark angels, but they weren't in the walls. They weren't anywhere. She lifted a shaking hand to her face. *What was wrong with me?*

It wasn't just Danforth, he had said; it was a lot of people. And it wasn't the people, not deliberately; it was feeling safe and getting careless, he had said. Could that be true? Could her mother's death have been *stupid?*

She felt a wail of anguish rise in her throat. *It's not stupid to me—but . . . but it was stupid, stupid and little and meaningless. It was. I didn't want to see that, couldn't see that.* She rested her arms in a circle on her knees and hid her face. *Stupid.* She wept then, a cleansing that struck deep into her heart and settled there, wept until her stupid nose ran and her breath caught in stupid hiccups, until she couldn't cry anymore.

Exhausted, Magda stumbled to the bunk and curled up on the yielding mattress, her face still streaked with tears. *Stupid.* She lay inert for a long time, staring at the opposite wall, remembering her mother. *She's gone. It's over. Even justice would not bring her back; it never brought anybody back.*

She took a shuddering breath and knew it was true. *But what do I do now?*

She closed her eyes and rested, too drained to think coherently. *Later.* She would ask Mr. Mack later, she decided, after she had apologized to him—*how could you apologize for that?* she thought, flinching from the memory of his cry as her knife slashed into his shoulder, but she would, anyway. Maybe he would forgive her. It was something to hope for—to live for.

He would be stupid to forgive her, but she thought he might. She smiled wanly. *Stupid—but a right kind of stupid, a good kind.* She would look for the other right kinds, too, she thought, and find them—somehow. Her breath slowed into an even pattern, then grew still softer, effortless, until she slept, at last without dreams.

Cargo-chain freighter Ceti Flag, *EuroCom registry, control room, 70 minutes after departing orbit at Wolf II.*

Jason intercepted the crowd of excited people outside sick bay before Danforth got a search started for the girl. The director was raving in their midst, shouting threats, for once possessed by a genuine emotion. Magda had scared the daylights out of him, and that just wasn't allowed, no, not at all. Jason pulled one of the admin people aside and, just to set up the play, asked what was going on, then pushed into the crowd inside the sick-bay door. Helena was nowhere to be seen; then he spotted her hiding out near the bed where Inga and Dr. Renfrew were working on Mack. Smart girl. Don't get asked and you tell no lies.

"There you are, Roarke!" Danforth shouted as he saw him. "Where is she?"

A dozen faces turned toward him.

"Who?" Jason asked benignly. *Flag* was just about to get even for Yves, he thought. You snotty bastard. Yes, sir.

"The girl! The girl who attacked me!"

"Girl?" Jason acted bewildered and saw the immediate response in the faces around them, like dye sheeting through water as wary eyes turned back to Danforth, suddenly speculative, horrified, even awed. The murmurs started a moment later. Danforth heard them even as he stared at Jason in shock.

"The girl!" he repeated uselessly. Jason looked back at him and crinkled his brow. Take that, Danforth. For Elizabet and Sanchez and everyone else who died from Central's stupidity. Somebody has to fall—and I'm taking you with me, as much as I can. He blinked at Danforth and glanced aside in puzzlement at the woman standing beside him. Games.

"I don't know what you're talking about, Director," Jason said. "What girl?"

Danforth's face flushed as he suddenly understood. "You can't do this, Roarke. I'll have your hide!"

"Do what?" Jason asked.

Danforth whirled and stormed into sick bay after Helena. Jason hurried after him, followed by the others crowding behind.

"Tell them!" the director shouted at Helena. "Tell them!"

Helena flicked a glance at Jason. "Tell them what?" she said flatly.

Danforth threw up his hands. "You won't get away with it! I'll find her myself!" He barged back through the crowd and vanished into the corridor.

"Better have someone go after him," Jason suggested. "He seems unglued." Helena shot him a bitter look and turned her back on him. Angry about Danforth? Or about his threat? Suddenly he tired of all the games, all the ways she jerked his heart around. Let her stay mad this time.

"I'll sedate him," Inga said calmly, then flicked a puzzled glance at Jason. Inga knew him too well, had picked up the false note in his acting. But she would like the irony, he thought. Maybe Yves would, too, enough to hate Jason less, enough to live with it after it was over.

"You do that," he said, and smiled.

They caught Danforth on the cargo-tin deck twenty minutes later—it was apparently quite a circus while it lasted. As Yves took the report over the intercom, he glanced suspiciously at Jason, just from habit. Jason crossed his arms and looked bland, then admired the starscape in the viewscreen. In screen-center Sol beamed in his golden glory, a tenth normal size at this distance just outside Pluto's orbit but beaming nonetheless, welcoming his errant children home.

Home. A good sound.

Jason wondered idly if stars made radio widgets, too, and how they might catch some if they did. Maybe Leland would know.

Yves keyed a button on his console and leaned forward to the transmitter mike. "This is *Ceti Flag*, EuroCom registry, returning from Wolf II ahead of schedule. Wolf Station has sustained flare damage, radiation injuries. Ship is returning with survivors of Wolf Colony. Request priority trajectory to Mars. End, Yves Merceau, commanding." He pushed the send button and sighed.

"Likely they'll tell me 'garbled message, please repeat.' "

"Well, they've got three weeks to get it right," Jason said.

Helena breezed in and gave a cool look to Jason and a kiss on the cheek to Yves.

Jason stood up. "If you don't need me, Captain, I'm going uplevel for a while." There wasn't much Magda could break in his room—if she felt so inclined—but maybe she had thought things over by now and could be safely sprung out of detention. He hoped so, for Mack's sake and hers.

"*D'accord,*" Yves said absently, and smiled up at Helena, showing too much as he did. "Uh, Jason . . ."

Jason turned back in the doorway.

"Crew meeting in two hours, dining room." Yves's dark eyes glinted.

"Sure, I'll be there."

Cargo-chain freighter Ceti Flag, *EuroCom registry, temporary sick bay, 2 hours after departing orbit at Wolf II.*

Mack looked up and saw Magda hesitating in the doorway. She saw him looking at her and almost fled, but he beckoned her vigorously over to his cot. Relief flooded into her face as she walked tentatively toward him. As if she thought he'd give her up, ever.

"Hi, Mr. Mack," she said shyly.

"Hi, girlie," he said lightly. Careful, Mack, do this right, he thought. "Got a boyfriend?"

She blushed and shook her head. Summers sighed, pretending deep relief. "Thank God, I don't think I could face that yet."

She reached out her hand and twined her fingers into his, then looked at the bandages on his other shoulder. "Does it hurt?" she asked in a voice so low he could hardly hear.

"Lots. But that's okay. How are you feeling?"

She shrugged a little. "Sad. I still don't have it all sorted out yet." She lifted her chin and looked at him squarely. "I still think he ought to die. He killed Mother.

But I won't do anything about it, Mr. Mack.'' She smiled sadly. "It would be stupid.''

She seemed to mean it this time. Mack's sigh was far softer, and genuine. "I love you, Magda.''

"I know.'' She bent over and kissed his cheek. "Mother was *so* incredibly dense.''

"Not when she had you, chick. Turn around and look over there.'' He winced despite himself as he lifted his injured arm and pointed. Magda turned obediently and stiffened as she saw Danforth in another bed along the far wall, snoring away.

"He's unglued,'' Mack said casually. "Happens to folks sometimes.''

"Mr. Roarke really did it? He really told them . . .''

"Yeah. They had to chase Danforth for twenty minutes, but they finally caught him on cargo deck somewhere. He shouted and carried on a while, but he gave it up finally. He's just played too many games for too long; nobody believed him, just like Jason said.''

"What will happen to him?''

"A little death.'' He smiled at her grimly. "Nothing he doesn't deserve—and maybe a lot he doesn't.''

"I guess so,'' she said stubbornly, and his heart turned over, looking at her, seeing her mother in the high cheekbones, the tilt of her jaw, that willful expression in her eyes. Elizabet had given him that look a dozen times before she had softened toward him, when she had finally begun to hope again, just a little—not enough yet, but a little. I'll take care of her, Elizabet, he promised her. I'll give her a good life.

Magda tightened her fingers in his and smiled down at him, the reason for everything worthwhile. He smiled back, feeling easy with her at last, not fumble-mouthed or heavy-handed, just easy, like a long journey ended.

"Love you, Mack,'' she said shyly, and looked down, avoiding his eyes.

"Love you, too, baby.''

Cargo-chain freighter Ceti Flag, *EuroCom registry, crew's dining room, 3 hours after departing orbit at Wolf II.*

Yves chased everybody but *Flag*'s crew out of the dining room and closed the door. "I put Leland on deck watch," he announced. "I want some things settled before we radio our supplementary report to Mars."

"Sounds good to me," Jason said affably. He got some coffee from the dispenser and sat down between Helena and Inga at the central table. Inga glanced at him with distaste, then shifted a little closer to Axel on her other side. Helena ignored him, her gaze fixed on Yves. Pariah time, Jason thought. Yves pulled out a chair and sat down across from Jason, then stared at him.

"I'll keep the bargain, Yves," Jason answered the look. "Don't worry your mind."

"What bargain?" Axel asked. Inga nudged him quickly. He looked at her in confusion. "What?"

"Off the ship," Yves said relentlessly, "and out of Ceti Transport."

Jason felt his temper rise a little. "I said I would. You've got it all." He took a sip from his cup and washed the coffee around his mouth, then quirked an eyebrow at Yves. "All."

"Danforth's sedated in sick bay," Helena said, her voice glacial. "We should discuss that, too."

"The threat still stands, sweetheart," Jason warned her mildly. "You hurt Mack and that girl and I'll see you never get your posting. That's a promise."

"I don't understand," Yves said. "What about Danforth? What posting?"

"You lied!" Inga blurted, staring at him. "He *was* attacked."

"Surprise, surprise. Yeah."

Inga looked thoughtful, then gave him a slow smile as she misunderstood completely. He could see it in her eyes: Roarke finally comes through on the loyalty, finally joins the crew, hip hoorah for Yves Merceau. Forget all the other reasons except Yves. He left her to it and took another sip of coffee. "Well, I'll temper my report about him," she said. "Let's not get too extreme." She pursed her lips. "Jump shock or something, strictly temporary, no expected recurrences."

"Jump shock?" Jason objected. "Ain't no such animal. What happened to your Hippocratic oath?"

"Or something, I said. My oath is just fine, Jason. Magda? Is that her name?"

"You don't know that, Inga. She's snapped out of it now—drug psychosis, Mack says. Give me that at least. Just let it alone." He made a mock bow in his chair to her and gave it all to her, too. Who the hell cared anymore? "Just keep it a little revenge for the captain, courtesy of the *Ceti Flag*. One last gift from first pilot."

She nodded, satisfied, then looked at Yves.

He saw Yves struggle with it, then glance at Helena and lose it. Yves's jaw set stubbornly. "I still want you off *Flag*."

"*That* you've made clear. I didn't expect anything else, not from you."

Yves bared his teeth at him. "All."

"That's a deal. Now, if you'll excuse me, former friends, I think I'll go check the tin line." He saw Helena look at him quickly, almost say something, then back off. Jason stood up and dumped his coffee in the sink, then left the dining room. Not one of them came after him, not one.

Loyalty, he thought bitterly. Yeah.

Cargo-chain freighter Ceti Flag, *EuroCom registry, crew quarters, 2 days after departing orbit at Wolf II.*

Jason lay comfortably on his bunk in *Flag*'s crew quarters, smoking a vile cigar. The cigar fumes rose in swirls and graceful arcs, then darted frantically from side to side as they neared their nemesis, the ceiling fan. Jason watched as the fan tore them to rags.

Some things never change, he thought.

He heard his door chime and turned his head lazily, then considered whether he wished to be interrupted. With more of the colonists brought aboard *Flag* as Inga adapted her biosystems, the corridors had become irritably overcrowded, not that the colonists misbehaved unreasonably. In fact, their attitude toward *Flag*'s crew sometimes edged toward the embarrassing, especially wide-eyed worshipful boys who sometimes followed him in droves. Well, two at a time, maybe. The door chimed again.

"Come in. It's open."

The door hissed open, and Helena stepped through, then hesitated with one hand on the doorsill. The automatic door tried to close, then racheted irritably in its sockets.

"Either come in or stay out," he advised her, and decided to inspect his cigar.

"I want to talk to you," Helena said.

"That's obvious. I said it was your choice, in or out." He took another deep breath of the redolent smoke, savoring it. Helena walked stiffly to the armchair and sat down. Jason frowned, not inviting the memory of other times she had sat in that chair, sometimes delectably. "So talk."

"Why are you still angry at me?" she asked, then caught herself as the question came out a little too plaintively. She shook back her blond hair and looked determined. "You go out of your way to avoid me, won't give me two words beyond 'yes' and 'no' and 'check that, please.' What have I done?"

"I'm not angry."

"Let's have a little honesty, Jason," she said with asperity.

"That's an interesting demand, especially from you. Let's just say I'm tired of games. Like 'I love you, Jason' on the cargo deck. Snotty poses and toss-'em-back insults are one thing, but lies like that are quite another. Your gambits are getting too rough, Helena. I don't want to play anymore. Okay?"

"But it was true!"

He gave her a sardonic look.

"Well, somewhat true—I just boosted the emotion a little. Maybe it's more true than you realize."

"If you don't know, Sheila, how can I know?"

"Drat you." She looked away and sighed, then twisted

her hands in her lap. "I'll quit cargo-chain, too, go with you. Would that prove it?"

Jason lay very still, watching his cigar smoke twirl upward. "You'd never forget what you gave up," he said slowly, not looking at her. "You'd always wonder if it was a mistake. That's not a great basis for a relationship, especially the way we fight already."

"I suppose you're right." She sighed softly. "I thought I'd offer, though, if it'd help."

He looked at her then. "More games?" he accused. "You knew I'd never let you quit cargo-chain."

"No, I didn't know," she snapped back. "I don't know why I'm even here. I don't know anything anymore." She stood up and glared at him. "Just forget it, Jase. Just forget everything." She stamped to the door and hit the release, then flounced out. The door hissed shut. He waited a few minutes, not moving, hoping she might come back and try again, dreading that she would cause them both more useless hurt. She didn't return.

He rolled to a sitting position and put the cigar in his ashtray by the bed, then wiggled his bare toes idly, left toes, right toes, left toes. They worked just fine. You never stop hoping, you old bear, he told himself. You never stop hoping for a way through the bars, out of the cage, back to the wild. Salmon streams, pretty she-bears to court and win, the tallest trees to climb, berries to gorge on, the mountains that never ended. He looked around his room at the same sights he had seen every time he woke for far too long on cargo-chain.

Games. Sometimes the best games were those you played on yourself. He picked up his cigar and clenched it hard between his teeth, then spread out again on his bunk. You old bear. He puffed a huge cloud at the fan and watched the fan tear the smoke to fragments, relentless in its animosity.

Good old bear. He smiled.

Epilogue

Ceti Transport admin building, Lowell City Square, Mare Boreum, Mars.

Six days after *Ceti Flag* returned to Mars, Jason stepped out of Ceti Central's administrative building, a boxy structure of glass and steel that stretched nearly to the city's bubble dome high overhead, and paused on the top step of a long tier that descended at flat and low increments to the street. A series of intent men and women breezed past him in and out of the wide building doors, heads down, brows wrinkled deeply with the bureaucratic wars. Jason amiably moved aside to the edge of the stairs, leaving them to it, then considered where to go. He felt strange out of a shipsuit, though the smartly tailored new jeans and wide-sleeved blouse suited him well—he had always liked red and decided that civilian clothes made a fine start on escaping a cage. Central had not agreed, not at all, and had written him up for being "out of uniform," one last parting shot before he dropped his resignation on Carson's desk.

He grinned as he remembered Carson's reaction. The old fart had stammered and flushed and sputtered for three minutes straight, then had looked at him suspiciously, most suspiciously. For three weeks, ever since *Flag* had made radio contact with Mars Control from Neptune's orbit, the media hounds had saturated the airwaves, expostulating, berating, hallelujahing, having a tizzy of a time. Ceti Transport had reeled, caught between the Scylla and Charybdis of media outrage about the flare disaster at Wolf II and glowing praise for *Ceti*

Flag's daring. Stammering and sputtering, Central had hastily promised sizable reparations for every surviving colonist, the pick of colony postings for the colony chiefs, a survey ship to UV Ceti and research money for Leland and his new drive, promotions and honors for the officers of *Ceti Flag*, and a third-rate bureaucrat's desk counting flimsies or such for Danforth. Jason expected that Danforth would survive—even Coventry had its limits when the media went wild.

"Mr. Roarke!" someone called. He turned and saw the young photographer below him on the steps. "Picture, sir?"

"Why not?" Jason posed and grinned wide for the camera.

"Thank you, sir!"

"Any time, son." Jason took a cigar from his shirt pocket and put it between his teeth, then sauntered down the steps. He strolled down the pavement, sniffing at the scent of Mars dust in the air. Even under a bubble dome, the environment teams couldn't keep it all out. Mars. He'd had some good times here on leave. At the next corner he dodged around a robot transport van careening down the street and jaywalked down PanUnion Avenue fronting PanUnion's offices and city hall, heading for the park square. Four acres of grass and trees, shaded walks, and occasional fountains buried in the center of the city, the park added a bit of green to the ever-present dusty red of Mars, a remembrance of Earth that youngsters raised on Mars usually ignored. Someday, on humanity's other worlds, the new worlds that now lay on Earth's threshold in every direction, those children might erect a Marsscape of red stone and dust, honoring their own memories of youth and home.

The park had the look of a Scottish glen and suited him. He stopped to light his cigar, then strolled onward under the trees.

He found a bench and sat down. Leaves rustled, swayed by the ventilation currents near the dome. A harsh red-tinted light glanced in from the miles of oxide desert surrounding the city; overhead, visible through the branches, the Mars sky was tinted a deep violet-blue and sparkled with a ghostly dust of stars even in dayside. He finished his cigar, looking up at the ghost stars, hunting for Leo and the Wolf star winking near his paw, then pitched the cigar butt at a trash receptacle. Hit it square; you can't lose, Roarke. He pulled out the newest flimsy from his pocket, for once a posting that tempted him. He might enjoy sharing ship with Isaiah and Leland on their way to UV Ceti for more drive research, even if it did mean twiddling on Mars until EuroCom had built Leland his fancy ship. Or he could let PanUnion bribe him with that colony posting at Alpha Centauri—money was always nice, especially *that* much money. Or he could marry that pampered heiress with the pornographic letters and let her pornograph him into happy satiety in her Riviera villa.

Of course, the hoopla and gasped admiration would wear off: every year had its new corps of media stars as fame moved on to new curiosities, new heroes, new villains. Some of the benefit might remain—in the future, Ceti Central's disaster planners would be a little less sublime about nasty possibilities. And the Wolf colonists would have a new chance at something better, something to make the price they had paid a less hurting memory. And Helena would have her senior pilot's posting, Yves his *Ceti Flag*.

What do you want, Jason Roarke? Will you ever know?

I won't go home to Earth, he decided suddenly. Mars is good enough, as a threshold, anyway. In a dozen years—I won't be that old in a dozen years—maybe the first *real* starliners will be launched, the ones for Gemini and Bootes and Puppis, the new worlds. I can go as a tourist, just to see. He leaned his elbows on his knees and studied the curling grass, green and soft and fragrant, beneath his boots.

He heard approaching footsteps, light and quick, as someone walked down the park path. He kept his head down, not wanting the necessary courtesy of a nod, perhaps a smile, to someone he didn't know. *Tell me, Mr. Roarke*, they would ask, *how many people died? What was it like, wondering if everyone would die? What was it like to give up everything you wanted, just to be a hero?* He started a little as the feet stopped in front of him.

"Why did you resign?" a young voice demanded, a voice he knew. Jason looked up and smiled. Magda shook back her long hair, a gesture that caught his breath for a moment, then put her hands on her slender hips and glared at him. "Why?"

"You're full of 'whys.' Comes with being young."

The yellow hair tossed again. "There's nothing wrong with being young. Besides, you aren't that old. How come you've got such airs about *old*?" When he didn't answer, she sat down beside him. "Why?" she asked more softly, her eyes focused intently on his face.

"I made a bargain," he said simply. "I decided to keep it."

"What kind of bargain?"

"The best kind, I suppose—a hard one, one with meaning. I hear each of the Wolf colonists is getting a sizable bonus; it'll give a lot of people a chance for a new start—like you. What are you going to do?"

"Go to college, probably here. Or are you going back to Earth?"

"No. Staying here a while."

"Then definitely here." She smiled. "I thought I might go into colony administration." The smile turned grim a moment, then flashed again into warmth, lighting her pretty eyes. "Are you going with Mr. Kendall on Dr. Leland's ship?"

"Where do you *hear* these things?" he protested.

"There are ways," she said loftily, waving her hand in the air. "Mostly Mack and Mr. Kendall have been talking about you. They wonder where you are; so did I. They have this *Mars Herald* reporter locked in the bathroom, you see, who wants to know *all* the Wolf story, especially the scandalous parts. They don't know what to tell him when they let him out, maybe next week sometime, and they want to ask you for advice. If you don't show up, they might tell the reporter practically anything, anything at all."

Jason leaned back and guffawed. "You're Isaiah's spy," he accused.

She shrugged. "I prefer 'emissary.' They're worried about you, Jason. So am I." Then she blushed, a clean wash of crimson up her throat and into her face.

"I'm too old for you, Magda," he said gently. "I'm old enough to be your father, as old as Mack is."

"Old again," she said in an exasperated tone. "Maybe. But not too old to be a friend—maybe? Or to let me be a friend. We both know the emptiness, I think." She looked at him with sober eyes, eyes that remembered too much. Young eyes that would not forget, not ever.

"I'd like that," he said, suddenly realizing it was true. His reward was the delighted smile that answered him. She bounced to her feet and held out her hand.

"Then come on, first pilot. Time's a-wasting. That reporter might starve before we get there, and then what will we do?"

"That's a thought, indeed. Would suit him right, the sod."

She laughed and shook her hair at him, then pulled him to his feet. Hand in hand, Jason and Magda strolled through Earth's garden and vanished into the streets beneath ghosted stars.

ABOUT THE AUTHOR

Paula E. Downing is an attorney and municipal judge in Medford, Oregon. She lives with her husband, fellow SF writer T. Jackson King, and four arrogant cat-persons in a large house on eighteen acres of wooded property a few miles south of Medford. Paula enjoys cross-stitch and needlepoint, reading, computers, devising new plans to keep local deer from eating her rosebushes, and pretending to garden. An Oregon native, Paula grew up in various towns along the Columbia River, and has lived among the forests, rivers, seacoast, marauder deer, and the mountains of Oregon most of her life. She has read and loved science fiction since her teens and began writing seriously on her own SF novels in her early thirties, eventually selling *Rinn's Star* to Del Rey seven years later. *Flare Star* is her second novel for Del Rey, with her next book, *Fallway*, scheduled for publication in 1993. She is currently working on a new novel.